The Risen Lands Duology

Book 1

The Witch's Catalyst

J. Cain McKrell

Published by Booksmithy at Smashwords

Copyright 2014 J. Cain McKrell

License Notes:
This book is licensed for your personal enjoyment only. This book may not be re-sold or given away without express written consent of the author. If you're reading this book and did not purchase it, or it was not purchased for your use only, then please return it to your favorite book retailer and purchase your own copy. Thank you for respecting the hard work of this author.

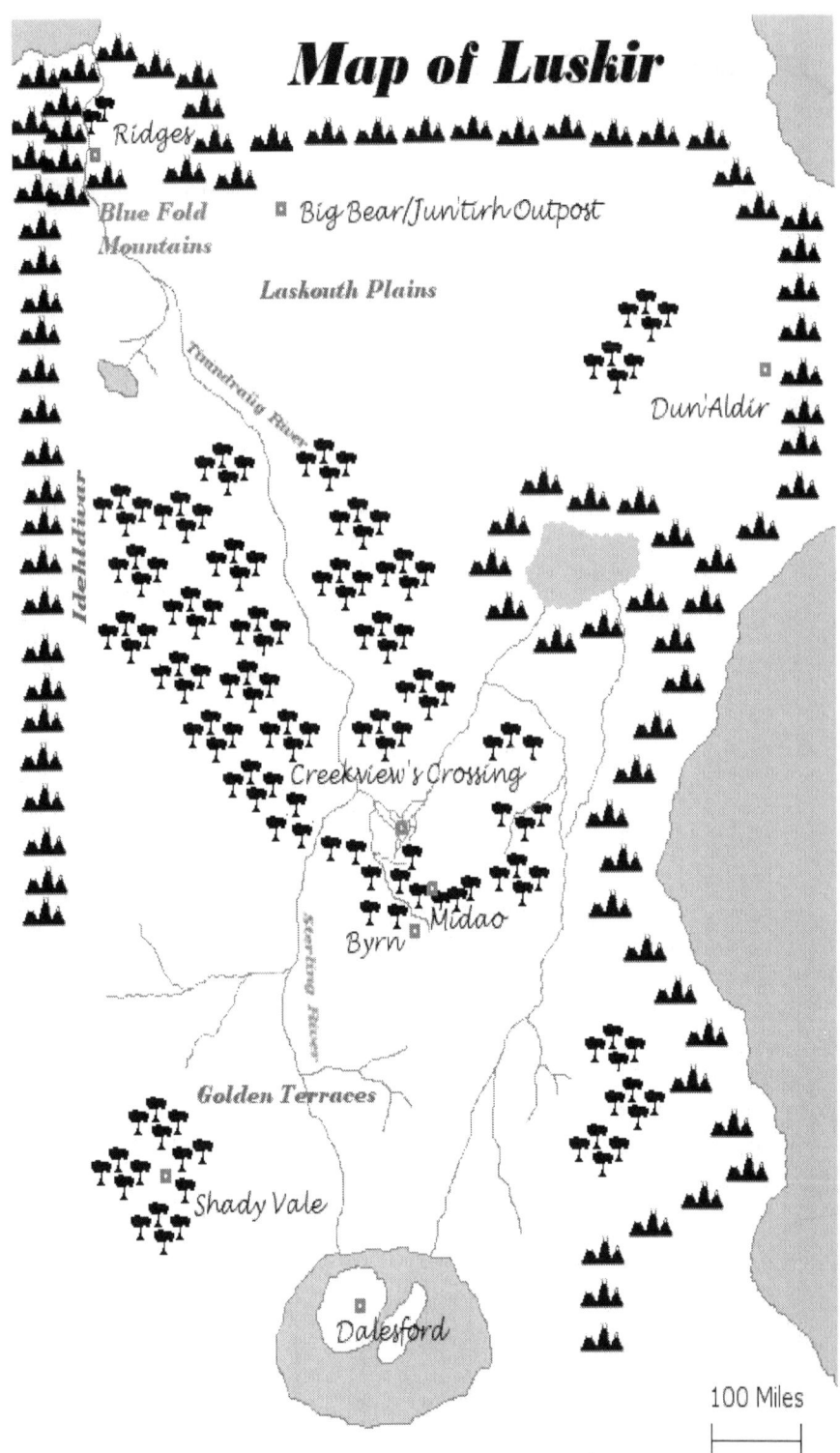

Table of Contents

Prologue

Chapter 1 – Boldstone

Chapter 2 – Preparations

Chapter 3 – Catalyst

Chapter 4 – Ten Days Out

Chapter 5 – A Delayed Return

Chapter 6 – Big Bear

Chapter 7 – The Best Laid Plans

Chapter 8 – Strange Return

Chapter 9 – Desperation

Chapter 10 – Contest for the Ridges

Chapter 11 – Brains and Brawn

Chapter 12 – Escaping

Chapter 13 – Longpost Road

Chapter 14 – A Summons Answered

Chapter 15 – First Impressions

Chapter 16 – Midao

Chapter 17 – Creekview

Chapter 18 – Cornered

Chapter 19 – A Time for Action

Chapter 20 – A Debt Repaid

Chapter 21 – Matters of Honor

Chapter 22 – Last Stand

Chapter 23 – Separate Paths

Prologue

His mind slowly awakened, confused and disoriented. Only a few moments ago he was some place else, though where he could not recall. It certainly wasn't here. He found himself in a chamber unlike any he had ever set foot in before. A sense of alarm ran through him, evoking a feeling that something was terribly out of place, but unable to discern what it was.

Gaining nothing from lingering about, he felt a need to move, even though he was unsure of where to go. There wasn't anything here, only an ever-present crimson hue permeating his surroundings that bathed the area in an unnatural light. Overcoming his hesitation, he chose a direction and set off.

He froze immediately, discovering the cause of his unease. Several moments of shock passed as he moved with mere thought, his body nowhere to be found. The incorporeal state drove him to the verge of panic, a feeling most unfamiliar to him. He was always in control, he was... Who was he? Again he felt confusion, unable to remember anything before waking only moments ago. Forcing himself to calm, he continued onward, seeking answers.

After a time, hours or days he could not be sure, frustration grew in him as he realized there was nothing, only the emptiness and pervasive red glow. Ahead the air seemed to become clearer, sparking in him a glimmer of hope. As he hurried forward he was abruptly stopped, running into a nearly clear barrier. Roaring in denial he instinctually threw himself at the wall with all the power of his thought, testing its give.

It did not yield in the slightest.

He sooner could have moved a mountain with his bare hands, had he still had hands. Vaguely he saw white points in the distance, beyond the barrier. They teased the edges of his memory, evoking an intense hatred, yet their nature remained elusive. They were important; he should know well what they were but couldn't remember.

Many days, perhaps weeks or years elapsed - he could not tell. The passage of time did not seem relevant here. He spent the endless days travelling along the perimeter of his peculiar cage, trying to piece together who he was and where he might be. Direction was difficult to determine, as he could float freely within his confines. It took a great deal of effort, but as time was no issue he carefully measured his movements. Eventually he was able to determine he was in a slightly elongated, hexagonal-like structure.

He often pondered the white points in the distance. They only existed towards one end, running along each side in a symmetrical arc towards each other. The points shimmered each time he pushed against the barrier, seeming to provide it strength in reaction to him. At times he seemed close to remembering what he once was, but the infernal lights in the distance would flash and he would forget once again. The only logical conclusion he could reach after what seemed an eternity was that he was a prisoner, and the white points beyond his reach were his jailers. They were the enemy.

More time elapsed. He tried without success to will himself out of existence more times than he could remember, putting an end to this eternal monotony. He couldn't starve or dehydrate himself as he didn't have these needs. Could he ever die, or was he doomed to an endless, mundane existence? On many occasions he raged against the barriers containing him, but it was always futile. The points of light would increase in brightness to match his intensity, lending their strength to the invisible wall. He would then launch attacks at the lights themselves, trying to crush them with his willpower. These would end in the same way, with the combined power of the enigmatic orbs rebuffing him.

One day something changed. A point of light inexplicably drifted away until it disappeared. Curious for the first time in ages he rushed towards the barrier; it no longer felt as solid as it once had. He immediately redoubled his efforts attacking the orbs, again he did not win but his loss was only by a narrow margin. They were now only eleven, not as strong as when they were twelve. His hope renewed, he rested for a bit. He could break them down eventually. After all, he had an eternity to work at it.

Years and centuries passed in much the same manner. Each moment was a struggle between him and the eleven orbs. Though he was continually defeated, he did not become discouraged. Eventually he would win out. They had to be successful each and every of their thousands of battles, while he only needed to see victory once. He had learned a few things in the time he spent here. For some reason they could not destroy him, and he could feel their fear of him growing. It fed him, giving him renewed vitality. With each assault victory grew closer.

His strength grew along with their fear, until one day it finally happened. At long last! Like too much pressure being applied to a stone, he suddenly crushed one of the orbs that had contributed to his imprisonment, causing it to explode into a million points of light and dissipate to nothingness. Panic and disbelief rushed through those remaining, and he reveled in it. The balance of power had tipped in his favor. The ten remaining were no match for him. Methodically, he began working to eliminate them.

Each one became easier to destroy than the previous. He basked in their imminent demise, and moreso in their awareness of their impending fate. How delicious it felt to obliterate them, tasting their fear as he grew in power. When only three remained, his memories, long blocked by the orbs, came flooding back to him in a torrent. He remembered, he remembered all of it. The knowledge of who he was in every minute detail rushed over him as if he were doused in cold water. Armies trembled at mere whisperings of his name, kings and queens cowered before him in fear. He was Kubathu, God-Emperor of the Vermillion Sands, Breaker of Souls.

He remembered…legions he ruled. Minds he dominated.

He remembered…betrayed by those he trusted. His soul torn from his body and trapped here.

He remembered…everything… the traitorous dogs!

He had always been quick-tempered and prone to fits of rage, but none compared to this. With a primal scream the three orbs, his watchers who had willingly placed themselves inside to guard over him, were decimated in a rush of energy. His prison reverberated for several long moments from the impact. It enraged him what those so-called magicians thought they could do to him and get away with it, locking him away like a criminal. They had deemed him too dangerous to continue his reign. Too dangerous? Perhaps, but only to those who plotted against him. He would show them just how dangerous he was.

With his captors eliminated it was time to reclaim his kingdoms, but the barrier still held, refusing to break. It shouldn't be possible… unless – the one orb that had vanished, somehow it must be maintaining the shield. His frustration renewed, he slammed against the shield several more times with all his might. It was a futile effort. His fury subsiding, he took a few moments to regain his composure. No matter, he thought. He could now sense what was happening outside of his encasement. His influence would again be felt in the land.

***

Another long scream was torn from him as he hung chained to the wall, his arms shackled over his head barely allowing his feet to touch the ground. His once fine royal blue robes were tattered and matted with blood and dirt. It had been weeks since he was captured, all the others in his group systematically found and executed. Hope was all but gone at this point, the sting of his failure worse than any physical pain he had endured over the last weeks. He was all that was left of the Magicus Celesti. The mighty Glaedrin was reduced to a shell of his former self, only being kept alive long enough so he could witness evil's triumph.

The witch sat on her throne directly across the grand chamber looking at him in self-satisfaction, enjoying the spectacle of his latest torture session. It was her doing that led to their demise, and to the terrible magic that was about to be unleashed upon the world. Despite all of their efforts, they could not stop Sevra from recreating the forbidden designs she had somehow uncovered.

Looking across the room he glared at her through pain-glazed eyes. He would almost have considered her beautiful regardless of her unusual appearance, had he not known how deeply evil this woman was. With skin so fair as to almost be translucent, the red of her lips provided the only hint of color. Her hair was as dark as the night sky stripped of stars, save for a slivered crescent of white.

Unable to bear the sight of her sadistic smirk any longer he used what remained of his faltering strength to survey his surroundings. Four large pillars stood in the center of the room extending high to the ceiling, squaring off a large area between them. Nearly filling the area was an intricately crafted network of silver and obsidian conduits, interweaved and coiled so as nearly impossible to follow with the eye. The contraption was only about a foot high and several feet across, but looked to contain miles of thin twisted metalwork. Moonlight filtered in through an opening in the ceiling directly above it.

Rising from her gilded throne, Sevra walked around the perimeter of the room, approaching him with the saunter of a cat ready to toy with an injured mouse. A thin smile spread across her lips, a smile of arrogance in her plans coming to fruition. The guard who had been tormenting him bowed his head to her and stepped off to the side.

"Soon, so very soon you will see the results of a century of my efforts. All of Luskir will be united by one power, under my command," she said to him coyly, gently patting his bruised face.

Sevra had gone to great lengths to ensure Glaedrin was fully subdued. Each of his fingers were broken to prevent him from manipulating energy with his hands. He was fed a vile liquid every hour on the hour that made his mind weak and confused. Able to neither think nor gesture a spell, he hung defenselessly to the witch's devices. Had he been able to speak he would have told her how foolish she was for what she was going to attempt, that there was no way to account for the unintended consequences of such a massive spell, or the lack of morality evident in controlling the minds of people in such a fashion. Better yet he would have liked to incinerate her with a mere thought.

Instead, he could only groan in response, his mind too muddled to form words.

"Oh, what's that – something to say my dear?" she asked, followed by a throaty laugh, "no, of course not Glaedrin. You will just watch. And see the extent of your failure before I let you die."

He looked her in the eyes, trying to offer a last attempt at defiance. He maintained his gaze only a moment before his head fell back down, not having the strength to continue looking forward. Before he slipped into unconsciousness his last sight was of the necklace adorning Sevra's collar. A string of six diamonds ran up one side, with five on the other and an empty slot where one once was. Each was fractured, flawed and broken though still beautiful. At the bottom of the chain and nestled in her bosom rested a large crimson gem, the cause of the calamity soon to be unleashed upon the world.

Boldstone

Snow devils sprang to life in the gusting winds across the northernmost plains. Glistening crystals swirled up into an unseen dance and vanished, reappearing at the wind's whim in an encore across the frozen stage. It was always windy in the Blue Fold, the mountain sides dominating the landscape this far north at the top of the world incessantly smoothed and shaped by the unending gales. Cold and indifferent, the wind rose over the stone that endured here for millenia, stoic and indomitable in defiance of the elements.

Seeming to blend with the stone around him, his face weathered beyond his twenty-two years from this harsh environment sat a man overlooking the landscape. From his vantage point sitting high atop the rock face of Boldstone Ridge, the highest of the five mountain ridges, the majestic beauty of the land he called home was not lost on him. The sun, low on the horizon, shone across the ranges comprising the Blue Fold Mountains. In the predawn light, endless shades of blue shone like glowing sapphires in the distance.

The man looked down past the encampments on the Ridges where his people lived during the more hospitable seasons, and beyond to the open plains below. During the winter, they migrated across these plains where the weather was less severe, surviving from hunt to hunt by shadowing the movements of the various herds.

Soon, he would be trekking onto the tundra once again in search of prey, doing his part to ensure the continued survival of the tribe. If there were a people made to thrive in a land most wouldn't dare to venture, it was the barbarians of the Blue Fold Mountains. Like the mountains themselves, they too were stoic and indomitable.

With the recent passing of his father, Jvard assumed responsibility of the four clans that comprise the Frostwrynn. There was relative peace among the clans residing in the Blue Fold range. Under the guidance of the Elders many disputes were settled before it came to aggressions between groups, and healthy-sized herds on the plains in recent years meant low competition for survival among the tribe. Jvard's father, Helstajvan had accomplished much in uniting the clans who shared this corner of the Blue Fold Mountains, as well as strengthening the bonds among his own clan.

Jvard began his descent through the footpath, bringing him away from the highest areas of the mountain, his reflections on his upcoming hunt, and back home towards Boldstone Ridge. This night Jvard and his hunting group would be on the move, and there were preparations to make and rituals to observe before departing.

The Ridges were bustling with activity. Only ten days ago had the last cold of winter broke and signs of spring were returning to the land. There was much work to be done, the hide tents and poles were carefully put back into storage for next winter on the plains, and repairs needed to be made to the permanent dwellings constructed on the Ridges that had been vacant for months.

Just beyond their mountain home to the northwest, a great river, the Tinindraüg, flowed during the warmer months of the year. A large area of the valley was shielded by the Ridges on one side, and another mountain range on its southern and western side. In this unexposed area, a great pine forest was able to grow whereas the rest of the north was largely barren or scattered with low vegetation. The plentitude of trees allowed the tribes to build several *Dhidvhel*, large hall-style houses that would be occupied by up to several dozen extended family members. Each ridge had between ten to thirteen of these halls, and one additional hall used for important meetings called the *Daärdvhel*, which referred to both the meeting and the name of the hall. On the fifth and highest level, a great hall was built known as the *Ingdaärðendvhel* for when all of the clans needed to meet.

The Ridges were an invaluable natural fortification, offering a highly defensible position from other groups in the Blue Fold Mountains. In the event of an attack, the few paths leading up to the different levels along the mountain were sealed off, while the cliff faces at each level created a daunting barrier. During an assault all clans would assist in the defense, and if the first ridge was breached a tactical retreat to the second would take place, all the way to the fifth ridge if necessary. The defense strategy was so successful in fact, that in the memory of the oldest tribesmen, and passed down in stories from their grandfather's grandfathers, attackers had only ever made it to the second ridge.

The Frostwrynn were somewhat unique among the various peoples of the Blue Fold Mountains. They did not live a completely nomadic existence on the plains as was to be expected of the northmen. The Ridges offered them a partial settlement where, though it was not an easy life, they had a few months of reprieve from the constant struggle for survival while moving on the tundra. This allowed them to grow larger than many of the other tribes, and have stronger affiliations among their own clansmen.

They even had some leisure time available - small teams took turns hunting to bring back food for all, while the others spent the majority of their time honing their battle skills. They drilled ridge-wide defenses as well as individual combat, each barbarian mastering a variety of weaponry. Astonishingly nearly one quarter of the Frostwrynn were literate, almost unheard of among the barbarians. Over the years, they managed to accumulate a small collection of texts, which they valued as one of their most prized belongings.

Jvard finished packing the essentials he would need for the upcoming trek and was ready to seek out his remaining tasks for the day. He decided first to find Garl, who oversaw the clan's move from the tundra to the Ridges. Garl enjoyed spearheading the task, and had borne this responsibility for many seasons. To most observers, the bustling activity would appear as loosely organized chaos.

A cacophonous blend of sounds carried over the Ridges: the stomping of men hauling new planks from recently felled trees on the hillside, the hammering of rooftops repaired and the chatter of children as they carried pails of water or chests holding various materials. The clattering of pots and pans joined in as massive quantities of food were prepared, all accompanied by the rhythmic sound of tools pounded into shape at the forge. To Garl it was not noise, but the essence of his people. All of these sounds merged into a symphony, and characterized the success of the clans and the level of community they had worked so hard to accomplish under the leadership of Helstajvan and now Jvard.

Approaching the center of the ridge, Jvard spotted Garl speaking with several clansmen. He was a hard individual to miss. Most of the barbarians were large, but Garl stood closer to seven feet than six. Dark blonde hair hung down to the middle of his back, while his face was covered with a thick beard reaching to the middle of his chest – both were interspersed with the silver of age rarely seen in this formidable land. His belly was ample, yet overall he had a hardness to him that demanded attention when he spoke. Gesturing at one of the *Dhidvhel* as he gave instructions, the men surrounding him nodded. One eye clouded with cataracts, Garl turned his head at the sound of snow crunching under boots. Seeing Jvard approach he dismissed the crew.

"Hoi, Jvard I'd been havin' my eye out for you most of the day!" he shouted over the din.

Jvard himself was a prime specimen among his people. Though not quite as large as Garl, among his kin he too was considered tall. To a southerner he would have towered. Thick boned and weighing nearly twenty-five stone, his speed and agility were surprising for a man his size, which he used to his advantage when engaging enemies whether they be beast or man.

"*Kveösjá*, my friend," Jvard replied in a greeting of respect, "how go the preparations?"

Garl paused and took an appraising look around, "Another day, maybe two, we'll be takin' back to business as usual. Most of the *Dhidvhel* only required minor repairs this season, a new plank in some sections, or a small patchin' of the roof. What of your plans?"

"Tonight we shall have the Elders call an *Ingdaärðendvhel* to greet the change of seasons. Afterwards I will visit the *Duchàlg* and receive their blessings for the upcoming hunt," he replied.

Garl nodded in consent, "A wise course, perhaps you'll gain some sight of your prey with the *Duchàlg*."

Jvard added, "They have ever shown their usefulness. We hope to be gone not longer than five days, but it always depends on the movement of the herds."

A concerned look came over Garl, almost fatherly, "Are you sure it's wise for you to be leavin' so soon, just back from the *Kleïntòr*?" Garl asked.

Soon after Jvard's father passed, the Frostwrynn and another nearby tribe, the Denórvja, had a territorial dispute. Before it escalated into a conflict, Jvard called for a *Kleïntòr*, a duel of honor between warriors whose victory would settle the matter. The elders on both sides agreed, and Jvard personally insisted on representing the Frostwrynn. His victory allowed his people to set terms in their favor.

"I am fine, my injuries were minor," Jvard replied, dismissing the concern with a small laugh.

"A few more scars will do you good I s'pose," Garl chuckled.

The two men clasped arms and parted ways, Garl back to his duties and Jvard moving along to the third ridge to organize the clan elders.

With two exceptions, all five of the Ridges had a similar design, each running east to west. At either end, several dwellings were evenly spaced apart. Moving in towards the center were food stores, pens for livestock, various tradesmen - tanneries, weavers, and woodworkers. In the middle stood the meeting hall, an expansive room large enough to hold the entire clan.

The first exception to the design of the levels was the third ridge. This level, aptly named the Shadow Cliff, was cast in a perpetual shadow by a jutting ledge on the fourth ridge, and was not wholly occupied by an individual clan. When in doubt, clansmen came to this ridge to seek out guidance from the *Duchàlg*, or spirit-seekers. The majority of Shadow Cliff was occupied by the *Duchàlg's* encampment, separated from the rest of the ridge by a tall wooden fence. Also on the eastern side of the *Duchàlg's* encampment sat a moderate sized building with little adornment, and it was here that Jvard was now headed. As a neutral ridge, this building was where the clan elders would meet on a daily basis for discussion, without fear of bias or favoritism.

Jvard entered the unadorned structure. At the back wall, an old man crouched down prodding at a fire built into a stone chute that allowed smoke to exit through the roof, a more recent innovation that none of the other clansmen completely trusted to be built in their *Dhidvhel*. To the majority of the tribe, a fire built inside seemed like an unnecessary luxury and outright dangerous. Seven additional elders were seated casually inside and talking softly.

Together, these eight men balanced the authority of the tribal chief; in this manner, no one leader could have absolute dominance over the group without their power being checked. If any decision made by the chieftain was unanimously opposed by the elders, it could be overruled.

The council was composed equally from the four clans. Two men, generally the oldest and wisest were selected to serve. Jvard entered, looking each of the elders in the eye before allowing a slight dip of his head. In turn, the eight men nodded back as one.

One of the elders rose, his face wrinkled and hair a shining white. His blue eyes still held a strength that had left his body some time ago.

He spoke in a deep, resonant voice, "Hail Jvard, son of Helstajvan. What brings you to our hall this day, have you come to turn the council on its head again so soon?"

Dagard had not approved of Jvard's last decision, so hastily seeking individual combat to settle their recent issue with the Denórvja.

Jvard ignored the slight, announcing what had brought him here, "Hail, Speaker Dagard, he who speaks for the tribe. I've come to proclaim that tonight we shall celebrate the Change of the Winds. May all of the clans forget their duties for a time, and may the Gods deliver us a bountiful season!"

The elders cheered and Dagard's mood brightened, clapping his large hands together slowly with mirthful laughter, "Wonderful, it lifts us all to veer away from our darker discussions to a more joyous subject. We shall begin the preparations immediately."

Word quickly spread that the *Ingdaärðendvhel* would be called for tonight. As sunset approached, the clansmen on the lower landings began ascending the paths to Boldstone Ridge. Throngs of people walked along the foot paths on the eastern or western sides of the Ridges to reach the topmost level. Every year after resettling into the Ridges, this special *Ingdaärðendvhel* was called, and was followed by several days of boisterous drinking and merriment in an attempt to please the deities of fertility and passion, Yvieona and her consort Fierengard.

Passion was a common trait among the barbarians, encompassing every aspect of their life, from their explosive violence in battle to their concise focus of survival on the harsh tundra plains. It was the song that echoed loudly in the hearts and minds of men like Garl, Jvard, and the rest of the tribe. Even as they made their preparations to settle into the Ridges they exuded a robust energy. Every act they performed, no matter how simple was executed with a single-minded intent to see it completed. When the song resonated loudest, most often in battle, the barbarians were known to accomplish feats that pushed the limits of what was accepted to be humanly possible. Stories spread over the centuries by the few outsiders who bore witness to their exploits, some exaggerated and others accurate, though all mostly disregarded as tall tales.

The four clans made their way to the center of the fifth level. The second exception to the design of the Ridges was the layout of Boldstone Ridge. At the center of this ridge stood the *Ingdaäröendvhel*, a structure built to entertain all four clans. The outer building was nearly three times the size of a typical *Daärdvhel*, and the remainder of the structure was carved directly into the mountain's cliff-face at the rear of the ridge. Eight tables each nearly a hundred feet long lined the inside, the tribesmen organized by clan at two adjacent tables. A dais stood at the rear of the structure from where the Speaker would make his address.

A crowd formed as they waited their turn to funnel through the gate-doors of the *Ingdaäröendvhel*. There was much jostling and a few blows were exchanged as the clans intermingled, but overall order was maintained. Approximately one thousand barbarians ascended Boldstone Ridge. Many Jdertusk, a boar-like creature but larger and more temperamental, were spit and roasting, and dozens of casks of ale were rolled inside.

The clans slowly funneled into the Great Hall, and soon filled the eight massive tables. Torches ran alongside the walls, and across the rear of the cavern behind the dais. Nine chairs lined the back wall, a throne in the center where Jvard was seated and four large chairs on either side where the clan elders were positioned.

Speaker Dagard approached the stand at the front of the dais, his hands outstretched beseeching silence from the crowd.

After a few moments he had the attention of the hall and began speaking in a seemingly magnified voice, "Hail clans of the Frostwrynn tribe – hail clan Rvestá, clan Kòdjak, clan Darcláw, and clan Jharta!"

After Dagard announced each clan it was necessary for him to pause a few moments, waiting for the uproarious cheers from the clan who was named to subside, "We have assembled today to discuss two important matters. First and foremost, with the passing of the last frigid gales of the season, it is now time to welcome the Change of the Winds!"

At that note, the entire hall boomed. Men shouted, mugs were clanged against tables and nearly a minute passed before the Speaker could continue.

"We will hold celebrations for two days, may Yvieona and Fierengard be pleased by the festivities. But before we raise our mugs we must discuss a matter of certain urgency. Igdahven, leader of the *Duchàlg*," the Speaker paused momentarily, gesturing at a robed figure, "has informed us he has foreseen a dangerous change in the skies. Though he doesn't fully understand its nature, he and the *Duchàlg* thought it prudent to bring it to the council's attention."

A curiously donned figure stood off to the side wearing a robe that looked to be made of hundreds of separate scraps of blue and gray cloth. His billowy sleeves were fringed with feathers, and several small skulls dangled from leather cords attached to a cincture around his waist. A wolf cap rested atop his head, its fur-skin draping over his shoulders.

The crowd grew uneasy and murmuring broke out among the tables upon hearing the Speaker's words.

Dagard gestured soothingly to the audience and continued his address, "Though we do not know exactly what the spirit-seekers have divined, given past events it is likely an attack from a rival tribe."

These last words Dagard accentuated and spoke with much derision. He was a master at manipulating the emotions of an audience to his desires; in his case, the role of Speaker was well earned. Attacks against the Ridges by a rival group were never successful and bordered on suicidal. Now that he informed the gathering of the potential threat and put an identity to it, it was time to soothe their worries so celebrations could begin.

He continued, a smile upturning the corner of his lip and a hint of venom entering his tone, "Of course, we all remember the last time our enemies had the gall to test the might of the Frostwrynn."

Again the hall erupted. They remembered well, and their emotions still ran hot from Jvard's recent victory over the very same rival's champion. Dagard was referring to the last attempt on the Ridges several years ago. In a particularly bad winter, the Denórvja, located several miles northeast, had outnumbered an advanced scouting group of the Frostwrynn on the plains and thought to take advantage. The small group sent two runners alerting the rest of the Frostwrynn to temporarily head back to the mountain, and then fell into a square formation. With their well-practiced tactics they were able to avoid being surrounded as they slowly retreated back towards the Ridges.

The Denórvja pursued, and made the ill-considered decision to continue the assault. Once at the fortifications, the Denórvja were forced into fighting uphill on narrow pathways with the entrances sealed off, while spears and arrows rained down on them. The Denórvja lost many that day, and were so weakened they barely made it through the winter. The Frostwrynn only lost three warriors. Jvard's decision to settle the most recent dispute with the Denórvja through an honor duel was in part made to spare them another difficult year.

"Whatever test and hardships are delivered unto us from the Gods, we shall prevail as we always do. Our scouts have not seen any hostile activity from other tribes, there is no reason we cannot continue our celebrations as planned. *Daün drovka du sôjn dravka*! As it comes, so shall we go."

***

Slipping away from the meeting during Dagard's speech, Igdahven returned to his tents on the Shadow Cliff to make last minute preparations for his meeting with Jvard. With his fire nearly dying out, the spirit-seeker pulled himself away from the workbench to fetch a few more logs. Tending the flames, he carefully placed two of them in the stone circle. He needed to keep the fire low but steady for the ritual. This tent, and a few others like it within their encampment were specifically designed for the ceremony he was about to perform. Each contained a table with various ingredients strewn about, a fire pit dug into the ground, and walls that sloped steeply to an open top at the center allowing the smoke to funnel out.

Igdahven, like most of the *Duchàlg*, showed signs of his gift for premonition at an early age. They were different than the other barbarians - without exception they were much smaller than their other tribesmen, and they embraced their ability rather than showing wariness towards it. Only seven out of the roughly one thousand barbarians on the Ridges had the gift, and once it began to manifest itself the child was immediately moved to the encampment on the third ridge to begin training.

Mumbling instructions to himself, Igdahven resumed his preparation of the mixture, the skulls dangling from his belt swaying back and forth as he bustled about. Within the hour, Jvard would be arriving at Shadow Cliff and Igdahven wanted to make sure all was ready for the Viewing. He hummed a jovial tune as he worked, Frostwyrm in the *Daärdvhel*, one of the more frivolous songs of the Blue Fold Mountain tribes.

The tune did little to cheer him though; he did not comprehend the visions that had occasionally flashed into he and his colleagues' meditations over the past few days and that lack of understanding disturbed him greatly. After Dagard's revelation of the *Duchàlg*'s divinations at his speech, Jvard would have many questions and Igdahven had few answers ready. As a spirit-seeker, it was his responsibility to forewarn the tribe of any misfortunes on the horizon, not being able to perform his duties adequately made him more agitated than a silverfrost with its paw in a warrior's snare. Hopefully some of these visions would emerge in the upcoming Viewing and Jvard could see for himself.

***

At the end of the Speaker's address, the celebration spilled out of the *Ingdaärðendvhel* and sprawled across the fifth ridge down onto the fourth. Jvard weaved his way through the crowds of people, pausing frequently to clasp arms, or accept an offering of drink or food. He did his best to greet each individual, but even the chieftain could not keep the *Duchàlg* waiting. Around him revelers imbibed in copious amounts of whatever was available: typically ale, wine, or for the braver souls an especially potent brew the barbarians called *drákna* known to sometimes cause temporary blindness.

He did not resent that though the rest of the clan was in the midst of celebration, his group was scheduled to perform the duties of the hunt. Nor did it ever cross his mind that as the tribal leader he should have special exemption from this responsibility. On the contrary, as chieftain he felt more pressure to perform well and set a high standard for the size of the return quarry. He would push the five men accompanying him to near their limits, because he would be pushing himself just as much in the upcoming days. Nearly ready to depart, he sought out the spirit-seekers in Shadow Cliff to see if there was any guidance to be gleaned.

Before the *Ingdaärðendvhel*, Jvard had learned of the recent divinations and questioned Igdahven to no avail. Their visions were indeed disturbing, but they were no more than sudden flashes that they described as "having many different interpretations." He shook himself away from deliberating on this news, if the spirit-seekers couldn't make sense of it yet he certainly would not be able to either. He needed to set his focus on something more concrete, what he would be doing for the next few days demanded his full attention. Arriving at the third ridge, he pushed the wooden gate open leading into the *Duchàlg*'s encampment.

Preparations

Jvard took a deep breath before pushing open the gate and crossing the threshold into the *Duchàlg* encampment. He braced himself as he passed through the entryway, the hair on the back of his neck standing on end. Though only a stockade fence separated their section of the settlement, they were a world apart from the other ridges. The very air seemed to take on a darker quality, the effect partly enhanced by the large piece of ledge from the fourth ridge looming over the encampment to cast it in perpetual shadow. A few large tents with high conical tops sporadically dotted the grounds, along with several piles of animal bones, and stone circles where fires were built.

Most of the barbarians found it difficult to hide their unease around the spirit-seekers, many simply avoided them altogether. Historically the peoples inhabiting the Blue Fold Mountains had always been skeptical of magic, at times to the point of irrational fear. It was said long ago among the barbarians that anyone displaying an affinity towards magic was Fel-touched. Sometimes these people were exiled, but more often than not they were killed on sight. Eventually people with the gift became accepted and sometimes hailed, filling the role of shaman. Over the past few hundred years as more barbarians continued to show signs of occult abilities they formed a society within their tribe known as the *Duchàlg*.

Jvard walked through the seemingly empty encampment guided by a series of torches. They led him to a plain tent made of cured hides. Unsure if this was where he belonged, he pushed the flap aside and entered. He was chieftain, after all, and didn't exactly need permission. Igdahven, his back towards the entry, was busy at his workbench preparing a mixture in a stone bowl.

"Please be seated Jvard, in front of the fire with the flats of your feet touching if you will," Igdahven instructed without turning around.

Jvard exhaled heavily as he lowered his massive frame to the ground, sitting as directed. Several minutes passed in silence as Igdahven continued working. Finally, Igdahven placed the bowl down on the ground a few feet away from Jvard. Walking over to the corner he retrieved a large pair of tongs, using them to pull a medium sized stone from the fire. He carefully placed the stone on the ground between Jvard's knees. He pulled a second stone out placing it on the ground near the bowl, and sat similar to Jvard.

Chanting slowly in a low, indistinguishable monotone, he threw a handful of powder into the fire casting the room into a bluish glow.

Igdahven continued his chant. The drone of his voice began filling the air, setting a steady rhythm reverberating through Jvard's head. The chant grew louder in Jvard's mind, spreading into his every thought. Soon the hymn seemed to fill the entire room causing everything else to fade away. Darkness enveloped him, and the hymn became the only perceivable sound set to the drumming of Jvard's heartbeat.

The chanting continued until he finally heard a distant voice instruct, "Breathe in deeply."

A loud hiss echoed as Igdahven poured the contents of the bowl onto the hot stones. Jvard opened his eyes, just then realizing they had been closed. Physical objects seemed dimmer and less substantial, their bodies, the stones, and the fire, all took on an immaterial quality. Wisps and streams of light and dark coiled around the room, often times drawn towards Jvard and Igdahven.

"Follow," Igdahven beckoned.

The two men, with Igdahven guiding, ventured out of the tent with mere thought and into the encampment. Again the insubstantial quality permeated all of the material, physical objects. Light and dark wisps continued to flow around all of the matter often focusing on either or both men.

Inside, only smaller flows were visible. Outside, they could see the true extent of the glowing and shadowed eddies as massive currents of light and shadow coursed through the sky. Smaller branches broke off in all directions, and broke off several times more filling their entire field of vision.

The spirit-seekers often came to this place in order to find answers. Generations ago they discovered through deep meditation they could enter this realm they referred to as the *Chàlgraäden*, or spirit realm. Hundreds of years of observation and trial and error allowed the spirit-seekers to build a working knowledge of the realm and the remarkable streams of light and shadow they called the *Duchstraüm*. They found that with practice, they could locate groups of people or animals by tracking the *Mináduchstraüm*, smaller divisions and branches of the larger flows of darkness and light. The more talented among them, Igdahven included, could even use these to pinpoint a specific person. One of the many uses the *Duchàlg* had for this place was to help the other barbarians narrow down the location of a herd more quickly, ensuring, or at least greatly improving the chance for a successful hunt.

"Come, this way," Igdahven said breaking Jvard's concentration on the glorious skyline.

In single leaps they bounded down from ridge to ridge. In a few quick steps, they were free of the ledges at the base of the mountain. Off they went across the plains, crossing miles of distance in mere moments. Occasionally Igdahven would pause and observe the movements of the *Mináduchstraüm*, noting which were moving steadily against the ones that meandered, as well as their speed and direction. Heading generally east, he turned slightly northward and resumed the rapid pace.

After many pauses to track the movements of the flows, change direction, or occasionally backtrack he located a large herd of Jdertusk. Small wisps of light and dark that had branched repeatedly from the main network of *Duchstraüm* curled around and among the beasts.

Jvard noted to Igdahven, "I know this area well. We are roughly three days out from the Ridges."

"Very well," replied Igdahven, "the herd looks to be continuing northeast, hopefully their direction remains predictable and you have gained some knowledge that will aid you in the coming days."

"Let us return home," Jvard stated, "I don't care to stay here longer than necessary."

The two men made the return trip to the Ridges much faster than their journey out to deduce the location of a herd. Within the span of a few thoughts, the landscape passing by in blurs, they were back on the Shadow Cliff. They reentered Igdahven's tent, returning to their physical forms and ending their brief expedition in the *Chàlgraäden*.

***

Assembled at the base of the Ridges, six men awaited for Jvard's arrival from the Shadow Cliff. This would be their team's first of three to four appointed hunts of the season. Due to the timing this year, they had to miss the celebration of the Changing of the Winds, but such was life; duty would always take precedence over festivity. Each man carried a moderate-sized pack, a mace or hammer, rope, a spear, and a few blades of different length. Three large sleds were brought along to use for returning the kill. Together, two men could drag a fully loaded sled many miles each day across the icy tundra.

Within the hour, the group spotted Jvard approaching along the eastern path off of the first ridge; even at this distance there was no mistaking his frame. Under the shadow of darkness and with his thick brown furs draped over his shoulders, he looked more like a great bear walking upright than a person coming down the path. Though the sky was still dim in the early hours, nights were beginning to grow shorter and dawn was trying to break through the cloudy morning. Jvard prayed the weather would hold for the duration of the hunt; they would be on the open plains at the coming of first light.

"*Kveösjá*, my brethren," Jvard called out when he was within range of his crew.

The men lightly touched their fingertips to their foreheads in respect. With the exception of one man he knew each of these warriors well, and had led each member of this team for at least three years, some longer. Jvard trusted all of them and knew them to be capable; their time spent working together transformed the unit into a finely tuned instrument that could only be achieved through years of shared experience.

A herd of Jdertusk, or other beasts encountered on the tundra, could quickly become dangerous adversaries against those who were unprepared. He had no such reservations about his hunting team. Each of Jvard's men had an awareness of everyone else in the group. They knew their individual responsibilities in the hunt, and could coordinate with one another wordlessly.

Jvard looked to the new member of the hunting party, a youth who had just passed his fifteenth name-day. The young man shifted under the scrutiny of the tribal leader.

He eyed him up and down for a long moment before speaking, "You must be Larik son of Glarid. You'll find us to be a group who works as one, the key to a successful hunt lies in teamwork."

Sensing the young barbarian's nervousness, he quietly leaned in so only Larik could hear and offered a piece of advice, "Watch. Observe. Think. You are both an individual and a member of the group – do not forget either. Look for opportunities to help and you'll find them, and never forget our strength lies in unity. You'll do fine."

Larik nodded vigorously, attempting to not show his nerves. He still had the lankiness of youth, not yet filling in the long limbs typical of the northern barbarians. Currently he stood a few inches over six foot, and still probably had several inches of growing left to do – though at the moment he looked to be more arms and legs than a newborn fawn and probably wouldn't completely fill in for a few years yet.

He had been looking forward to joining a hunting team for what seemed like an eternity, and could barely contain his excitement that the opportunity was now upon him. To be able to join a hunting party was a rite of passage among the barbarians, signaling that a young man had finally come of age and could assist in the continued survival and well-being of the tribe. Larik was determined to prove himself, though now with a tempered enthusiasm after Jvard's advising words.

Out on the plains, the landscape was largely unvaried. Shortly after venturing out, a pale orange glow broke over the horizon as first light welcomed the day. Looming far to the east was yet another mountain range, deceptively distant because of its towering heights. Jvard set a purposeful pace to the northeast, hoping to catch signs of the Jdertusk herd before it made any drastic changes of direction from what was indicated to him by the *Duchàlg*. He estimated the expedition would take roughly six days, two and a half days out, and three and a half days returning to compensate for the additional burden of the kill they would be hauling.

Hours passed by as the party moved across the tundra. Occasionally they passed by patches of dense brush, or twisted, low growing trees stubbornly clinging to life, unable to root properly in the frozen land. It took a certain amount of fortitude to survive in the Blue Fold, even among the plants and animals. Life either adapted to the harsh conditions, or succumbed to the elements.

Jvard's group traversed the terrain like they were born to it, moving as naturally as a bird taking flight or a wolf-cub at play in the frigid snow. They maintained a fast pace for hours, drawing on a strength only the barbarians seemed to possess that allowed them to stave off fatigue. The pounding of their footfalls set a cadence in their minds, and once they fell into a comfortable pace the cadence became a center of focus eliminating all other thought. There was only the rhythm, driving them forward as if of its own accord.

Catalyst

Her moment of triumph had arrived. It had taken over one hundred years travelling the world, eliminating those who stood in her way, searching far and wide to seek out the obscure, ancient designs. Any loss of life was inconsequential to her in the face of what she stood to gain.

Guided by divine inspiration, she perfected arts that were forgotten for millennia. The might of a God was on her side, instructing her, offering her direction when all seemed hopeless. He taught her how to cheat death itself so she could see this task complete, and see centuries more as the undisputed Empress once her plan came to fruition.

Smiling, Sevra glanced over to Eldora, the Duchess of Dun'Aldir, First Seat of the Luskiran Council. The Duchess smiled back vacantly. While the people thought Eldora to be the most influential person in all of Luskir, her mind had not been her own for nearly two decades. Sevra was the true source of power in the city of Dun'Aldir. After unleashing the spell, the entire land would be hers to command unabated – and once she eliminated the council, there would be none to oppose her.

Waiting the past few weeks had been the most difficult part in her long journey to see the ritual complete. All of the preparations had been ready for months, but she was instructed to wait for just the right conditions. With the arrival of the equinox along with volatile weather moving in, her God told her it was time to disperse the powerful magic. She was going to imbue the very air itself with her spell; two large, converging storms would serve as the perfect delivery method.

She wanted all to bear witness to her moment of glory. Her personal guard, the Devoted, lined the room, each mentally broken to be fully acquiescent to whatever she desired or commanded. Eldora sat by her side, eagerly awaiting what her most trusted advisor was about to reveal.

Also in attendance were the two commanders from Sevra's private army, the Drakvnar. Guard-Captain Ramnar and First Lieutenant Kempf both stood as still as statues, monitoring the room. While Ramnar was not under the spell that affected the Devoted, his loyalty towards Sevra was every bit as strong. He fully believed in and supported her vision, and carried out her will without question. Ramnar led the Drakvnar, those of the True-Blood, and had the respect of the thousand men under his command.

While Ramnar oversaw the day to day operations, it left little time for him to maintain discipline among the whole of the Dun'Aldiran forces. That was where Kempf proved his usefulness; shorter, heavy-set but muscular, Kempf performed the unsavory duties that may have otherwise sullied the reputation of Guard-Captain Ramnar. Kempf had no such reservations about how others regarded him. He thoroughly enjoyed his work, making an example of anyone who dared step out of line. There would likely be a period of turmoil after her plan was put into action. Ramnar, Kempf, and the rest of the True-Blood would need to be ready to quell any unease.

Among all of the imposing figures in the room, one stood out above the others. Urstaag, her prize from the north, remained silent behind Sevra with furs hanging loosely over his shoulders. The man was a full seven feet tall, and more closely resembled a bear standing on its hind legs in the dim lighting. He rarely spoke, and as with her other fifty personal guards, he demonstrated an unwavering obedience to her.

Unaffected by the same spell she used to break the Devoted, Sevra initially had difficulty with the formidable giant. She was forced to resort to more exhaustive magic in order to rein him in, but he was worth every moment of the struggle. Always at her side, anyone who had to speak to the witch woman always found their gaze shifting to Urstaag. His presence alone was oftentimes enough to set her opponents off balance.

It was unusual for Sevra to have so many people within her inner sanctum. Normally, if she even suspected someone having been here she would have called for their execution immediately. Tonight however, was different. The fruits of her labor were at hand, and secretly she relished in the thought of others witnessing the terrifying display of power that would soon take place.

Moonlight began to filter in through an opening in the ceiling, supplementing the light thrown by the thousands of meticulously arranged candles to illuminate the device at the center of the room. It was nearly dizzying to look at the item, silver and obsidian metals so masterfully interworked it seemed as if it were one continuous piece.

She briefly reflected on the ordeal it had been to retrieve the spectacular filigree. She was guided to its location in the middle of the Vermillion Sands, nearly losing her life in the process. To think that there were actually people still living in that barren wasteland, watching over the relic; she would be repaying them in due time.

The instrument had to be painstakingly restored. Only the finest artisans were commissioned for the project, and discretely removed afterwards to maintain its secrecy. All of it had been possible through one means, divine intervention. Without the God given instructions she never would have found the artifact, figured out how to restore it or learn the necessary rituals to use it.

As a young wizard's apprentice, some one hundred and forty-nine years earlier, she began hearing the voice that brought her to this moment. Convinced she had gone mad, Sevra cloistered herself away for many months afraid and ashamed, until realizing that her studies were advancing more quickly than was normal. The voice frequently offered corrections and advice, telling her things she wouldn't have known otherwise.

Then, it offered her more.

The advice turned into tantalizing visions of power and promises of immortality; it was all within her grasp. The only thing it asked in return was that she eliminate the wizard she apprenticed under, and retrieve the necklace as her own... from then on they were as one. Her lips parted a bit as she caressed the ruby at her neck, recalling when she came into its possession and how far she had ascended.

Her God-granted abilities set her apart from the others who thought themselves to be wizards. Delving directly into the realm that they could only touch upon, the power she wielded was beyond their limited capabilities. As far as Sevra knew, there were no others who could walk in both the realm of spirits and the physical world, moving wraithlike from one to the other. She allowed herself to slip into this state now; the physical world losing its color, the sounds in the room dampening.

Dark streaks of energy only she could see filled the chamber. Their counterpart, strands of a pure silvery white were only present in one concentrated area, leaving her feeling somewhat vexed. She brushed aside those implications, allowing the limitless flows of energies at her disposal to wash over her. Soon she would be reaching outward to call upon both varieties of energy in vast quantity.

Proceeding across the room she stopped in front of the light currents. They led her to Glaedrin, representing the last of the magical order she had been in a private war against for the past twenty years. What a pathetic creature he now was, defeated in both mind and body. His suffering truly pleased her. Though Sevra considered herself to be peerless, he was the closest there was to her level of skill.

"Soon," she whispered to him, "I'll let you die, but not before you witness what you worked so hard to prevent. Your spirit will be mine, extending my years and terminating yours."

Glaedrin could see Sevra was not entirely among them, that she transcended to a state more conducive to magical efforts. As a wizard he too journeyed into that realm, though admittedly not with the same fluidity and duality Sevra could manage. Since his capture, he had been completely sealed away from it. There was little left for him to fight with, but he could not stop until he no longer drew breath. He spent the better part of his life tracking Sevra's every move, and he knew her better than anyone else alive.

He knew her confident exterior was a mask covering the weakness of her vanity, and that her life had not been her own in over a century. He knew she understood, yet still refused to accept the nature of the spiritual realm. He knew she could not see the choices she had made throughout her life were dictated by evil and not her own. He knew he would soon be dead and had to make a last attempt to fuel her doubts. He knew what he needed to do.

Summoning the last remnants of his strength he spoke back to her, "There is good and evil Sevra, the end never justifies the means. You've observed the realms and can guess at their workings. Look about you, tell me your eyes do not deceive you."

A flash of anger distorted her features, quickly passing.

"I do not guess, wizard. I know all, I see all," she snapped, "I'd kill you now, if I didn't know how much pain bearing witness to your own ineptitude will bring you."

"I pity you, Sevra, no more than a pawn to a being more twisted and wicked than even yourself. I'm sorry this happened to you," he said with calm conviction.

Sevra reached out and latched her hand onto the side of his face, her nails digging into his skin until she drew blood. Shaking with rage she wished to strike him down, but composed herself and turned away. Delaying her gratification just a while longer so he could witness her triumph would bring him more pain than she could ever inflict upon him physically. Putting Glaedrin out of her mind, she was instructed by her God that the time had arrived to begin the ritual.

Despite her efforts to devote herself fully to the task at hand, she couldn't help but find part of her mind wandering towards the seed of doubt planted by Glaedrin. The words the wizard spoke were pure nonsense; she was not delusional. The evil lived within those who could not see that she had been personally selected by a deity for this mission. The act she was about to perform would be a historic moment, remembered for all time. She would unite Luskir and eventually the entire world. There would be no more war once all people were drawn together under her banner, their only option to submit to her rule. They would all bow to her.

***

Kubathu stirred deep within the gem about his bearer's neck. Overall he found Sevra largely underwhelming, though easy to manipulate and suitably competent to reach his ends. Playing on her pride and vanity was the simplest way to guide her towards his goals. He had convinced her he was a God communicating directly to her as his "chosen", and she never questioned it. Her supreme ego allowed her to unequivocally believe she was selected to lord over all mankind.

Foolish girl.

Once she put the necklace on he had direct influence over her actions, each day gaining more control. Over a century of pulling at the witch's strings led them to this moment. Finally they had come to it; he would soon reclaim his kingship and lands he was bereft of so long ago. After tonight's task he would only need to find the missing diamond maintaining his prison, then he would again walk the lands.

Sevra, he whispered. *The time is upon us. Open yourself to me so I might guide you.*

As time passed he had earned the woman's trust, increasing the amount of control he dared exert over her. He reached through his encasement, the close proximity of her and the necklace allowing Kubathu to delve into her mind. He could sense her defenses lowered, granting him access to use her as a vessel for his power. Only he knew the exact details of the ritual about to be performed, though he shared what was necessary with Sevra to receive her compliance. Pushing into her mind, he sensed a great deal of turmoil in her at the moment. The so-called "wizard" she was speaking with seemed to have her agitated.

Her emotional state weakened their connection, though he could still manage to guide the energies as needed. Before being imprisoned in the gem, the ancient spirit was a master of mental subjugation, giving him an advantage over any adversary he faced. He also had a fascination for blood, his macabre interest going beyond the simple act of watching people bleed out, though he did find that exquisite. Occasionally he would slit the throat of a slave simply to watch the vital fluid spill from them.

He also studied blood from an academic standpoint, and found a creative way to combine his two passions. Not every person's blood was the same, there were many different kinds. Through years of experimentation he found, in some cases, he could bind his magic directly into a person's veins, eventually producing the same effect as if he struck with a mental attack. As the blood coursed through the victim's body, over the course of a day or two he gained the same control over the individual as if he had assaulted them directly.

This revelation led him to think about the possibility of spreading the magic on a massive scale. The spirit realm granted him the solution. Because it was all encompassing of the physical world, he only needed to inject his designs into the large currents of energy that ran through the skies. The currents would carry it through the air for him, compelling thousands upon thousands to his control as they breathed in the magic and it circulated through their bodies. The intricate metallic device before him, the *masjkiena*, was his tool for concentrating and feeding magic back into the currents. Retrieving it from the ruins of his former empire had been unexpectedly difficult, but Sevra performed the task admirably.

For the first time in two millennia he began performing the ritual. In his time, Kubathu was widely regarded as the most powerful living magus and to this day possibly the most powerful who ever lived. He turned brother against brother. Armies hostile towards him imploded on themselves as officers sabotaged their own strategies and soldiers once allied fought each other. The world was brought to its knees before him until he was betrayed and trapped by the Magicus Celesti. Soon they would all again feel his influence.

He began guiding currents in through the open ceiling, using Sevra to direct more energy than her frame could nearly handle. He poured it all into the *masjkiena*, light and dark torrents flooding through the interweaving silver and obsidian metal. The currents would take time to pass through the device, signaling the most critical part of the procedure during which he would apply his psionics to the flows before they redirected back into the spirit realm. On the fringe of his awareness he sensed Sevra becoming increasingly agitated, still railing against the earlier words of Glaedrin.

***

Sevra grew sullen at relinquishing control of her being to such an extent, only on a few occasions had her God demanded it of her. Though she didn't like it, she understood the necessity. She was pushed aside to a back corner of her mind, now sharing it with the powerful presence that had guided her throughout her life. Attempting to focus on the ritual proved difficult, the wizard's words still stinging. She was nobody's pawn; yet here she was relegated to a small nook of her consciousness while the God-being took control of her body. The more she thought about what Glaedrin said the more enraged she became, simmering until she began to boil over.

Intense shockwaves coursing through her body drew her from her brooding. As she refocused on the ritual, she realized the deity had arrived at the next step in the process. No longer did he pull in large amounts of energy, but instead layered spells delicately into the *masjkiena*. Curious, she tried to watch closely; if she understood properly this was the element that would make it possible to enter the minds of the victims. There was a very light touch to the God's work, almost as if he held back on this portion of the magic.

Determined to prove the wizard wrong, that she was more than a dupe in someone's larger plans, she decided she would sit idle no longer. Certainly she could partake in the ritual by lending her strength and insight at this juncture. It was her body after all doing the work, and she had amassed more knowledge in her unnaturally long life than any magical being on record. After watching for a time, she came back to the forefront of her mind alongside the deity. The casting didn't seem overly complicated, it was time for her to show her strength. She silently applauded herself as she replicated the master's flows perfectly, with much more power than he was delivering.

***

Kubathu sensed Sevra retaking portions of her mind from which he shut her out. He had arrived at the most delicate piece of the ritual, infusing his mental attacks into the currents that would soon re-enter the spirit realm. The sheer precision involved and need for his complete concentration prevented him from sensing her motives. Suddenly she duplicated the spell, pushing far too much of her will than was called for. He was momentarily dumbstruck; she had used a hatchet when a scalpel was needed, and then drove the magic home with a sledgehammer instead of the small tap of a jeweler's mallet.

Nooooooo! Do you have any idea what you've done? The entire spell effect would be ruined because of Sevra. Frankly, even he wasn't sure what the full ramifications of her actions would be. The beauty of his spell laid in its subtlety, manipulating the minds of the victims to work towards his ends, the same as he showed Sevra to take control over her guards, but on a larger scale. The brute force employed here could have decimated a small army. He wrested full control of Sevra's mind away from her, though he was unsure how to proceed. It was too late to abort the ritual, one would sooner stop an avalanche by trying to stand in front of it.

There was no other choice but to continue the spell. He did his best to adjust his work before the last phase began where the energy would be redirected into the world currents. Despite his best efforts, it was beyond repair. As the energy completed its passes through the *masjkiena* Kubathu resigned himself to the fact that the night was a disaster. There was nothing for it but to wait and see what effects would take place over the coming days.

You have failed miserably Sevra, know that what you have done brings us into uncharted territory. In disgust, he allowed his essence to recall back into the necklace.

***

Sevra felt the spirit exit her mind, severing its communication. She called out to it, but received no response. Her eyes darted back and forth as she fully returned to the physical world, everyone in the room looking to her expectantly as they anxiously awaited the result. Momentarily unsure of herself, she bit her lip in trepidation. This was all Glaedrin's fault. He knew just what to say to her, somehow he knew and he made her jeopardize the ritual. Her gaze fell upon him when she fully arrived at her senses, and he grinned back at her! The old man was crafty to his core. She erupted in a fit of rage, striking out at him. She would add his life force to hers, it was the least she should do to him after his guile.

Glaedrin was pleased with himself in the end. They always said a wizard's wit was his most powerful weapon, and without his magic to rely upon he still managed to disrupt Sevra's plans using only his words. He had no way of knowing exactly what had transpired, but he could read it in her face something went wrong. Judging by her demeanor it went very wrong indeed. In his final moments, Glaedrin tried to think of more pleasant things. One of his guilty pleasures was playing at cards, he always enjoyed the challenge of getting the most out of what he was dealt. He believed he did that tonight. It wasn't much of a hand to play, but he played it as best as he possibly could.

Being one of the few people to know the true nature of the necklace, and observing Sevra's dysfunctional need to exert her dominance, he rightly guessed the dynamic between her and the ancient spirit. Kubathu was truly in control between the two of them. While Sevra, who in her own right had become fairly dangerous, was still in the end subservient to a greater power. He could only hope his well-placed words ultimately caused irreparable damage to the evil act they were trying to commit.

A green stream emerged from the witch linking to him, stifling his breath. His eyes drooped and head nodded down, no longer able to support it as all of the strength drained from his muscles. It felt as if his very skin were becoming too heavy, sagging grotesquely. His final thought was that he played his last hand masterfully, he could only hope it was enough.

***

Something was different. Though Igdahven could only speculate at the inner workings of this realm the *Duchàlg* called the *Chàlgraäden*, he had been here many times and saw immediately that a significant transformation had taken place. For as long as he had been coming here, the major streams of light and dark remained consistent in their positions. Thinking back on the hundreds of years of tradition passed down among the *Duchàlg*, he had never even heard stories of the *Duchstraüm* shifting in such a way.

After Jvard's departure onto the plains, Igdahven was determined to find answers to the disturbing visions that haunted the *Duchàlg* over the previous days. He decided he would forego the celebrations of the rest of the tribe and see if he could tease out some information from this riddle. However, coming into the spirit realm he was taken aback by its changed appearance and left with even more questions.

The currents of light remained in relatively the same positions, but many of the visible dark currents across the sky seemed to make a complete ninety degree turn, all flowing towards the south. Previously only a few ran in that direction, and the countless others ran in a variety of all possible courses. Now every single dark current raced south. Worse, they had made a definite increase in speed as well, flowing nearly twice as fast as the lighter currents. Whatever was happening, it was unprecedented – and did not bode well.

Ten Days Out

Lowering its massive maw and sniffing the ground, excitement coursed through the creature. One sunrise ago it sensed a pack of the thick-hide-long-tusks encroach on its territory. It enjoyed the taste of these beasts and would have otherwise run off in pursuit, but another scent approached on the drifting wind, the unmistakable smell of two-leg-tundra-roamers. To the creature, meat was meat no matter how it chose to amble about, but it had an instinctual hatred towards the two-legs that had hunted its kind to near extinction. Rather than pursue the long-tusks, it would lie in wait and let its meal come to it.

Retreating to its den of low brush it settled in, tucking its thick paws and hindquarters under its fur covered frame. The beast prided itself on masking its appearance among the drab arctic landscape; so adept it was it could often kill a pointy-eared-cunning-eyed morsel before it even knew it was about to be eaten. It would wait, as quiet as the falling of snow until the tundra-roamers arrived.

***

A day and a half had passed until Jvard finally saw signs of his quarry. The tracks on the nearly frozen ground matched the size and direction of the herd he intended to find, he was certain he was now moving along the correct path. The best he could tell, the tracks and droppings were fresh; within the next day they should be able to sight the herd.

The colors of winter still dominated the land. Even late into summer it was typical for snow to remain in patches. It had been overcast for days, and flurries were beginning to fall intermittently; if Jvard didn't spot the herd soon he feared the hunt may end in failure. Presently, brown stretches of ground and the occasional dense copse of underbrush intermixed with larger sections of white. Rarely, bits of green could be seen emerging from the barren landscape. The group again increased their stride after stopping to examine the impressions left from the herd. Travelling on, they skirted around a large thicket, not even aware of the white mound that rose up as the last of them passed by.

Covering the rear of the hunting group, a slight sound demanded Daltvnar's attention. A veteran of Jvard's team, for years he preferred taking up this position so he could see everyone out before him and judge for himself where he might be needed. He was the group's tactician; though he was not considered the greatest fighter, tracker, or hunter by the standards of the tribe, he was well-rounded and excelled at lending aid where and when it was needed the most. It was what he did best.

Peering over his shoulder at a slight rustling he wasn't quite sure if he heard or not, instinct alone saved him at that moment. A massive fur-covered arm swiped at his head as he turned, giving him just enough time to angle his body and divert the blow to his shoulder. Even so it was a terrible impact, tearing flesh from his side as it spun him around and knocked him to the ground. The beast moved in ready to complete its kill.

The group halted and turned about immediately hearing Daltvnar cry out. Fanning out in a semi-circle with Jvard charging in from the center they approached the sudden threat that had appeared. Several cries to Kuldárhik, the ancient god of battle, were made as four throwing hammers thudded in from different directions, causing no real damage but interrupting the creature's intentions. The two men on the outsides of the formation drew their spears and charged in as well.

Jvard was astonished to see a silverfrost bear before him. The last time he heard mention of one he was merely a child; it had been suspected of causing significant loss to the tribe's food stores. A formidable foe, silverfrost bears were two-thousand pounds of teeth, claws and fury that seemed to border on hatred. The beast reared up to its full ten foot height and issued a roar of challenge.

The two spearmen remained at their full weapon range, cautious of the animal's incredible strength. Even with the distance afforded them by the spears, if not careful they could still fall victim to the long limbs of the silverfrost. They worked in unison with each other, coming at the bear from both sides to keep it off guard. Jvard and the other two men grabbed an additional throwing hammer off of their belts, readying to line up their shots. Larik, standing back in awe of the monstrous creature, froze wondering how he could possibly harm it. Sensing the futility of launching an attack, he remembered Jvard's earlier words before they departed on their trek, *look for opportunities to help and you will find them.*

Running over to the injured Daltvnar, he pulled him to a safer distance from the fray while everyone else was occupied. It was a small role to play, but likely saved Daltvnar's life.

Three hammers rang home as the bear was engaged with the two spearmen. Its thick hide seemed to absorb two of the blows and render them harmless, but the third struck it just below the neck causing the beast to wince and turn its head to the side. The spearman on the left took advantage of the sudden opening, driving his weapon into the silverfrost's upper chest. The bear reeled in pain and angrily retaliated, suddenly lurching to the side to bowl over the second warrior, and snatching his weapon in its powerful jaws in one swift motion. With a quick thrash of its neck it wrenched the spear from the barbarian's hand, crushing it and casting it aside like a twig. Now unarmed, he stumbled backwards, desperately attempting to gain some distance. The bear in its lust for blood immediately pursued, and was met by the loud crack of an axe splitting into its skull. Crashing to the ground, the beast never even registered the blow that ended its life.

Jvard placed his large foot onto the base of the creature's head and gave a mighty heave on his axe handle, taking a few attempts to extricate it.

"Well," he said, "it appears they are more than myth."

His men let out a small laugh, mostly one of relief that the situation had ended without any major casualties.

Daltvnar, standing though favoring his left side added, "I'll be fel-touched if I ever hear someone say silverfrosts don't exist. Once this heals I'll have a scar to prove it!"

The men nodded in agreement, they were all surprised to see one of these animals. Jvard now had a choice to make, the meat from this beast was more than acceptable for a single hunt. Should he return home or continue pursuing the Jdertusk? Wanting to set a high standard, he didn't have to think long.

Jvard issued his instructions, "Daréic, you and Daltvnar begin cleaning and quartering this animal, we'll leave a sled with you for you to begin hauling it back to the Ridges when you are done. The rest of us will continue after the Jdertusk."

"Is it wise to split us up Jvard?" Daréic asked, "You know how ornery a herd of Jdertusk can be."

Seeing the obstinate look in Jvard's face, Daltvnar added in, "At least send the boy back with Daréic, if you're dividing the group you should have experienced men at your side."

Jvard thought over this concern but rejected it without having to deliberate for long.

"No, it will be good for the young man to see and learn how to properly hunt one of our main food sources. The more of us who can provide, the better it is for the tribe as a whole. One day perhaps Larik will be leading a hunt of his own, he should learn how to do it right."

Still breathing hard from the fight and continuing to sweat, Daréic gave in. "Have it your own way then, I'm a bit spent at the moment anyhow," gesturing at Daltvnar he added, "Dal's not lookin' so great himself."

Daltvnar was leaning over, hands on his knees, panting for breath and growing slightly pale. "The injury must've taken a bit out of me. C'mon Daréic, let's start prepping the haul. I'll be fine, I just need to run it off. Jvard, perhaps you'll catch us up on the way back. If not we'll be seein' you in a few days at the Ridges."

With that the men parted ways, Jvard leading his group of five while Daltvnar and Daréic prepared to take the kill home.

***

Jvard's group let out a collective sigh of relief as they finally spotted the Jdertusk. It had been nearly three days since they split after encountering the silverfrost; Jvard had not anticipated the herd straying off as far as it did since he and Igdahven spotted it in the spirit world of the *Chàlgraäden*.

"Ten days," he groaned softly.

Jvard hadn't realized he had spoken aloud until he saw the confused look on Larik's face. "Our excursion will have taken at least ten days from start to finish," he elaborated.

He hoped to be out maybe five days, a week at most.

"It never goes quite as you plan, remember that Larik," Jvard added with a smile, trying to keep spirits up though no one was really complaining.

They had a saying up in the great North, *Daün drovka du sôjn dravka*, "As it comes, so shall we go." A few days longer than planned on the tundra was only a small inconvenience to the barbarians.

With the herd in sight, but not so close as to startle them, the group made their preparations. These hunts took great precision and coordination. Even when executed perfectly with a full group there would be ten passes at most. With five men, they would be lucky to get five or six attempts on the beasts. Each man removed his pack, extra furs, and weapons except for a spear, throwing hammer, and sharp knife. Jvard fetched several small vials out of his pack containing a dark red, pungent liquid. Each man carefully poured small amounts onto their hands, working the liquid onto their faces, necks, and under their arms.

"This will mask our scent," Jvard explained to Larik, "the Jdertusk have poor sight, but a keen sense of smell. We'll be able to get closer this way."

Moving with a stealth that belied their stature, they approached the Jdertusk. When they were within a few hundred yards, three of the men went around wide to the opposing side. Their job was to redirect the herd once the hunt was underway. Jvard and Larik began the frontal approach in what would be their first attack. They managed to come within thirty yards before one of the beasts suddenly lifted its head and sniffed the air.

Letting out a series of grunts and squeals, the herd was alerted to their presence. Employing the standard strategy for a Jdertusk hunt, Jvard and Larik sprinted forward and heaved their spears. Jvard's spear hit home, catching one of the animals in the rear leg, bringing it to the ground. Larik's throw went slightly high, landing harmlessly among the beasts. The two men dashed in pursuit of the fleeing herd, Larik silently cursing himself.

The Jdertusk scattered ahead, quickly outpacing the pair. Lying in wait was the remainder of the hunting team, positioned to attack the beasts from the side as they approached. One of their spears found its mark, dropping another Jdertusk instantly. Ideally they would have also made the animals turn to allow Jvard and Larik to catch up for a third volley at the beasts. However, with only three hunters devoted to redirecting such a large herd, they were unable to perform the task correctly. Jvard's team would have to settle for a moderate haul of only two Jdertusk.

"Larik, gather our packs and bring them over to the downed animal," Jvard directed as he went to finish off the beast he initially injured.

With the packs retrieved the others began breaking down the kill. The animals were skinned and cleaned immediately, and then quartered for easier transporting. While the men began this task, Jvard unfolded two double hide sheets, soaking them thoroughly with a waterskin. The sheets quickly froze in the cold air, and he placed one of them down on the sled. More water was poured onto the butchered meat to rinse and form a frozen layer around it, protecting it from spoilage. Moving it onto the sled, the second frozen hide was set on top. Ropes were tied off to it, and four of the men began dragging the meat back home to the Ridges. Larik, disappointed in himself at missing his shot at a Jdertusk kill, pulled the empty sled.

***

Exhausted, Daréic and Daltvnar continued home, lugging the sled that held the enormous silverfrost bear. Something felt wrong to the two men, they couldn't understand why it had grown increasingly hot over the past two days. Sweating profusely, they continued placing one foot in front of the other. At times their vision narrowed to a point and occasionally spots floated before their eyes.

"Keep marching on Dalt, we are stronger than this hunk of meat we're dragging about," Daréic tried to say encouragingly.

Daltvnar nodded as he stumbled and regained his footing. Normally when exertion set in he would be able to find a steady pace and push through, priding himself in his ability to overcome the elements, his own tiredness, or whatever else this unyielding and resplendent land he called home threw his way. This time however, was different. The rhythm pounding through his head was clashing out of time, and discordant melodies disrupted his thoughts and weighed him down. They were nearly there, the base of the Ridges rising in the distance after three long days of arduous labor. He was determined to make it the rest of the way.

"We're there Daréic! Perhaps now we can get some rest," Daltvar said turning to look at his companion.

But to Daltvnar's surprise, Daréic had collapsed. Alarmed, Daltvnar looked to his friend then back to the Ridges. The mountainside focused in and out, becoming cloudy and clear in rapid succession. He felt concern when he was able to look again toward the Ridges in the distance. Were those all people lying out in blankets, why were they at the base of the cliff and not settled down in the security of the Ridges? He took two steps towards Daréic, when the ground rushed up unexpectedly to meet him.

A Delayed Return

Darkness settled in long before Jvard decided it was unsafe to push any further for the night. He wanted to make up as much distance as he could and return to his duties atop Boldstone Ridge. They were roughly two days out from home, close to the area where they encountered the silverfrost bear nearly six days ago. Daltvnar and Daréic would have already been back at the Ridges for days; initially, Jvard had hoped to return on their heels.

Using some of the vegetation from the nearby thicket formerly inhabited by the bear, the men cleared an area of ground and built a small fire. They allowed themselves to indulge for an evening and cut a flank from one of the Jdertusk quarters, switching from the usual dried meats that sustained them on these hunts. After feasting, Larik stood up and moved closer towards Jvard. Respectfully, he touched his fingertips to his forehead as Jvard looked up at him. Jvard gestured with his hand, inviting Larik to sit.

After a few moments together in silence, Larik pointed towards the mountain and said, "Jvard, home is on the Ridges, but we're as comfortable out here as up there. Not that we mind, but why do we push so hard to return a day or two sooner?"

Jvard smiled, "It may seem selfish of me to want to return quickly. To you and the other men a day or two may not matter, but I have many decisions to make every day for the good of the tribe. Being gone nearly a ten-day is too long."

The fire cracked as the two men sat staring into the dancing embers.

"I can't believe I missed the Jdertusk," Larik blurted out suddenly.

Jvard pulled his eyes away from the flames, staring at the young man, evaluating.

"Back in the hunt, when we made our first assault. My spear sailed high over the group," Larik further explained, growing uncomfortable under the leader's scrutiny.

"It happens to the best of us, sometimes you just miss," Jvard said, sweeping his arm out around the campsite, "we've all been part of hunting forays that were disastrous. The herd might get startled early and slip away entirely, or everyone misses and the turners fail to redirect them. Many things can go wrong."

Jvard gave Larik an appraising look, trying to gauge the young man's thoughts, "Don't worry yourself. Two Jdertusk is an acceptable catch, especially in addition to the silverfrost."

Larik nodded, and again touched his fingertips to his forehead before walking over to his bedroll. He was still disappointed in himself for failing so badly in front of the chieftain. His next opportunity, he would show Jvard he could do better.

The men turned in for the night, waking early to continue their journey home. Morning revealed a thick black smoke above the horizon towards the east, in the direction of the Ridges. The group slowed to a standstill, an unsettling feeling sinking in as they feared what the smoke could mean. Without speaking, they looked to Jvard for direction.

"Leave the sleds. The meat is frozen, we will come back for it later!" he shouted as he doubled his pace across the plain.

The barbarians moved with a hurried stride throughout the day, covering many miles. They did not pause to eat, and only occasionally took small sips from their waterskins. They slowed to a walk briefly every few hours to catch their wind, never stopping. Had they been fully rested, they may have been able to do a straight run of the sixty some odd miles that remained. However, after nine days of exhausting themselves on the plains even the barbarians began to tire. Towards the evening, the Ridges finally came into view over the expanse of flat land.

Jvard and the men could clearly see the smoke originating from their cliffs. Dismayed, they continued through the remainder of the day and into the night, running when they could, and walking when they couldn't. Battling through their exhaustion, they kept moving. In the dark they were forced to a walk, the thought of stopping to rest not crossing their minds.

The sun rose yet again marking the second day of their frantic pace. A crimson hue broke the darkness, piercing the clouds and stretching across the skyline to bathe the land in a reddish tint. The rich blues reflecting off the mountains contrasted with the surreal red of the sunrise, creating a startling panorama that existed only in this corner of the world. It was a spectacular sight, but also a deadly one. Jvard and all the peoples of the North recognized that the sky in this condition typically signified a dangerous storm approaching.

As the hunting team arrived at the stretch of land leading to the Ridges, they were met by a puzzling scene. From their vantage point about a mile away it looked as though several hundred men and women were milling about at the base of the cliff. Other figures on various ridges moved aimlessly while buildings near them still smoldered. A few hundred feet off to their side was an abandoned sled. The men began to sprint toward the Ridges.

"Wait!" Jvard bellowed.

They halted mid-step, confused by their leader's command. While looking over the situation, Jvard had an overwhelming sense of wrongness. An almost tangible hum in the air replaced the familiar harmony of the barbarian's daily tasks on the Ridges.

"Something is amiss, come look at the sled," he said pointing over in its direction.

As they approached it, they could see the hide canvas that should have been covering the top was several yards away, leaving the meat, or what was left of it, exposed to the elements.

"What do you suppose got into this?" one of the men asked.

The question was met with silence. Mostly bones, gristle, and a few scraps were all that was left of the enormous silverfrost bear. Jvard didn't have an answer; the bear alone should have been enough meat to boost his clan's foodstores for several days. How does over a half ton of raw meat disappear? Moreover why was it still out here on the plain and not brought up to the Ridges days ago to finish prepping for storage?

"Let us go see what everyone is doing out here in the open," Jvard answered.

Larik felt the unease of the group, had he been alone he would have been frightened by the oddness of what was going on around him. The other three men moved up ahead, anxious to return home. He decided he would stay by Jvard's side; Jvard seemed to be walking a bit slower, more cautious. Just being in the large man's presence could inspire confidence, in this land of uncertainty the chieftain was a singular point of stability. By Jvard's side, Larik was not afraid.

Jvard frowned as he walked the last mile between him and his people. He wanted to run forward but tones of alarm were ringing in his mind, intuition warning him to be cautious. His crew ran ahead, except Larik who stayed slightly behind, mirroring his movements. Dozens of barbarians near the cliff-base turned their heads up to sniff at the air, and as one they broke away from the main mass and began moving forward.

Jvard froze.

Even at this distance he saw the overall wrongness, the abnormal movement to the group. The three members of his hunting party continued towards the Ridges, now tens of yards ahead of Jvard and unaware of the perversion of nature rushing to meet them.

Finally, the three barbarians came to a standstill, realizing something was out of place. The throng rushing at them gained speed, coming towards them at a fair clip despite their awkward gait.

"By the Gods," one muttered as they drew their weapons.

They were close enough to see their brethren in detail. The skin of the horde took on a pallid tone, sickly and rotting. Their movements were jerking and ragged as they lumbered on, as if they could not quite find the coordination to sprint. The most unsettling feature was the eyes, cold, glazed over and lifeless.

"Get out of there!" Jvard yelled.

It was too late, his men had already committed to battle and were caught unaware by the sudden attack. Jvard and Larik watched in horror as the three were overrun and swarmed by the mob. The men's screams could be heard over the grunts and moans of the pack, which only attracted the attention of the hundreds more of the affected tribesmen gathered by the Ridges. An occasional fount of blood flew high as the horde appeared to feast on the men. It suddenly became apparent to Jvard what had destroyed the meat on the sled.

Realizing the danger they were in, Jvard's first priority was to move to safety and make a plan to get onto the Ridges. Perhaps he could lure the group away and allow Larik to reach the cliffs in order to seal the pathways. With only two of them their options were limited, but it was their only chance. What madness had plagued his tribe? Motioning to Larik, Jvard attempted to signal him back and indicate they should temporarily retreat.

Larik forced himself to rein in his rising panic, disbelieving of what he saw before him. What were those things gorging themselves on his comrades? The worst part was that behind the ghastly appearance he could recognize some of the abominations as members of the tribe. He put his fear aside and allowed the pounding of his heart to push everything else out of his thoughts. His blood hammered through his veins to the steady cadence of his pulse. He was a warrior, a barbarian with an inborn ability for battle that was rivaled by none. With Jvard by his side, they would be unstoppable. He would make Jvard proud, refusing to embarrass himself again like he did in the Jdertusk hunt. Upon seeing Jvard's signal, he drew his spear and charged forward.

To his horror, Jvard saw Larik begin running in the wrong direction. He made a desperate leap, fully extending in an attempt to intercept the foolish young man. He fell short, landing empty handed, flat on his chest. Yelling an oath, Larik charged forward into the mass. Many of the creatures, unable to push their way into the feast turned their way towards the sudden noise. They moved forward as one, seemingly indifferent to the rage of the charging barbarian. Driven by a single need, their only desire was to feed.

Larik met the first one by driving the tip of his spear through its midsection. He delivered the blow with all of his power, driving the thing back several feet. It made no move to defend itself, and seemed unperturbed by the injury that should have proved fatal. With the spear still through its belly it stretched its arms out in frustration towards Larik, unable to reach him past the spear. Larik found himself quickly losing ground, unable to withdraw his weapon from the creature as more began to close in around him.

In desperation he dropped the spear and grabbed for the hunting knife at his belt. Grasping it just in time, he slashed at the neck of one to his right as he backpedalled away. They both continued pursuing him, though by any logic neither should have still been standing. Another approached from his left, and several more were moving towards him from all directions.

Jvard hastened back to his feet, drawing his axe from over his shoulder as he raced ahead. He could no longer see Larik through the crowd that surrounded the youth. The last sight of him only a few moments earlier showed the young barbarian's situation looked dire. He chopped viciously at the fiends before him, sometimes connecting with two or three in a single blow.

The hits should have felled nearly any man, but these things before him in the guise of his kinsmen ignored the slashes and continued their advance. Frustrated at their persistence, Jvard redoubled his efforts, unleashing a flurry of vicious swipes while trying to ignore his revulsion. His attacks gained him nothing as two creatures would replace the one he just destroyed, and more began to work their way around him despite the pile of bodies accumulating at his feet. He was forced to move backwards in order to avoid being flanked, the screams of Larik following his every step.

With a final sweeping arc of his axe, he knocked several of the creatures back and allowed the swing's momentum to spin him about, breaking away into a sprint across the plain. Maintaining his speed as long as he could, his leg muscles began to burn in protest. Only when he thought he would pass out did he slow down. Chest heaving, he looked over his shoulder and slowed to a more sustainable pace. He had gained some distance, but was still being pursued by nearly a hundred of the beings. It was critical for him to circle back around to the Ridges, but upon looking at the horde behind him, he could not see any feasible means of doing so.

The creatures moved faster than he anticipated, many times forcing him to turn and fight if they came too close. A swift strike to the skull seemed to be most effective; he tried not to look at the faces of those he recognized as he delivered the blow.

Jvard's instincts screamed at him to turn around and battle his way through to the Ridges, but he knew to do so was beyond foolhardy. If he turned back now he would surely not last long. Dead, he couldn't help anyone – and more to his worry he began to doubt there was anything to return to. Whatever happened back on the mountain, it looked like his clansmen were unable to secure the cliffs. Those things had not only been at the base, he also spotted a few walking about some of the higher levels.

Continuing southward, his pace was slightly fast for comfort in order to maintain his distance from the group. As he covered ground, it gave him time to think and for the gravity of his situation to sink in. In all likelihood, his entire tribe was wiped out. As large as the group chasing him was, it was only a fraction of the numbers he had seen at the cliff base. Everyone he knew was gone in the blink of an eye with no explanation. What happened to his people, and what were these things? From his brief encounter all he could tell about them was they appeared to be only motivated to feed, and incredibly difficult to kill.

He pushed aside the questions he could not answer. There were more immediate concerns that needed his attention, first and foremost was how long could he continue running. Risking another glance back, he saw he was still being pursued. How far would they give chase, could they run on indefinitely? He could not run to the ends of the earth, eventually he would tire and have to face the inevitable. There was a settlement nearly two days away, a trading post established to accommodate miners of the southern ranges of the Blue Fold Mountains. *"Daün drovka du sôjn dravka,"* he whispered softly to himself. He would make the long and difficult run, it was his only chance. As it comes, so would he go.

Big Bear

Finally he could let his sleeves down and relax. Well, perhaps just a little at least, he mused. It had been three years of hard work establishing this town, and setting up an environment that if not quite thriving was at least financially stable up here at the edge of the world. Walt Whirten was a man that always went his own way, did things by his measure. He had walked away from much and managed to attain success a second time in his life. He took pride in that. By his estimates, he should be able to turn a handsome profit this year.

Filling out the last note on his ledger for the evening, he opened the top drawer of his desk to retrieve his pipe and tabac. All goods in and out of the Jun'tirh Outpost, or more commonly referred to by the townsfolk as Big Bear, were carefully tracked. A small tax was levied on each transaction that went towards the operational costs of the town, and more importantly, financed Walt's prosperous and independent lifestyle.

He reached into the inside pocket of his robe for one of his favorite contraptions, a tiny metal box with a flint head filled with the smallest amount of a volatile powder. He had discovered the powder in his younger years as an alchemist, and lost his eyebrows on several occasions while developing it. Puzzling out how much to put in his light box to get a small flicker and not a miniature explosion had been equally adventurous.

Angry shouts from outside his window distracted him from finishing up his work. He grumbled to himself after the brief moment it took to recognize the source of the commotion; it sounded like McRenzy was up to his usual antics. It had become a habit with that man of late, bellowing at one person or another like he had lost his last bit of sense. "Well McRenzy, let's find out who's done you wrong this week," Walt uttered to himself.

Walt walked the few steps from his desk to peer out of the second story window down the street. This vantage point provided him with a view of his entire town; from here he could look to his right along the main road, to his left past the town walls and into the wild plains, or straight ahead over the low buildings to the streets beyond. He set his focus across the street to find Aubur McRenzy in a blind rage, shouting at Mrs. Cleary, the town baker. Aubur was a hefty, unkempt man, tall and oafish. With long wild hair, a crazy gleam in his eyes and a grizzled beard he could strike an intimidating presence.

"Your husband's encroached on my territory for the last time I'll tell yeh!" McRenzy shouted, red-faced and spitting, "You tell 'em.."

Hands on her hips and chin jutting forward, the much shorter Bella Cleary did not back down an inch, being so bold as to poke a finger into his chest and interrupt him, "Now you listen to me! Speakin' to a lady like that. If you have a problem with my husband you take it up with him!"

Aubur reared his arm back as if to strike the woman, and Walt had seen enough. While Aubur's actions alone were offensive, it was the distraction from his pipe that had truly raised his ire.

Walt yelled from the window, his voice booming down the roadway, magically enhanced and deafeningly loud, "McRenzy! I've about had it with your disruptions in my town."

Aubur jumped back startled, looking for the source of the voice that was reverberating throughout his head and all around. When he gathered his senses he gazed over towards Walt's home.

"This is none of your concern Walt, why don't you bury your face back in your books and stick to your own bus…"

His words froze as a thin line of fire shot towards his beard, igniting a small portion of it.

Aubur let out a high yelp, desperately patting his beard with both hands as Bella tried and failed to stifle a giggle.

As Aubur managed to put the flames out, leaving behind a few smoking embers, he shouted as he walked away, "I'm not afraid of you or your tricks wizard, I've a right to my gains as much as you, you hear me?"

He nearly continued ranting, but a look from Walt seemed to change his mind. The two stared at each for another moment before Walt slammed his window shut, satisfied that Aubur's blustering had run its course.

"Idiot," He mumbled as he sat back down with his pipe.

He had a plentitude of ways he could have dealt with the abrasive brute. With one as simple as him, he probably could have taken over his mind and made him do a jig in the street if he wished. Or outright engulf him in a ball of flame. The thought of a conflagrated McRenzy dancing in the middle of the street brought the corner of Walt's lips up in a small smile. He was only entertaining his imagination however, that kind of violence and blatant display was not the way he chose to do things. Aubur was only a fool after all, people like that existed in the world and that's all there was to it. It wasn't Walt's place to determine if they should be allowed to or not.

Sitting back in his recliner, Walt puffed on his pipe which had gone out during the commotion. Sighing, he looked over to his desk where he had left his ignition device. With a shrug he pointed down at the pipe, igniting it with his magical gift. It took substantial more effort than retrieving the flint and powder box, but he was comfortable and didn't feel like getting up again. Continuing to mull over what made Aubur McRenzy's gears turn, he realized the man reminded him of someone he knew from his younger days at the Magicus Celesti, a center of learning of sorts located far to the south.

The Magicus Celesti took in people like Walt, those born with an ability to harness the elements at their most fundamental level and transform it into a physical manifestation. They taught that the world functions like clockwork, driven by a balance of positive and negative energy. Some individuals, the Celesti as they called themselves, had a natural talent to draw from these energies.

Walt recalled a young brash wizard at the Magicus Celesti who took joy in having these abilities. Not because it granted him a higher understanding of the natural order of all things, but because the young man believed it set himself above others. What was it about Aubur that reminded Walt so much of the other wizard? Superficially they had little in common.

Walt snapped his fingers as he realized the connection; it was the sense of entitlement shared by both men. Much like the brash wizard who thought himself better than others and could justify any of his wrong doings, Aubur had the same delusional quality. The world owed him, and he used that invalid reasoning to condone any number of his despicable actions.

Pausing a moment, Walt gave some thought to the order he had put out of his mind for the past several years. He never did finish his training. Eventually, Walt grew disillusioned with the Magicus Celesti and its teachings. Though he left early and in many ways still had much to learn, he outshone the others in many respects. He felt his colleagues had a profoundly flawed view of the nature of their abilities. From his perspective, they were working within a framework that imposed unnecessary limitations. The well source from which their powers derived was trained to be funneled as a trickle, while Walt saw it having the potential of a cascading waterfall.

"A limited mind leads to a limited view," Walt considered aloud, something he would say frequently while he was lost in thought. Taking another deep draw from the pipe he considered the various roads he had travelled in his life. Overall he was content with his choices.

When the Celesti began talk of the end of the world and a coming apocalypse he decided it was time to part ways with them. He never fully trusted them, despite spending several years on their grounds. Too much time reading tomes by a candle had obviously turned their brains to mush. The order had been planning something big, what it was Walt was not able to discern. From the level of secrecy involved, and the whisperings he had heard it didn't seem like anything he wanted to be a part of. He left the organization one night without looking back.

Returning to his window, Walt looked out to his town below. The sun was beginning its descent behind the tall mountains in the distance, reflecting a bluish tint unlike anywhere else seen in the world. Soon the shadows from the Blue Fold Mountains would cast over the town, causing an early darkness. Walt smiled, yes, he was content with the decisions he had made in the past and the new life he had carved out for himself.

With a yawn, Walt began his evening ablutions. His earlier display with Aubur had cost him a fair amount of energy; tired from the exertion, he closed his window shade and retired to his bedroom.

***

His wish had come true, and the moment it did he wanted nothing more than to take it back. He didn't really mean it, he was just angry at everyone. Always being the odd one out, the last one picked, passed over and brushed aside certainly took its toll. Devin had moved to Shady Vale when he was only seven, never quite making friends in the five years since he had come to live with his mother's distant relative. All he knew of his parents was that they were from a city far to the east, but when they both died during an attack he wound up here.

The village itself was set deep in a clearing in the woods. The community was not built from a well-designed blueprint or plan. Log cabins sprawled here and there, dirt pathways formed over the years in highly travelled areas, and the town center eventually developed from where people found it easiest to meet and go through their daily chores. While not the most efficient, its layout was aesthetically pleasing, as if the town had blossomed right alongside the trees.

Many travelling through this part of the world were unaware of the existence of this town; rolling hills and terraced farmland surrounded the woods, and miles of trails through the forest led to the small village. Only those local to this area paid any mind to those who dwelled there.

Sunlight filtered in through the trees, casting a speckled glow over the houses and town square. Devin sat alone at the base of the single statue in town, an effigy of the village founder. At the base read a single line, "There is nothing so valuable as a place to call home." The solitary statement made the boy feel all the worse. Normally at this time of day, the village would be bustling with activity. Water would be hauled, clothing washed, livestock tended to, all of the activities that kept the town alive. Instead, it was eerily empty and quiet.

"It's all my fault," Devin whispered to no one in particular as he absent mindedly tossed his favorite stone between his hands.

He glanced over to the town hall, looking through a window to the only other person who wasn't sick. He didn't know how he could live with himself for this.

Myrna Vitano shook her head in disbelief. In all her years she had never seen anything quite like this. It was amazing how quickly the world could be turned upside down. Every single person in the village had fallen ill, except for herself and the Dawlson boy. Illness sweeping through the community as the seasons changed was not uncommon. Some years it could be particularly bad, and mostly everyone would be wracked by fever and body aches at one time or another. Having the entire town become violently ill at once was something altogether different. Perhaps the last three days of rain and everyone remaining inside helped spread a flu that had been brewing; she had never seen a storm so bad in her life.

Though she was doing her best for these people, their prognosis was not hopeful. The condition of the townsfolk was rapidly deteriorating despite her best efforts and years of practice in medicine. She had a knack for tending the ill; with much experience to rely on, intuition, and some trial and error she had saved quite a few people where others had given up all hope. Combined with her caring persona, she found her calling in life.

She came down from Creekview's Crossing over ten years ago when they reached out for a healer. A young girl had been sick for months, bedridden and growing thinner and thinner. She succeeded in curing her where all of the so-called doctors and professionals had failed, and learned much in the process. Returning to Shady Vale two years later, she decided to stay permanently in the charming, unique village. The privacy and slow pace of life here suited her well. It must have been six or seven years since she even left the forest.

This was by far the most unusual sickness she ever encountered, in both the severity at its onset and rapid progression. Inside the town hall, each of the fifty villagers were unconscious and laid out on blankets on the floor, everyone with a dangerously high fever. She crouched down to check on Mr. Sadler, the village cobbler. Brushing away a strand of silvery blonde hair that had fallen in front of her face, she sighed audibly at the man's condition.

Lifting back an eyelid showed his eyes had begun to turn yellow. Broken blood vessels ran across his face and around his temples like lines spidering across shattered ice. Similar symptoms could be seen among many of the ill. She reached for the man's wrist, taking it up to check his pulse. It was racing far too fast. She desperately thought through her prior experiences, struggling for some hint of what might cause these symptoms in conjunction.

Fits of violent coughing and choking from many different sources in the room interrupted her inspection of Mr. Sadler. Myrna ran to the next distressed patient and froze short with a gasp.

"Devin! I need you in here!"

Myrna was at a loss. Did the boy not hear her calling? More violent fits were wreaking havoc on victims throughout the room. Jordi Walsh, a kind woman who seemed to always have a fresh pie cooling at her window sill, was the first of those she tended to after the fit. The woman's face had turned completely pallid, nearly gray. Eyes bulging and rolling, she gasped her last breath. If it was any consolation to Myrna, the woman looked to be completely unresponsive and bereft of her senses; she could only hope she did not register the pain. After checking the other patients who fared the worst, the same fate befell them as well.

Outside, Devin heard he was being called back in. The last few days had been a waking nightmare of assisting Myrna in tending to the ill. His mind raced with panic, he wanted nothing more than to run away. Did he have enough time to sneak off? Where would he go? He knew one thing; he could not go back in there again.

The door to the town hall opened, and Myrna stepped out to look around. After a brief moment she spotted him still sitting by the statue. Her eyes met his; he felt like a deer caught in the aim of a hunter. She began to ask why he hadn't answered her and in that second, unable to face what he had done, he took off.

Puzzled, Myrna hesitated. What would make Devin run off, should she chase after him or go back inside to see to the ill? What in the good spirit's name was going through his head? With a glance back at the makeshift hospital, she set foot after the boy.

She greatly underestimated how fast he could run. She made the decision to leave town hall thinking she would catch up to him in minutes, but nearly an hour had passed as she chased after him. She was close to him and consistently saw signs of his passing, or glimpses of him in the distance where the trees weren't too dense. Several times she had thought to give up pursuit but each time she did, she'd change her mind thinking she was close to catching him.

Up ahead the tree line briefly ended and led into a small clearing. Just as she thought she couldn't run any further, she sighed with relief seeing Devin hunched over, his hands on his knees and sandy blonde hair like a mop over his eyes. She approached him, both of them breathing heavy. Gently but firmly she grabbed him by the shoulder, in case he tried to run off again.

"Devin, everyone back home is sick, some have died. I need your help. What would make you run off like this, do you have any idea…"

He cut her off with a flat statement, "It's my fault they're dead."

She stood upright upon hearing him say that, not knowing how to respond or what he meant. What could the boy have done?

"What do you mean, it's your fault?" she asked slowly and carefully.

Not able to look at her he answered nervously, talking faster and faster as he went, "Three days ago, we were all out playing. Well, I was watching and the others were playing. They saw me, and I hoped they would ask me to play with them but they didn't and they told me I should just go home no one likes me anyway and…" he began to cry and choke up as he spoke, Myrna shushed him and put her arm around his shoulder.

Devin collected himself after a moment, and was able to finish, "They've never liked me and they're always mean, so I wished they would all die. But I didn't really mean it! I was just angry…"

Catching on to why he was upset, Myrna shook her head, "Oh hush now, that's just a coincidence. You can't make someone sick just by wishing it."

"But I…"

"Trust me, I know you didn't mean it. Believe me, it's not your fault. I've been healing people well longer than you've been alive. Don't you think I'd know if you could wish someone sick?"

The boy nodded at her.

"This is something altogether, *different*. C'mon, let's walk back to town and see what we can do. I have to warn you, it wasn't looking good when I left to chase you all over creation, and it'll probably be worse when we get back," Myrna finished.

The two walked side by side back to town, subconsciously taking their time. The boy, reluctant because he didn't fully believe it wasn't his fault, and Myrna afraid to see what she would be walking back to.

The Best Laid Plans

"Aubur, even a light-blinded fool can see you're being unreasonable on this," James Cleary wasn't one to mince words, but considering the grizzled man's outburst at his wife the other day, he had lost nearly all his patience.

Frankly, it took every bit of restraint for James not to launch his fist into the man's face. Walt chose to mediate the dispute between the two men before it came to that. A large mining vein had been discovered that bordered the two men's territories. In reality, it split the boundary so well it was nearly indeterminable to whom it belonged.

The group had been trying to negotiate for nearly an hour with no success. James was fully supportive of dividing the mineral haul from the vein fifty-fifty, Walt's first suggestion. When that was rejected by Aubur, he also supported Walt's alternate suggestion of making minor adjustments to the boundaries so both men would have equal access to the large vein. Walt had maps prepared to ensure it was fairly divided. That too, was immediately dismissed by McRenzy.

"Well Walt, you might as well go to the shed and take a few of those powder barrels of yours, and blow the whole vein sky high and see whose side the rocks land on," James said sarcastically, "Aubur here won't be happy unless he has it all to himself."

Aubur almost seemed to brighten at that idea, until he caught onto the sarcasm. After that he looked to be on the verge of an outburst.

Walt cut in before giving him the opportunity, "Because our suggestions do not suffice, do you have anything to propose, Aubur? Something that would satisfy both parties?"

Looking in turn at Walt and James, Aubur scowled. He didn't have a suggestion that would satisfy both parties, because even though Aubur himself couldn't see it, he was only interested in what benefitted him the most.

Finally, he threw his arms up and said with disgust, "Go ahead and decide whatever it is you want! It looks like you're both intent on pulling one over on me anyways, jes' like always. I've listened to the two of you enough for one day."

At that he stalked off from the wizard's meeting room, out of the house.

"Well Walt, call me a pessimist but I don't think that's the last we'll be hearing from McRenzy," James said dryly. "Mark my words, I feel a storm is coming from this."

Walt nodded his head in agreement.

Nearing sunset, James said farewell to Walt and made his way home after staying to share a drink with the wizard. He wasn't pleased with the result of the meeting, but then again Aubur's reaction was entirely expected. If things didn't go how Aubur wanted he went out of his way to make anyone else pay for it.

James exchanged many friendly greetings along the way back to his house. Practically all of the residents new each other and he was generally well liked and respected among the community. Down the road he spotted Aubur standing on the corner of one of the more seedy taverns in town, flask in hand. Without giving the man a chance to approach him, he continued along his way, ready to retire for the evening.

***

Flecks of light and dark swirled about, circling around him and then quickly flittering off to disappear out of sight. When he thought they had vanished, leaving him in a void of nothingness, it would quickly start over again. An unusual, pale glow entered Walt's bedroom, providing a colorless light to the darkness. Unable to tell if he were seeing his room or imagining it, he decided not to dwell on it. Were his eyes closed? Of course they were; he was sleeping. Wasn't he? Rising from his bed, he was surprised by his lack of weight. Trepidation was at the forefront of his emotions, but the sensation felt oddly natural here.

Blinking, he found himself no longer in his room, the open plains endlessly stretching out before him. Walt now realized that he was neither sleeping nor awake - though it was like dreaming, or something close to it. The pale glow grew, threatening to pull him back to the waking world. He pushed it away, straining to remain in this dreamlike state that he recognized, having been here before on rare occasions. It was a very tenuous balance; focus too much and the concentration would wake him, but if he was careless he might float away into a regular dream. The light and dark strands continued to drift about him. Only out here, they grew and stretched into long wisps spreading across the plain.

He could feel the raw power the currents contained, almost reach out and touch them with his mind… No, he'd done that once before and found himself sitting upright in bed, pulled away from this place.

The strange glow intensified, again beseeching his attention. *Odd*, he thought, *that doesn't belong here.* He ignored it for the time being, willing himself to stay and explore this place that felt both foreign and familiar.

Speculating on the nature of the strands of light and darkness, their infinite blackness and vibrant white, he allowed himself to get lost in their dancing display. What were these things, were they sentient or simply a part of nature? Did they have needs, desires, or serve some kind of purpose? He had so many questions and so few answers.

Groups of strands spiraled upwards, catching his eye. Instinctively he looked back down... *Don't look up*, he thought to himself. *If I look up I'll wake up, it always happens that way.* Only he felt as if he could look up, the sky would provide him with answers and he'd have a deeper understanding of this place.

The pale glow returned yet again, growing increasingly brighter until it washed over him. He tried to push it away once more, but it was beyond his control. He could have sooner stopped a river from flowing. The wave fell over him in a tsunami of light and fire.

Walt woke with a start, the glow of flames intense outside of his window. Cursing, he ran over to view its source. Remnants of his dream were quickly forgotten as he peered down the roadway to see the church set ablaze. Throwing on a robe and still donning his nightcap, he raced out into the street. The fire was too intense to approach, leaving Walt to join the group of onlookers standing at a safe distance. Buckets of water would do no good here, and Walt couldn't hope to conjure what was needed to quench the conflagration. All they could do was pray the wind didn't pick up and spread the flames.

On the other end of town, unseen due to the diversion, Aubur loaded two large barrels into his wagon and headed towards the mountains.

By early morning, the blaze began to die down and the light of day revealed no serious injuries. Only skeletal fragments of the once fine building remained, a few charred beams looming over a pile of burnt rubble.

"Bless the good spirits we were able to get out quickly, we are safe and that's all that matters," Pastor Ildaradi said to the crowd that had come to offer condolences, blankets, and food. He and three young men were in the building the previous night, and luckily all managed to get out in time.

Dark soot stained the pastor's white robes and filled the lines beginning at the sides of his eyes. Well into his middle years, he had aged gracefully. He grew up an orphan in the great city of Dun'Aldir, another nameless victim of the Feuds of Succession. He got by through stealing, fighting, or whatever was necessary for him to survive. Turning his life around as a teenager, he devoted himself to preaching goodness to others. With a squat, wide face that was nearly always smiling, his positive mood and gentle way was quite infectious. The church burning down seemed to roll off his shoulders, he worried about it no more than he would a hangnail.

"Daro, may I see you for a moment," Walt called over from the smoldering debris.

The preacher turned his head, excusing himself from the crowd and moved to join the wizard. Walt intently inspected the ground, his long white hair partially concealing his face and hanging uncharacteristically unkempt about his shoulders. Puffing his pipe furiously and muttering all the while, Walt steadily grew angrier. Daro in typical fashion showed concern for the wizard.

"My friend, these kinds of things happen. It will be rebuilt and resolve itself. How would we find our strength if we were not tested like this from time to time?" the preacher implored of the wizard.

The wizard interrupted the pastor's attempt at comfort, "No, no Ildaradi. You are correct, this is but small in the grand scheme of things. What I want to know is who did this? This was arson."

Daro was taken aback, his face turning grim, "Are you sure?"

"It's as clear as a north summer's day is long. Look here," he said, gesturing to various spots on the ground, "this dark grease is remnants of oil. Do you see?"

Straining to see what the wizard pointed towards, the preacher shook his head, "It all looks the same to me."

"Allow me to assist," Walt replied.

Pointing at the ground, he concentrated a moment until a red tint began to spread along the charred floor. Soon it spread to the entire perimeter of the building, and several more lines running back and forth across the center were revealed. Daro looked to the wizard questioningly.

"Simply applied a little heat, my friend, causing what was left of the fuel source to reactivate a bit," Walt responded to the unspoken question, "this is where the oil was spread before starting the fire. Someone came in here and doused the building, this was set intentionally."

***

Only a few miles north of town at the base of the mountains, the camp outside of the mines was a chaotic mass of people and wagons that somehow functioned to support the operation on a daily basis. Throngs of people moved about their business as food vendors were setting up to get ready for midday lunch. General supply wagons were pulling in while wagons full of minerals headed back to town with their haul. Several teams sprawled across the half-mile stretch of the mountain range, allowing the miners in the deep to do their jobs as efficiently as possible. Inside, miles of twisting and turning caverns were being excavated. When one area was exhausted, the whole campground would shift down to the next section of the expansive range.

Far inside a tunnel, crewmen were hard at work on the newly exposed mineral vein. Dim light from oil lanterns provided limited vision, and team members tied rope to each other to avoid getting lost as they travelled to their work site. The rhythmic sound of picks on stone rang through the corridors in the otherwise silent depths. This team was in luck, the vein was one of the richest any of them had ever worked on.

"I'll tell yah what, we're making money hand over fist in here, but the great powers help us this's backbreaking!" one man grumbled half-heartedly.

Mumbles of assent were heard among the crew as they continued, but it was more in bluster than revolt. Sure, many of them would rather be doing something else given the choice, but the truth of it was they were drawing a larger pay than they could otherwise imagine.

Adding to the already hazardous conditions, this particular position inside the cavern had been contentious as of late. The crew hard at work with their picks were under the employment of James Cleary, but a rival crew had crossed their path on several occasions in this section. Thankfully today, they were nowhere to be found. Some border dispute was taking place; the men didn't concern themselves over it. They simply struck their picks where the boss pointed and he said he'd work out the disagreement. Overall the men liked working for James, as they considered him to be a fair, honest employer.

Inside the camp, James took inventory of his group's supplies, tallying the cost in his head. He'd need to get a list made up and over to a wagoner, because they were running low on just about everything. Most needed was oil and black powder, but they could also use a few more mining picks, a new wheelbarrow, and a few replacement parts should any more of their tools break. Nearing the afternoon, James began heading toward the mine to check on his crew and assist with the heavy lifting. Most of the other crew bosses avoided the mine work, but he liked to show his men he wasn't afraid of or above doing any of the work himself. He knew respect was earned not given, and his crew genuinely worked hard for him because they respected him. That, and more importantly, he paid them well. After delivering his list to the caravan, he descended into the mine.

***

"Well ain't this odd," Kris bellowed, "they accident'ly put some grain where the black powder should be."

A large, nearly perfectly round man, Kris had worked in this warehouse for almost two years. Normally he went unacknowledged throughout the day, the man liked to talk quite a bit, and loudly. Once a miner, an explosion too close to his head caused him to lose most of his hearing. The other workers learned to tune him out over time. This statement however, got the attention of the foreman. By his record he should have had thirty barrels of the volatile powder. There were indeed thirty barrels, but two of them were incorrectly packed.

"I'll note it down as a mistaken delivery, not sure how the driver mixed this one up. Just set those aside for now, we don't even store grain here," the foreman instructed his worker.

***

Rubbing his fingers lightly against his temples, Walt continued reviewing the paperwork in front of him. It was amazing the sheer amount of goods that came in and out of Big Bear, and the amount of paperwork it generated. Organizing the transport was quite a challenge, verifying the accuracy of the ledgers was equally difficult. He could have hired a clerk to perform this task, but he needed to be sure it was correct. Turning a profit wasn't possible if the revenue and costs weren't balanced properly. After all, how could he know if he was making money or not if he didn't know what he was spending? It boggled Walt's mind how many businesses he had seen fail because the owner had overlooked that simple principle.

Nearly approving the set of documents before him, he stopped signing and retrieved his red ink when he saw a small discrepancy in the inventory report. The barrels of powder he manufactured didn't balance to what was left on hand; circling the mistake he handed the documents off to the courier waiting at his side, noting for the warehouse to investigate further.

***

The soft ding of pickaxes striking stone reverberated in the distance, disturbing the heavy silence that permeated the underground. James made his way through the dark earthen corridors towards his territory. He didn't have a particular love of being underground, frankly he did not know any man who did. To him, this was all about working hard and providing for his family, as well as giving the men he employed a means to do the same.

A second noise interrupted the steady rhythm of metal ringing against rock. It was the soft sound of footfalls echoing throughout the caverns, accompanied by the dull grating of wood dragging on stone. *It could be my crew moving some equipment into place*, he thought. Nearly impossible to pinpoint a noise in the maze of corridors, James put it out of his mind and continued forward. He didn't notice the line of powder at his feet, or the man in the distance running off into the shadows until it was too late.

Powerful explosions rocked the mine, eliciting startled gasps at the camp outside. Rocks slid down the mountain, some rather large causing people to scurry to safety. Many confusing minutes passed by, some running to a safe distance while others ran to the cave entrance unsure if they should enter to help. All the while teams of laborers periodically exited the mineshaft with all haste.

When the dust settled and a semblance of order was restored to the camp, a head count was taken and a team sent in to survey the damage. James and his entire group were unaccounted for, as well as three other individuals.

***

Walt paced back and forth along the length of his study with a furrowed brow. His mustache bobbed up and down synchronously with the furious puffing of his pipe. Two days had passed since the tragedy at the mine that left eight missing and presumed dead. Activity at the worksite had ceased, essentially shutting down the town as well. He received paperwork this morning confirming that two barrels of powder were in fact unaccounted for. Between the church fire, the missing barrels, the explosion, Aubur's dispute with James, and that it was only James and his crew missing, it was easy for Walt to put the ugly pieces together.

The town had not yet figured it out, but then again most did not know the church fire was intentional, nor that equipment was unaccounted for. Only Walt had all of the information bundled up in a convenient package. The whole situation smelled of Aubur. Walt would track him down and tear the truth from the man's mind with his fingers if necessary. Dismissing the thought, he fixed himself a cup of tea. It shouldn't come to that. Taking a seat at his desk he began penning a letter.

***

"We will be holding a vigil near the worksite at sunset, in remembrance of those who were lost," Daro announced to the townsfolk gathered outside of the husk of a building that was once the church. The wind was beginning to pick up in earnest, a cold rush of air and clouds moving in reinforcing the solemnity of the day.

Bella Cleary sobbed softly at the death of her husband while her friends tried to comfort her. Tears were being shed among the people for the loss of their friends, husbands, or relatives. Towards the rear of the crowd, Aubur stood uncomfortably.

"The procession will begin shortly, please gather your things and join the caravan at the north gate," the preacher instructed.

As the gathering began to disperse, a messenger arrived bearing a package. Breathless, disheveled and nearly frantic, his eyes scanned the parting crowd. He had one instruction, deliver the letter by any means necessary. It was his mission, his sole reason for being. He felt as if he had a needle stabbing at his brain, and the only way to remove it was to make the delivery. Seeking out Aubur, he spotted the man hurrying down the road. Heedless of those around him, he vaulted ahead to intercept his path. Aubur stopped short at the courier who suddenly appeared standing before him, arm outstretched holding a leather-bound document.

He nearly yelled at the deliveryman, just from the shock of having someone appear in front of him so quickly. He refrained though upon seeing the urgent, panicked look on his face. He cautiously reached his hand out to take the package, eyeing the strange courier the whole time. Taking it in a quick motion, Aubur backed away a few steps before turning around and continuing along his way.

Finding himself standing in the middle of an empty street, the dull fog cleared from the messenger's mind. He was wearing his delivery uniform. *Odd*, he thought. Today was his day off. How had he gotten out here? The last thing he remembered was being in his house preparing a meal. It was quite disorienting for him that he was standing in his kitchen one moment, and the next he was outside in the road. Confused, he slowly walked back home.

Out of everyone in the street, he had received a delivery. It made Aubur feel good, important. Looking at the letter in his hand, he nodded to himself with satisfaction. He felt it pulling at him, beckoning him to open and read it. Instinctively, his guard went up; but curiosity overrode his caution. Nearly discarding the letter, he stopped himself. He couldn't bring himself to let go of it. *There could be important information in it*, he thought to himself. Perhaps he should read it right away.

Floorboards creaked as he walked down the hallway towards his room. Dust and dirt covered every surface, and the paint was chipped or peeling in most places. Many of the rooms were no longer lived in, a few doors hanging askew on their hinges. The building itself was in a general state of disrepair, Aubur didn't care much about it. He didn't own the building, so it wasn't up to him to fix any of it.

Entering his room he tossed the bounded document onto a table, and removed his jacket, carelessly casting it aside. All of those fools would be making their way to the memorial by now. Not him, those people got what they deserved. With them out of the way his life would be a bit easier. He sat down in his chair, looking at the letter for a moment. Somehow the world felt drab and colorless without the letter in his hand. Before he knew it, he was holding it once again. Better yet he should read it now. Removing the document from its binding, it read in a flowing cursive script:

Dearest Aubur,

I cordially invite you to my residence at your earliest convenience. We have much business to discuss and I find myself in need of your assistance. Your cunning wit and intelligence are truly needed now more than ever to see the town through this trying time.

Warm feelings flooded through Aubur as he read the letter, the foreign sensation making him uncomfortable. He went back over the first paragraph several times, savoring each word before continuing.

You are who I seek, Aubur, for I know the truth of you. If you keep an open mind to my suggestions you will find great profit.

Your friend,

Walt Whirten

Walt was his friend, a darn good one - his only friend for that matter. Now where did that thought come from? Didn't he recently have an argument with Walt? No, that can't be right. *He knows I'm the best crew boss around*, he said to himself as he tried to justify his newfound friendship with Walt. He would take him up on that visit, and found himself eager to hear what the wizard had to say.

***

It was only a short wait for Walt after he sent out the document. He had placed a substantial amount of spells both on the courier and the letter, leaving him fatigued. Wanting to take care of this quietly and discreetly, he was very careful in his methods. Suddenly, he felt a mind open up to him. A link of energy connected him and his contact; everything was moving along as planned.

Not yet done with his tasks for the day, anger fueled Walt where he would have otherwise preferred to rest and recover. Aubur was a threat to his operation. Two days' worth of revenue lost, a building burnt down, and materials stolen. Not to mention he killed a few people in the process. No, this simply would not do. Walt would confirm the truth of the events from the last few days and bring the man before justice.

Heavy footsteps outside followed by a door creaking told Walt his target had arrived. The connection he seeded to Aubur's mind through the letter was already strong, so little effort would be needed to completely delve into thoughts.

"Let's see what depravities that hovel of a mind is holding," Walt mumbled as he casually walked down the stairs to greet his guest.

He found Aubur standing in the foyer, looking around purposefully. A self-satisfied smile came across his face as his eyes fell upon the wizard.

"Please, follow me to my study," Walt bade as he gestured towards the adjacent room.

Quick to oblige, Aubur appeared eager to get to business. That was a good sign. The uncharacteristic smile and friendly demeanor told Walt he was deeply under the spell's control; normally Aubur was as ornery as a bear in a prickle patch.

"Have a seat, my good man," Walt told Aubur, highlighting his words with an ingratiating grin, "I've asked you here today…"

"I know why you've asked me here Walt," Aubur interrupted arrogantly, "It's simple, I'm the best at what I do and you need me. You want me to oversee more of the mining operation, and I can tell you it's a good decision."

Interruptions normally were not tolerated by Walt, however in this case he let the man ramble. He did his best to feign interest, adding an "aha", "oh my", or widening his eyes as the conversation dictated. Aubur continued on for several minutes detailing why he was better than his rivals, appearing delighted to have such an interested audience. As he continued, Walt pulled out a small golden pocketwatch, lazily spinning and dangling it. Side to side, back and forth. It was quite a stunning piece. Walt allowed himself to enjoy its beauty for a few moments as it elegantly caught and reflected the light.

Walt hastily returned his attention back to his task when he noticed the growing silence, and nearly chuckled. Aubur had slowly trailed off, his eyes being drawn towards the watch. The weak-minded fool was already entranced and he didn't even have to directly call attention to the instrument. Usually a bit more manipulation was required, the lack of challenge was bordering on cruel, Walt thought.

"Well, best be on with it," Walt said as he stood up and approached his subject.

Before him, a nest of darkness writhed about Aubur like an agitated den of snakes. Drawing on his power, Walt projected thin silvery tendrils that penetrated the blackness, setting them swirling about Aubur's head. He went in closer, proceeding through it with a business-like demeanor. The darker energy itself wasn't evil, it just seemed to attract and bind itself in greater quantity to those who were. He reached out and touched the dazed man's forehead, fully entering into his mind.

Images and emotions flooded through Walt, melding with his own thoughts and experiences. Sharing minds in this manner could be dangerous; if not careful it was easy to lose one's own identity among the other person. Walt didn't want to bring anything into his own being that didn't belong there. He cautiously poked and prodded into Aubur's recent memory, catching flashes of his actions. Flames erupted as he ran off into the night. A lock was carefully picked, barrels stolen.

Black filaments began to creep through Aubur, threatening to surround Walt's presence.

"What is this, here?" Walt thought. He had never seen anything quite like it. Was this some kind of defense Aubur was subconsciously enacting?

A shockwave pulsed through Walt, not originating from this joining of minds but from somewhere external. It felt as if he had been spun around and turned inside out, the very energy that granted him power shifting about tumultuously.

As quickly as it came it was gone. Somehow Walt managed to maintain the connection to his subject. However, the dark webbing began to spread, suffocating him like thousands of tiny spiders. This certainly was not initiated by Aubur, the man's brain was quickly being destroyed by the foreign body. Walt pushed against it, desperately creating barriers to keep it from invading his own space. It stopped just outside of the mental barricades he placed, but continued rampaging through Aubur's body and brain. Not yet done with his task and safe for the time being, the wizard created more seals of energy in an effort to halt its spread. He did his best to contain the invading entity, managing to block it off at every direction and trap it in a section of Aubur's mind.

Exhausted, he stopped for a moment to admire his handiwork. What looked like a three dimensional web of shimmering light encapsulated a pulsing black series of knots. What in the spirits was that? Satisfied his barriers would hold, Walt continued searching through images of Aubur's recent activity. He confirmed his suspicions, Aubur set off the explosions in the mine that led to the deaths of several men. He would be executed for murder.

Strange Return

Daylight waned, and the low sun filtering through the thick copse of trees caused a premature dusk throughout the forest. Hours passed as Myrna and Devin slowly walked back to the village center. Normally there would be torches lit to provide extra light while folks finished up their tasks for the day, or young children would play amidst the last bits of daylight before being called back home by their parents.

There were no fires. There was no sound.

Arriving at the center of their woodland community they were greeted by darkness and silence. Myrna didn't realize she had stopped moving until Devin nearly walked into her. Didn't she close the door to the town hall before she left to chase Devin?

The faint sound of bleating sheep caused her to frown; it seemed as if something had gotten into the pens to disturb the animals. Her initial inclination was to check on the people she had been tending to in the hall, but she felt fear at the thought of going inside. Deep down, she knew many would be dead. Motioning Devin to follow, she delayed the moment she didn't want to face and walked beyond the building towards the noise. The bleating grew louder, and drawing closer they heard the distinct sound of gnawing and tearing of flesh.

"It's just a wild animal gotten into the pens, Devin. We'll scare it off, and then go see how everyone is faring," Myrna whispered down to the boy.

Myrna moved closer towards the pens, squinting at the hunched over mound among the animals. The figure stood, still facing away from her, and she involuntarily took a step back. A bloody hand reached down, tearing more flesh from the half-dead sheep in front of it. Grey, pallid skin with many sores and bruises covered the creature. It paused in its feast, raising its head slightly to sniff the air. It turned around, its yellowed eyes meeting Myrna's.

It was the mayor.

She quickly put her hand over Devin's mouth, stifling his cry of surprise.

Before leaving to chase the boy, the mayor had been close to death. He was up and about now, but by no means did he seem himself. To Myrna it felt as if an eternity passed as they stared at each other. After a long, tense moment, the thing finally broke its gaze to return to feeding. Myrna dragged Devin along, back around the building.

"Did you see, did you see? He's one of the Grey! I wished them dead and he came back as a Greyman!" Devin rambled.

"Hush now!" those are just stories meant to scare children," Myrna chided, "I'm sure there's some explanation..."

She anxiously watched the door to the town hall creaking back and forth in the breeze. Devin looked at her while she stood away from the building, unsure of what to do. Were the others still alive, what had happened to the mayor? It was growing darker by the moment, and soon they wouldn't be able to see anything at all. She had to check in on them, she finally decided.

"Stay here, I'll be right back," she whispered.

Devin began to protest, but she was already moving towards the town hall. She didn't get very far, only taking two steps forward before she froze again.

A hand reached through the doorway, its fingers working slowly as it gripped the frame. The door opened the rest of the way, revealing a woman with her shoulders hunched, peering out with a vacant look in her eyes. A terrible stench wafted towards Myrna from the building. Even in the dim light, Myrna could tell something was horribly amiss.

Cautiously, she took another step forward.

Another figure appeared behind the woman in the doorway, and then another. Soon they poured out of the town hall, pushing and shoving each other to funnel through the narrow entrance. Myrna's face paled and she spun on her heel, grabbing Devin and dragging him away by the collar as she ran.

The faces of the people she had known for years had been replaced by ghastly caricatures of who they once were. Whatever happened to them, it wasn't natural. Even though her first instinct was to try and help them, it was overridden by a stronger sense that they were in danger. She didn't need to pull for long until Devin was in a full sprint along with her. After gaining some distance along the trail leading out of Shady Vale, they stopped for a moment, panting to catch their breath. Looking back, it didn't seem as if they were followed.

"We'll go stay out at one of the farms for tonight, and check back in the morning, maybe things will make sense with the new day," she told Devin.

"You can come back if you want," Devin replied as he shook his head, "I made them all into Greymen, I can't come back."

"Devin listen to me, you didn't do this. We don't know what has happened and there is no such thing as the Grey..."

"Then what happened to them?" he interrupted.

Myrna pursed her lips for a moment, ready to argue further. Instead she sighed and shook her head. She didn't have an answer for the boy.

Walking along the trail proved difficult with the lack of light. Myrna stumbled a few times, nearly rolling her ankle on the uneven ground, while Devin found himself accidentally veering from the path and tracking through the brush. Though there were no signs of pursuit, they both felt unnerved and set a swift pace for themselves. Sometime in the middle of the night, they reached the edge of the forest.

Under the open sky, the starlight revealed a farmhouse in the distance. With a last look back, Myrna felt reasonably sure they had not been pursued. Feeling safer out of the woods, they walked the rest of the way towards a barn to seek shelter.

Had they arrived during the day, they would have seen golden fields and the rich dirt of worked farmland stretching for miles. Over time, the rolling hills had been painstakingly leveled, and the view at sunrise made this area aptly named the Golden Terraces. Given their current circumstances, Myrna did not think they would have time to appreciate its beauty in the morning.

Crossing through the field they approached the barn doors, luckily unlocked. Only a stone's throw away was a small, one story house with a chimney. Myrna signaled for Devin to be quiet; the last thing she wanted was to wake the farmer whom she assumed would be sleeping at this hour. She gently touched Devin on the shoulder, motioning for him to go inside. As they entered the barn, a horse whickered at them, stomping its foot down lightly to let the strangers know it was there and perhaps that they didn't belong. The smell of animals and the warmth of their body heat greeted them as they moved in further. At the end of the stables, a small wooden ladder was latched in place, granting access to the hayloft where the two curled up and slept fitfully for the night.

Images flashed through Devin's dreams in rapid succession. The Grey pursued him through the woods, somehow drawing closer every time he looked back. He tried to run, but his feet kept getting tripped up by roots writhing up from the ground in front of him. Falling, he watched helplessly, unable to move while lifeless hands reached towards him... the image changed to the mayor devouring the sheep, then yet again into all of the villagers lying on the ground before the statue, slowly, jerkily rising.

"You did this to us, Devin," they groaned. Devin mumbled in his sleep, unable to escape the disturbing nightmare.

***

Thump. Thump. Thump-thump. Thump-thump.

Its eyelids spasmed and flickered.

Blood rushed back into decimated muscles, air refilling ruined lungs. An arm twitched with motion, a leg jerked. Yellowed eyes snapped open, and its head slowly rose to look about. It had no thoughts or emotions, only primal instincts and a desperate, insatiable hunger driven by a futile need to replenish its desecrated body. It stood shakily, wobbling like a fawn emerging into the world. More were standing up around it, but it heeded them only enough to determine they did not smell edible. It hungered for live flesh, not necrotic, rotting tissue.

There was nothing here to feed on. It didn't quite feel disappointment, as that was too complex of an emotion for the thing's reanimated brain. It felt a great urgency to seek and explore, to find something it could devour. Wandering about the perimeter, it encountered a doorway and exited the structure, with scores more following behind.

Hundreds of scents assaulted the being as it breached the entranceway. Two forms stood off not too far in front of it, smelling of warm, fresh blood. More smells of fresh meat came from the trees and surrounding woods, and from somewhere off to its side. It turned its head back and forth to further test the air. Those scents were less appealing than the two before it, but savory nonetheless. Its moment of distraction cost it as the pair ran off, causing a growl of frustration to escape its lips. It didn't matter, there was more to be had nearby. It could always pursue its more preferred prey afterwards. Nearing the limits of its ability to plan and think ahead, it decided that's what it would do.

***

Devin woke with a cry, clutching in his hand the small stone that he had with him as long as he could remember. Myrna was already sitting up watching him.

"It sounded like you didn't sleep well," she said to him with concern as he rubbed his eyes.

He quickly put the stone back into his pocket, hoping Myrna didn't see it as he sat up. Disoriented from sleep, it took him a few moments to realize where he was. Last night's events slowly came back to him when he fully awoke, and he remembered why he was in the hay loft. So it wasn't all a dream. Greymen were real. He wished everyone dead, and then they turned into the Grey.

Before he could respond to her, the door to the barn burst open. A man spoke in a calm, raised voice, "Ya'll come on down from there now, don't try hiding I know you're up there."

Myrna slowly sat up, hands raised showing she was unarmed.

"We don't mean any harm," she answered.

"Who's that with ya? Both of you stand up so I can see, easy now," the man instructed.

Devin slowly stood to join Myrna, and saw the middle-aged farmer in overalls with a crossbow trained on them. He lowered it slightly as he realized it was just a women and child.

"Here I thought I had robbers about, you two ain't robbers are ya now? Naw, I suppose you wouldn't be," the man concluded, "What're ya doing in my barn?"

"Could you please lower that thing?" Myrna asked, her tone not pleased that she had a weapon pointed at her.

"Uhh, sure, my name's Jarid. C'mon down and let's go talk inside," he said apologetically. He placed the crossbow down on a table and followed his guests out of the barn.

Inside, Devin sat quietly as Myrna proceeded to tell the farmer about the previous night. Incredulous, he had many questions that Myrna could not answer. Devin knew, or at least thought he knew some of those answers. He kept quiet though, not mentioning that it was all his fault. He didn't want the farmer to think he was a bad person. That and Myrna seemed to get mad at him every time he mentioned it.

"We just wanted to get out of there and go back this morning in the daylight. It didn't seem safe to stay last night," Myrna said after recounting her tale.

Jarid ran his hands back through his short graying hair, not sure if he should be concerned by the story, or if the woman in front of him had lost her mind. Come to think of it, his boys had gone south into the city of Dalesford a few days ago. They should've been back by yesterday. No, he was sure they were fine, probably just found a bit of fun and dilly-dallied longer than they should have. He'd have to give them a talking to when they returned.

"Well, what you two decide to do is your own business I s'pose," he said, trying to offer a smile.

"You're welcome to stick around and make yerselves some breakfast if you like, I'll be off working the fields - and reckon you'll be gone by the time I get back this afternoon?" he added with a tone of finality.

Working his way through the field, Jarid thought about the strange encounter he just had. That poor boy, quiet little fella he was. He thought it unfortunate the kid was stuck and caught up in some scheme with a mad-woman, whatever her motive was; it wasn't any of his concern and he wanted no part of it. He had fields to tend, and that was the only burden he cared to carry. She did seem to truly believe what she told him. He hoped she'd find herself some help someday, fix whatever malady was toying with her pretty little head.

Just as he was beginning to convince himself all was well, and the disturbed woman would soon be off his farm and out of his mind, he saw a few people in the distance limping out of the woods. He was getting on in years, and his eyesight wasn't quite what it used to be. Squinting, he could clearly see these good folks were injured.

Maybe there was a hint of truth in the lady's story and there was trouble brewing in Shady Vale. It was a strange place full of strange people as far as he was concerned, but they might be having some kind of emergency. *Best do the neighborly thing and see if they needed help*, he figured. He felt like he had to make amends anyway for drawing a weapon on the woman and boy.

"You folks doin' alright are ya?" he shouted over when he was close enough to be heard. Now that fella didn't look good at all, his head looked like a melon left too long on the vine. The farmer squinted a bit harder. Even though he didn't receive an answer back, the person began moving towards him.

"I said are ya..." terror struck the farmer as he was finally able to distinguish the features on the being approaching him. The man looked ten days dead. He turned to run, tripping and falling over himself several times. Another one of them approached from the side, and another yet. Sensing the fresh kill before them they darted forward in a frenzy of biting and clawing. The man let out a final scream that was cut short as teeth tore into his neck.

After his harrowing night and terrible sleep, Devin realized how starving he was, now that he and Myrna were able to sit and relax for a while. They took Jarid up on his offer of breakfast, Myrna finding some eggs and frying them on a skillet. Just as they were beginning to relax, a scream split the peaceful silence as they sat down to eat. Devin ran outside to see the source of the commotion, looking back towards the woods where the sound came from. Myrna followed behind, yelling after him not to run off. He couldn't see exactly where it came from, but saw enough to know they were in danger again.

"No, no, no," he whispered to himself, trying to hide his head in his hands. The Greymen had followed them from the forest and now wanted their revenge for what he did. Part of him hoped last night wasn't real, but the sight before him quickly dashed those hopes. He looked to Myrna, who gasped as she followed him out of the house. Dozens of what were once the villagers of Shady Vale headed in their direction. She moved towards them as if she wanted to examine them.

"Myrna let's just go they're scary," Devin implored.

She wasn't so sure, maybe it was just part of their sickness and they could still be helped.

"We might be able to do something for them, if I could just get close to one and see…" Myrna said aloud, more to herself than to Devin.

Devin shouted back, "Didn't you hear the farmer screaming? It had to be him. We have to go!"

The raised voices attracted the attention of the creatures. Before they had only been meandering in the general direction of the house, now they had the prey in their sights. Seeing the change in their intent, Myrna had second thoughts about getting closer to one.

"Quickly! To the barn," she told Devin.

"Do you think they won't find us in here?" Devin asked as they scurried the short distance to the barn.

"We're not staying. Help me saddle up the horse, we have to go now," she answered.

Bridling the horse as fast as they could, they were ready to be off. Before hopping up behind Myrna, Devin spotted the crossbow the farmer had left on the shelf. Next to it was a tin can full of bolts. Myrna let out an exasperated noise as he grabbed them but she said nothing. Exiting the barn, Myrna was pleased the animal was more on the docile side, the last thing they needed right now was to be thrown off.

They left just in time, with the Grey nearly upon them. Seeing the faces of the villagers close up, Myrna was glad of her decision not to approach them. They looked ravenous, mindless, with arms outstretched in anticipation as they stumblingly ran towards them. Heading due east, they passed over more farms and fields, riding several miles until they reached Longpost Road. From here, she could head north back to Creekview's Crossing where she lived many years ago, or south into the city of Dalesford. She chose to go north, to the town she once called home.

***

Wind gusted along the mountainside where the town gathered, the cold air stinging their sullen faces. They watched as the man in brown robes walked out to the front, his cherubic features strained with sadness. He would provide words of comfort to the people of Big Bear, as he had so many times before.

"We have come today to celebrate the lives of those who were taken away from us. The wounds are still much too fresh, the grieving undone, to see past our own pain," Daro paused as the mourners looked to him. The entire town had come to the memorial at the base of the mountain, in honor of those lost in the mining accident.

He continued, "Today, let us remember these men for who they were, the goodness in them and the joy they brought to us."

Sobbing could be heard amongst them, while others were somber but accepting of the fact that life in the northlands was dangerous, even moreso for those who made their living through mining. Pastor Ildaradi resumed his speech, the lull of his voice set to a comforting cadence left the gathering immersed in his words. A few women lost consciousness, perhaps overcome with grief.

Daro showed concern, but continued as others quietly tended to them. More people fell to the ground, the number increasing rapidly. Now alert that something was truly wrong, the preacher interrupted his eulogy and came forward to help. More people dropped where they stood, unconscious and dangerously fevered. The preacher appeared unsure of what he should do, very few were left standing scattered among the fallen. After a moment, Daro made his decision to unhitch a horse from a wagon and make haste back to town.

***

Returning from his brief excursion into Aubur's mind, Walt quickly moved to inspect his subject. He had not yet regained consciousness, which wasn't a particularly good sign. Walt reached out to lift back one of Aubur's eyelids, and drew his hand back as he felt the intense heat radiating from the man. Fever was burning him alive.

Hours passed and Aubur was still unresponsive. Now that Walt looked closer, he saw his skin had taken on a greenish hue and dark lines spread out around his temples. He was going to bring the man's crimes before the town and have them deal with him, but perhaps he should just put the villain out of his misery here and now. No one would really show concern if Aubur went missing, his absence would be welcomed by most. He dismissed the notion; it wasn't his role to be judge, jury, and executioner. As justified as he was to be rid of the nuisance, they were civilized people and procedures had to be followed.

The door suddenly crashed open in the main room, "Walt, we have an emergency, the whole town…" Daro trailed off as he made his way through the foyer and stumbled onto Walt standing over Aubur's unmoving form, falling silent at the odd arrangement.

"Please, continue," the wizard implored, as if it were completely normal for him to have an unconscious man sprawled out on his table.

"Ah, nearly all the people have fallen sick up at the memorial service," he answered.

Though he wasn't quite sure what he experienced with Aubur, Walt immediately suspected an underlying cause to both of the occurrences.

"Tell me, did this happen about three hours ago?" he asked.

"Yes," Daro replied, still trying to catch his breath, "I rode back as quickly as I could to inform you."

"Is Aubur alright?" he asked when the wizard went silent for a few moments.

"Oh him, I never would have classified him as alright. As far as his current condition, he's probably worse than his usual self," Walt answered dismissively.

That left Daro with a confused expression, and ready to ask more questions. Walt on the other hand, had larger concerns with this new development. He went to his office and retrieved a small suitcase as he continued speaking.

"Come, let's go see to everyone. Aubur will be fine or he won't. But I think he's been afflicted with whatever everyone else is going through. We'll see what there is to be done," Walt said somewhat assuredly to Daro.

Questions burned through Daro's mind as they approached the northern mines. They rode hurriedly, not giving them much opportunity to talk. The wizard seemed to have some inkling of what was going on, but then again Daro thought, Walt always did seem to know what others did not. Daro flexed his hands several times as he gripped the reins, trying to keep them from stiffening. Though the weather was finally beginning to turn, a mild chill could still be felt in the air. Given the current circumstances, the coming of spring did not do much to lighten his spirits.

The condition of the townsfolk greatly deteriorated in the several hours Daro was gone. Upon returning, the few people who were not afflicted had grown increasingly worried. They decided it was too many people and too far to transport them back to town, so they began moving the sick into the front chamber of the mine. That was all they could really do. Immediately, people approached Walt as they saw him coming, waylaying him with questions, requests, and information. He held his hands up for a moment, beseeching silence.

"Please, just show me the way to the sick and I'll see what I can do," was all he said in a calm tone.

Inside the mine, Walt saw the full extent of the malady. They had dangerously high fevers, and all were unresponsive. Walt was unsure what good he could do, he couldn't delve into these people as he had with Aubur. He was fairly certain that would be a bad idea given their current state, not to mention the careful planning that had taken place with Aubur to create a basic foothold into his mind. At any rate, he was far too tired from his earlier endeavors to try that again without rest.

Walt found himself confounded, which didn't happen very often. He couldn't cure their ailments; he had no talent as a healer. But perhaps he could try to figure out what was happening to them without further taxing himself. Along with his training at the Magicus Celesti, Walt also received a thorough education in the workings of the world. It wasn't always best to rely on magic, considering how physically exhausting it could be. Applying a bit of science could be useful here, he reasoned.

Given the commonality of symptoms and timing, Walt worked from the assumption they were affected by the same sickness as Aubur. He was able to glimpse the toxic nature of the affliction while sharing minds with him, how it had travelled through his blood and attacked his brain. He supposed he could carry out an examination of their blood, allowing him to see if it yielded anything similar to what had attacked Aubur.

Inside of the suitcase he brought were several empty vials. The few people still standing watched Walt with curiosity as he took a dozen of the small tubes and made minor cuts on the forearms of the sick, collecting many samples of blood. They all looked to him expectantly when he stood up, appearing done with his work.

"Could someone please fetch me two bowls, about so big around," the wizard asked as he put his hands apart to demonstrate the size he wished.

"And also a skin of water!" he shouted as a few men ran off to get what he wanted.

The idea was fully beginning to take form in Walt's head while the items were gathered. Using a technique he learned from the Magicus Celesti, he created a purely neutral strand of energy from opposing elements, referred to as a skimmer for its various diagnostic applications. He added a vial of the blood to the bowl, and an equal amount of water. Then, taking a small, shiny black stone from his pack he ran it across the skimmer several times before pushing it into the bowl with the blood. He twirled it around with the motion of his finger without actually touching it. Satisfied, he raised it out of the bowl with a hand gesture. The skimmer had gone in white, and came out a deep red color. What was left in the bowl was a black, foul liquid.

"This explains a few things, at least," Walt said aloud, getting the attention of the nearby group.

When they looked to him questioningly he elaborated, "You see, the bowl should be clear now after the test, or perhaps slightly light pinkish at most."

Everyone still looked confused.

Walt sighed, seeing he would need to explain further.

"Many things make up a person's blood. There are various liquids, oxygen, and even metal. The red color comes from the metal in our blood. Once I magnetized the energy with the stone, it was able to attract the metal in the blood, and thus the color. What should be left is a clearer liquid, but here we have this," he said, pointing at the bowl.

They looked in to see the black puddle left in the bowl.

"This – is some kind of foreign body and shouldn't be here." Walt finished.

Walt very carefully poured the black pool into the now empty vial, and delicately put it back into his pack along with the other samples of blood.

"Well, are they going to be okay?" Daro finally asked for the group as Walt seemed to be no more forthcoming.

"Frankly, I do not know. All I can say with certainty is something has bonded into their blood that doesn't belong, and it seems to be unnatural. It happened a few hours ago, and happened both up here and back in town, to Aubur to be specific," he stated matter of factly.

"So you don't know what it is, and don't know if they'll be okay?" a man shouted accusingly from the gathering.

"Correct. But we know more than we did twenty minutes ago and that is a start," Walt said, in a tone meant to shut down any argument.

Sensing he was about to be assailed with questions, he put an end to the conversation, "I am tired, and need rest if I'm going to do any good whatsoever."

And it was the truth, as a result of his magical endeavors throughout the day, Walt was physically exhausted.

"It is late, I suggest you folks stay here with the ill, they may just get better on their own. I'll watch over the town and you can send a runner back with messages as necessary through the day tomorrow," Walt offered.

Not hearing any comments or argument, Walt nodded his head and returned to Big Bear.

The next morning Walt was awoken by a knocking at his door, accompanied by the urgent calling of his name. He could have slept hours more, the spells he had employed yesterday left a strained feeling behind his eyes. When he arrived home the previous night, he was surprised to find Aubur missing. He had expected to find him unconscious in the same place he left him. Before turning in for the evening, he scoured his home and parts of the town to no avail.

"Please hold, please hold, I'm coming," Walt shouted down the stairs.

He opened the door to find one of the men from the mine come to deliver news.

He was completely out of breath and pale, "They've all died Walt, all of 'em," he blurted out.

"Dead..?" Walt repeated, not sure if he had heard correctly.

"Daro is up there giving the last rites of passage," the messenger responded.

Walt was completely taken off guard. He had assumed because Aubur was apparently up and about, the others would be too. Nearly the entire town, gone? This was unprecedented, all of those families, the town he built, many of the people in their prime. It was too much to comprehend in a single moment.

Walt nodded, "I'll wait back here in town for the survivors, and address them tonight," he stated flatly, unsure of how to digest the news.

The afternoon came and went, followed by sunset with no sign of the survivors. Walt began to grow worried, after this many hours he should have at least had another message sent to him by now. He allowed himself to believe they were taking their time grieving, and would return on the morrow.

Another day passed, and yet another. Walt lost himself trying to analyze the dark vial; though it obstinately held its secrets from him. Every time he tried to probe it with a skimmer it felt as if he were trying to untie a knot while his fingers were covered in slick grease. Any apparent openings molded and reformed, denying him from getting beyond a superficial measure.

After two days, he could no longer attempt to stay busy and deny something was horribly wrong. He decided he would need to ride out and see what happened. It had been flurrying on and off all the while, and at that moment the sky darkened and wind howled. Lightning crashed as snow began to fall in droves. The sun had risen with a deep blood red hue that morning; Walt knew many ocean-goers and other cultures deemed this sign as a coming storm, though he didn't put much stock in that belief. Today however, it seemed to prove true. He let out a deep "harrumph," frustrated with himself for his indecision over the previous days. He could have at least had some answers, good or bad, but now he would have to continue waiting until the vicious spring storm passed.

***

Visceral visions flashed before him, both disturbing and strangely alluring. He felt a rush of exhilaration as he sat nearly atop the animal, pinning it down with his knee. It was still alive, somewhat at least, jerking and twitching in the last throes of death. Smears of the animal's blood marred his face and chest, leaving him with a profound feeling of satisfaction. There were others with him huddled around it, feasting and equally enraptured.

He reached in for its throat, tearing through flesh, muscle and cartilage, causing its artery to burst which only set the group into a greater frenzy. Savoring the moment, he held the ruined trachea in his hand while the others tore through the animal's stomach into its innards. It looked exquisite to him; as he admired it, he thought it superior to the finest cut of meat he had ever laid eyes on. He wanted to take a bite, desperately needed to, but something felt oddly out of place. A nagging feeling told him he had to look down first, only then could he partake in the feeding. Every time he tried to ignore the feeling, it returned even stronger. Regrettably, he gave in and looked upon the kill to see not an animal, but the face and body of a man. Revulsion roiled through him, and he dropped the chunk of meat from his hands.

Aubur woke with a start, filled with a hunger beyond any he had ever experienced. Though he couldn't bear to admit it to himself, there was a lingering sense of curiosity from his dream. The need for the flesh he didn't get to partake of stayed fresh in his memory, leaving him with a sense of yearning he didn't want to think about. With an involuntary shudder he stood, but then froze when he saw the skin on his arms and hands.

His skin was no longer white, but a pallid yellow, almost greenish color. In a panic he pulled his shirt over his head, revealing his chest and shoulders to have the same discoloration. The ample belly he was accustomed to was gone, replaced by the sight of protruding ribs. How had he lost so much weight? A smell of rot overpowered his senses, like walking into a room and discovering an animal that had been three days dead. It only took him a moment to realize he was the source of the malodor.

Finding a chair he collapsed into it, in shock from seeing his decrepit body. His head throbbed fiercely and he was wobbly on his legs, though the pain seemed to be subsiding and his strength returning with each passing minute. He couldn't quite remember, but he had the distinct feeling he had come very close to facing death. It took him many seconds to remember his own name; everything he tried to recall seemed as if it were in a fog, and he had to forcibly reach through it and drag the memory back into his being.

With his fragmented recollection, he remembered he had been excited to come here, to Walt's house, but why would he want to see him? He hated the wizard. Not for the first time, he indulged himself in a fantasy of choking the life from Walt, watching him reach out helplessly gasping for air he could not get, bringing him to within an inch of his life before devouring the flesh from his bones… a feeling of revulsion grew in the pit of his stomach, concerned why that last thought ran through his head.

It was about a business deal, Aubur suddenly remembered. Money, more specifically getting more of it, was the only thing that would have gotten Aubur excited to come here. Of course, Walt would never have brought an opportunity to him, they openly despised each other and there was an entire line of individuals Walt would have sought out first. Then Aubur recalled the letter carrier, with the ridiculous note to come see the wizard. That was where things grew unclear. Grimacing, he realized Walt had tricked him, and did this to him as some sort of punishment.

Again he stood up, fighting through the weakness in his limbs. He was going to have it out with Walt this time, consequences be damned. The wizard was going to fix him back to normal or one of them was going to die today. He stepped outside, and overestimating how well he had recovered, stumbled down the stairs. Cursing, he spit out snow and climbed back to his feet, thinking perhaps he should rest a bit more before seeking out the wizard. He was still weak, completely famished, and growing hungrier by the second. Deciding to find food first, then Walt, he stopped dead in his tracks when he heard the whisper.

"*Dun'Aldir*," it said.

He jumped left, as if someone had touched his shoulder. Seeing no one there he spun the other way.

Still there was no one, "who said that?" he demanded.

Alarmed, he realized he was alone. Not just in his direct vicinity, but it dawned on him the entire street seemed empty.

The whisper came again, "*Dun'Aldir*," this time more insistent.

Aubur was no longer sure if the voice was in his head or coming from somewhere around him.

He let out a yell in frustration, and wandered down the street. No wagons were nearby, nor were there any people passing time at the tavern or running daily errands.

"What the hell is going on!" he roared.

Again came the whisper.

This time, he closed his eyes and tried to take a few calming breaths. After a few seconds he began to relax, until he felt an itching, tickling sensation near his abdomen. Lifting his shirt to scratch at it, there was visibly nothing there. He felt something though, like a string tied just inside of his midsection, gently tugging him.

"*Dun'Aldir*," the voice insisted.

"Who are you!" he yelled, looking up and around.

Deciding he would ignore it, he continued through the town, or tried to. The pulling grew stronger, and the whispering more urgent. Curious, he moved in the direction of the tugging. A sensation of pleasure spread through his body, emanating from the invisible line pulling at him. It rewarded him, like an obedient dog following a command.

The whisper came again, soothing, "*Dun'Aldir*."

"I ain't going to Dun'Aldir, damnit!" Aubur protested.

Shortly, he discovered he was wrong. He became physically unable to ignore the command. When he tried to move a different direction than the pulling sensation dictated, nausea nearly overwhelmed him. Against his wishes, he soon found himself outside of the town, and confirmed he was indeed heading in the direction of Dun'Aldir. Even though every step was against his will, he slowly but surely began the long walk to the capital city.

***

Many tense, silent moments passed for Sevra as she tried to come to terms with the full realization of her mistake. She considered herself an intelligent person, but this was beyond her grasp. With her personal guards, the Devoted, under her psionic domination, she could see through their eyes and give them commands from any distance. Most importantly, she could trust her life to them. If she closed her eyes, she could see each of the fifty men she had subjugated as if a pinpoint on a map. The spell was supposed to do that en masse across the countryside, affecting all of those whose blood was composed in such a way that made them susceptible. Over the course of the last decade the divine being who guided her had prepared her for what she should experience at this moment, but she felt nothing, and He had been silent for hours after the casting.

She looked over to Glaedrin, the last of the Magicus Celesti, now dead on the floor. This was his fault. She wished she could kill him all over again.

"Nobody moves, nobody speaks!" she shrieked, seeing some of her guests growing restless.

They shrunk back into their seats, looking uncomfortably at each other. Her guests would remain still, at least until she had some reasonable estimate of what happened.

A loud crash caused her to whip around, "I said nobody…" she began to yell, but stopped short when she saw one of her personal guard had collapsed.

Anger clouded her vision. The stupid ox of a guard couldn't even remain standing for a few hours? She stood up from her dais, approaching the fallen man with the intention of kicking him further senseless, venting some of her frustration. Before she reached him, however, her anger turned to dread when nearly all of her Devoted collapsed to the ground. The Duchess of Dun'Aldir slumped from her chair also, falling haplessly to the floor. In the next few minutes her remaining personal guard collapsed, as well as a few guests.

The fifty points of light in her mind that connected her to them all blinked out, no longer did she feel a connection to their minds.

Urstaag, standing in his ever-present position behind Sevra, watched as the Devoted fell to the ground. Somewhere, very distantly, he thought he should feel concern for them. After all, he had sired each of them, as well as all of the roughly one thousand Drakvnar who comprised the commanding elite of the Dun'Aldiran soldiers. Technically he was their father, but had long been devoid of any such emotional attachment. Well into his fifth decade of life, he would be considered old for his people, and was beginning to feel it despite his large, powerful stature. Most of that life he had spent under Sevra's control; the land that was once his home he could no longer recall. He did not go to any of the fallen Devoted, instead waiting by Sevra's side should she find need to command him.

Hours more passed, while Urstaag and the others stood or sat silently in the open-skied chamber, not daring to move. Sevra appeared to grow increasingly agitated, constantly checking each of the Devoted and muttering to herself too low for anyone to hear her words.

She stood from her inspection and with fists at her hips, almost pouting she said, "They've all died."

Her demeanor shifting dangerously, she yelled, "All of you go, in two hours I want a count of everyone in the city who has expired!"

They sat, still quietly watching her as each person waited for someone else to get up first.

"Now!" she screamed.

Chairs scraped against the floor, and the room filled with the noise of footsteps and voices as they scrambled out and issued instructions to one another. With the room emptied, she retreated to her throne, to sit and think.

"This is your fault, Glaedrin," she said petulantly at the dead wizard as she passed by, kicking his corpse.

She sat, struggling to accept the gravity of her situation. The spell had been a complete failure, her fifty Devoted all dead in one fell swoop along with Eldora, her connection to the Luskiran Council. She had worked so hard to master control over them, all for nothing! Her God had still not spoken to her since the debacle, and that was what worried her most.

When all seemed darkest to her, a single point of light entered her mind, providing a sliver of hope. It was distant, far distant. Closing her eyes, she focused on the single beacon, probing it with her mind as she had grown accustomed to with her Devoted. It was a man, a rather vile one from the feeling it exuded. Had the spell worked properly, this she imagined is what she should have felt but with tens of thousands more individuals.

She delicately reached her will out to the point of light, guiding him gently but firmly towards her.

"Dun'Aldir," she beckoned to him.

He would arrive in a few days, the meager opposition he offered no more than a mite against the full weight of Sevra's will. It would have to do, and when he did show up she would find out why the spell only seemed to affect him.

Desperation

A full day had passed since Jvard began his race south. Above, black clouds were woven together by webs of lightning skittering along the sky. Snow fell in bursts, at times whiting out his view. Every few minutes, when visibility allowed, he would look back to reassure himself that he was preserving the few hundred yards separating him from the horrors that wished to tear him apart. Fatigue had long ago set in, but he forced that somewhere distant to the back of his mind. The percussion of his footfalls was the only sound he heard over the driving winds, his rhythmic breathing the full center of his attention.

Miles of landscape passed him by, barely registering to his vision. There only existed the thundering of his pulse, steady breathing, and legs pumping in endless repetition; his consciousness had room for nothing else. He refused to acknowledge the intrusive thoughts of what had become of his people.

Whenever the chieftain was absent and the clans needed a leader, they always looked to him. It had been true in the time of Helstajvan's reign, and so too in that of Jvard, son of Helstajvan. He didn't care much for making decisions for others, but understood people listened to and respected him. He had seen his kinsmen through some rough times in battle, but this was a foe he did not understand. A full third of the tribe had become deathly ill with no apparent cause.

Speaker Dagard approached, entering the meeting house on the third ridge to give him an update.

"Garl, we've moved the afflicted men and women down into tents at the base of the ridge as you've asked. Hopefully no more will fall," he reported.

"What of the sick? Can't anythin' be done for their condition?" Garl inquired.

"The Duchàlg, the ones who aren't infected themselves at least, are out among the stricken learning what they can," Dagard replied.

Garl grunted in response, dismissing the Speaker.

At this rate, Garl began to worry how much of the tribe would be left by the time Jvard returned.

It had been a terrible night, at times the wind gusting strong enough to shove Jvard off balance. Explosions of light crashed through the darkness, sudden flashes revealing the creatures still full in pursuit. He paid them and the storm no heed; his singular purpose only to keep moving. The sun began to rise, delivering an end to the storm and revealing nearly a foot of snow left on the ground.

The cadence that had been the center of Jvard's focus resounded in his head like the drums of war, driving him onward. As robust as the barbarians were, few of them would be able to travel this far without pause. Jvard kept moving without dwelling on how long he had been running. To start thinking about it would do little for him other than make him realize how tired he should be.

Settling into their pace, Jvard no longer looked back every few minutes. Now comfortable he was keeping his distance from them, he would only check occasionally. He continued to suppress thoughts about his tribe. This catastrophe was not natural, someone had done this to them and he would live to find out who. His panic was kept at bay only by the knowledge that the sun would be rising over the Ridges as well, he prayed that what remained of his people had also survived the storm.

Igdahven strode slowly through the field of the stricken, shaking his head. So many already dead; the malady had moved through them with incredible swiftness. Of the Duchàlg, only he and a young apprentice were not affected. Those who remained did not look like they would last much longer. They were burning from the inside out, fever rampaging through their bodies. Hours before their painful death the victim's skin took on a pallid color.

Pain wracked the victims as Igdahven moved person to person, administering a mixture of herbs to help alleviate their discomfort. It only offered them a small solace. Sighing softly at his ineffectiveness, he decided to return to the meeting house and break the bad news.

"I am sorry Garl, there is nothing that can be done for them," Igdahven sadly announced to the council, "those who have not passed will likely fall as well within the hour. A darkness has overcome them, infecting them through to their blood."

"A darkness?" Garl questioned.

"I've been as thorough as I can in my examination of the victims. While viewing them in the Chàlgraäden, they are infused by flows of pure darkness. Even examining their blood in the spirit realm shows signs of the taint," Igdahven answered.

Garl sat silent in thought. For the first time in his long life, he was unsure of himself and how to help his people. How would he explain this to Jvard when he returns? Worse, what if the hunting party was infected before they left, and they fail to make the return journey home?

The sun climbed high into the sky, and was well into its descent towards dusk. Jvard's head throbbed from the rhythm that had spurred him onward for the past day and a half. Reaching over into his pack, he pulled out some remaining scraps of dried meat, eating as he ran. Occasionally he would bend down and scoop a handful of snow into his waterskin, his body heat eventually melting it allowing him to drink without stopping.

His concentration began to deteriorate. Memories of his tribe seeped in from his subconscious, threatening to infiltrate his singular focus. Fighting with every stride he held on to the steadiness of his steps, inhaling and exhaling his only concern as the countryside passed him by. To Jvard's dismay, his pursuers did not falter, did not tire. They dogged him relentlessly, his only choice was to keep moving as long as he could.

It was a complete and utter disaster. Suddenly and without warning a full third of the tribe died within an hour of each other, when only three days ago everyone was in perfect health. Garl sighed audibly as he tried to come to terms with the abrupt loss of lives. Most of the women, children, and the barbarians themselves were lamenting their departed loved ones down in the field, leaving the Ridges nearly empty.

"What of all the bodies?" Speaker Dagard asked into the silent meeting hall.

"What do you mean what of the bodies!" Garl snapped, "they will be buried at the base of the mountain as is our tradition."

"My apologies, Garl. But we do have a real concern on our hands with organizing this many burials. This is unprecedented, and we want to make sure the disease spreads no further," Dagard replied. The Elders nodded in agreement.

Garl abruptly left the hall, stepping outside and walking along the fence of the Duchàlg's encampment to the edge of the ridge. The second and first ridges spanned out before him, followed by nearly the entire tribe scattered out among the field at the cliff base. To think how joyous everyone had been only a few days prior at the festival of the Changing of the Winds, and now this.

Darkness fell across the tundra as Jvard raced through Darcláw's Gap, a long ravine bisecting the southern Blue Fold

Mountains. Half a mile to either side, twin peaks gradually ascended and expanded across the horizon to separate the northlands from the rest of the world. These landmarks hardly registered as Jvard continued his desperate run. At times, the path would unexpectedly dip, or loose stone hidden under the snow shifted beneath his feet, making it difficult to maintain balance. Some of his pursuers fell in these areas, thoughtlessly trampled by those behind them. They would not remain down for long, rising again as soon as the rest passed over them.

The steady tempo guiding Jvard through his long trek began to unravel, its sonority clashing in dissonance. He started to tire, his concentration all but shattered. The impurity of the melted snow began to cramp his stomach. Drawing on his last reserves he forced himself onward, allowing thoughts of his clansmen to penetrate the near trance-like state he had fallen into during the run.

The unstable rhythm that guided him for days was replaced with a fire of rage. Visualizing his brethren somehow transformed into these monsters and turning on the rest of the clan fueled the fire; having no distinct enemy to lay fault on only further enraged him. He would not let himself falter when he had already come so far, the thought of revenge pushing him to continue while his body tried to revolt against him. If he were to fall here, he would not be able to pay those back who did this to his people. He could not allow that.

A mournful wail emanated from the field, splitting the night. Garl, looking out from high atop the third ridge lowered his head in sympathy. Never in his life had he seen such a travesty befall his people. They had lost tribesmen in battle, to the elements, and to other sicknesses over the years, but nothing like this. Another cry rent the night air, followed by another. Garl looked up with curiosity and concern. The wails turned into screams of agony as pandemonium exploded across the field.

Everything seemed to happen at once. Gasps of surprise were transformed into startled screams. People looked over with interest towards the commotion, unable to see what was happening among the crowd, while others began fleeing in panic towards the Ridges. After several long moments of confusion, the source of terror became clear as loved ones who had passed only hours before began to stir across the field. The dead had risen.

Disbelief and shimmers of hope were quickly shattered as it became apparent the Risen were not who they once were. In an instant, grieving family members became prey to a frenzied, unthinking mass. Garl made all haste down the trails to the cliff base.

"Arm yourselves! Guard the through-ways!" Garl yelled to anyone he passed still on the Ridges as he made his way down.

By the time he reached the base he had a few dozen warriors by his side, instructing half the group to the west end, while he led a group to the east. Crowds of people attempted to funnel through the narrow passage, the process painfully slow in the disorderly retreat from the field. The warriors lined up along the passage, guiding the crowd through while fending off the assailants. After many bloody minutes, any survivors were back on the Ridges, the gates secured. Garl looked out onto the field, hundreds of the Risen moving towards the first ridge, while hundreds more of the tribe lay dead on the field.

Stumbling in the dark, Jvard descended out of the mountains through Darcláw's Gap, onto the Laskouth Plains. He could not see the unholy beings behind him, but knew they still followed. On shaky legs, he deliberately pushed his pacing so they did not close the distance in the night without his knowledge. In the blackness, Jvard could not see his own hands let alone the ground he was running on. Several times he lost his footing while hitting uneven ground, nearly tumbling and using all fours to keep from pitching forward. Every uneven step sapped more energy from him that he could not afford to lose.

The sun began its ascent again, marking the completion of Jvard's second day running. Beyond tired, he could no longer keep his right arm up properly and clutched at a stitch in his ribs with his left. He had been praying to Kuldárhik for hours, not for a way out of the situation, or to die well, but for a chance to be granted vengeance for the loss of his people. Without his tribe he was merely an empty shell, and did not feel truly alive. All he asked from his deities was to be given the chance to be an instrument of death against those who had caused this.

Sealed off from the field and base of the cliff, the clans had time to regroup within the safety of their Ridges. Over half of the tribe had been decimated, hundreds dead after their encounter with the Risen. Nearly a hundred more were injured on the field, mostly with minor bite wounds but a few were severe. The Risen themselves continued to amble about, while the surviving tribesmen hoped whatever afflicted them was only temporary and might soon pass. As Garl stood at the gate on the first ridge, looking through the slats into their vacant, hungry expressions, he did not hold this hope. They attempted to push and pry their hands between any small gaps to no avail, often tearing skin from their fingers, showing no concern for their own flesh.

He began to believe that nothing remained of his former kinsmen. As much as he wanted it not to be true, it was difficult to deny what was before him. They appeared to be no more than mindless, reanimated husks. Mindless, that seemed a fitting name for them to Garl. A frown creased his features and he lost himself in a fit of anger. Raising his sword level with his shoulder, he thrust it straight through a space in the gate directly into the head of a creature and through the shoulder of the one behind it. Withdrawing his weapon, the thing fell flat, but was immediately replaced by another in an endless stream. The face that took the place of the one he put an end to was a face he knew well, and the shock of recognition returned him to his senses. Turning in disgust, he stalked up the ridge without looking back, heading for the Daärdvhel on the second level that had become their command post.

Still being pursued, Jvard gauged the distance between himself and the horde. Had they gained ground since he last checked? Behind him, he was startled to see the great southern Blue Fold Mountains seem so small in the distance. Swallowing hard, Jvard struggled with the realization that he had left his people.

His heart skipped a beat, his measure nearly broken.

Ahead, a palisade rose up out of the flat landscape. He turned direction slightly to head for the outpost, if he could only last a few more miles. His muscles rebelled with every stride, beginning to tremble as he trekked through the deep snow.

The crashing rhythm that drove him forward no longer sounded, and sheer exhaustion thwarted his ability to rely on anger alone. Fatigue had finally bested him; he was well beyond what he could demand of his body and spirit. His vision started to flicker as he continued towards the lone settlement on the plains, no longer able to tell if his eyes were closing or his sight beginning to fail. He continued moving as long as he could, until it seemed an explosion rang in his mind, the world turning into a million points of light rushing towards him as he was enveloped by blackness. A final thought fluttered across his mind. *My clan*, he lamented, *what has befallen them?*

Contest for the Ridges

Though a battle had not occurred on the Ridges in years, Garl once again donned the role of commander like a set of well-worn hides. He knew how to structure the defensive force properly against an assault. He tried not to think of the fact that the enemy this time was his own kin.

"Bring those too injured for fightin' to the third ridge, the rest of the clans gather your warriors on the first," he commanded of the Elders to inform their individual clans, "women and children should go up to the fourth, get another wall between 'em and the horde."

The Elders nodded their understanding.

"It will be done. Should those things break through, our men will be ready for them," Speaker Dagard assured the stand-in chieftain.

Hours slowly crept by as the clans took hold of their positions, the air on the first ridge blanketed with quiet tension as they waited. Every noise seemed amplified in the silence, and sights more vibrant to the heightened senses of the anxious tribe. As they looked through the gate at their former tribesmen, their vacant, hungry expressions were almost unrecognizable. The fire that kindled the hearts and spirit of the barbarians was gone from those on the field; they were only shells of their former selves. They continually pressed against the barricade, the combined weight of the mass causing it to groan and creak under the stress. The knowledge that these things had once been their kinsmen was almost too much for the barbarians to bear.

"These are no longer your brethren!" Garl bellowed to the men on the first level as he swept his arm out towards the field, "A maliciousness, an evil is spreadin' through them as an avalanche rages down a mountain. They are no longer your brothers, your sisters, your mothers or your fathers. They've died; some fel workings have twisted them into a walkin' travesty. Should they come through that gate you must all do your duty to protect the tribe!"

Garl needed to bolster his men, they had to show their inherit strength that allowed them to exist in the unforgiving northlands if they were to survive this ordeal. If his instincts were accurate, they had a long few days ahead of them.

Working through the night, Igdahven treated the most grievously injured in the makeshift infirmary at the *Duchàlg* encampment. He and a young apprentice, Naÿrja, were the only two spirit-seekers remaining. The young girl having lost both of her parents left Igdahven feeling obligated to take her under his wing. She had cried silently through most of the night, until overcome by exhaustion. Currently she was sleeping by the supply table.

Applying his tincture on the wounded seemed to do little to help them. His nine patients had all lost consciousness, many of them missing substantial pieces of their flesh from the bites they suffered. Those injuries alone did not fully explain their condition, however. He moved over to one victim and placed the back of his hand on their forehead; his fever had only grown worse. *Must be a result of the infected wound,* he thought.

Reaching back to his medicines, he sighed and muttered softly to himself, "I simply don't know what else I can do to help you any further."

Hopelessness began to overtake him as he dug around in his supply kit, searching for anything that could help bring down the fever.

A stirring noise from behind caused him to look up from his rummaging.

"Ah good! You've awakened!" Igdahven exclaimed as he turned back around, and to his delight saw the patient sitting upright.

***

A loud crack resounded across the Ridges as the wood of the gate gave in and created a small opening, its integrity finally failing. The push of the crowd on the field continued driving forward, threatening to completely tear it down. Worse, the condition of many of Garl's warriors, nearly half of the two hundred remaining, had suddenly and without explanation deteriorated within the last hour as they waited for the inevitable. They could hardly stand let alone swing a weapon. Begrudgingly accepting that he only had half of the men he thought he would, Garl ordered all able-bodied fighters into position. The barbarians were not dismayed, accustomed to changing their plans as need dictated.

Garl instructed the recently sickened warriors to evacuate up to the second ridge as the Risen hurriedly filtered in through the gate's breach. The ill were in retreat, while the narrow path up from the west gate filled on both sides with barbarians, forming a gauntlet along the entrance from the field.

The first creature lurked through, the skin on its face pallid, blistered and peeling. A grey film covered its eyes, obscuring their color and creating a sickly cast in its visage. Hissing as it glanced back and forth, it attacked the man on its left. The barbarians quickly pounced, five polearms immediately thrust into the creature's abdomen, chest, shoulder, and neck. Already choosing their next target, the fighters scrambled to adjust as they realized their first enemy still approached, seemingly unaffected by the multitude of wounds it suffered.

They finally felled it as one man thrust a spear through its eye socket, but not before it managed to sink its teeth into the throat of its original intended victim and tear away a large piece of flesh. The barbarian attempted to yell out in pain, the noise coming out in a gurgle as he grasped his ruined neck and collapsed to the ground. The remainder of the gate suddenly burst inward, several of the creatures pouring through the opening.

Bedlam ensued as more of the walking horrors filtered through the gate. Soon every barbarian was engaged in combat; they had not anticipated the resilience of this particular foe. Garl issued a curse, yelling for his men to fall back. Normally this style of retreat from ridge to ridge was highly effective, keeping his men alive while making the enemy pay dearly for the ground they gained. The problem was these things did not die like they should have. This enemy seemed to not feel pain, or even seem aware they had been wounded.

Looking around he saw many of the Risen with arms hacked off, deep gashes across the throat, or impalements through their chests. Yet they continued approaching, while only a few were silenced on the ground with deep wounds through the skull. The barbarians were trained to attack the upper torso. It was the largest, least mobile target on a person. In this case, it was an ineffective strategy.

"Their heads! It's the only way to stop them, attack the head!" Garl shouted above the commotion.

It was no use, his kin were slowly being killed off by the larger persistent group. In a few minutes his men were outnumbered nearly five to one against an enemy that did not recognize when they should be dead. Garl managed to rally twenty men nearby into a line as they hastily moved towards the second ridge, incorporating any clansmen they passed into the formation. The men near Garl quickly adapted their combat methods, crushing skulls or severing heads to put an immediate end to the abominations.

Approaching the pathway to the second ridge, the file transformed itself into a 'V' formation and continued backpedaling towards the entryway. The section was tenuously secured, the last of the Risen in the immediate vicinity dispatched. Other than Garl's organized squadron, the rest of the ridge had broken into disordered combat. Several yards away, dozens of the beings approached a group of three barbarians who were already sorely pressed.

"Fall back!" came shouts from men in the formation, "secure the second ridge and regroup!"

Seeing they would not disengage in time, Garl held off the retreat momentarily to see to the three stranded men.

"Hold yer position, two with me!" he hollered above the din.

Garl was old by the northerners' standards, no longer standing out as the strongest or most agile among the tribe. What he lacked in youth he made up for with experience. He knew when to act, when to hold back, and could feel the pacing and visualize the unfolding of a battle down to its hours, minutes and seconds.

Before him, the three warriors only had seconds remaining if he did not intervene. He rushed forward, not boisterous or daring, but strong, steadfast, and with efficiency of motion. Hurling a throwing hammer end over end at the leading creature, he collapsed its skull while hastening towards his endangered comrades. Ending the charge with a vicious lateral sweep of his sword, he took the heads of an additional two. The pair of warriors in Garl's wake soon caught up to join the fray, hacking and slashing to create an opening to safety for their struggling clansmen.

"Go, Go, Go!" Garl barked as he pulled the men back towards the secured pathway to the second ridge. The 'V' formation opened up, breaking into two files allowing Garl and the rescued men through. Four spearmen held the assailants at bay in the narrow pass, driving their weapons into the leading mass. The throng pressed in behind, pushing back against the spearmen with its combined weight and forcing them further up the hill.

The rest of the barbarians withdrew to the safety of the second ridge, while the four men slowly backed up the trail. Desperately holding on to their spears, they strained with all their might in an effort to withstand the collective force of the Risen pushing against them. After what seemed an eternity they crossed the threshold to the gate, their clansmen slamming the portal shut and barring it. Peering down to the first ridge below showed many barbarians would not make the retreat.

***

Excitement and hope filled Igdahven at seeing his miraculously revived patient. "I'll just spread this medicine across the wound on your chest," he stated merrily, his thoughts preoccupied with the effectiveness of his concoction.

As he reached out towards his patient, his hand froze midway when he noticed the expressionless look in its eyes. It growled softly as it peered about, left and right. Igdahven followed its gaze, and saw all of the sick around him beginning to stir. Fully coming to, it lunged forward at the spirit-seeker, falling short as Igdahven pulled back.

All nine people under his charge began to awaken, but not as they once were. In the instant before they could gain their bearings, Igdahven rushed over to scoop up Naÿrja and ran down the hill to warn Garl. Breathing heavily, he rushed away from the encampment with the sleeping child in his arms. Beginning to stir, the girl flickered open her bleary eyes.

"What's happening?" she moaned.

"Shhhh, just hold still for a bit, we'll be safe soon," Igdahven answered.

Looking across the ledge to the levels below, he wasn't certain if that would hold true.

***

Yet another puzzle to contend with, Garl thought to himself, silently fuming. Now that he and what was left of his troops were momentarily safe on the second ridge, they were able to breathe for an instant and evaluate their predicament. Their relaxation was short lived, however, as they looked across the ridge. To their shock, the entire company of ill troops Garl evacuated only minutes before lay unresponsive on the ground.

Running over to the fallen men, Garl and others began checking for pulses, breathing, or any signs of life. Dismayed, they found none. Nearly a hundred men who were perfectly healthy other than suffering a small scratch or bite earlier in the day now lay dead. The welfare of his people was in Garl's hands and it all was quickly falling to ruin. The entire tribe had been cut down to under fifty warriors and roughly two hundred women, children, and elderly currently taking refuge on the fourth ridge.

"What in the Fel Wastelands happened to them?" Garl questioned angrily.

Though he was not particularly looking for a response, a young man stepped forward. Garl recognized him from clan Kòdjak of the first ridge, though he was unsure of the youth's name. Short by the standards of the tribe, and not quite filled in, the lad shifted nervously. He was not one to put himself at the center of attention, nor did he wish to address a tribal leader.

"Speak your mind," Garl bade the hesitant young man.

"You see, as it is… well, all these men that were sick I mean. They had a thing in common," the young man finished apprehensively.

"And what might that be?" Garl asked, attempting to hold on to his remaining thread of patience.

"I think all these men were down in the field earlier, in the first attack," he answered, "at least I recognize running beside quite a few of them."

"So all these men were in the field, as were many of us. How does that hold meaning?" another voice added to the growing murmurs.

"You can see for yourselves, all of these men in particular look to have been injured while they were down there. Look, here, and here," he said while gesturing towards various wounds.

Garl leaned in for closer inspection. Sure enough each of the five bodies he viewed had a bite mark on some area of the victim, mostly the shoulder or neck.

"Jahnnal, Gléandrigh, you two start checkin' the rest of the bodies for bite marks," Garl ordered. "Fine job lad, what is your name?"

"Adran, sir," he replied, lightly touching his fingertips to his forehead in salute.

Unsure of what to make of Adran's revelation, Garl stowed it away as potentially important. Planning the group's next actions correctly was of utmost importance, their very existence depended on intelligent decision-making. They certainly couldn't go back down the hill at the moment. Continuing upward to the fifth ridge seemed to be the only option, though eventually they would be putting themselves into a corner. A yell in the distance drew Garl from deliberating his limited choices, and attracted the attention of his men. They quickly spotted the source of the disturbance, though they could not quite make out his words.

Igdahven half stumbled down the hill to the second ridge with Naÿrja in tow, holding onto his hand. He waved his free hand wildly as he shouted to the group of warriors who were safe on the second ridge; there were so few of them standing. Why were so many lying down? The few standing could not have possibly carried that many injured so quickly to safety, Gods willing they were only injured. He felt as if he were sluiced in a cold, late spring deluge as the answer dawned on him. If not for what was chasing him down from the third ridge he would have frozen in his tracks.

Instead, he yelled more urgently as he ran toward the group with all haste.

Even at this distance it was easy to distinguish the form of Igdahven racing down the pathway. The long patched robes, wolf-skin cap, and belt adorned with various dangling skulls was unmistakable. Garl instructed his men to wait while he jogged out to meet the frantic Igdahven, and the child he held in tow.

Watching as their leader strode off, the men all turned to see what urgent news Igdahven might be delivering. The group walked a few dozen feet closer, coming to a stop and standing casually in a rough semi-circle.

"What do you suppose that madman is sayin'?" Gléandrigh inquired of his clansman.

"With that one, anythin' is possible. Whatever it is, I doubt it's good," Jahnnal answered, shaking his head.

The men watched as Igdahven frantically waved his arms, talking excitedly at Garl. Garl seemed to reply, causing the spirit-seeker to become even more agitated if that were possible. Igdahven threw his hands up, frenetically gesturing back towards the men. Garl turned to look, the disbelief apparent in his body language even to his men standing hundreds of feet away.

Curiosity and murmurs of confusion spread among the men at seeing Garl's reaction.

Adran turned his head and muttered to the fellow behind him, "Looks like more bad news is…"

Abruptly ending his statement, he desperately threw up his arms in defense. A man who was dead only a moment before bore down on him, groaning unintelligibly. It took him to the ground, Adran managing to lock his arm over one of the creature's while grabbing its throat with his other hand. In terror, he attempted to hold it at arm's length while it worked its jaw in frenzied excitement. Adran, at best, was only competent in a confrontation. He was not exceptionally strong as most of the northerners, and was one of the few barbarians who did not naturally excel in combat either armed or unarmed. His fear grew as he began to tire. Its breath putrid, the once dead tribesman still had much of its former strength and was determined to sink its teeth into Adran.

The struggle ended suddenly as an axe vertically split the head of the creature nearly in two, splashing gore in a wide radius. It collapsed lifeless onto Adran, who scrambled out from beneath it. All around, the once-dead men began to stir. A leg flickered, an arm twitched, necks and heads slowly raised from and lowered back to the ground as they acclimated to their state of reanimation. Some of them had already stood up and began ambling towards the men. Uncertainty threatened to split the warriors, as some looked to back away while others were ready to charge in.

"To me! To me with all haste!" Garl shouted across the ridge, motioning widely with his arm.

The men decisively turned about, following the order without hesitation as they sped across the grounds. Most of the creatures were still disoriented and had not quite yet given chase. They reached Garl in a few moments, who quickly set his men to action once again.

"Up the hill, last two men through barrin' the gate. No questions, nine to kill up ahead!" he barked, relaying only the bare essentials of the information he had received from Igdahven.

The group quickly obeyed, moving through the next secure point on the Ridges. They were now backed up onto the third ridge, abandoning the first two as a lost cause. Knowing a confrontation lay ahead, Adran allowed the others to pass through first as he decided he would help set the gate. Though he wasn't a coward, he knew would not be the most effective to rush through and engage in battle. If he allowed the others to go first while he secured the barrier, he felt he would be doing his part.

Passing through the entrance, there was no time to rest as the nine Risen once under Igdahven's care rushed towards them. However, with Garl's warning the barbarians were ready. The first thirteen men through the entryway moved forward, and rather than rushing ahead to meet the attack fell into position and waited. After their first experience on the field, and then seeing more combat on the first ridge, this group of warriors knew what to expect.

Contrary to the belief of most civilized lands, the barbarians were quick to learn. In addition to their tenacity, they often displayed their adaptability and cunning in battle. Subconsciously they had already inferred much about this particular foe, this time allowing the threat to come to them.

Setting their spears forward, the front line aimed high for the neck and head rather than the body where they would typically point their weapons. As they expected, the creatures blindly lurched forward with no regard for the sharp spearheads. The contingent forced the spears forward, each of the five men taking down one of the Risen with their thrusts.

The front line was momentarily exposed as they retracted their weapons and four more of them followed in. A supporting column shifted forward, slashing with swords and axes while their comrades repositioned themselves to be less vulnerable. The strategy was successful, and soon the small group of the Risen were dispatched. Their faces grim, the barbarians did not rejoice at the minor victory. The third ridge was secure for now; but in light of all they had lost and the tenuous state they found themselves in, there was little to celebrate.

***

"We must destroy the remains, Garl. And quickly. There is no other choice," Speaker Dagard insisted.

A few men voiced their agreement, while others broke out in heated argument.

Garl raised his hand commanding silence, "We cannot desecrate their bodies, and on a hunch at that. It goes against our ways," he said slowly with conviction.

"Then you put us all at risk, you've heard Igdahven's account, as well as seen for yourself what happens when someone is bitten by one of those… things." Many nearby sided with his reasoning.

Dagard continued, "A difficult decision needs to be made, and you must –"

"Silence!" Garl roared, interrupting his opponent and drawing the eyes of nearly everyone on the ridge.

"We're not havin' the time for this. Do you truly have the desire to mutilate the bodies of your brethren, destroyin' that which is sacred? Move the bodies down to the third ridge, beyond the gate. They seem to be disorganized, they won't be breakin' through again unless a few hundred of them press against the frame, and that doesn't seem likely at the moment," Garl argued.

"I do not think that wise, what if…"

Garl interrupted, speaking softly, "I think we all know what is going to happen to them, but on the chance we're wrong, this is doin' no harm. Quickly now, let's get those bodies to the third ridge."

In the end, they were unable to go through with what they all felt needed to be done. Upon moving to the fourth ridge, where the clans took refuge, they found an additional thirty who had died mysteriously within the last few minutes. They quickly confirmed the dead had suffered various bite wounds that by themselves should not have been life threatening. Additionally, it was discovered two of the warriors received similar injuries while battling on the first ridge, presenting Garl and the remaining tribe with an even deeper dilemma as these men were still conscious.

A more important argument ensued regarding what to do with the two bitten men who were already beginning to develop mild fevers. They sat at the outskirts of the fourth ridge, calm despite the gravity of the decision being made for them. Neither of the barbarians thought to try to flee, or lessen the severity of their predicament to their kinsmen; they knew what fate awaited them and accepted it, as well as the danger they posed if they were to try and conceal their injuries. They would have rather faced their death a thousand times than to bring such dishonor upon themselves.

The disagreement intensified, with Garl and Dagard toe to toe, yelling until their faces were as red as the morning sun on the day of the storm. Garl did not know what should be causing him more anger, that Dagard wanted to kill the two men on the spot or that two of his kin were fated to die in such an inglorious manner. The two warriors' lives were nearing their end; the only options available to them were to be cut down by their own or tied up, fall ill and die only to reanimate as one of those monsters. Both choices left Garl feeling as a blood traitor to those he was supposed to protect. His people were meant to meet death with honor, not as a precaution.

Igdahven tried to think of any other solution, sensing the dispute could soon turn to hostility. Naÿrja began tugging at his sleeve.

"Not now," he chided, brushing the girl away absently, "we're discussing an important matter."

A few moments later he again felt another tugging at his robes.

"By the Gods girl! You are going to be sorr…" His words were lost as he looked down at Naÿrja and allowed his head to follow where she was pointing. The two bitten men, not yet defeated by the illness, ran to the edge of the fourth ridge and leapt down the steep incline to the third. They half stumbled and half rolled, regaining their footing on the lower ridge, somehow uninjured. The remainder of the tribe moved to the edge of the cliff, watching the progress of the warriors.

While the tribe argued their fate, the two men resigned themselves to their impending demise.

"Are you ready, Hammás?" Rikkar asked his companion.

Hammás nodded back.

The pair did not speak other than those initial words, communicating an immeasurable understanding between each other with no more than a look.

As the argument raged on and fully drew the attention of the tribe, they casually slipped away unnoticed. They felt the Gods were with them in their decision, granting an awareness of each other and the world around them. A level of clarity neither had previously known presented itself to them in a revelational chorus of sights and sounds, heightening their senses. Leaping down the ridge they somehow found their footing on the nearly vertical drop, recovering from the fall in perfect timing to continue their frenzied pace, matching each other stride for stride. Scaling the wall with agility unbefitting their large statures, they climbed over to the second ridge and picked up fallen weapons.

Howling to Kuldárhik, the two men fought back to back, guarding each other and moving with a single-minded purpose of destruction. If they were to die it would be on their terms, with a song on their lips and the lust of battle in their hearts. They moved with the speed and grace of a pair of ridge cats, dancing through their enemies, killing with each fluid motion they made. If a foe was not in their direct path they simply avoided it, while those that were, fell with unerring precision. They cut their way through countless of the Risen, becoming lost to the sight of those standing on the fourth ridge. The watching barbarians prayed for them from afar, willing their strength to the two renegades through a primal bond as old as the tribe itself.

Though they did not down every enemy they encountered or go out of their way to engage, they worked in a determined straight line downward to the first ridge. Each maneuver was performed with flawless, brutal efficiency. The chorus grew to encompass every cut and slash they made, every brilliant counter and evasion. Minutes passed as they carved their way through the first ridge, out into the field among the sea of undead where they became lost from view. In a crescendo of violence, the chorus became all-consuming and they knew no more.

"Elders, which one of you identify and claim those men?" Garl asked, the entrancement at an end.

Elder Damas stepped forward, representing Clan Darcláw. "They were of mine, Hammás and Rikkar," he declared proudly.

"When this is over, may their names be sung in triumph to their sacrifice this day. For now, we have much work to do," Garl replied sorrowfully.

***

Two sleds were available usually reserved for hauling the kill from a hunt back to the tribe. Garl ordered them brought out for the grisly task of transporting the bodies down to the empty third ridge. In most situations the barbarians were a highly pragmatic people, but regarding their fallen kinsmen they held certain beliefs. They refused to destroy the bodies, yet could not keep them nearby on the likely chance they would reanimate. Also they would not dishonor the bodies by piling them deep onto the sleds, only transporting four at a time on each which greatly slowed their progress. When circumstances allowed, they hoped to retrieve the bodies for proper burial.

With the first and second ridges lost, Garl's focus was on securing all available resources up to Boldstone Ridge. Two groups of six were assigned to transport the dead to the third level, while the other groups were charged with carrying food, weapons, and all other wares. A head count was taken, confirming the tribe had been nearly destroyed. Forty-six warriors remained, along with one hundred fifty-seven women, children and those beyond the years of battle. Though they hoped for a reprieve as the day neared its end, it was not long until tragedy struck yet again.

"We're doing right by these people, whether you agree or not," Darvik scolded his long-time friend and fellow clansman.

"No point in arguing anymore, what's done is done. The quicker they get back with the sleds the better and we can be done with this. Only a few more trips to be made," Gregor replied, "far as I'm concerned these bodies aren't going to be at rest much longer."

The Ridges were once again full of activity as it would be at any other time. Only on this day, the tribe was solemn and silent as they worked. An owl hooted, almost mournfully in the distance as the sun made its descent in the sky.

"There's always the chance we've got it wrong, we can't let fear lead us to abandon our ways," Darvik insisted.

Gregor only grunted absently in response.

Raised voices from the third ridge interrupted their conversation. They ventured over to the edge to look below.

"Motherless son of a..." Gregor muttered, allowing his curse to trail off.

Down below, tribesmen slowly backed away from the sleds and let out cries of alarm. Extremities of the bodies being transported began to twitch and slowly show signs of life, as the corpses that were already moved began to rise. The warning spread among the tribe as more people began to realize what was happening.

A call carried across the third ridge, "Stop what you are doing! Retreat back up top!"

The Risen seemed to be in a momentary state of disorientation, acclimating to their newly reanimated state. The barbarians took advantage of the delay, quickly fleeing.

Captivated by the scene, Darvik and Gregor's gazes were focused below. Darvik's instincts saved them at that moment, a sixth sense prompting him to turn around. There were still ten corpses that needed to be brought down, now ambling towards them and reaching out hungrily. His startled cry alerted Gregor to their immediate danger.

Darvik, with his back to the edge of the cliff and the first of the creatures upon him, had nowhere to run and no time to unsheathe his short sword. As it closed in ready to lunge, Darvik fell flat to his back with the reflexes of a warrior, grabbing the tunic of his former clansman and rotating as he neared the ground. He pitched the creature over the ledge to the ridge below, where it climbed back to its feet, seemingly unfazed after its rough fall. The two men had few seconds to spare as the other nine Risen approached, and they were unsure whether to flee left or right.

A voice, echoing across the Ridges shouted, "To the east! Everyone on the third and fourth, safe passage to the east! Get to Boldstone now!"

Garl watched the horrendous scene unfolding, berating himself for his foolish hope and putting his remaining clansmen in further danger. Filled with rage he began issuing commands, setting up a defensive line with several men leading up towards Boldstone Ridge. His voice echoed across the mountain, seemingly unnatural in volume.

There was no hesitation remaining in the barbarians. All curiosity, doubt, and confusion about the Risen had been left at the massacre in the field below. The tribe immediately stopped their work and headed toward the safety of the highest ridge. They ushered their people to the top level, their quick reaction preventing further losses.

"Keep them at bay, don't let any of those things through!" Garl instructed his line as the last of the remaining clans passed through the barricade.

A handful of the Risen managed to follow in, but were quickly disposed of as the group of warriors fell back into Boldstone.

"Lock and secure the cursed gates," Garl grumbled, "begin movin' the supplies into the *Ingdaärðendvhel*, we'll take refuge there.

Three men go check that the west gate is still secured."

And so it went that for the first time in the tribe's history a hostile force had taken over up to the fourth ridge. Sealed away inside the Great Hall on the fifth, Garl silently fumed as he deliberated on how he was going to keep his remaining people alive.

Brains and Brawn

Big Bear Outpost was empty and silent. The only noise breaking the stillness of the air was the soft sound of falling snow. A storm like this typically shut everyone indoors and created a vacated appearance, but this time the town was truly desolate; days had passed since Walt saw or heard from anyone. The storm was finally beginning to ebb after nearly a full day of white-out conditions. Roads, buildings, and fields outside of the town walls were covered in a pristine white blanket, the serenity of the landscape contrasting the chaos of the storm that left it behind. With the snow over a foot deep, Walt had a difficult decision to make about travelling northeast to the mines.

Wading through the snow to check on the horses proved to be a challenge. Each step was an effort, with his feet sinking deep on every stride. By the time he made it to the stables, his robes were wet and feet cold from snow getting into his boots.

"I seem to not be properly dressed for this nonsense," he sighed.

He grabbed a saddle from the rack and began outfitting his favorite horse, Tulip. He enjoyed this particular beast. She was older, mostly chestnut with patches of white along her shoulders and chest. Most importantly she was a bit on the gentle side. He didn't need a horse that could burst through a wall, or might give a good bite just because it felt in the mood to. Yes, Tulip was just his speed.

While he finished saddling the horse, he looked out of the open stable entrance to the untouched grounds. There were no prints in the snow other than those he left. There wasn't a patch of surface anywhere that wasn't covered in white. How could he possibly think to get up to the mine in this? The normally three hour trip would likely take all day, if the poor girl could even make it that far. Walt groaned again in frustration.

Some powerful wizard, he thought. He couldn't figure out what was wrong with everyone, couldn't stop them from dying, and couldn't figure out how to get to the survivors that should've been back days ago! He kicked his foot through the snow in frustration, only to set himself hopping when the flimsy toe of his boot struck a buried rock. Hobbling, muttering and cursing, he retraced the steps back to his house. Upstairs, he went out to his balcony for the hundredth time over the last few days to look out towards the mines.

Again he was greeted by the endless sea of white. A few trees stood here and there, and no signs of life were seen anywhere. Walt paced as he thought about this new predicament, the horse certainly wouldn't make it out very far in this. Those who hadn't perished were still stranded at the worksite as far as he knew. Why they would have delayed beyond the first day was beyond him. They should have come back to make preparations for burials, and figure out how to move on from this.

Walt found himself on the other side of the balcony, looking towards the uncivilized lands. Further east were more outposts like his, thriving on the rich mining provided by the expansive Blue Fold Mountains. To the west, Darcláw's Gap led into a series of plateaus populated by wild men, and even further west, the Idehldivar, a seemingly impassible mountain wall. His settlement was the last in line, a final stop for those who wanted to be away from civilization but still part of a town.

Questions poured through the wizard's mind as he paced, what illness plagued his people? Where had Aubur gone? Should he risk travelling to the mine or stay put a few more days? Going for days on end without getting any closer to answers was beginning to infuriate him. A flicker of motion broke him from his deliberations. He turned his attention fully towards the wild lands. There was definitely something out there, far away on the plain. Squinting, he couldn't quite tell what it was; it looked like hundreds of dark specks marring the otherwise undisturbed field of white. While on a ship once, he had seen an instrument that allowed a person to view far in the distance. The captain had said it was quite a rare piece, refusing to part with it despite Walt's prodigious offers. He wished he had it at this moment. Having no other alternative, he sat, waited and watched.

Nearly an hour passed before he could say with certainty the specks were growing larger and heading in his direction. It took nearly an additional hour before he could determine a solitary figure out in front of the rest of the pack, and shortly after that confirm it was in fact people running his way.

If things weren't strange enough already... either one berserk barbarian is leading a troupe of them towards my little town, or a hundred of them are angry with one and chasing him in my direction, he thought. Either way, he didn't care for the position he suddenly found himself in.

What would they be doing coming south, on the tail of a blizzard nonetheless? No time in recent memory had this many of the northerners come out of their secluded mountain ranges. During particularly lean winters a few might come out to trade furs for food, or other materials they couldn't procure themselves, but this group certainly didn't look like it wanted to barter. The sight of the barbarians could perhaps explain his people's extended absence. If the survivors had somehow come across this group, he could expect they won't be returning at all.

From what he knew of barbarians, Walt was fairly certain he was in great danger being caught in their path. There weren't many options available to him; he could sit and wait for them to plow through town, looting and pillaging. They'd likely kill him in the process. He could ride out to meet them, perhaps scare them off with a display of magic. If what he heard was true they were wary of people like him. That option didn't sit well with him either though, if it came to a fight he could take down maybe one or two, perhaps ten. He'd be overrun shortly after that though.

There is the lone man out in front, he considered.

He just might be able to stun him a bit, and drag him back to town with the horse before the others lagging behind could catch up to him. It was risky, but he would then have something to bargain for his life with. That's what he would do. He wouldn't be caught haplessly waiting for those brutes to decide his fate. Quickly, Walt ran up to the western gatehouse to open the large steel portcullis. When he had this town designed, he knew the dangers of being so far north. A thick steel gate and high stone walls did much to stymy an invading band, as long as there were people around to guard the walls.

After opening the gate, he scurried back to the stable to retrieve Tulip. He thanked the spirits for his timing, already having her saddled up and ready to go for when he thought he was leaving to the mines. Taking a length of sturdy rope, he sped off through the gate towards the approaching force. Walt wagered this was the first time barbarians had seen a lone horseman riding towards them rather than away. On second thought, this may very well be the first time anyone did such a thing. It certainly was a bold plan, he had yet to work out if it was decisive or bereft of sense.

The horse labored through the deep snow as it raced beyond the gates. Froth soon formed around its mouth from the exertion, the animal working extra hard to meet Walt's demands of speed. He figured he could push her long enough despite the conditions; they didn't have too far to go. A trail of snow kicked up behind Walt as they blazed their path, racing slightly from the south to cut off the barbarian. Walt had to hit him fast and hard, and make haste back to town.

He frowned upon drawing close to the invading force. The lead man seemed to be moving with a grim determination, lacking the frenzied gleam of one intent on killing. His eyes were set forward as he relentlessly put one foot in front of the other, as if he was driven on by the thundering of the Gods themselves. In contrast, those behind him appeared to pursue with a ravenous, mindless lust. Their features were gruesome, were they wearing war paint?

Nobody even seemed to notice Walt. The frontrunner stumbled several times, picking himself up and carrying on despite his obvious exhaustion. He was undoubtedly an exceptional specimen, even at this distance Walt could see he would appear as a twig next to an oak tree if they were to stand side by side. Did this group run all the way from the Blue Fold? *No, not possible*, Walt thought, though he couldn't think of how else the sight before him came to be.

Gathering up his courage before losing his nerve, or worse the barbarians turning and spotting him, Walt slowed Tulip and began to draw his focus inward. He stayed aware of his surroundings only so much as to not fall from the horse. Once he achieved a clear mental state he could feel the world of energy beckoning to him, waiting to be drawn through the eye of a needle and bent to his will. The pool was a part of him and all about him, an all-encompassing presence he only had to reach into. He drew as much of the energy into him as he could hold, finally releasing it as a dense ball of air the size of a fist at his target. It felt to Walt as if the magical projectile met a layer of resistance before striking home, like trying to hit a fish in a pond with a rock. Nevertheless, the barbarian collapsed to the ground, whether from exhaustion or the blow Walt wasn't sure.

The sun was already well in the sky, bringing a warmth to the day that hadn't been seen in many months and causing Walt to sweat as he labored. The storm of the previous day was winter rebelling against its yearly end, lashing out in its final death throes. The snow was quickly becoming wet and heavy from the rise in temperature, hampering Walt's movement. He had to hurry, or the horde would be upon him. Up close to his target, Walt dismounted and set to work securing rope around the giant barbarian's legs. He was grateful the large man was unconscious. The barbarian's ankle seemed nearly as thick as Walt's thigh, his great size leaving the wizard to question how he would manage to handle him once he awoke.

Tying off the rope through the saddle straps, Walt leaped on Tulip as quickly as he had ever mounted a horse. Less than a hundred feet separated him from the terrifying mob. Now that they were in his proximity Walt could clearly see something was amiss.

The group had a staggered, uncoordinated lope to their strides, their facial features a horrendous mockery of a typical human's. And the smell! It was worse than a midden heap in mid-summer. Walt made a quick apology to the barbarian for what he was about to do and sped away with the horse, dragging the barbarian's unconscious form behind him.

Racing back to town he hoped he didn't cause too much injury to his captive, dragging him through the snow as he was. Luckily it was deep and soft, protecting him from most of the bumps and abrasions of the ground. Galloping through the entrance, and once again running up the gatehouse steps to seal him in and them out, an odd thought occurred to Walt. He had this portcullis built in fear of invading barbarians, and here he was dragging one in behind him.

The host outside of his town desperately wanted to get inside, but the walls and gate were nearly impenetrable without basic siege equipment. Walt anxiously watched the mob pressing in on the gate; to his relief they didn't seem to be trying to organize a way to breach. At the moment they only seemed capable of mindlessly pressing themselves against the barrier. Walt would have loved to examine some of these creatures. Though they looked like they were once human they did not appear so now. A sinking feeling grew in his stomach as he began to make connections between this and the events over the last few days. With a bit of time he could confirm his suspicions, but first things first, he had to see to his new guest.

***

All five of his senses rushed back to him in an instant, reminding him he was still alive. Sunlight pierced in through the large entrance, stinging his eyes. The dull smell of livestock was masked by the aroma of roasted chicken, reminding Jvard of how hungry he was. A horse whinnied from somewhere close, setting him on edge until he saw it was behind a stall. Was he in a stockpen? Fully awaking, he looked about with a scowl as he rubbed the itchy straw from his shoulders that had worked itself into his skin.

He glanced down and saw a large fowl prepared on a platter, causing him to drop his immediate concerns. Greedily tearing into it, the entire bird was gone in under a minute. As he licked the grease from his fingers, he realized he probably ate a bone or two by accident as well. Nearby was a large bucket of water that he lunged for from his hands and knees, drinking like a man who had been wandering a desert for days. With his basic needs sated, he was able to think more clearly and wondered who might have put it there. The last few days at first had seemed only a dream, but he began to remember the horribly transformed faces of his kinsmen. He rushed to his feet, though he seemed safe for the moment he wanted to know where he was and how he got here.

After taking three steps he felt a sudden pull on his leg. A shackle around his ankle attached to a thick metal chain in the wall prevented him from moving more than a few paces. Roaring in anger, he tugged viciously at the chain a few times to no avail. He stopped suddenly when he looked up and saw an old man in the doorway, watching him.

"I was starting to think you were never going to awaken," the old man said to him.

Jvard didn't reply, the hair on the back of his neck standing at the sight of the robed figure. He had a similar feeling while near one of the spirit-seekers. Only this was different, more intense. Being close to one of the *Duchàlg* was discomforting, while something about the man before him made his skin itch.

"Ahh, I see you were hungry, that is good," the old man said into the silence, appearing a bit uncomfortable with the lack of conversation, "I can bring you more if you like."

"Why am I chained?" Jvard demanded.

"Just a precaution, only a precaution," the man told him, waving his hands in front of him in appeasement.

"I'm terribly sorry for the arrangements," he continued, gesturing to the stables before them, "you see, I think I would have had a better chance of carrying the horse upstairs into a proper bedroom than you."

"Release me," Jvard stated, ignoring the attempted humor and knocking his fist against the metal ring in the wall that secured him to the chain. The stable shook from the impact.

"I'm afraid I can't just yet, not until I'm certain you aren't a danger. You see, strange things have been happening of late. I am Walt, what might your name be northman?" Walt asked, attempting to draw a few words from the barbarian.

The barbarian didn't respond, instead fixing the old man with a stare. A low growl began to issue from deep in his chest as anger swelled in him, he didn't have time for the old man's nonsense. He needed to find out what happened to his tribe and who was responsible. Without revenge he would never regain the favor of his Gods, or be allowed entry to the Great Hall when he exited this life. A chieftain abandoning his clan earned the highest disgrace possible among his people. At the moment, chained in a room and not even knowing who his enemy was made the possibility of revenge seem very distant.

Daün drovka du sôjn dravka, he reminded himself. As it comes, so shall we go. His immediate need was to get free. After that, well, he would contend with what the fates put forth. He allowed his anger to fuel him as the blood drummed up through his temples and gorged his muscles. His thoughts devolved into a frantic primal state as his pulse thundered a wild rhythm. He was a trapped animal, in need of escape.

Walt watched in amazement as the barbarian exploded into a rage. He wanted to turn and flee but he was captivated by the spectacle before him; he had read accounts of the ferocity barbarians exhibited in battle and the fear they inspired in their enemies. Witnessing it up close was altogether different. The very air around the barbarian seemed to tingle, a wildfire on the brink of ignition. What was he thinking when he originally intended to capture this beast before him, and was it his imagination or did the barbarian seem even larger now? The sudden snap of the chain from the wall broke Walt from his entrancement. With a high pitch yelp he turned and ran from the stable, Jvard close on his heels.

Cursing his inquisitive nature, Walt reproached himself for his foolishness. He couldn't help it, the sight he had just witnessed ran counter to much of what he thought he knew. By all records barbarians were leery of anything magical, yet if what he observed didn't involve magic he would eat a toad. Instead of forming up a defense or attempting to disable the northerner before the situation grew out of hand, he decided in his infinite wisdom that he'd rather take the moment to study him!

Where should he even run to? He realized he was moving towards his house until he began to think what little use that would be. Sure he could lock a door, but the barbarian would probably smash through it like it were made of kindling. Risking a glance back, he saw his escaped captive no longer followed him. Instead he was walking over to the portcullis separating the mob of barbarians from the two of them. Walt slowed to a walk and finally stopped, standing with his hands on his hips watching the northerner. Confident that he wasn't going to try to tear him apart, at least for the moment, Walt carefully began to walk back towards his guest standing before the gate. The barbarian had stopped just out of arm's reach of the creatures now surrounding the town, staring at them in what appeared to be sadness and pity.

"Begging your pardon, I believe we should put our differences aside for the moment as there are larger problems going on," Walt said as the creatures pushed up against the gate, fervently reaching their arms through the grating.

"I am Jvard, son of Helstajvan," he responded after a brief pause, not taking his gaze from what were once his kinsmen.

"Welcome to Big Bear, Jvard, son of Helstajvan. You'll have to forgive me for not extending my hospitality to your group," Walt stated dryly.

Jvard continued staring ahead, not offering a response.

They stood for a time, watching the people outside of the gate. Walt decided he would remain silent and observe, wait and see what Jvard would say or do. He must have had many questions, and though Walt had much on his mind he refrained from speaking until the barbarian had an opportunity to express his thoughts. It made for a long, quiet evening. After what seemed an eternity, and just as Walt was nearing to give up waiting for Jvard to break the silence, he finally spoke.

"Where are all of the people who dwell here?" he asked.

"Up at the mines, off aways in that direction," Walt said as he pointed towards the northeast, "mostly all of them fell ill and died, the survivors haven't yet returned."

"How long ago did they..." Jvard began, but was interrupted by Walt holding up a finger.

"It has been several days," Walt answered, but held off further questions, "I too have many things I wish to know. Now that I've answered two of your inquiries will you indulge me with some answers?"

Jvard, more agreeable now that he was no longer chained to the wall, nodded in assent.

"How is it that you came to my doorstep, barbarian?" Walt wished to know.

Recounting his ordeal, Jvard described how he returned home overdue from a hunt only to find his people transformed. They harried him for days as he fled south, much of it a blur to him. He left out that he was the chieftain of the most dominant tribe in the north, best to not share too much personal information with this man he didn't yet trust.

"And that's when I awoke near your horses, perhaps you can fill in how I came to be there," Jvard said as he finished his tale.

"I saw you several miles out, you looked as though you could use a hand. You collapsed as I was a few hundred feet away and I dragged you back into town; my apologies for the bumpy ride, though I don't think you noticed," Walt told him, not exactly lying.

He figured it best for the moment to omit that rather than offer the barbarian the help he needed, he clunked him in the head instead.

Jvard looked thoughtful for a moment, slowly nodding as he registered Walt's words.

"Then I am in your debt, old man," he acknowledged.

Walt dipped his head slightly, pleased with himself, "You're too kind. We're safe for the moment, why don't we continue this conversation indoors where the surroundings are less unseemly."

Walking towards his house, Walt paused as he realized Jvard stopped following him and had returned to the gate once again. Perplexed, Walt went back to his side.

The wizard tried to explain to Jvard that it had been a trying few days, that he had only just come to and should allow himself some rest, but trailed off as Jvard shushed him dismissively. He was left sputtering as the barbarian moved in closer to the gate, peering intently through the throng. Walt harrumphed, setting his beard into a bounce. Getting hushed in his own town; he had half a mind to light the barbarian's hair on fire.

Ignoring his host, Jvard again looked at the scores of creatures at the gate. These men and women were his responsibility, and he had failed them. He recognized most of their faces, men he once fought beside, laughed with and shared meals. His face paled as he saw one man in particular a few rows back. How could that be?

A prickling sensation ran up the barbarian's spine, stealing his attention. It felt as if sharp steel were being dragged through stone next to his ear. He turned to see Walt quickly twirling his finger, causing a flame to disappear like a child who shouldn't have something and was trying to hide it behind his back.

"Ah, no harm intended, just looking to get your attention for a moment," he said somewhat sheepishly to Jvard's consternation.

So he was dealing with a fel-touched magician. Jvard knew he had been uncomfortable around this man for a reason. He would have to be careful, every one of his people knew those who directly touched the elements were not to be trusted. They were a cowardly lot, each and every one. If he wasn't careful he'd end up involved in some scheme concocted by the crafty devil. Perhaps he already was, the thought dawned on him. Jvard grew concerned, what if this whole ordeal were some wizard plot he was caught up in?

Jvard decided not to let his concern show; if the magician were up to something Jvard might have an advantage letting the felborn think he had him unawares. Pretending the flame winked out before he saw it, Jvard beckoned Walt over to him. There was a very disturbing sight among the creatures he needed to reason out.

"Look at the man back there, the one missing most of his flesh," Jvard pointed out.

Walt looked over and thought he saw who Jvard was referring to. He shuddered involuntarily at the sight of him. Most of the skin was torn from his face and torso, and one of his arms was missing.

"That is Larik, son of Glarid. I saw him die," Jvard stated flatly.

He continued at Walt's questioning look, "He was on the hunt with me, when we returned to the fields before Boldstone Ridge he was butchered by those things. Now he is walking among them."

Storing away the implications of the barbarian's words, Walt thought it best to remove themselves from the immediate situation and think it over when their minds were fresh.

"Let's get inside. We have much to think on, and the answers will come in time," Walt suggested.

The two men retreated to Walt's home, escaping the world outside. They made their way into the dining room, where Jvard sat heavily in an ornate chair. Walt sighed, worrying about its structural integrity as it creaked beneath the northerner's weight, but it seemed to hold. Walt began to prepare a meal as his guest sat, leaning back with his hands over his face.

Jvard's head was pounding. He really did need a few days of rest after his flight, to clear his head a bit and focus on what to do next. Walt finished roasting another bird, looking pleased with himself in how it came out. He frowned a bit though as he looked at the size of it, then at the size of the barbarian. Sighing again, he tore off a drumstick for himself and placed the rest of it in front of Jvard along with a jug of wine.

After eating in relative silence, Walt spoke up, "I think we should turn in early, and look at this with a fresh perspective in the morning. I trust you won't try and kill me in my sleep?"

"I feel like I should be the one concerned about whether or not I shall wake again, *old man*. But no, I have no intentions of harming you. At least not tonight," Jvard answered with only a hint of mirth.

"Good. Then I shall see you in the morning."

***

Opening his eyes, Walt found himself standing on the open fields outside of town. The darkness of the night was broken by a dim gray light, though it was impossible to determine its source. Immediately he recognized he was not truly here, at least not in the physical sense. He had been coming to this waking dream more often of late. Ever since his people disappeared he'd journey to this place where energy ebbed and flowed like the tides of the sea, and could be not only felt but seen. It was different tonight, very much so. He vaguely saw the forms of the hundreds of beings surrounding his town. They were less substantial though, merely apparitions of their bodies as they appeared in the waking world. Nothing flowed about them which proved strange in itself.

Every living thing had dark or light wisps of energy interacting with it, the fundamental source from which life and magic flowed; these had nothing. They might as well have been rocks or sticks. As confused as he was, struggling to make sense of recent events, the one truth he could be certain of was the things surrounding his town were only husks of men. There was nothing alive about them in any sense. Walt walked out among them as they aimlessly meandered about, trying to gain insight into their motives. He was unable to determine one other than they wanted to get through the gate. Suddenly he wanted to be away from the lifeless things before him, anywhere else.

The thought occurred to Walt that because he was not physically limited by his body at the moment, he was likely not restricted by the laws of motion either. He concentrated on a location in the distance, visualizing himself there and moving to it. In response, the landscape pulled and stretched towards him to reform around the spot he had chosen. Pleased, Walt tried again and again, each time moving further off onto the Laskouth Plains.

Distancing himself from the hideous creatures surrounding his town put him at ease, but he grew concerned when a dull throbbing began to spread through his mind as he moved further away from his resting body. More notably, his incorporeal form became less substantial until he moved closer back to town and the feeling subsided. Experimenting, he travelled in each direction with the same result. He quickly reasoned that his sleeping body was the center point and he could only move so far from it. That revelation was a bit dismaying, he had started to hope that he would be able to wisp himself away towards the mines and discover what happened to his people.

Finding a comfortable distance away on the plain, he lingered a moment to observe the swirling dark and light flows that made magic possible. They were nearly everywhere, fluttering in and out of existence in the middle of the air, surrounding trees, and above his town. This basic energy formed the elements that he could call forth and manipulate to his will, though the experience taxed him heavily. A flicker of motion in the distance caught his eye, putting him on alert. It looked like a person, appearing with the same ethereal quality he himself took on here, but as soon as Walt was certain he spotted the man, he vanished. He looked about in futility trying to locate him again, and his apprehension increased when he was unable to do so.

Nearly losing hope, by happenstance he saw him again moving purposefully among the lifeless beings outside of Big Bear. Walt drew himself quickly towards the town in the same manner he had travelled earlier, covering great distance with a thought to instantly reappear within yards of the stranger. The being turned abruptly, obviously startled by the wizard's sudden appearance.

Walt had never seen anyone quite like him; a wolf head and skin sat atop his head, while he wore a patchwork robe that swayed and flowed with each subtle movement. He was only able to view the stranger a brief few seconds before he darted off again. This time Walt was able to track his direction and attempted to keep pace with him. They raced northward, the mountains streaking by them in a blur as they crossed vast spans with each stride. The throbbing in Walt's head returned, coming on with ferocity as he moved further away from his sleeping body. It was too late for him to turn back. He travelled beyond the limits of his strength, fading out of the realm of spirits and finding himself awake in bed.

The following morning Walt awoke still tired from the previous night. His body had slept, but the hours spent in that other world did not allow him to truly rest. That was the first time he had ever seen another person in the dream world, having no explanation for it he put the event out of his mind for the moment. Downstairs, he found Jvard already awake frying eighteen eggs over a skillet in the living room fireplace, as he had the previous three mornings since his arrival. He sighed audibly as he thought the barbarian would either burn his house down or consume all of the food in a matter of weeks.

"If one were to rise as late as you on the tundra, he'd soon starve or become a meal himself. Though you're rather bony, perhaps you'd be safe," Jvard said flatly upon hearing Walt come down the stairs.

Walt offered a grimace in response, "Is it any different outside from yesterday?" he asked.

"There is no change," Jvard replied, "they're still trying to get inside, or wandering about the walls."

"What are your plans, barbarian? You showed up on my doorstep, but I have no idea why in particular you came here or where you go from this point forward. Though we should have a few days, or weeks even, we can't stay behind these walls forever," Walt inquired.

Jvard took a deep breath, his thoughts turning introspective.

"My intention was to reach safety. What were once my kinsmen stayed on my heels for two days, I needed to escape and this was the nearest place," he said after thinking a moment longer, "those people were my kin and clan, and I failed them. I seek redemption, *wizard*. But I'm not sure where I'm going, or where to begin looking."

Hiding his surprise, Walt stroked his beard for a few minutes. The emphasis Jvard placed on calling him wizard did not escape him. So, the northman was more observant than he let on. Though much of barbarian culture was unknown, their distaste of magic users was fairly common knowledge. Frankly he was astonished that Jvard hadn't reacted more negatively towards him.

"I believe I can be of assistance in that regard," Walt said into the silence, "you see, there is an order of which I was formerly a member. They may have foretold this disaster, though at the time I thought they were simply mad."

With that, he had Jvard's full attention.

Walt continued, "Let's head outside, there are a few things I'd like to confirm today. Your assistance would be useful, if you'd be willing to lend a hand?"

Jvard nodded his consent, eager for anything that might help discover what happened or who was responsible.

"Should I find a few more answers, I can piece them together with other knowledge I've gleaned," Walt added, "perhaps then we'll have a starting point."

Wiping yolk from his chin, Jvard stood abruptly and ventured outside. Walt stared for a moment before following, dismayed that there was not a scrap of breakfast left for him.

"You want me to what?" Jvard asked incredulously upon hearing Walt's plan.

Living in the unforgiving realm of the Blue Fold Mountain Range that Jvard called home, he had survived many brutal experiences; even so, this idea caused his stomach to sour.

"I need to examine their blood, as well as one of their brains," Walt reiterated.

Jvard scowled again at the thought. He had been doing that a lot since breakfast.

"Well this is what I need to find more information, and to be honest this sort of thing isn't where I excel. You agreed to help me, did you not?" Walt reminded the barbarian.

"So I did," Jvard answered, "how would we even go about this?"

"It'll be too awkward to try and pull one through the gate, and we certainly can't open it," Walt answered, "we'll have to pull one up over the wall and do it then. There's an axe in the toolshed."

Jvard's scowl deepened. He didn't like the sound of the plan at all, though he didn't have a better alternative. Not only that, they still hadn't figured out what happened to Larik. The young man had not been originally afflicted, yet here he was walking among the Stricken. Consequently, Jvard was hesitant to put himself in reach of one of them. Who knows how contagious they might be.

"Let's be on with it then, the sooner we have answers the sooner we can make decisions," Jvard said begrudgingly.

"That's the spirit. I suppose..." Walt offered.

After visiting the tool shed to grab a simple axe and fashion some rope into a lasso, they proceeded up through the gatehouse onto the wall. They looked out across the field into the sea of decaying flesh. The smell from the creatures had certainly grown in intensity, becoming nearly unbearable. Putting aside his displeasure, Jvard made several throws before he finally managed to catch the rope under the arm of one and around its shoulder, pulling it taut. He tried to aim for someone he didn't recognize, butchering someone that he knew well would have been too much for him to endure.

Jvard pulled the thing about three quarters of the way up the wall, slowly tugging it away from the rest of the crowd. He wasn't quite sure who it was, and didn't care to look too closely to try and figure it out. As he pulled it towards him, it reached out to him growling and thrashing its arms about. Jvard braced himself as he shifted the rope into one hand, wrapping it up around his forearm a few times as he tried to hold the creature in place. It swayed back and forth from its desperate motions while it dangled along the wall. With his free hand, Jvard hoisted the woodman's axe. Raising it over his head he tried to time the sway of the creature with the swing of his axe, with the intention of splitting it into the thing's head.

Careful, careful!" Walt called out.

"I'm okay," Jvard replied, his voice slightly strained.

"I meant with the subject, but yes you too," Walt answered back, drawing yet another scowl from Jvard.

With a loud crack, Jvard drove the axe home. The creature no longer struggled, and swung faster from the impact until Jvard regained control of it. Lifting it onto the wall, Jvard set the corpse down heavily. Grimly he put one foot on it and yanked on the axe handle. It pulled out with a sickening noise drawing groans from both men.

"There's plenty of blood for you. I'll leave you to manage the rest," Jvard said as he tossed the body inside the town walls to the ground below, exiting through the gatehouse and stalking off.

Walt watched as Jvard walked down the street, not entirely sure where he might be going. He probably just needed to cool off a bit, clear his head. Killing the stricken person must not have been an easy thing for the barbarian. A shame, he was hoping to get a little more assistance to complete his task today. He sighed heavily as he went back home to retrieve his pack of alchemy materials.

His preference would have been to perform the examination somewhere more suited to the task, or at least in the stable where he could have used a table and organized his equipment. The ground outside would have to do though, he wasn't interested in dragging the corpse through town to a more appropriate location. As long as the weather continued to hold he shouldn't have any problems. Clearing away an area of snow, he laid his pack out near the body, along with a pail of water and several bowls.

His first order of business was to collect some of the blood while it was still fresh. Careful not to touch the body, he picked its arm up by a sleeve and made a longitudinal cut along the length of the forearm, starting at the elbow and running down to the thumbside of its wrist. He placed the arm over one of the empty bowls, letting the blood spill into it. Pleased with the ease he accomplished this, he took a deep breath before moving onto his next task.

Using a pair of tongs, he carefully removed pieces of the brain through the head wound Jvard inflicted. This was not the kind of work he was accustomed to, but did his best to maintain his composure through the process. He reminded himself he would be rewarded for his thoroughness, it would be worth the trouble for the information he hoped to gain. Looking away as he reached in and dug around through the skull, he told himself it could have been worse; he did not have to put much effort in to opening up the skull any further, Jvard seemed to have done a fair job of that.

The difficult portion of his tasks complete, Walt looked closely at the pieces of tissue in one of the bowls. He turned them over several times with the tongs, looking at each one individually.

Admittedly, Walt recognized this wasn't his area of expertise. He had known a few people who devoted their entire lives to studying various parts of the body. It was a bit too morbid for his taste, there were far more interesting things in the world to him than poking and prodding at a cadaver. Even with his lack of experience in this area, he was able to determine part of what he was hoping to, now to inspect the blood.

Gingerly he moved the arm out of the bowl, leaving him with a large pool to work with. Sitting cross-legged on the ground he pulled the bowl back a bit, along with an additional bowl to give himself some room to work away from the corpse. He let his mind empty, drifting away until he was in the place of calm emptiness where he could call forth his power. He pulled at the small strands of energy available to him, collecting them and rearranging it into a skimmer, a completely neutral element to use for his test. Breathing heavily from creating the silvery elemental strand, he took out one of his special stones to magnetize it, in the same manner as the ritual he completed days before at the mine.

At a flick of his wrist he sent the skimmer into the bowl, moving it through every inch of it. He withdrew it after a few moments, directing it into the empty bowl. He was left with a pool of black liquid, the same result as when he performed the test days ago on his people. Satisfied, Walt now believed he had solved what happened to everyone. Now he only needed to figure out how it happened. Knuckling his back, it was hard for him to believe the entire morning had passed while he worked, the sun high in the sky marking how much time had elapsed. Hearing Jvard's heavy footsteps approaching, he turned to greet him.

"Excellent timing, I believe I now have some answers to share," Walt said as he turned to see Jvard approaching.

"Don't look so surprised," Walt said while chuckling at Jvard's expression, "I told you I'd come through."

"Your answers may have to wait. I think your townsfolk have returned," Jvard responded ominously.

Walt jumped to his feet, his face slightly pale. In a split second he decided his materials were safe on the ground for the time being, and he beckoned Jvard to lead the way. Whereas Jvard arrived through the western gate, a similar entrance existed along the northeastern side of town that Jvard seemed to be leading him towards. Struggling to keep up with the large strides of the barbarian, Walt began to feel a stitch in his side attempting to match the pace that was casual for Jvard. Arriving at the wall, they climbed a set of stairs that allowed access to the top.

Looking to the field below, Walt's heart sank as he saw many of his former citizens in the same condition as the invading barbarians. They were still a few hundred yards away, but he could tell it was them. Both men silent, they walked down below to the gate to wait for their approach.

"I am sorry, barbarian," Walt said softly.

"For what?"

"I didn't give thought to how the sight of your people like this might affect you. You have my apologies," Walt offered.

Jvard merely grunted impassively in response.

As the Stricken approached the town, their movements jerking and faces pallid, Walt felt regret that he wasn't able to do anything more to prevent their condition. He had desperately wanted information regarding what happened to everyone, but was hoping for something other than this. A quick count left nearly half of his townsfolk unaccounted for, offering him some hope that they may have escaped elsewhere. Soon the northeastern wall was pressed upon nearly as much as the western side of town. A thought of survival punctured through his grief as Walt realized they were now completely surrounded.

He tried not to look into the faces of the men and women he once knew, now an unthinking mass. The worst were the few children among them in the same state, their eyes lifeless as they reached through the gate with a greedy zeal towards Walt and Jvard.

"They're plague stricken," Walt said suddenly.

"You mean this is a disease, what do you know of this?" Jvard asked, further alarmed.

"I'm a man staring at a painting one color at a time, I see many of the parts but it's not making a complete picture," Walt answered, "come, we have much to discuss."

They returned to the scene of Walt's examination, Jvard lagging behind as they approached the bowls and corpse. The wizard urged a hesitant Jvard closer. Overcoming his distaste for the magic that must be involved, he peered over Walt's shoulder into a bowl full of a black viscous liquid.

"This was withdrawn, in a sense, from the blood of the victim," Walt stated, "it does not belong."

He allowed Jvard to look at it a few moments before continuing, watching as he saw curiosity seeping into the barbarian's features.

"I performed a similar ceremony a few days ago when my people were only sick, not whatever they are now. During which, I procured this," he said as he reached into his pack and pulled out a vial he had collected of the black fluid, "though I don't know what it is, it shares the same essence."

Jvard exhaled heavily, "This doesn't tell us much," he said, almost disappointed.

"By itself, no. I know more though. Here, look," the wizard added as he carefully moved pieces of the brain around with the tongs. "As far as brains go, I think this is typical."

Jvard offered Walt an incredulous look.

"Some folks I used to know had odd hobbies," he gave as a limited explanation.

"This however, is not typical," he continued while examining a blackened piece of tissue, "the blood carries the plague up into the brain, where it necrotizes, that is, kills the tissue."

Holding up a finger Walt held off the barbarian's question, "Nearly a week ago, I was inside the mind of a criminal, attempting to draw the truth from him. I believe, in a coincidence, the plague struck at that time – I felt the presence trying to overtake his mind, so I sealed it away to continue my work. At the time, I had no idea what it was. But after others became ill and seeing their blood, the two separate events seemed connected. This brain tissue is further confirmation."

Jvard was perplexed, "How did all of this happen so widespread at the same time? It makes no sense."

"I was using magic to investigate the man's mind. While I was working I felt a fluctuation in the power I draw from, something like I've never felt before. It was like watching a river suddenly reverse the direction of its flow for a time. Someone did this, with magic, and it had far reaching affects," Walt concluded.

"What of the order you were involved with, you said they spoke of this happening?" Jvard asked, finally feeling like they might be getting somewhere.

Walt furrowed his brow as he thought about how to respond. When he abandoned the order, he was still only an initiate, the lowest designation available. Perhaps he could have climbed through the organization's ranks, but his interests always seemed to be elsewhere.

"They were a very secretive group, the Magicus Celesti," he finally responded, "unfortunately, I was not privy to much of their information. However, word did begin to spread amongst them that a growing power was developing in the east, eventually the talk grew to ridiculous heights of a coming catastrophe. If this is related, it seems they were right."

"Why did you leave them?" Jvard prodded.

Walt decided there was no harm in being truthful, "Again much of what they did was shrouded in secrecy. I grew distrustful of them and left in the night. Frankly I thought they were spreading rumors to gain support for their own private war with another group."

Jvard chuckled mirthlessly. So, the wizard himself didn't trust other wizards.

"It appears there is nothing for either of us up north any longer. We're rather isolated here, most importantly we should find how far reaching this plague is. Of lesser consequence, my enterprise is a failure with no people to run it and I suspect you are now a chieftain without a tribe," Walt said abruptly.

"You're recommending we leave," Jvard replied, stating the wizard's thought for him.

Walt nodded.

"Given the current circumstances I think the Magicus Celesti will at least forgive me, though they likely won't extend a warm welcome back. They are far to the south, through the Golden Terraces but I believe they will have more answers," he said.

Jvard was hesitant about the proposition. Should he dare trust the wizard, and worse his former cohorts?

Sensing the barbarian's hesitation, Walt added, "Worse, a scheduled caravan should have arrived here two days ago from Creekview's Crossing. I fear they may be affected by this as well. We are safe here for the time being, but will run out of food before long."

"We should take the food with us and go, then," Jvard decided, "no sense in staying here trapped to eventually starve behind the walls."

"My thoughts exactly," Walt agreed, "we'll stay a few days, you still need a bit more rest and it will give us time to prepare for the journey. Also we're almost completely surrounded, we'll have to think of a way to escape."

"There's one more thing we should discuss, wizard," Jvard said.

Walt looked to him questioningly.

"Larik. He didn't seem to be affected when all chaos broke loose. Yet there he is, one of the plague-stricken," he answered, gesturing towards the walls.

Walking over to the gate, Walt looked out among the victims. He spotted Larik; he wasn't easy to miss, as deformed as he was with large chunks of flesh missing.

"It looks as though they really tore into him. I'd suggest not letting them make any contact with you," Walt warned after thinking a moment, "whatever this is, it spreads through the blood and I would guess, can pass from them to you like many other illnesses. That would explain Larik's presence out there."

Two days passed uneventfully, Jvard anxious to be on the road. He came here because he had no other options and was unsure of what to do next. Walt had thrown him a sliver of hope, as slim as it was. If he had to trust a group of fel-touched, tainted wizards to find vengeance for his people then so be it, and woe onto them should they try and deceive him. Mentally he was beginning to wear down, the things outside of the gate being in such close proximity caused him anger, sadness, and grief all at once. He spent hours at the gate looking into the faces of the men and women who were once his kin, reminded of his failure as their leader and that he was now truly alone. Part of him hoped some flicker of recognition would come back to his people, but it was in vain. There were no longer souls behind those vicious eyes. Being on the move would give him a sense of purpose.

In between sessions of despondent staring through the gate and fits of violent rage to vent his frustration, Jvard assisted with packing a wagon for their travel. Several casks of water were gathered, and they emptied out the stock houses of cured meats.

"Even with as much as you eat we should have plenty for a few weeks," Walt commented to Jvard as they went over their plans.

While running south, Jvard had lost his magnificent half-moon axe at some point. It seemed minor compared to the loss of his people, but it was a weapon he revered greatly. In need of a replacement, the town of Big Bear did not have much of a selection. For the moment, he decided on a simple sledgehammer he found in the toolshed. Hefting the fourteen pound hammer, the weight felt comfortable and controllable in his grasp. Though he was used to an axe, given the enemies they were likely to encounter the hammer made more sense. The last thing he needed to happen was become surrounded by the plagued with his axehead stuck in a bone.

They had still not worked out how they would make a clean break from town. Counting over one hundred and seventy of the plagued surrounding them, they found themselves in the middle of a quandary. With their impending departure quickly approaching, Walt suggested they try to thin out the crowd before they attempted to flee. Jvard was initially opposed to the idea, he did not relish the thought of slaughtering his former kinsmen unless it was in immediate defense for his own life. In the end he agreed, but only if they began at the northeastern side of town where Walt's people, the former citizens of Big Bear, now surrounded the walls. Walt shrugged as if it made no difference to him. He had already begun detaching himself from viewing them as human, where the barbarian still seemed to be struggling.

As they approached the gate, Jvard stopped short and urged Walt forward.

"Lead the way, wizard," he invited.

Jvard wasn't fully supportive of the idea, but he understood Walt's reasoning. Because it would be unwise to go beyond the gate and wrecklessly swing his weapon about, he'd let Walt handle whatever he had in mind.

"This way then," Walt said, leading them up the stairway to the top of the wall.

Watching as Walt slipped into a meditative state, Jvard's skin itched just standing near him. He was extremely uncomfortable being so close to someone using magic, but forced himself to stand and watch. Walt opened his eyes directing his hands outward, lines of fire extending out of his fingers. They caught a few of the plagued, causing them to conflagrate immediately. Walt breathed out heavily, placing a hand on a knee as he observed his handiwork. Many emotions ran through Walt at the moment, mostly pity and sorrow mixed with a small amount of morbid hopefulness that he could bring their numbers down. After only a few seconds however, the only feeling shared by Jvard and Walt was horror as the fire failed to destroy them.

Flesh melted from their bones, creating a sickening stench as their bodies charred. Several more caught on fire and they went into a frenzy, issuing howls as they clashed into each other. When the flames settled down, they were left with features even more terrifying than before. Though they reacted, it was no more than disturbing a hornet's nest. In the end, no real damage was done to the Stricken by Walt's attempt.

"That was the worst idea I've seen come out of you yet, wizard!" Jvard yelled between coughs, his eyes stinging from the smell.

His nerves were on end from the harrowing display. There was one particular moment when the wind picked up that Jvard thought the entire field would be set ablaze, or the fire would spread into the town.

Jvard had enough, it was time to go.

"Are you ready to leave wizard?" Jvard shouted, springing into motion.

Blinking in confusion, Walt was not quite sure what the barbarian was up to.

"Get the wagon to the front gate and hitch up the horses, old man!" he directed, offering no explanation.

Walt huffed, choking on his words. Before he could form a sentence Jvard was already moving fast down the street, leaving him to do as the barbarian commanded. Well, now was as good a time as any to be leaving. He hustled after Jvard, making his way towards the stable to ready the wagon and horses.

Jvard veered off towards the butcher's shop, two streets over from Walt at the stable. Much of the meat was now beginning to spoil. He certainly wouldn't eat it, but it should do for what he had in mind. There were many animals already quartered as well as an entire deer that had been left hanging to bleed out. Jvard twined up all twenty quarters of meat available, giving about four feet of line on each one. Throwing the deer over his shoulder he ran down the road, dragging all of the chunks of meat behind him.

"What are you doing..." Walt began as he saw Jvard finally speeding past him, with a deer across his back and dragging enough meat behind him to feed an army.

"I'll lure them away, once it's clear open the gate and start heading out. "I'll catch up," Jvard instructed.

"But..." Walt stammered.

"Do you want out of here or not wizard, just see it done!" Jvard shouted.

Not waiting for a response, Jvard darted up through the gatehouse onto the top of the wall. The wizard was fully caught up in Jvard's whirlwind of action and there was no choice but to agree. Jvard dangled the quarters of meat down along the wall, slightly out of reach of the plague-bearers. It did not take long to draw their focus as they ravenously reached for the hunks of meat. They grew frustrated, completely fixated on the meal that was just beyond their grasp. Jvard dangled it up and down, teasingly, while he yelled for their attention.

He ran along the length of the wall, leading them away from the main gate back towards the northeast entrance where the other group of the Stricken roamed. Soon his bait had their attention as well. With each and every one of the creatures fixated upon him, he hoisted the meat back up and dropped the deer from his shoulders. Spinning in a few circles, he let the strings fly out to their full length. Faster and faster the hunks of meat whirled around as he gained momentum, until he finally angled them upwards and let them fly. They sailed out nearly thirty feet, causing a feeding frenzy among the horde. Quickly, he rolled the deer off of the wall to buy him additional time.

Though it was a lot of meat, Jvard would not have much time. A mob that size would quickly devour what he had thrown out to them. He sprinted back across town, running as fast as he possibly could. The other entrance was temporarily clear, Walt having opened the gate as Jvard asked. As he approached, he saw that the wizard had a horse hitched to the wagon ready to go and another on a tether. Jvard, not familiar with riding, jumped into the back of the wagon and urged Walt to move forward with all speed. They left the town of Big Bear heading south. Walt looked back with bitterness, his once promising venture crashing to an end. All of the people he had met and befriended, now gone. Jvard instead looked northward, filled with sadness at leaving the only land he had ever called home.

Escaping

Somehow he was still alive. He didn't know how but he had survived, though he was no longer sure if that was preferable. He watched nearly the entire population of his town die in the span of two days, only to come back as horrific remnants of who they once were. Those who didn't fall ill suffered a worse fate, being viciously torn apart and devoured by those who had reanimated. He alone survived, by mere chance Daro Ildaradi found himself in the right place at the edge of the encampment to allow him to flee, while the others were trapped amidst the confusion. Having no other alternative, he ran northward through Darcláw's Gap into the untamed lands.

That was nearly seven days ago. Since then he had been through a brutal snowstorm, many days spent running, and moving instinctually on very little sleep. He thought he had found salvation upon seeing a group of people on cliffs in the distance, but as it turned out he was mistaken. It was a tribe of barbarians more likely to kill him than extend a hand to help, but he had no other option than to seek their aid. He hastened forward, waving his arms and calling out for help as loud as he could. It was better to put himself at their mercy than continue on as he had been.

Moving closer, their peculiar behavior brought him pause. The figures no longer appeared as dots on the hillside, he could clearly see their forms as they walked aimlessly about the topmost level of the cliffs. As one, the gathering of people turned towards him.

"Dear spirits," Daro whispered.

He stopped running forward, falling silent. Tense moments passed as the group in the distance stared in his direction, and he looked back, hoping they somehow didn't see him. The stalemate was broken as the mob began their rambling, growling descent down the terraced levels of the cliff. So it wasn't only his people who were affected. This had happened elsewhere, whatever it was. Daro couldn't turn back as he still had many of the former members of Big Bear at his heels, and he could no longer go forward with the group in front of him. With the south blocked by impassible mountains, his only choice was to continue northward.

As he had so many times in the past, Daro prayed to his God for guidance. He was not familiar with this territory, and he did not know how much longer he could continue on. The only thing he could do was go in the one direction available to him and hold fast to his faith. Running beyond the ledges he was presented with a sudden drop-off leading down into a valley. It was so steep that in normal circumstances he wouldn't dare try to descend it, however these were not normal circumstances. With only a brief hesitation he took his first few steps. He struggled to keep his legs under him, involuntarily gaining speed as he stumbled down the hill.

No longer able to maintain his balance, he fell, rolling down the precipice. Rolling over rocks and various brush earned him several bruised ribs and an injured shoulder. When he finally came to a stop, he was within a copse of pine trees, the first trees he had seen since entering the barbarian territories of the Blue Fold Mountains. He gritted through the pain of his injuries, looking back up the hill to see a host of the undead vermin falling over each other down the dangerous slope. With no time to rest he continued onward, the sound of rushing water offering him encouragement and a direction to follow.

The noise of water falling grew ever louder, drowning out all other sounds as he followed a stream back to its source. Water crashed down thirty feet over a ledge, splashing his face with cold droplets. Fearing he was trapped, relief washed over him when he spotted a pathway not too far away that led upwards. He followed it all day and all night, and again the next day without rest.

His journey was beginning to take a toll on him. Not only physically, but mentally he was changing, adapting. His body became ragged, his features once full of cheer were now haggard and haunted. Yet he was not ready to lie down and die. A fanatical zeal had overtaken him, allowing him to push beyond his limits. Being alone for several days, pursued by walking abominations drove him closer to God, making him stronger.

Walt had inspected all of these people when they fell ill, why didn't he warn them? It was obvious magic was involved somehow, the wizard must not have been forthcoming with his discoveries, maybe even having a hand in this. After all, how well did he really know Walt? The entrepreneur was always distant and a bit aloof. This could have been some experiment gone awry. Faith in God was all man needed, Daro reasoned. Regardless if Walt played a part in this or not, people dabbling in things they didn't understand always led to disaster. Magic was certainly to blame here. He cursed the wizard's name as he ran, and all those who brought this atrocity upon him. Once he got off of this mountain, he would hold them accountable.

Eventually he came to a juncture. Heading due east would have brought him around the back way towards the Ridges, while to the southeast flowed the mighty Tinindraüg River. The river, flowing miles upon miles all the way to the southlands, could serve as a great marker for him. Maybe it would even deter his pursuers from following, hide his scent if that's how they managed to track him so well. He decided the river was his best and only option. It would deliver him from this wasteland and back to civilization.

***

Two days had passed since they had heard any sounds from outside. The ever present growls and scraping at the door subsided, and finally disappeared altogether. Was it a ruse to lure them outside, did they possess that kind of intelligence?

"I say we risk a look," Dagard suggested.

After several days trapped inside of the meeting hall, many agreed, eager to leave the confining space and see the sunlight again. There were however a few rumblings of disagreement to be heard.

"You're thinkin' it's just fine to open up that door and let those monsters pour in? Have some sense Dagard," Garl admonished, "Igdahven, is there any way you can tell if they're out there?"

"If they were people, yes," he replied, "but these things have no traces of life to speak of. In that sense, they might as well be invisible to me."

Garl frowned deeply, disliking the choices he had been given of late. The clans were his responsibility now, and he watched them dwindle from nearly one thousand strong to the roughly two hundred who stood before him. Here he was, faced with yet another decision to make that could cost lives. The majority of his people were beginning to feel cloistered in the dark hall for so long, and were more than willing to see if leaving was an option. Garl begrudgingly made up his mind.

"Women and children move to the back," Garl instructed, his deep voice resonating in the hall, "every person able to swing a weapon form a ring two men deep between them and the door. I'll open it and see what's goin' on. If anything goes wrong get that door shut, and Igdahven you're in charge."

If anyone was going to be harmed by a decision he made, it would be Garl himself and not another one of his people. When everyone was in place, with him at the door and the warriors fifteen paces behind him, and the rest of the tribe against the far wall, he opened the door. Sunlight flooded the room, stinging their eyes that had become accustomed to the dim torchlight. Garl instinctively put his hands up, momentarily defenseless until he could adjust to the bright light. He boldly stepped forward through the doorway out into the open, giving his people the opportunity to safely close the door if it came to that.

He scrambled to the side, looking left and right with the anticipation of an imminent attack. Fortunately, the attack never came. As his eyes began to acclimate, all that he saw was an empty ledge of bright snow. None of the Risen were in sight, and looking down over the Ridges out across the field showed no sign of them. He walked back in front of the doorway to issue the all clear to his men, but beckoned only Igdahven and Dagard to follow him while the rest remained behind.

Garl was perplexed, why had they suddenly left? Accepting the favorable turn of events, he put that question aside momentarily. By his count, they were long overdue some good fortune. With Dagard and Igdahven following, they carefully ventured off the Ridges far out onto the field below. The snow tamped down from hundreds of footprints left a confusing trail to recreate, but eventually Igdahven discerned their assailants moved north, around the cliffs. They followed the trail for a time, until they reached the hillside overlooking the pines.

"However they got down there, they'll have a hard time getting back up," Dagard commented.

"Looks like we can rest easy for a time," Garl agreed, "they'd have to go all the way aroun' northeast and back south to us, or go west through the mountain passes back over to the Ridges. Either way we need to take advantage of their absence. Let's return home."

Retracing their steps through the open plain towards the Ridges, Garl paused, realizing Igdahven was no longer by his side. Instead, he was forty paces back, looking southwards thoughtfully. Though the weather was turning favorable, deep snow still covered the ground. A large storm must have passed through while they were sealed in the *Ingdaärðendvhel* at the top of Boldstone. Before Garl could ask what he was doing, Igdahven began muttering to himself and moving about agitatedly. Garl watched as the spirit-seeker walked several steps in one direction, then another and another.

"Over here!" Igdahven finally called out.

Garl rushed over, with Dagard directly behind him. Two bodies lay in the snow, each with gaping head wounds and many vicious blows to the body. Igdahven wasn't sure exactly who they were, but the faces were familiar and recognizable as belonging to one of the clans from the Ridges. Dagard gasped while Garl issued a stream of profanity as they saw what had attracted the spirit-seeker's attention. Exploring further, they found it was not only the two, but a large scattering of corpses all with split skulls and various missing limbs.

As they dug through the snow, the bodies they discovered created a meandering trail to the south. The longer they followed the trail, the further apart the bodies were found. At first the victims were severely mangled, hacked and slashed almost unrecognizably. As they continued along though, the three reasoned out the killer became more efficient, finishing them off with a solitary gash to the head. The three barbarians were fairly close to each other, each combing through their own sections of snow as they tried to puzzle out what happened. It was Garl who found the final corpse, with Jvard's resplendent double-headed axe buried deep in its skull.

Later that night, the council was largely split on how the tribe should proceed now that they were no longer trapped. Igdahven stayed relatively silent throughout the discussions, he preferred to see where everyone else stood on the matter. Garl and several men argued they should go after Jvard. Dagard disagreed, commenting it was foolhardy to divide the remaining survivors in order to chase after someone who may already be dead, which Garl refused to believe. Yet others argued they were no longer safe on the Ridges, and should relocate.

The noise in the hall rose as the three different groups shouted their opinions, their voices echoing across the walls creating a dissonant cacophony. Igdahven shook his head, it never ceased to amaze him how people thought they were better arguing their point by trying to talk louder than the next person. In contrast to the slow crescendo of bickering that developed into a sustained din, it ended in a crashing silence when Garl issued a guttural growl accompanied by driving Jvard's axe through a table, fully breaking it in two.

"Enough!" Garl shouted, demanding the attention of the tribe, "I'll be going after Jvard, it's the least he'd 'ave done for any one of us."

He looked around for a moment before making a noise of disgust and stalking off. Igdahven quickly followed after him, and reminded himself of Garl's conviction. Garl would always do what was right by his heart; thinking only got in the way of making the important decisions. Igdahven had to make sure the tribe didn't get caught up in the whirlwind that was Garl and be led down a well-intentioned but inevitably self-destructive path.

"Garl, slow down!" Igdahven called out as he passed through the doorway outside.

"So you're coming with me then? Good, your unique tracking skills will come in handy, all this blasted snowfall…" Garl answered, only half-paying mind to Igdahven while stuffing gear into a pack.

"Stop, Garl," Igdahven said imploringly. He continued past the towering man's glare, "Everyone needs you here, do you really want to go off and leave Dagard overseeing the tribe?"

Garl paused for a moment. He wouldn't want to entrust the tribe to Dagard for long, the man was too callous for his liking.

"Give me a day or two. Now that we know Jvard might be alive and a direction to search, perhaps I can find answers for you tonight," Igdahven pressed.

Garl stopped what he was doing, thinking it over.

"Bah, I'd prefer to sleep under my own roof tonight, spirit-seeker. I pray you find me answers, and soon," Garl said, leaving the threat hanging in the air, "come see me once you have information."

With much work to do, Igdahven walked to the empty *Duchàlg* encampment on the third ridge, retiring to his dwelling on the Shadow Cliff. If Jvard was still alive, Igdahven had the best hopes of locating him. Anyone else would have to search for days through the snow, but in the realm of spirits they called the *Chàlgraäden* he could cover a much more expansive area. Travelling alone tonight, he could skip the elaborate rituals; as one of the *Duchàlg*, he had the ability to enter into the *Chàlgraäden* merely through meditation.

Darkness fully enveloped the Ridges while Igdahven sat cross-legged in front of a fire in the middle of his hut. Smoke drifted upwards, dancing and swirling in patterns until it exited the room through a small funneled opening in the ceiling. Igdahven blinked in a rhythm while watching the swirling smoke, with each successive blink drifting further and further away from the fire to a place somewhere internal. At last he felt his spirit disconnect from his body. It was a familiar sensation for him, not altogether comfortable though not necessarily painful either.

The spirit-seeker opened his eyes to a muted world. There was a general lack of sound, a falling weapon would land with a dull thud rather than a metallic ring, and the footfalls of a nearby person were almost silent. Color was nearly absent, showing objects and living beings as grey shadows of their actual forms. Physical barriers or distances meant little as well; with a thought or single leap Igdahven could travel a great distance, covering miles in seconds.

In no time at all Igdahven reached the area where Jvard lost his weapon. That in itself did not bode well; the axe had belonged to his late father and Jvard would not have parted with it lightly. There were no additional signs here that Igdahven had not seen earlier in the day, based on the alignment of bodies it was easy to determine they were headed southward. He didn't have much of a trail to go on, but it made sense he should continue in that direction. The only route to travel in these parts was through Darcláw's Gap, and further down to Jun'tirh Outpost. The spirit-seeker had never attempted a journey that far from his physical body, the distance would surely test his ability.

He had his doubts, but there was nothing for it but to try. Garl needed information, and if he didn't get it this way, he would end up placing himself and potentially others at risk to find it. The seasoned barbarian cared for Jvard like he was his own son. All that Garl needed was the slightest inkling that their young leader was alive and he would set off after him, throwing all other worries aside. Then again, Garl would likely try to do the same for any member of the tribe. Where Dagard's motives were carried out through skillful oration, Garl's actions derived from somewhere guttural and primal, leaving others with no choice but to be swept up in his wake. The difference between the two men was that Dagard manipulated emotion, while Garl created it.

Continuing towards the Gap, Igdahven felt the connection to his body weaken. He had been moving for a fair amount of time; even considering the great distances he could cover with each leap it was still very far to his destination. Focused on the task at hand, he hardly registered the signs of life that dotted the landscape. Telltale wisps of light and dark gave away the deer, rabbits, and other wildlife scattered throughout the area. What greatly disturbed Igdahven was the complete lack of energy that had surrounded the reanimated tribesmen. There was no sign of life in them, he was convinced they were truly the dead risen. As to how or why it happened, he was stymied.

Finally passing through Darcláw's Gap, he began to have doubts that he would find anything useful. Worse, it was a struggle every second to remain in this realm while he was so far from his physical form. Immense pressure built in his head, resulting from the effort needed to not fade from the *Chàlgraäden* and return to his body. Having come so far, he pushed himself a little farther to inspect the outpost town. Proceeding to Jun'tirh Outpost seemed the most logical choice. Had Jvard come this way it was the only place to go, short of traveling at least twice the distance again to the next settlement south.

Soon the strongly fortified walls that encapsulated the small town came into view. Immediately he knew something was wrong, scores of people were outside of the town yet none had the signatures of energy that defined something as living. He looked up, wanting to gather his thoughts for a moment. The *Duchstraüm* continued to flow in the wrong direction, adding to his discomfort. The large dark rivers in the sky all ran to the southeast, while the light streams were moving in all directions as expected. It had to mean something, at no other time the *Duchàlg* were aware of did the *Duchstraüm* change so drastically and rapidly.

He moved in closer, walking among the field of the Risen roaming outside of the town walls. He was dismayed to see this group belonged to his tribe, they must have split off south while the others returned to the Ridges. The walls didn't appear breached, why were there no people in the town? Igdahven leaped ahead among the buildings, hoping to find some answers.

He was pleased to find that he was incorrect; there were a few signs of life nearby. Not far away he located a pair of beasts in a short, squat dwelling filled with hay, and they looked well cared for. Wisps of dark and light swirled about them, showing they were real, living creatures. He walked back outside to take a good look around. The streets were all empty, most covered with untouched snow, though a small area was cleared in front of a large building and near an alleyway to the next street over.

An odd sensation crept over Igdahven, along with a sudden rush of air coming from behind. Turning, he tried his best to approximate its source. A house with a balcony was directly in his line of sight; looking to be as good a place as any, he blinked himself up to it. Familiar feelings rose within him, drawing a wide smile and cackling laugh from the spirit-seeker. His ability to track individuals relied partly on recognizing the person's unique imprints they leave in the *Chàlgraäden*. Like a scent that stirs up a forgotten memory, the imprint nearby triggered recognition in Igdahven. It was the spiritual footprint of Jvard, he was alive and very close by.

Elation coursed through Igdahven as he hurried towards the doorway. He could barely maintain his presence in this realm so far from his body back on the Ridges, but he would hold on. His excitement soon turned to caution as he passed through a white mist to enter a room adjoining the balcony. Laying in a bed was an old bearded man; though his body was resting he was far from inactive.

Oddly there was no spirit inside of the man, but it was not the same lack of life similar to those who had been afflicted. This person was very much alive, his soul was just not currently present.

Dark and light wisps enveloped the old man, cocooning his still form. The white mist from the balcony originated from him, and Igdahven noticed it extended out over the fields outside of town. Guessing him as the source of the disturbance he felt earlier, Igdahven cautiously backed away from the man.

He could sense Jvard nearby, but the vast amount of energy in front of him obscured his exact whereabouts. Growing weaker with every passing second, he decided it better to find out who this individual before him was. Igdahven walked back out to the edge of the balcony, following the trail of mist leading into the field of undead. In the span of a thought he was back down among them, hurriedly seeking the anomaly.

He had never met someone from outside of the *Duchàlg* who could visit this realm unaided, if he was not mistaken that person was somewhere nearby. The spirit-seeker had a sinking feeling Jvard was somehow mixed in with this old man, and that he was of the tainted blood. The *Duchàlg*'s abilities were limited to walking the *Chàlgraäden*, seeking answers and guidance. One who could directly touch the elements of nature were dangerous in the extreme, thankfully none had been born among the barbarians in many generations.

The mist he had followed from the sleeping form began to dissipate. Disappointed, he turned back towards the town hoping to at least locate Jvard before he was forced back to his body at the Ridges. Igdahven jumped nearly a foot in the air when he saw the old man had been right behind him, his wolf-skin cap sliding askew. Immediately he darted away, heading towards the mountains. The old man pursued him, matching each giant leap into the distance. Pressure in Igdahven's head mounted to an unbearable point. He felt silly as it struck him that there was no need to continue fleeing; allowing his concentration to falter, Igdahven blinked out of the *Chàlgraäden*, returning to his body on the Shadow Cliff.

Longpost Road

"Ya'll be careful now, there's queer things goin' on around here these days. Watch out for those pale-men," the old farmer said as his guests returned to the road.

A few days had passed since Myrna decided to take Devin north to her hometown of Creekview's Crossing. She didn't feel safe among the small, secluded farms scattered along the Golden Terraces. By her estimate, a city would have the necessary resources to stay secure.

During the day they travelled along Longpost Road, and most nights camped not very far from it. Their road meandered high on top of the hillside, often further away from the farmlands that stretched out to either side. The vantage point allowed them to see far out below, and it looked as though the disease, or whatever it was, was not isolated to Shady Vale. Occasionally in the distance, they saw a solitary man or group of men wandering, their movements too awkward and intentions unclear. In these parts, anyone outside who was not retrieving wayward cattle or working the field looked suspicious.

Word had spread among the locals that danger was present in the form of mindless, roaming creatures in the guise of their neighbors. It took some time for the scattered whispers to become more than rumors, and a few days more for the rumors to gain acceptance as fact among those who lived in the expansive Terraces. But in the end, they all saw the truth of it. Many good families were lost to the creatures, and more lost still until it was realized a bite was fatal and transformed loved ones into something else. The farmers had taken to calling them Pale-men due to their complexion.

Their losses seemed great; however, if the locals knew the extent of the destruction elsewhere in the world they would have seen they handled themselves rather well. Most of the farmers had never travelled further than a few miles from their homes, and took for granted the way they lived. They spent their lives enduring droughts, working from sunup to sundown without complaint and assumed the rest of the world did the same. Many of the farmers had more mettle than any soldier and more smarts than a scholar, but most importantly came to each other's aid without question or hesitation. Others might have called them brave, but they just assumed it the neighborly thing to do.

The young men quickly formed a watch and militia to protect the farmsteads, while the older men organized the patrols. At nightfall many families would converge to one farmhouse to sleep in groups under a protective watch. Myrna and Devin found themselves taking shelter at one such farm as they approached the border of the Terraces. A part of Myrna wanted to believe that she and Devin could be safe remaining here, but deep down she knew that to be a sentiment more likely to get the two of them killed. Though out of danger for the moment, the farmer's nerves were frayed and their sense of security fleeting.

Everyone was on edge, false alarms interrupting Devin's sleep more than once during the night. As he lay there wide awake well before dawn, he couldn't help his curiosity at the sound of the watchmen talking. He looked over to Myrna, fast asleep, before slowly slipping out of his bedroll as quietly as he could manage. Once up, he took another look at Myrna, who shifted slightly before settling back onto her side. Now that he was out of bed, he felt a little foolish. Those soldiers wouldn't want him nosing in their business, whatever it was. But they didn't seem to take notice of him, so he stayed for a while and listened to their conversation.

"I'll say it again, one of those pale-men gets a hold on you and you're done for," Devin overheard one of the guards, a burly man in his middle years saying.

Another man, tall and lean answered him back, "I don't know, I think it's just people being scared. You know how stories'll spread when people are all riled up."

"You're bein' dense man, I saw it with my own eyes. That group of pale-men overran the Daniel's farm five days ago, killed the whole family. The father though, he didn't die right away. He only had a small bite on his forearm, but the next day he damn turned into one o' the bastards."

"Sounds awfully farfetched to me," another man at the table said.

"Believe what you want, but I'm tellin' yah don't even let the damn things touch you. Why I..." The burly man trailed off as he finally noticed Devin, who had been intently listening to the conversation.

"Get back to bed, youngin!" he shouted, "This ain't a story for children's ears now."

Nearly jumping out of his skin, Devin turned back towards his sleeping bag, only to bump into the sternest looking person he ever saw. He wanted to move around him but found his legs wouldn't cooperate.

"I was just..." he stammered.

Devin looked away under the scrutiny of the farmer, unable to hold eye contact with him.

"You're the boy traveling out with the lone woman," he stated.

Devin nodded, nervous of the stranger. He had an air of command about him that Devin was unaccustomed to; nothing would have made him happier at that moment than to just sink into the floor and disappear.

"Look up, boy. Always look someone in the eye when you're speaking with them," he said, firmly but without anger.

Devin risked a glance upward. He was surprised to find the man was older than he expected, with short greying hair that seemed incongruent to his otherwise vigorous appearance.

"Come, sit down. I wish to speak with you," he said as he ushered him to an empty table. Devin began to regret ever having left his bedroll as he looked back towards it longingly.

"I understand you and Myrna will be leaving in the morning, travelling north," he stated.

"I spoke with Myrna earlier in the evening," he added, seeing Devin furrow his brow at how a stranger might have known that.

"I don't agree with her choice to leave, but can't say with certainty that she'd be any safer here," he continued.

Devin gasped involuntarily as the lighting allowed him to notice the long scar running from the man's temple, down his cheek and under his chin.

Seeing the boy's reaction, the man smiled lightly and said, "There are many dangers out there, many here too these days, for that matter."

"How did you get the scar?" Devin asked, finally summoning up the courage to speak.

"I was a soldier," the man answered, "long ago, before I came here and settled down. So there is no one else travelling with you and Myrna?"

"It's just us," Devin answered quietly.

He chuckled slightly, without humor, saying something too low for Devin to make out.

"I knew she was being evasive when I spoke to her earlier," he said, trying to keep his tone level though a touch of harshness seeped into it, "a boy and a woman, alone on the road in these times. And how do you plan to keep yourselves safe? You're too small to use a sword properly."

"I have a crossbow," Devin shot back defensively, "I haven't used it yet though."

At the next table, the other watchmen laughed at the response, causing Devin to hang his head a bit lower.

They cut short at a glare from the former soldier.

"That's a good weapon for you to have," he said to Devin, and spoke up slightly louder and directed towards the other group, "a bolt can kill anyone, any size no matter who is pulling the trigger."

"Go get it, and meet me in the barn," he ordered, trying not to sound exasperated, "maybe I can show you a thing or two that might help save your neck one day."

Devin spent the remainder of the night in the back of a dimly lit barn, receiving shooting lessons from the stranger who seemed quite knowledgeable.

"Where do you keep the weapon?" the soldier asked Devin.

"In my pack, folded up in my bedroll," he answered.

"And think for a minute why that's a bad place for it," he bade the boy.

"It could get damaged," he answered after a moment.

The man shook his head, asking him to guess again.

Several more moments passed, "It'll take too long to get if I need it?" he asked more than answered.

The man held up his finger, "That a boy," he said.

"From now on you'll always carry it in this," he told Devin as he got up to retrieve a tangle of leather straps and buckles from a pile of equipment.

"Take it, I have more gear than we could ever use here," he added at Devin's hesitation.

He handed it to Devin, who looked as though he had no idea what to do with it.

"It goes around your leg, put that strap around through the slot. The pouch here'll fit ten or so bolts in it, always keep it full so your ammo is at hand," he instructed as he proceeded to show the boy how to properly wear it, "now it's always only a split second from your reach. A split second can be the difference between life and death, remember that boy. You can keep it hidden under your cloak wearing it like this."

He had Devin remove the holster and put it back on a dozen times, until he was able to do so without putting thought into it. Then he had the boy holster the weapon and draw it.

"And again," the man instructed, over and over.

Devin holstered and drew the crossbow no less than a hundred times.

"Can I shoot it yet?" Devin asked, growing tired of the exercise.

"I was going to move you along to that shortly, but do it twenty more times because you asked," the man said.

Devin sighed and did as he was told, while the stranger moved towards the back of the room and set up a dozen cans against the wall.

"Okay, enough. Wait until I'm back next to you," he said after lining up the cans.

He then showed Devin how to load the weapon, and the various pieces of the device.

"Line up your target looking down the sight, and keep your back elbow up. Good, just like that," he commented when Devin's form looked appropriate.

Managing to hit a few of the cans they set up as targets, Devin was quite pleased with himself. His instructor offered him little praise though, instead prompting him to reload faster and keep his hips aligned with his shots rather than twisting his torso whenever possible. The initial excitement Devin felt soon faded as he began to grow tired and frustrated at the task. His arms and shoulders began to ache from levering the string back into place on each reload.

More concentration was demanded of him than Devin was accustomed to, but the man did not relent at his complaints. Another hour passed, and then another as Devin mechanically reloaded, aimed, and shot at the tin cans. Having woken up in the middle of the night was starting to take its toll on him, he was nearing his breaking point when the man finally allowed him to stop.

"If you come back through here and you need help, ask for Harrington. I'll come if I can," the stranger offered, "a little more practice and you'd make a fine soldier, young man. Be off now, try and get some more sleep before your leaving."

Devin thanked him, even if it was a bit forced. Now he almost regretted having gotten up at all in the middle of the night. He only wanted to see what the grown-ups were doing, not get dragged through a night of exercise. In a few short hours he would need to be travelling and he felt so tired. On the other hand, it was the first time someone taught him how to do something and it left him with a small feeling of pride he hadn't yet experienced in his short life. As he left the barn, he walked a little taller than usual. Returning to his sleeping bag, Myrna was still soundly resting a few feet away. It seemed no sooner than his head hitting the pillow that daylight had fully broken and it was time to be off.

Rubbing his eyes, he awoke to overhear a watchman talking to Myrna by the doorway. His entire right side from his chest and shoulder down through his forearm was sore from all of the reloading, as well as the muscles on the left side of his abdomen and most of his back. He sincerely hoped he wouldn't have to use the crossbow at all today. Quickly he strapped on his holster, placing the weapon in it and tucking it away under his cloak. It made him feel more grown up, maybe he didn't regret the impromptu lesson he received the previous night after all.

"Sure you won't stay..." Devin heard the watchman saying as Myrna was shaking her head.

"C'mon Devin, have some breakfast and it's time to leave," she said, breaking off her conversation with the guard when she saw the boy approach.

As they were ready to leave, the man on duty stopped Devin, holding a small burlap sack out to him, "Wait, Harrington told us to give you this. And to remember to always keep your holster filled, and retrieve the bolts whenever you can. They'll run out faster than you think."

Inside the sack was a quiver with nearly fifty steel-tipped bolts. Myrna made a tsk noise as if she disapproved, but said nothing. Devin mumbled a thank you, a bit embarrassed from being the focus of attention. They left the house together, bidding the farmer farewell and expressing their gratitude for his hospitality. The sun was already climbing well into the sky as they began the next part of their journey.

Myrna wanted to believe she could stay in this area, and that it was well protected. Unfortunately, she did not think that was the case. The large open spaces left her feeling small, vulnerable and exposed. A city would have better organization and resources by her reckoning. She also no longer thought that the Pale-men were only a local problem, and didn't hold out hope that if she went far away their worries would be solved. Whatever happened in Shady Vale and the Golden Terraces was probably occurring elsewhere.

"A city will have walls, and experienced guards. Maybe even the royal army has gotten involved at this point," Myrna said to Devin, not for the first time.

He nodded as they left the Golden Terraces behind them, placing his trust in Myrna. Devin was all too eager to be away from Shady Vale. As a result of Myrna's chiding, he had stopped blaming himself aloud for turning everyone into Greymen. Unfortunately, it didn't stop him from thinking it. What if it was like this everywhere, how could he go on knowing he caused it? Reaching into his pocket, he quietly pulled out a pouch with a drawstring that was tied to his belt.

He walked for a bit holding the pouch with his shiny stone inside, gaining some comfort from it. The sparkling, clear gem had been the only possession he ever had, and he kept it very secret. His mother - his real mother, not the woman who watched over him in Shady Vale, had given it to him before he had to leave. At least, he thought she had. He had been very young at the time and couldn't quite remember. There were a few other rocks in the pouch that he had found and fancied, but none gave him the sense of security of his special stone.

"Devin, why don't you walk the horse for a while," Myrna asked.

Quickly placing the pouch into his pocket, he walked ahead to take the reins from Myrna's hand. They had been taking turns the last few days riding, as well as walking along with the animal to give it a rest and stretch their own legs. They didn't know the horse's rightful name, so they had taken to calling her Honey for her solid light brown color and sweet disposition. They had to be careful on some parts of the road, they were rather high up and at times their passage became narrow with no safety fencing on either side.

"Are you sure we're going the right way?" Devin complained as they marched across the hillside, at times pushing overhanging branches out of their face.

"Yes, very sure," Myrna sighed, "as sure as I was the last three times you asked."

"I thought you said this was supposed to be a main road…" Devin quit his griping in mid-sentence, after walking through a spider's web, the sticky strands passing over his face and chest causing him to groan and spit.

Myrna couldn't stifle her laughter, *that ought to stop him complaining for an hour or so*, she thought.

"Like I've told you, this road could take you all the way north to the Laskouth Plains, or south along the Sterling River to Dalesford. It's not very well traveled here though. It'll open up in a few days when we get further along."

Devin didn't answer, frowning as he tried to wipe the webbing from his mouth.

By dusk they fully exited the lower-lying region of the Terraces. Stone walls ran for miles, most were markers for properties that had been long abandoned and currently belonged to no one. The landscape was dominated by the green of high grass that had overtaken the unworked fields. Small cliffs arising from the hilly terrain added touches of grey to the palette. Occasionally a flock of sheep could be seen grazing in the distance, but there were no signs of the shepherd.

Myrna made a few attempts at small talk with Devin. She hadn't felt like they bonded much given the amount of time they had spent together. When not complaining, the boy gave mostly one or two word answers, making conversation difficult. Eventually she gave up altogether at trying to force it; he would speak more when he was ready.

"We should stop here for today, Devin. It'd be better to clear out a spot and set up while we still have some light," Myrna suggested.

Devin wholeheartedly agreed, glad that he would soon be off his feet. His legs ached more each day, and his soreness from the previous night only added to his discomfort. As the sun began to set they had flattened out an area of grass and laid out their bedrolls. Myrna drove a sharp stake into the ground, and tied Honey off to it so she wouldn't roam too far.

"We should be coming up through some villages soon, Byrn and Midao most notably," Myrna said with as much enthusiasm as she could muster.

"What if they're like what happened at home?" Devin asked.

"We can't think that, have some hope that things are okay somewhere," she responded with forced cheer, though she had doubts herself.

Devin abruptly got up and moved over to his bedroll, "I'm gonna go sleep," he said as he lay down and turned away, leaving her somewhat surprised and alone with her thoughts.

Lying for a time with his back turned to Myrna, he pretended to sleep. After a while he heard her settle into her bedroll, and the rhythmic breathing of her drifting off soon followed. Maybe they should have just stayed back at the last farm, rather than chancing it out here on their own. He had little hope that they left the Greymen behind them in Shady Vale and the Golden Terraces. Somehow when he wished everyone dead, it came true. The only conclusion he could reach was that he was a bad person. Worse, he couldn't even talk to Myrna about it because she yelled at him every time he brought it up. He made all those people into monsters, and they had killed innocent people. Ultimately, it was all his fault. Why should he deserve to live when he was responsible for so many people dying?

Feeling worse than any time he could remember, he found it difficult to fall asleep. As he had so many times before he pulled out his secret stone, looking for comfort.

Odd, he thought.

It was warm to the touch, almost as if it had been sitting in a pot of hot water. Usually it was cool, or at least no warmer than his hands if he had been holding it a while. Though it caused Devin some concern he gave little thought to it. He found holding the stone calming, allowing him to fall into a fitful sleep of disturbing dreams.

Opening his eyes, Devin arose to a dimly lit room with statues of men lining the walls. The stone was almost flesh-like, every detail down to individual wrinkles carved in full detail. *No, not statues*, he realized as he moved in close to inspect one; these were actually people, standing perfectly still as if stuck in a moment of time. He stepped back, towards the center of the room and continued staring at the unmoving beings.

A thumping sound coming from the opposite end of the chamber spun him around. The thought occurred to him that he was dreaming, but despite how much he wanted to, he could not wake up. It didn't feel safe here. *Maybe if I close my eyes, it would all disappear*, he thought. After a few seconds he risked a small peek, barely squinting with one eye. To his dismay, everything remained as it was. The thumping grew louder, more intense, demanding he no longer ignore it. He crossed the room, the people remaining still, but following him with their eyes. At the end of the room was a large red sarcophagus built onto the wall, a deep blood red that nearly gave the impression it was freshly painted and still wet. Devin reached out to touch it, surprised to find it was dry. As soon as his hand neared it, another thump emanated from within, startling him.

The knocking intensified, nearly throwing the lid off. Whatever was inside wanted to come out, and Devin couldn't allow that to happen. Panicking, he ran around the room trying to get help from the people, but they had transformed. They were no longer humans, but Greymen lining up against the walls. Devin stumbled backwards, nearly falling across the room into another line of the creatures. They continued to remain motionless, only watching him. He regained his composure when he realized they didn't seem too interested in him, and returned to the sarcophagus that now looked like it might break apart from the vicious pounding. Desperately he pushed back against the lid that was being forced open from the inside. He was not strong enough, it was slowly forcing its way out.

No, he thought, *it can't get out*. But he couldn't keep it contained, he was powerless to stop the inevitable.

Devin woke with a start, drawing a deep breath. Thankfully the dream he thought would never end was over. If it was possible he felt more tired than he had before he went to sleep, as if he had actually been pushing against the heavy stone lid all night. Myrna sat directly across from him, watching with concern. As he began to stir she moved closer to him, putting her hand up against his forehead. He tried to push away, but she insisted and fixed him with a look.

"Well, you don't feel warm," she said.

"I'm fine," he lied.

Truthfully he did not feel too well, and was in a cold sweat from the nightmare. He realized he was still holding the gemstone in his hand that he had fallen asleep with. His palm ached from how tightly he had been gripping it throughout the night. He needed to distract Myrna so he could put his secret stone away.

"I could use some breakfast," he said.

"All right," Myrna sighed, turning around to prepare some food, "but I'm worried about you. You've been having quite a few bad dreams the past week. Probably not unexpected though considering all you've been through."

She paused and turned back to him, "You know if you need to talk I'm here for you."

"I know," he answered, using the moment she turned away to quickly place the stone back into its pouch.

"We should be coming up on Byrn, maybe by the end of the day if we're lucky," Myrna said cheerfully as they ate breakfast, "hopefully all will be well, but we should be careful."

"Have you ever been there?" Devin asked, genuinely curious. He had moved to Shady Vale from far away, but he was so young the only place he ever knew was their isolated town in the woods.

"Yes, many years ago. It's a nice little village, much bigger than Shady Vale," she said with a touch of sadness, the thought occurring to her that their home was no more, "but it's still only a village."

Neither she nor the boy had proper time to grieve the loss of their town, she realized. That alone was probably causing Devin a fair amount of turmoil. *Poor boy*, she thought. *He's lost the only place he could call home, if he even ever felt at home there.*

"It'd be nice to stop there for a while if we could. I'm so tired of walking," Devin said through a yawn as he strapped on the holster for his crossbow.

At Myrna's insisting, they returned to the road and continued northward. Devin rode Honey for a time, his feet aching from their long days of travelling. The sun was beating down from the clear blue sky, making the day unseasonably warm for spring. They passed no other travelers on the road, the only sound the loud hum of insects buzzing among the high grass off to their sides. No longer a dirt trail, the road had opened up wide enough to be able to accommodate a single wagon.

By late afternoon, a soft rustling sound put Myrna and Devin on alert. They stopped to listen, but each time they did the noise also ceased.

"It's probably nothing, just a small animal," Myrna offered, "being alone on the road can start to play tricks on you, best not let our imaginations run wild."

Devin nodded, relaxing a small degree. It was easy to grow paranoid walking through the endless miles of countryside. This wasn't the first time an odd noise had startled them. Night time was the worst, not being able to see made them conjure images worse than reality could present. Often the sounds seemed as if they were coming from right next to their tent or bedrolls.

Unexpectedly, Honey reared up, nearly breaking away from Devin's grasp on the reins. He was lucky he decided to take a break from riding and walk for a time, if he had been on the horse he very likely would have been thrown.

Myrna frowned at Honey's behavior. It was unlike her to lose control, being such a docile creature. She and Devin both stiffened when the rustling returned directly in front of them. When a rabbit hopped into the road, pausing to look at them they both nearly laughed aloud.

"Well how about that. Here's our big scary monster that's been terrorizing us today," Myrna giggled.

With a grin Devin quietly tried to draw his crossbow. It had been many days since either of them had eaten any meat. The rabbit's ears twitched as it seemed to sense his motive. Devin thought it was going to dart away, any rabbits he had ever seen were incredibly skittish. He ever so slowly raised the crossbow, inching it from the holster. His lips were slightly parted, tongue pressing against them in concentration while he drew the weapon free.

Myrna screamed in terror when another creature crashed through the grass onto the road, the rabbit bounding away. Devin stumbled backwards, falling over as Honey broke free from his left hand and ran away. The crossbow dropped from his right hand and landed a few feet from him. One of the Grey had wandered onto the road, intently focused on tracking the rabbit. It paused almost as if it was surprised to see two people before it. Quickly forgetting about the rabbit, it showed far more interest in the larger meal. The Greyman lurched forward, a gleam in its eyes at its good fortune.

 Standing only a few feet from the thing that had once been a person, Myrna wasn't sure what she should do. After a slight hesitation, she attempted to run ahead, but had her foot knocked out from under her by the thing as it grabbed for her. Devin watched in horror as the Greyman managed to scurry forward and grab her ankle before she could get a safe distance away, causing her to fall forward to her hands and knees. Desperately she tried to get her feet back under her, but couldn't as it grabbed a hold of her foot again and began pulling her in. Realizing she wasn't going to break free, she rolled over onto her back and kicked the Greyman in the face with her free leg. The blow pushed it backwards but did no real harm, only gaining her a moment before it was on her again.

 Devin didn't even register that he was yelling Myrna's name, his composure unraveling at the sudden stress of the situation. After several valuable seconds wasted in panic he realized he should try and do something. He looked around for a rock, or anything he could use to hurt it. Spotting the crossbow on the ground, he felt extremely foolish it didn't immediately occur to him to retrieve it. For some reason he thought of Harrington watching him, disapproving. Finally working through his initial shock, he scrambled for the weapon.

 The creature was now upon her, its putrid breath in her face, the smell of decomposing skin causing her to gag. She struggled to keep its head away from her, driving her hand up under its chin to try and control its neck. With her other arm she grabbed its wrist preventing the Greyman from pinning her down. Unfortunately with both of her hands occupied it still had one arm free to hold her down by her coat. It was only a matter of time before the Greyman would break free of her tenuous grip.

 A small cloud of dust accompanied by a dull thud sounded off from the ground near her head, and then another. A third quickly followed, this time a solid thunk spattering gore onto the ground next to her. After two misses, the last shot Devin fired off entered through the back of the Greyman's shoulder and exited clean through its neck, taking a good chunk of its throat along with it.

The injury seemed little more than a nuisance to the creature though, paying it no more mind than a fly buzzing about a vulture as it tried to scavenge a bit of carrion. However, the impact of the shot caused it to lift its head and look back across the road towards Devin, giving Myrna an opportunity to reach a fist sized rock not far from her. She grabbed it, wasting no time slamming it into the distracted Greyman's head. Dazed, it rolled off of Myrna and fell onto its side. Devin watched with a transfixed sense of horror tinged with disgust as Myrna repeatedly bashed the creature's head until it was unrecognizable, her survival instincts overcoming her fear.

Just as abruptly as it had begun, the nightmare was over. Myrna collapsed to the ground sobbing while Devin's response was equally intense; though outwardly he showed little reaction, inside he struggled trying to resolve what he had witnessed and his role in the skirmish. Having never seen such a degree of violence, he didn't know how he should respond. Looking at Myrna now she didn't seem the same woman he had been travelling with, he would have never imagined her capable of doing what she just did.

As the minutes passed by a profound feeling of shame settled in, replacing his shock. Since they left Shady Vale, Devin had frequently daydreamed of playing the role of hero during their long hours on the road, envisioning scenarios where he fended off dozens of Greymen, protecting Myrna and the various farmers they came across. Having the truth of his weakness so bluntly laid out before him was a crushing blow. Had he been attacked instead of Myrna, the thing probably would have killed him. He was unable to handle one of the creatures when it wasn't even interested in him, if any more had been about, he and Myrna would likely be dead. He was no hero, just small, scared and alone.

Myrna's sobbing finally began to subside as she came to terms with the attack. She had never before killed anything, even accidentally stepping on an insect sometimes caused her regret. Of course, her life had never been threatened in such a way. The more she thought about it, the stronger she concluded that she didn't have a choice in her action. That fact provided little comfort, however, and she was still left with an ill feeling in the pit of her stomach. She looked over at Devin, who had a mortified expression on his face. The poor boy! She was certain this was the most terrifying thing he'd probably seen in his life. Sadly, she had a strong feeling it wouldn't be the end of their ordeals. Finally able to trust her legs beneath her, she stood up.

"Devin," she called over.

He stiffly walked over to Myrna, brushing his sleeve against his eyes. Standing before her he couldn't tell what she might be thinking or if she was upset with him. He stood there, feeling awkward and alone. Myrna embraced him tightly, pulling him in close for a long time.

"I'm sorry," he managed to say in a choked-up voice, and she told him everything was okay.

As they were about to leave Devin remembered what Harrington had told him, always retrieve his bolts.

"Hold on," he asked Myrna, before turning around and looking for his two missed shots.

Quickly finding them, he saw the third in front of the motionless Greyman. It was coated in blood and gore, having passed clean through it.

"Maybe you should leave that one," Myrna said in a strained voice, "It's not worth wasting water to clean it off and who knows what you could catch from touching that."

"Yeah, it smells awful," Devin agreed, the stench from the corpse rapidly growing worse.

They walked together well through dusk, both hesitant to stop and eager to move away as far as possible. Honey had not yet returned, and neither of them saw any sign of the animal. Both Devin and Myrna found themselves constantly looking to their sides, or back over their shoulders. Small noises nearby were no longer necessary to put them on alert, they felt that at any moment they could be set upon without warning. Myrna wondered if the feeling would diminish or if this was their new reality, constantly living in fear between one attack and the next.

It was well past sunset before they decided to stop for the evening, as much as they wanted to keep moving they had the sense to realize it was far more dangerous for them to stumble around in the dark. Reluctantly they set up camp under a tall tree, covering themselves over with their bedrolls and not bothering to put up their tent. They sat shoulder to shoulder against the large trunk, leaning into each other as much as the tree.

Neither found much sleep that night, wary of any sounds or imagined sights. They sat in watchful silence, both too afraid to make any noise. As the hours rolled by their fears proved to be for naught, the night passing uneventfully until coyotes in the predawn hours created a ghastly cacophony. Even with Devin and Myrna's familiarity to the sound of those animals, it still further set their nerves on edge. It had lasted nearly twenty minutes, a mixture of barks, howls, and high pitch crying that set their hearts racing.

The sound of grass rustling nearby amplified their fear ten-fold. Devin's anxiety grew to a breaking point, Myrna throwing her arm across his shoulder as she sensed he was getting ready to run.

"Wait!" she brusquely whispered.

The steps sounded too quickly and close together to Myrna's more experienced ear for them to be caused by a person. A gentle nickering confirmed her suspicion, immediately followed by Honey walking up to them and nuzzling his large head against both of them in turn. The danger around them still felt all too real, but the return of the horse did much to lift their spirits. Mercifully the coyote's wails died off, fading into the distance. As the sun rose forming a slit on the horizon, they wasted no time packing their things and returning to the road. Neither had slept much, but their desire to be off far outweighed their drowsiness.

"Not too far ahead, if I remember right," Myrna had said for the third or fourth time that morning.

The road transformed from a flat, endless stretch into gentle rolling hills dotting the countryside. Each time they reached a crest Myrna expected to see the village laid out before them in a valley below, and was consistently disappointed when they were presented with more road to travel. They were getting close, but the monotony of the trail made it difficult to gauge exactly how much further they had to go.

"Ah, finally!" Myrna exclaimed as she reached the top of the next hill, looking down at brick and stone houses nestled together in small bunches.

From their vantage point, Byrn sat huddled at the base of a large bluff, the rustic village stretching across rocky grassland and low ledges. A small river ran from the northwest, one of the dozens of branches of the Tinindraüg flowing alongside the edge of the community before breaking off to the east. The modest dwellings, though charming, had little variation among them. Their similarity and overall layout suggested they were constructed at the same time with each house meticulously placed where it was meant to be.

The trail to the village winded down the hill for nearly two miles, Devin urging Honey forward in his excitement to be out of the wilderness. Something seemed out of sorts to Myrna, though what it was she couldn't exactly tell. Perhaps she was only being paranoid because of the ordeal from the previous day. As they drew closer, it became more obvious what was bothering her. No noise came from the village, nor was there any smoke from cooking fires or workmen, and there was no sign of people out and about. A village this size should almost feel as if it had a life of its own, but as they made their approach it just felt dead and empty.

"Slow down, Devin!" Myrna called out.

He turned back, bringing Honey to a stop and dismounting.

"What is it?" he asked, startled by the urgency of her call.

"I think something is wrong," she said, "look around, where is everyone?"

Devin's heart sank as he looked around and the truth of Myrna's words dawned on him. It was far too quiet, even at this distance they should see some activity.

"What do you think we should do?" he asked after being silent for a time.

Myrna closed her eyes, rubbing her temples. By the spirits her head ached, why couldn't anything be easy? Making decisions when she had no idea what to do, and holding on to a sliver of hope that the end of their journey would lead them somewhere safe was beginning to wear her down. A lack of sleep over the past week did not help matters.

Until yesterday she felt generally safe, but after the attack she realized how vulnerable they were out in the open. The only protection they had to rely on was Devin's crossbow. *And he's only a boy, it shouldn't be up to him to keep us safe,* she thought. Sighing, she opened her eyes. There was nothing she could do about it now, best if they deal with what was in front of them first and worry about the rest later.

"Let's go in a little closer, quietly. If there's trouble we'll ride away," she told Devin.

Moving down the hill they cautiously approached the town, passing by a few small, empty farms along the way. Nothing looked out of the ordinary; an axe was left in a large stump where someone had been splitting wood, bales of hay were piled outside of a barn, a field was freshly plowed to grow newly planted crops. The only problem was there were no people or animals in sight.

"That's a weird place to put blankets out," Devin said as he spotted a fenced-in area.

A pile of white and brown was visible from the road where Devin indicated. Concerned, Myrna moved in for a closer look.

"Those aren't blankets, Dev," Myrna whispered.

Looking closer they saw scraps of animal skins piled up inside of the pen. Spatters of blood marred the furs, and bones that had been picked clean lay strewn about.

"I think this was a goat pen," Myrna said, frowning while she looked around.

Poking a stick at some of the skins, underneath she saw a few skulls, femurs, and rib cages all without a scrap of meat left on them. She didn't have to put much thought towards what had done that to them.

"Let's keep moving," she said, "I don't think we can learn anything more here."

Passing by a few more small farms, they entered into the village proper. The same silence and empty stillness greeted them as they walked down the graveled streets, past deserted homes and stores. The town was essentially one large square, sporadically intersected with roadways wide enough for a carriage to pass. Taking their time, within a few hours they walked every inch of the roads. They began to relax somewhat after traversing the entire town, becoming increasingly confident that it was vacant. Occasionally they saw signs of a hurried departure, tools left out in the open, or clothes left on lines to dry in the warm air.

Deciding there was little more to see outside they ventured into some of the homes, all of which were empty. Again signs were present of a hasty departure. Pots and pans were left over cooking fires, and most people's possessions were still in the house instead of taken away with them.

"What do you think, Devin?" Myrna asked as they exited the fourth house they checked, hoping to get a few words out of him.

"Nobody's here, that's for sure," he answered.

Devin continued to think about the devoured animals from the farm, his forehead creased with worry.

"Do you think Greymen did that to the goats?" he asked.

Myrna nodded, seeing that Devin was trying to puzzle information together that she had already solved.

"And it looks like the Greymen are no longer here," she prompted, using his term for them.

Devin thought for a moment before asking, "Do you think they stayed behind and ate all the animals, then left somewhere?"

"Exactly," Myrna said, glad Devin was able to think it through, "come on, follow me," she instructed.

She led them towards a large barn at the western edge of town, set apart from the other houses. An overbearing stench greeted them before they got too close.

"Ugh, what is that smell!" Devin yelled out.

"This is the slaughterhouse, I noticed it while we were walking earlier," Myrna explained, "we should look inside."

Devin stayed back as Myrna approached the door. She looked back at him as she realized he didn't follow, fixing him with an unimpressed stare.

"Really Devin, you're going to let me walk in all alone?" she said, somewhat teasingly.

"But it smells so bad," he replied.

Fairly convinced the structure was empty, Myrna slid the door open. She didn't really want to go in, but if she was to be certain Greymen had been here, this would tell her. Confident they were alone, she still felt it prudent to cautiously step back after opening the door. No sounds came forth which she considered a good sign, but she couldn't tell what was inside as she peered into the darkness. Devin stepped up beside her and they waited, listening intently. Hesitantly, Myrna at last stepped through the doorway. The malodorous scent greatly increased as she breached the entrance, causing her to gag.

A light sound of hurried footsteps rushed towards her, though she couldn't see as her eyes struggled to adjust to the dark. Frantically she screamed and stumbled out of the doorway, back into the open daylight. Bracing herself for what might approach, she breathed a sigh of relief when a large tabby cat raced out of the barn and brushed her leg as it ran by. It took several more minutes until she was able to calm herself and work up the courage to head back inside.

Again stepping through the doorway, she stayed near the entrance until her vision acclimated to the low light. Many hooks hung from the ceiling, presumably once holding the devoured animal carcasses now scattered on the floor.

"I don't think anyone's been here for a while. These remains have been laying here for days, judging by the odor," she yelled back outside to Devin, her voice muffled through her sleeve.

"What?"

"Oh just get in here for goodness sake!" she hollered.

"Why did we even need to come in here?" Devin asked, finally entering the barn.

"Because," Myrna explained peevishly, "like you said the Greymen probably were here, ate all of the food and left. If we continue confirming all of the animals and meat were torn into, we can assume that is true."

"Well I guess that makes sense," Devin muttered, equally annoyed from her tone.

As they circled back through town they found more evidence of livestock that had been eaten alive, or uncooked meat stripped to the bone. It became obvious, at least to Myrna, that all of the people had fled while the Greymen remained behind to devour any piece of flesh they could find before moving on. The lack of available meat reminded her that their own food situation was becoming strained. A few pieces of stale bread and jerky were all they had left to split between them.

Although it was unsettling roaming through an abandoned village, it seemed to be safe. As tired as they were, Myrna and Devin welcomed the opportunity to be off the road for a day or two. Choosing one of the houses to stay in, as a precaution they piled furniture in front of the door and hung blankets over the windows. They settled in for the night in an actual bed for the first time in weeks.

"Come on, Devin, we have a lot to do today," Myrna said as she shook the boy awake the next morning.

He groaned a bit and rolled over, not showing much interest in getting out of bed. Not in the mood for sluggishness, Myrna took a firm grip of the blanket and yanked it from Devin in one swift motion.

"Next step's a cold bucket of water kiddo," she said in all seriousness, "time to be up, I'll be outside."

Finally joining Myrna and Honey in front of the house, Devin tried to rub the sleep from his eyes. It had been so nice to not have to lie on the hard ground for a change.

"What did you want to do today, I was hoping we could just rest for a bit to be honest," he said.

"We need to keep looking around," she answered, "just because we haven't seen anyone yet doesn't mean there isn't anyone hiding around here. That and we should try and find some things that might be useful for us on the road."

"You want to steal from them?" Devin asked incredulously. The suggestion wasn't something he'd expect to hear from Myrna.

Myrna didn't answer right away, thinking through how to explain it, "Things aren't normal right now Devin, they'd understand. We have to think about our survival. If someone isn't using something and we need it, we have to take it. I'd hate to say it, but Harrington was right back at the farm. It's dangerous out here."

They spent the day rummaging through houses, looking for any signs of people or things they might need. Devin felt awkward at first going through someone else's belongings, but after a few hours it felt no different than doing chores back in Shady Vale. It surprised him how quickly it became normal to him. By mid-afternoon they had replenished their food supply after finding a bakery, and each found a pair of daggers they pocketed and a bow and quiver for Myrna after checking through an entire block of homes.

"This looks like it could be promising, Dev. The Spring Blossom Inn," Myrna said as they reached the next street they planned to check, reading the sign in front of a large building.

The inn opened up into a large room filled with mahogany tables and chairs, a bar area, and a raised floor to the rear that featured a piano. A very thin layer of dust had settled on everything, intimating that the room hadn't been used in at least several days. Myrna pictured on a regular night how charming it must have been, the tables filled with people drinking and chatting, the aroma of dinner being prepared, maybe a singer or storyteller to provide entertainment. A sickening feeling came over her as she realized how far removed from ordinary this was. Would their lives return to the way they were anytime soon or was this only the beginning?

Devin began heading upstairs while Myrna busied herself going through the various drawers and cupboards. As he reached the top step, a wall of odor nearly caused him to tumble backwards. He forced himself through the anteroom and into a long hallway, with many open doors along the left and right walls. A strange low hum was present as he walked down the corridor, continually increasing and decreasing in intensity. It seemed to come from everywhere, making it difficult to determine its exact source.

Unsure of what the noise might be, Devin carefully peered around each doorway in turn as he walked by. Nearly turning around to wait for Myrna, he determinedly changed his mind and mustered the courage to explore on his own. The source of the noise became clear when he looked into the third room on the right, a swarm of flies covering a body on the floor. Pausing in the doorway he gagged a few times, struggling to keep his last meal from coming back up. It was hard to tell the exact extent of the injuries to the corpse, but it was obvious they were severe. Bone was exposed in many places, with most of the flesh torn off. Even the person's face had been largely ripped away, exposing an empty eye socket. Most notable about the body was its size; it must have been the largest person Devin had ever seen.

He forced himself into the room to get a closer look, inspecting a suit of black armor piled in the corner. It was equally oversized and made of hard but pliable leather, and next to it was a halberd as long as Devin was tall. Keeping one eye on the body, he tried to lift it up. Barely able to heft it, he couldn't imagine how anyone could actually wield this thing. He set it back down, accidentally dropping the heavy weapon and causing a loud clatter. He turned around quickly at the noise, almost as if he expected someone to be standing there and chide him for his foolishness. But there was only the lifeless corpse in the room with him, unmoving and quite dead. Leaving the room he hurried back downstairs, his courage spent and interest in exploring the other rooms lost.

"Myrna!" he called out, "I found someone!"

Startled, she stopped what she was doing. Before she could speak he began explaining hurriedly, "He's dead, all the way dead."

Rushing up the stairs behind him, she entered the room Devin pointed out. Doing her best to ignore the smell, she approached the body while he waited in the hallway.

"I don't think he's from around here," Myrna said as she left the room, "he looks like a soldier of some kind, though I didn't see any insignia."

"Was there anything else up here?" she asked, "you should have stayed near me rather than running off on your own. You know how dangerous that was."

"I haven't looked yet," Devin said, slightly abashed, "I stopped when I found him."

Checking the other rooms, they found more bodies through three more doors. Myrna had no idea who they were, but seeing four large men with the same armor confirmed her suspicion they were part of a group.

"Last room," she said to Devin as they proceeded along the corridor.

The final door was the only one that was shut when they arrived, all of the others were wide open. Ready to check the only remaining room, she stopped herself when she heard a soft thump from the other side. The thump was followed by a scratching, dragging sound, and then repeated. Myrna wasn't quite sure what to make of it. Telling Devin to step back, she opened the door while standing off to the side and peeked in.

She put her hand to her mouth, stifling a gasp and resisting the urge to vomit, then she quickly shut the door.

"What is it? Myrna, what was in there?" Devin asked, nearing to panic from the noises he heard when the door opened.

"It's not something you need to see," she said firmly, though she was visibly shaken, "go downstairs and I'll take care of this."

"But what…" he began.

"Just go!" she interrupted with a tone of finality.

Devin exhaled heavily and threw his arms up, turning away and stalking down the stairs. Myrna waited until she heard his footsteps retreat all the way down, and then returned to the door. Drawing the bow she had retrieved earlier in the day, she fitted an arrow and jerked the door open. Backing down the hallway as fast as she could, she anxiously waited with the arrow trained on the door. The thumping noise starting again, followed by the soft dragging sound and another thump.

An ashen, blanched hand gripped the doorframe low towards the floor, the gnarled fingers flexing and pulling. A head with long black hair peered around the corner of the door at foot level, as it shot its other arm out into the hall, sniffing the air. It turned its head and looked at Myrna, the skin of its face overly drawn like leather stretched too tightly across a drum. Silently it worked its mouth before issuing a low growl, struggling to turn itself about. With a frenzied zeal it pulled its upper torso into the hallway, inching its way towards Myrna.

The creature no longer had a lower half. Everything below its navel looked as if it was torn away, its entrails grotesquely trailing behind it as it propelled itself forward. Seeing the creature allowed Myrna to resolve in her conscience that these things were no longer human; any person suffering such an injury would not survive. Not only was this thing moving, it didn't even seem to be feeling any pain.

Doing her best to maintain a semblance of composure, Myrna released the breath she had been holding and let the arrow fly. It struck the creature in the neck, but if it hurt the thing it did not show. The jarring impact slowed the monster, but only for the brief moment that it took to regain its balance. Fighting the urge to panic, she focused on nocking another arrow. With a shaky hand she reached into the quiver. It took her three tries to notch the next arrow to the string as she fumbled around, with each passing moment the Greyman dragging itself closer and closer.

It was too much for Myrna to take; she had used a bow many years ago, but that was shooting at a target that wasn't intent on killing her. No longer calm or collected, she released the arrow and turned to run without even bothering to see if it hit or not.

"Run for it Devin, get out of here!" she shouted while hastening down the stairs, taking three at a time.

"I'm downstairs already!" he shouted back, annoyed at being forced out of the hallway and unaware of what Myrna was dealing with.

"All the way out!" she shouted, suddenly downstairs beside Devin and sprinting towards the door.

Surprised, Devin looked over at her and then at the stairs to see the top half of the Grey Man darting forward, gracelessly sliding down the steps. Making an indecipherable noise, Devin ran past Myrna and straight out of the door into the street. He didn't stop running for two blocks. Myrna, directly on his heels, fortunately had the sense to untether Honey on their way by.

"Where were its legs?" Devin shouted, finally stopping and panting for breath.

He paced, needing to do something other than standing still while he tried to get the sight out of his head. Myrna had nothing to say for consolation, she too was speechless with shock.

"I know we were hoping to rest a few days Dev, but who knows what else might be lurking around," Myrna said, catching her breath.

"Let's just go now, I want to leave," Devin said, beginning to sob, "I don't want to be here, I wanna go home."

The stress of the previous days finally pushed him beyond his breaking point. Devin began to cry in earnest and walk around aimlessly. Myrna's attempts to calm him down were ineffective, and she had to settle for guiding him in the direction she wanted to go. They briskly walked north out of town, Myrna pulling him along more than walking with him. It wasn't until they were far out of town that Devin regained some self-control. He realized he had been unconsciously gripping the diamond in his pocket, not noticing until then how warm it felt through the pouch.

They gained as much distance as they could from Byrn before nightfall. Luckily the next village, Midao, was not too far away and shortly after that they would reach Creekview's Crossing. After their latest experience, however, Myrna did not have the same optimistic outlook she once held about their final destination. As they set up camp for the night, just thinking about what might be waiting in Midao made her nervous. Nearly a quarter mile from the road, under a small copse of trees they set up their sleeping bags. Devin had settled down somewhat, but he still wasn't very talkative. Sitting with his arms wrapped around his knees, he looked forward with a vacant stare.

"It'll get better soon," he vaguely heard Myrna tell him.

He didn't respond, his thoughts were somewhere miles away. Every time he closed his eyes he saw that living torso, dragging itself towards him. Against his leg he held the shiny stone, hidden away in the palm of his hand. Usually it provided him a sense of comfort or strength, but tonight it only seemed to feed his worries. It was almost hot to the touch, further adding to his concern. After a time he mumbled a goodnight to Myrna, and lay down to sleep.

Lightning crashed as rain poured down, the flashes revealing a sea of Greymen lumbering towards him. Most were missing large patches of skin and flesh while some were altogether missing limbs, others yet were legless like the creature from the inn. Devin lay on the ground with the mud forming up around him, burying him and trapping him in place. He tried to scream but no sound came forth, while the horde relentlessly ambled forward.

With each flash, the Grey crept closer. The mud was now up to his neck, pinning his arms to his sides, and the pressure at his chest began to suffocate him. Another crash of lightning revealed them standing over him, leaning in and sniffing the air before him. Their eyes widened with a hollow glee, working their mouths hungrily as they appraised the meal before them.

"Wake up!" Myrna shouted, standing over Devin in the pouring rain.

She had gone beyond gentle nudging and calling to him, moving on to yelling and shaking him roughly. Devin's unresponsiveness began to worry her greatly, the deluge alone should have woken him. Intermittent explosions of thunder and lightning drowned out her voice, but she hardly took notice of it. His pulse and heart rate felt fine, if a little fast, but he still remained montionless. She looked into his face, perfectly still and unmoving. Dread overcame her, what if he was having some kind of reaction to the stress and didn't wake? She had seen it before, someone unable to deal with a traumatic event and falling into a stupor for weeks or even months. There she sat, staring at him and holding onto him closely in the downpour, unable to do anything else. Her relief was so great when his eyes began to flicker and slowly open that she let out a sob she had been holding in.

"Why didn't you wake up, I was so worried!" she exclaimed, hugging him tight.

But still he didn't move or react, Myrna slowly realizing all was not right. She pushed him back to arm's length, looking into his staring eyes. Finally coming around, his vision adjusted as if seeing Myrna for the first time.

Fixating on her, he spoke with a slow, strained voice that seemed not to be his own, "My time is running short. The others… all gone."

Devin?" Myrna murmured, even more upset than before, "What are you saying?"

"Keep it away from Him. The diamond… it can't be allowed near him or all is lost," was the only reply.

"Devin!?" she shouted, an uncontrollable tremor entering her voice.

He offered no further response, his eyes closing as she repeatedly yelled to him. Myrna tried to drag him somewhere more sheltered, but the sparse trees made it difficult to find relief from the torrential rain. Devin again appeared to be sleeping normally, though nothing Myrna did could break him from his slumber. Falling down against a small tree, she pulled Devin up onto her lap to get him out of the dirt. There was nothing more she could do except for sit, and wait.

She found no sleep for the remainder of the night. Everything was soaked and covered in mud, and Devin's comfort was her only concern. The rain did not relent, forming large puddles around them. In the early morning hours, Devin finally began to stir. Myrna sat up straight noticing him move, watching him cautiously.

"Gaah, everything's so wet!" he bellowed, quickly getting to his feet when he realized he was huddled up closely with Myrna.

Myrna couldn't help but smile, glad to see him up and acting like himself.

"Are you okay? I couldn't wake you when the rain really started coming down," she said, wiping some tears from her eyes. She didn't want to mention his strange behavior during the night.

"I'm fine," he answered, feeling slightly awkward while she stared at him probingly, "are you crying?"

"No, I'm fine," she lied, "do you remember anything from last night, talking in your sleep? Maybe a bad dream?"

He thought for a moment, "No, not really. Maybe a small dream about the Greymen, but it wasn't too bad."

Truthfully it was one of the most terrifying dreams he had in a while, but he tried to appear untroubled by it while talking to Myrna.

Deciding not to press any further, at least for the moment, she suggested they collect their things and go back to the road. She would keep her concerns to herself for now. Devin was probably having a hard enough time as it was without her heaping more worries onto him.

"We can't possibly get any more soaked and miserable than this. Might as well cover some ground while we're being drowned out," she suggested, offering a weak smile and looking forward to moving on towards the next town.

They gradually changed direction as the road began to turn eastward. After many hours of walking, a small branch of the Sterling River came into view, running adjacent to their path. The trail became more heavily wooded than the area they left behind. Everywhere they looked was the green of grass or leaves, the only other color present was the brown of the narrow dirt road fading into the distance. Large oaks and pines were scattered along the path while dense forest lay only a stone's throw away to the east, and across the river to the west.

Puddles began to form from the heavy, ceaseless rain. At first, they had taken care to walk around them. After a time the pools of water became so frequent, and because they were already soaked to the bone, they no longer saw the point and just walked straight through them. They passed by a few small homes along the way, Devin almost hoping they would stop. Each time though Myrna continued by without pausing.

"Is it much further?" Devin asked while he looked longingly at the shelters they walked by.

"Not too far, luckily the villages are close together. It'll be nice to get out of the rain, that's for certain," she answered.

"Why don't we just wait it out at the house we passed?" he asked.

"We don't know who lives there Devin, or where they are, or what we might find in there. Things are strange right now but we can't just go breaking into homes," she responded with no room for argument.

"But we did at the village," Devin answered, confused.

"That was different," she said.

"How?"

"It just was Devin, we'll be there before nightfall if we keep moving," she said in exasperation, not really having a valid explanation of what was different about it.

Myrna had considered stopping in one of the shacks they saw, but readily dismissed the thought. There didn't appear to be anyone living in them at the moment, which made her wonder what might be inside or why the people decided to leave. Whatever their reason, she didn't have the desire to investigate after what happened at Byrn. She just wanted to get somewhere safe as soon as possible. Even though she was trying not to show it, she was worried greatly about Devin's behavior the previous night. Talking in one's sleep was not unheard of, but the way he had spoken seemed like something else entirely. She looked up the road to him, he seemed perfectly fine today as she watched him pull Honey to a stop up ahead. He scratched his head and turned to her with a confused look.

"Do you see those white bumps up there?" he asked.

Catching up beside him, she squinted to see what he was looking at. It was far off, but she did see white mounds standing out in stark contrast against the green of the woods ahead. The gentle downhill slope of the land allowed them to see far into the expanse before them, though the grove of trees they approached blocked their view of the next village beyond.

"Yeah, I do see it," she confirmed, "I can't tell what they might be though."

If Myrna felt it was necessary, they could walk around the trees ahead. Unfortunately, that would add on an additional two days before they reached Midao. The oddity ahead seemed inconspicuous, at least from this distance. It wouldn't hurt to risk getting closer so they could further evaluate it.

"C'mon Dev, let's get a better look," she said, moving forward.

After nearly an hour of walking they were able to determine the white shapes they saw were the canopies of a broken down caravan. A few hundred yards away they paused, the fear they felt at Byrn and when they encountered the Grey Man on the road returning in full.

"The village is only on the other side of the woods, right along the road," Myrna said, thinking aloud, "I think we should try to go through if we can…"

"Ow!" Devin yelped, quickly drawing his hand up towards his mouth.

"What is it?" Myrna asked.

"It's nothing," Devin evaded, putting his hand behind his back, "I must've turned my wrist funny or something."

The look on Myrna's face showed she obviously didn't believe him and was not in the mood for any nonsense. She grabbed his left arm before he realized it, pulling his hand over to inspect him despite his protests.

"Devin! This is a burn on your hand, a pretty bad one. It's welting up!" she reproached, "how in the blessed spirits did you do that to yourself?"

The boy didn't seem to trust adults very much, the last thing she wanted was to force him to talk and risk pushing him away. However, she needed to know how he burned himself. It made no sense, and she was unwilling to add it to her growing list of worries while Devin seemed to be hiding something.

Devin labored to think up a lie she might believe; they hadn't had a fire in several days, it was obvious by the blister forming that it happened only a moment ago, and he had nothing else on him that could possibly cause a burn. The only option he had was to tell the truth. With a deep sigh he removed the pouch from his pocket.

"My mom gave this to me," he said, showing it to her.

Feeling the heat coming from the stone through the pouch, Devin upended it onto the ground rather than taking the risk of another burn. Myrna gasped at the clear diamond nestled in the dirt, steam rising from it in wisps when she looked closely.

"That must be worth a fortune!" she blurted out.

Almost embarrassed that was the first thing she said, she covered her mouth with her hands. It was true though, the large, perfectly formed gem must have been one of a kind. A cold tinge of fear ran up her spine as she thought about the words Devin spoke the previous night and the gemstone at their feet.

"And you've always had this stone?" Myrna asked.

"As long as I can remember," Devin answered, "it started getting warm a few days ago. Now it's almost too hot to touch."

Myrna bent down and tapped her finger to it. The diamond was certainly hot enough to cause a burn. Taking the pouch, she scooped the stone back into it, and placed it into Devin's backpack.

"I'm glad you showed it to me, Devin. I think it's a very important stone. Never tell anyone else about it and keep it safe in your pack," she said.

"You wouldn't know where your mother got it from would you?" Myrna thought to ask as she was tucking it away.

He shook his head.

"Mmm, I suppose you wouldn't," she said softly to herself, "that's alright, let's move along and try to see if we can get by up ahead. I'm glad you showed it to me, Devin."

Both riding Honey, they remained alert while they slowly walked by the wagons on the side of the road. All was quiet, the only sounds the steady patter of rain and the muted hoof beats against the wet ground.

"Over there!" Devin whispered, as loudly as he would dare.

A pair of black boots stood out from behind one of the wheels, sticking up straight as if a man were lying down behind the wagon. Myrna veered away from the road, directing the horse down the slight embankment towards the caravan.

"Myrna, let's just go!" Devin implored, not having the slightest interest in exploring.

"Shhh, it'll be only a minute," Myrna argued, "if we find out what happened here we might get a glimpse of what we're walking into."

The owner of the boots was revealed as they moved around the wagon. It was another man in black armor, his skull bashed in and skeleton exposed in many places. Another four bodies were scattered nearby, each bearing similar injuries. As they worked their way around the broken down caravan, fourteen more bodies were found, six of them gigantic men in the same armor. Devin promptly leaned over in the saddle and emptied out his stomach.

"Sorry," he muttered, wiping his mouth.

"Don't worry about it," she said, hardly paying any mind to him sicking up.

She continued her inspection of the area while Devin looked around impatiently, eager to leave.

"Those big men, they're dressed the same as the ones we saw in Byrn. I think everyone from the village came up in a larger group, maybe they were guards from somewhere. They ran into some problems here though..." she continued, fully absorbed in trying to make sense of what might have happened.

Devin bobbed his head slightly against her back. It was hard for him to pay attention to her, most of his focus was on trying not to throw up again from the proximity of the bodies.

Tilting his head up, he let the rain wash down his face. The coolness of it felt good on his skin, helping to calm him and settle his stomach. It was almost relaxing, closing his eyes to hear only the rainfall and pretending it was just another normal day, before he had wished everyone dead. If he tried hard he could imagine he was back in Shady Vale, sitting at the porch watching the water slide from the roof in droves.

His brief daydream shattered with Honey rearing up and springing forward, leaving him scrambling to keep his grip on Myrna and stay atop the horse. Her terrified neigh pierced the silence, the noise jarringly vibrant in the soft rain. Where Myrna and Devin failed to see the Greymen, they were likely saved by Honey's sense of smell. Myrna managed to regain control of the animal amidst the trees and lead her back onto the road. Looking backwards, they saw what had startled the horse as various forms crawled forth from the caravans. Most fell haphazardly onto the road as they exited the wagons, but quickly pulled themselves up and loped forward in pursuit. Without needing much encouragement, Honey galloped along the road into the woods, towards Midao.

A Summons Answered

For the first time in her unnaturally long life, Sevra felt truly alone. Since she was a young woman she knew she was different, special in some way. When a divine being chose her, it was confirmation of that fact. Now, her God had not communicated with her for many weeks, its last message being one of displeasure towards her failure.

Adding to her solitude, all of those minds she had rooted herself into were gone, most likely a side effect from the botched spell that should have given her more power and influence than anyone dared dream. Once holding domain over royalty, soldiers, and key officials, her network was reduced to one man who at this very moment neared the city. She would meet with him later this afternoon, and find some answers.

The dream of having the lands under her dominion would be salvaged. She could have given up when the spell went awry, or when she lost favor of her God and He abandoned her, or when the city was nearly overrun with the Infected. To the contrary, she was more determined to still have everything she desired. Dividing the True-Blood into groups, they first secured their fortress, and systematically worked their way throughout the city. The job was not yet complete, but progress was being made in securing Dun'Aldir for the citizens who survived.

They didn't need to know she caused the disaster that nearly destroyed all of Luskir, but Sevra certainly would make sure they knew she was their savior. The loss of Eldora, her contact within the Luskiran Council, was but a trivial setback. She only needed the council to convene one more time to execute her new plan. Under the pretense of rebuilding and responding to the recent calamity, and with the way clear into the city, the council agreed to accept Sevra's accommodations in Dun'Aldir. Though things hadn't gone according to her original plan, by the end of the day Sevra would be declaring herself Empress - once the small matter currently before her was dealt with.

Proceeding through her courtroom, she entered into the adjacent meeting chamber where the Luskiran Council had already gathered.

Addressing them with a rehearsed speech, she stated, "Before we begin, let us take a moment of silence to remember Eldora Al'Deir, First Seat of the Luskiran Council, last in line of the house Al'Deir. Though she fell victim to the disease that has ravaged our land, her spirit is still among us. We will forge ahead to brighter days, and restore Luskir to its former splendor."

Sevra watched as the seven present members of the council respectfully bowed their heads in reflection, duly noting one seat was empty. Pushing aside her annoyance of the missing party, she pushed ahead with her plan and would deal with his absence later.

"All non-essential members please exit back into the courtroom, and we will seal the meeting to the council," Sevra requested.

Though meetings typically remained open, it wasn't unusual to excuse non-council when matters were discussed that required utmost confidentiality. All of the personal escorts, servants, and guards left the room, leaving the Luskiran Council alone in the dimly lit chamber. The heavy, stone door slid shut, audibly locking into place behind them.

"I have one critical piece of information to share with you all," Sevra began, pacing slowly around the table.

A scratching sound and series of shuffling noises caused some of the men and women at the table to look at one another in curiosity. It faded as quickly as it came on, and they returned their attention to Sevra, eager to hear what she had to say.

Sevra froze at the sound, grateful that it did not linger or cause any major disruption. She wanted to take her time, enjoy the moment she was in. All eyes were eagerly on her, desperate for the information she hinted towards in the spell-laced letters she sent out to them, imploring them to hold an emergency session. Sevra promised them a way to restore order, and that she knew the cause of the disease ravaging the countryside as well as its remedy. She looked at each council member as she spoke, enjoying their ignorance of the subtle influence she held over them.

"The infection that has spread across the land is in part, magical in nature. I alone, know the way forward," she said, enjoying the alarm her statement caused.

They looked to her for an answer.

"Let me provide more clarity on the matter. Your services are no longer necessary," she told them bluntly, moving to the wall opposite of the door.

They looked shocked, almost hurt.

One of the councilmen broke free of the enchantment, looking at Sevra as if seeing her for the first time this day, "Enough of your damn games, woman! I've never cared for having you lurk about our meetings, but Eldora was always insistent. Now tell us for what purpose you have gathered us here!"

"The purpose of having you here is to inform you all that you are now obsolete, useless, not needed," she answered, pressing in one of the stones on the wall until it slid away beyond reach.

The floor opened up, sending the table and councilmen crashing fifteen feet below. Sevra had made preparations for this meeting, having additional walls built in the basement where she had her men capture and place dozens of the Infected. Startled cries from the drop were replaced by screams of terror when they realized they were not alone in the makeshift pit. Injured or dazed from the fall, most of the council members were hardly able to stand, let alone defend themselves from the ravaging, once human creatures.

Sevra, satisfied by the screams and various sounds coming from the pit, casually walked from the meeting chamber back into the courtroom. The stench of blood that greeted her told her before she even had to look that the Drakvnar had done their part as well. Massacred before her were the entire entourage and guard for the council, ambushed unexpectedly as they left the meeting chamber.

"Well done Ramnar," she remarked to the Guard-Captain, smiling and wiping away a streak of blood from his arm.

"We managed to take them by surprise, most were dead before they even drew their weapons," he responded.

"Not quite all of them though," she commented, reaching up to teasingly drag her nail over Ramnar's open wound.

He lowered his head, shamed to have suffered an injury to such a lesser adversary.

"Tell me, has my other guest arrived yet? By last reports he was nearing the city," Sevra asked, eager to find answers to questions that had preoccupied her mind for weeks.

"Very soon, he was seen not long ago approaching the city. Empress, my men tell me he looks to carry the infection, but he is still with all his faculties," Captain Ramnar informed her.

"Make sure he gets here safely, and clean up this mess so I can entertain him properly," she said, carefully maneuvering her way among the bodies and pools of blood.

Returning to her throne at the end of the courtroom, Sevra sat regally and waited while the Drakvnar removed the bodies. After a few tense weeks, she finally started to feel in control once again.

***

As much as he tried to resist, Aubur found himself resolutely plodding to the capital city of Dun'Aldir. He once encountered a family in a wagon passing by him on the road; upon sight of him the children screamed while the driver gaped openly and sped the horses along faster. Other than the sporadic traveler, the road east was surprisingly empty. It wasn't until he came through a small village outside of the main city that he realized he was not a well man.

Cutting across an empty field towards a scattering of simple wooden houses, Aubur felt suddenly vulnerable, exposed out in the open. Paired with the thought that he was being strung along to Dun'Aldir by someone or something only increased his unease. A rustling from the bushes near the first house he approached startled him. He was relieved when he saw it was only a dog, its ears back and tongue lolling out as it looked to Aubur, almost expectantly.

Never a friend to animals, Aubur's first impulse was to kick the dog for scaring him, but then decided he wouldn't mind some company after being alone for so many days, even if it was just a dog.

"Come 'ere pooch," he said gruffly, making a poor effort to sound friendly.

As the dog came closer, its disposition changed. It stopped in midstride; with three feet on the ground it froze, not daring to land its fourth paw down. Ears coming up, suddenly alert, it recoiled slightly.

"Come on now," Aubur said, more forcefully, extending his arm out.

A deep hunger came over Aubur, much like the one from his disturbing dream. *Could probably break its neck*, he thought, *wouldn't even need to cook it...*

With a low whimper the dog bounded away, swiftly turning around and running off into the distance. It made Aubur furious, mostly at Walt for doing this to him, but also at the world and everything in it, and that it was now his lot in life to wander as some hideous thing that scared children and animals. He was worse than a leper.

Entering the village, he was again surprised to find it mostly empty, though he did see a few men huddled low to the ground across the street. He stood and watched them for a time, unable to determine what they might be up to. *Maybe playing at a game of dice*, he thought. They seemed excited and engrossed in whatever it was. Not having eaten for days, maybe they could tell him where he could find some food.

Walking up to them from behind, Aubur carefully approached the four crouching men. He cleared his throat loudly after it grew apparent they weren't taking notice of him. Slowly they stood and turned, revealing a mutilated husk on the ground. Their hands and faces were marred with the animal's blood, although the empty boot he saw nearby told him it wasn't an animal. These people were eating a dead man, and at that moment Aubur decided the world had gone mad. Putting his hands out, he slowly backed away from the four men. They all shared the same gaunt, jaundiced appearance that had befallen Aubur, but there was a difference. The stares from the men were vacant, their movements jerking and uncoordinated as they moved towards him and sniffed the air.

"I don't want any trouble," Aubur stammered, caught off guard by their appearance and behavior.

In reply, the creatures groaned and hissed as they drew nearer to him.

"Easy now," he said carefully, still backing away.

They continued their advance, and slowed to a stop inches away from Aubur's face. They looked at him almost with confusion, but it was difficult for Aubur to tell exactly what they might be thinking with their inhuman features. He squeezed his eyes shut involuntarily, turning his face away as the thing's disgusting breath wafted in front of him. Feeling the creature withdraw a few inches, Aubur opened his eyes and continued watching the four men. After their brief inspection, they appeared to have lost interest in him and returned to the corpse at the ground. The insistent pull to Dun'Aldir nagged him once again, demanding he make haste. Interrupted by the directive, he stopped in mid-kneel beside the desecrated husk, falling backwards in horror upon realizing what he was about to do. Running in terror and disgust, Aubur continued towards the city looming on the horizon.

***

Still captive in the ruby cell about Sevra's neck, Kubathu was brooding when he felt a sudden change in his surroundings. The walls seemed more pliable, stretching against the force of his will. For the first time in weeks his interest had been piqued, drawing him out of his listless drifting across the prison that was his home for last two thousand years.

The days immediately following the botched spell had been suspenseful; he knew their plan hadn't worked as intended and death was likely imminent for those affected, but in his wildest dreams he didn't think it would have caused their reanimation. He explored the potential of continuing their work and reestablishing contact with Sevra, but the reanimated forms turned out to be nothing more than shells of men, unthinking beings that were completely uncontrollable and ultimately useless.

Watching Sevra scramble in panic as scores of her Devoted resurrected into mindless creatures brought him some satisfaction, had they actually gotten to her, he may have even found it entertaining. He determined at his earliest opportunity he would find a new host, the witch was no longer of value to him. This new entity that had arrived, however, he showed potential; the way everyone recoiled at his mere presence made Kubathu long for a physical form in which he could inspire such awe. Listening intently, he began formulating his own plans.

  Aubur's approach was well known to Sevra from the instant she began guiding him towards Dun'Aldir. Over the last few days she informed her guards, making sure they allowed him to pass through the palace grounds that had been locked down and secured since the turmoil. He zeroed in on the witch-woman as he entered the throne room, feeling the pull she exerted as if she had a rope around him. There was a collective gasp as he approached Sevra, guards subconsciously tightening their grasp on their weapons and servants scurrying to safety. Pausing halfway through the room, he ignored the stares and addressed the one who summoned him.
  The soldier escorting him roughly grabbed him by his shoulder in an attempt to force him to kneel. He brusquely shoved the hand away, his unsettling, jaundiced gaze setting the guard back a step.
  "Is there a reason you dragged me across the entire blasted countryside, woman?" he said while looking directly at Sevra, knowing instinctively it was she who was responsible.
  Her guards quickly converged towards him, but Sevra called them off with a wave of her hand.
  "Come now, that's not a proper way to greet your master," she teased, drawing a frown from him, "but we'll get to that later. After all, tonight you are my guest of honor. Why don't you have something to eat, you must be famished."
  He was starving; if his emaciated look of skin drawn tight over bone wasn't enough of an indication, she could also tell through her connection to him.
  A wide variety of food was brought to him, the servants fighting the urge to shrink away from his smell and appearance as they drew near. Despite his loathing for being forced to march all the way to Dun'Aldir, he accepted the provisions and ate voraciously without hesitation. Disregarding the vegetables, breads, and cheeses, he gorged himself for hours, devouring pounds of meat until his stomach grew distended. The servants looked to Sevra, who signaled to continue feeding him until he had his fill. Aubur's only lament was how overcooked he found the pink slabs of beef.

"Now that you've been sated, tell me your name," Sevra instructed.

Aubur emitted a loud belch and a moan of satisfaction from the meal, and then fell silent as he placed his arms behind his head.

"Look at me, at this ruined, hideous body of mine. There's nothing worse you can do to me than what I've been through. I don't feel like telling you anything, darlin'."

"Tsk tsk," Sevra sounded at his obstinacy, "you have potential to me at the moment, though it is up to you to choose what to do with it. Whether you wish to cooperate or not, I have ways to extract the information I desire."

He looked at her with his yellowed eyes. With the same sickened appearance, smell and rotting skin as the Infected Ones, he obviously had fallen victim to the spell that had gone awry. How was it that he survived?

"Very well," she said, seeing no answer forthcoming.

As she stared back at him, Aubur felt a tingling sensation slowly spreading behind his eyes. Through the spell that granted her influence over him, Sevra could touch his mind in nearly any way she saw fit. She teased him with the promise of pleasure, hinting that she could grant him more or end it on her whim. Like a carrot dangling in front of a packhorse, he only had to tell her what she desired to know and everything he ever wanted could be his. He tried to resist her, but as the seconds elapsed the temptation mounted.

"Everyone, please clear the room," Sevra instructed.

The room emptied in seconds, servants and maids scurrying off, while the small group of Drakvnar she had chosen to replace her fallen Devoted filed out last. Urstaag, remained standing stoic and silent behind the throne; any orders to leave Sevra's vicinity did not apply to him.

She looked on in amusement while her newest specimen vainly attempted to resist her compulsions. If she desired she could have continued on with this method and shortly have the information she wanted. But that wouldn't be thorough; he needed to understand his role in their newfound relationship.

"It works the other way too, you know," she said silkily, cutting off the thread of pleasure she had been feeding to him, "pain can be just as great a motivator as pleasure."

What started as a small prickling turned into sharp twinges of agony, stabbing daggers into Aubur's mind. His teeth clenched and his eyes began to water at the pain mounting inside of his brain. He thought the pressure was going to fracture his skull as he grasped at his head.

"Aubur! My name is Aubur!" he shouted, desperate for the pain to stop.

Cutting off the flow of energy, Sevra bared her teeth at him in a smile.

"There, now we are making progress," she told him with mock sincerity.

She allowed him to catch his breath for a minute, but did not ask any further questions until the silence began to make him uncomfortable. If she asked what she wanted to know at this instant, there was no doubt he would tell her. There was more to this, however, than obtaining information. She needed to break his spirit; sending him on his way after forcing a few answers from him would only cause him to harbor resentment and anger. Like all of the others she had broken before, she needed him to be grateful for every second she wasn't causing him pain, that it was an extension of her kindness he wasn't being tortured at any given moment.

Before Aubur could fully collect himself she forced another jolt of pain into him, bringing him to his knees. He clutched his head as small drops of blood began to form at his nostrils.

"I'll tell you anything! Stop, no more!" he managed to cry out between throbs of agony.

"I know you will dear, but that's not really the point of this, is it?" she told him.

Tomorrow she would find out as much as she could from him, and hopefully come to an understanding of why he was still alive while thousands upon thousands of others affected by the spell were dead. Tonight though, was about breaking him down. After that, if she found use of him perhaps she would let him live. Seeing his pathetic form writhing on the ground, she thought most likely not.

The next morning, Sevra progressed through the bowels of the palace, winding her way through the cellar and to the dungeons beyond. Before proceeding to the second level, she paused at the hastily constructed chamber she had used to rid herself of the council, peering through a gap in the construction. The sight brought a smile to her face; of the council members who weren't completely devoured, they were now plague-touched themselves, vacantly drifting across their cell in search of more fresh flesh. She applauded herself for the delectable way she disposed of them. Silent assassinations might have sufficed, but that left too much potential for loose ends. Taking care of them all at once was efficient, and the results clearly evident before her. Seeing the last looks of terror on their faces had been far more rewarding than leaving the task to someone else.

Stopping in front of the locked room where Aubur was being held, she heard him scurry towards the back wall at her approach. It seemed he was already responding well to the previous night's training, learning a proper fear and respect. Opening the door revealed him cowering in the corner, and upon Sevra entering he pushed himself further against it as if he wished he could disappear into the wall. Last night, she had forbidden him from speaking, forcing pain onto him whenever he tried to answer her questions. At the same time, she punished him for not divulging what she wished to know.

"Please, let me tell you," he begged, hardly waiting for her to cross through the entrance.

Despite the atrocious smell, Sevra calmly entered the room, standing with her arms folded in front of her. Taking her silence as a cue to continue, Aubur hurriedly began to answer the questions she would not allow him to respond to the previous night.

"Walt Whirten did this to me, from Jun'tirh Outpost, er, Big Bear we call it. He's a trickster, uses his devilish magic to get his way all the time."

Sevra had mainly come here with the intention of breaking the man down further, but Aubur earned her full attention.

"Tell me more," she demanded.

Pleased that he was satisfying his new master, Aubur continued to tell her everything he knew about the magician. He told her Walt had come to Big Bear from the south, but he wasn't sure from exactly where. He described what he meant when he said Walt used magic, explaining anything and everything he had seen the wizard do that was beyond the ordinary, from conjuring fire to mind control.

As Sevra received the full story from the despicable specimen before her, her face grew grim. Sensing her mood turning dangerous, Aubur hurriedly talked faster and faster, trying to give the witch every scrap of information he could to please her. It only seemed to increase her fury until she could no longer contain it.

Reaching out she grabbed his head in her hands. Aubur tried to squirm away, but had nowhere to go with the wall behind him. She tightened her grip on him, but also clasped her mind around his. Delving into his thoughts she verified the truthfulness of his words, seeing all of the interactions Aubur had with this Walt Whirten person, hearing every word and imprinting his face and voice into her memory. Aubur screamed soundlessly, pain exploding throughout his body. Kneeling, he wanted nothing more than to curl up into a ball to try and allay the pain, but Sevra holding him in place did not allow it.

Another wizard! She had been so careful eradicating each and every one of those who would stand in her way. The Magicus Celesti, who covertly opposed her for decades, and the disciples they brought into their fold she hunted down and eliminated, sometimes personally.

She bore down on her grasp of Aubur's mind, her anger transforming into a consuming need that could only be sated by squeezing the life from the wretch. One thing saved him at that moment; there was another presence in the room that had his own designs for the despoiled man.

"Sevra!" she heard, a voice filling every corner of her mind.

Her God had returned, after weeks of silence he finally came back. She nearly dropped to her knees in relief.

"With your other pets gone, are you so foolish as to destroy the only being truly under your dominion?"

Immediately Sevra released her grip on Aubur, shocked and overjoyed her God was once again communicating with her. Unmoving, but still breathing, Aubur slumped to the floor unconscious.

"You've come back to me!" Sevra stated aloud, tears forming in her eyes.

"For the moment, but know this. Your pride brought nearly all to ruin. Should you fail to return stability to the land under your undisputed reign, I will seek out someone else who can."

"No! I can, I've already put much in place, the ruling council is eliminated, I…"

"I've been watching, I've seen every action you've taken and know every thought that led you to them. I'll continue watching, do not make another mistake."

Sevra felt the presence exit her mind, leaving her world feeling once again empty. Looking to the form on the floor, she groaned in disgust, wishing she could have killed the loathsome, rotten being. As she turned to leave the room, Aubur began to cough, spitting up blood and struggling to breathe while lying on his back. With her foot she roughly rolled him onto his side, but breathed a sigh of relief herself when his breathing returned to normal.

She had been so careful, working methodically to eliminate any who even had the slightest inkling of an ability to oppose her. How had one slipped through the cracks, and how much did he know?

Completely infuriated by the time she returned to her throne room, she had Urstaag gather her Guard-Captain and First Lieutenant.

"And fetch an artist as well, a good one!" she yelled to him as he was on his way to retrieve the men. If her soldiers were to find Walt Whirten, they'd need to know what he looked like.

She needed to mobilize the True-Blood immediately, there was much work to be done. This rogue wizard had to be captured so she could extract his secrets and dispose of him. Those who could wield magic were too dangerous to be left unaccounted for, and she had been too careful for such an oversight to bring all of her work to ruin. Her route to sole supremacy was nearly clear, but there was still a member of the ruling Luskiran Council missing, the one man who did not make it to the meeting. Now was the time that she should be proclaiming herself Empress, not wasting time with the myriad of obstacles trying to stop her. Already adjusting her designs, maybe she could prove her legitimacy among the people as well as take care of her other problems at the same time.

"We are at your service, Empress," Ramnar announced upon entering the room, saluting and standing at ease.

"Tell me, how many men are at your disposal?" she demanded of him.

Ramnar tallied the numbers in his head quickly, "Roughly nine hundred of the True-Blood, after losing a hundred to the sickness. Additionally, five thousand cavalry and nearly twenty thousand soldiers are at hand."

"I have important orders for you Ramnar, as well as Lieutenant Kempf," Sevra instructed, "you are to leave one hundred of your elite here in Dun'Aldir, along with half our force of soldiers."

Ramnar nearly raised his eyebrow in surprise.

"Take a quarter of the soldiers to Creekview's Crossing and its outlying areas," Sevra continued, "and the last of the men will go southwest, all the way to Dalesford to evaluate the condition of the city and aid the people in any way they can."

"Empress, we were barely able to reclaim our own city, parts of it are still lost to the Infected," Ramnar argued, only risking to offer his opinion if he truly felt it necessary.

"Half of the city's army, ten thousand soldiers plus most of your Drakvnar, are at your disposal to do with as you see fit. That is more than you should need if you delegate appropriately. There are other tasks you must accomplish while you are out as well, and I'm holding you personally responsible for them," she snapped, "listen closely because they are of utmost importance."

Ramnar bowed his head in obedience, awaiting instructions. When they were not forthcoming, he risked a glance to view Sevra looking beyond him, and turned at the sound of footsteps from behind. Urstaag had returned, the crumpled collar of a nervous man in his ample fist.

Not so gently Urstaag tossed his burden onto the floor, paying him no more mind than if he were a sack of grain. The man began to rise up from the floor, but at a glare from the giant remained on his knees.

"Good, the artist has arrived. I hope you are competent at your craft, we'll be spending the afternoon together and for your sake it better not be a waste of my time," she told him.

The man blanched at the prospect, looking like he wished he could sink through the floor and disappear. Sevra appeared to not notice him any further while she continued her instructions to Ramnar and Kempf.

"During your travels, you are to spread the message that Empress Sevra is returning peace and security to the lands. Everyone must know it is through my mercy and guidance that their lives and land will be restored to prosperity. Do you understand?"

Ramnar bowed his head low, acknowledging her instructions. "Secondly, you are to capture, *capture*, mind you, a man by the name of Walt Whirten. He could be anywhere along the Blue Fold Mountain Range, southwards to Dalesford or somewhere inbetween. All of your men, soldiers, anyone under your command shall be on the lookout for him. It is critical he is found and brought to me, he is extremely dangerous to us."

"Lastly, you'll need to assassinate Radford Roltain should he still be alive. He is the last of the Luskiran Council and was not in attendance. It is important you make it look like an accident," she instructed, "he'll likely be in one of the backwoods towns that he caretakes outside of Creekview's Crossing. It should not be difficult to find him."

With his marching orders set, Captain Ramnar saluted once more and left with his First Lieutenant to organize the endeavor.

As they left she looked at the artist, narrowing her eyes. She had forgotten he was there. Such a pity; she now hoped he was competent enough to do the job she had in mind for him, but not so good that he would be missed. With a look to Urstaag, he dipped his head ever so slightly back at her, understanding what would need to be done.

***

Setting his sights to the topmost ridge, Igdahven sought out their interim chieftain to share what he learned the previous night. Jvard was still alive! Garl would be thrilled to hear the information, but he had to be careful how he told the old barbarian. It could be dangerous for the tribe; Garl would likely set out after him without thinking of the consequences to the clans, or what was left of them. After near decimation, now was certainly not the time for the Frostwrynn to be scattered and leaderless. Then again, it would be far more dangerous for him personally if Garl found he had withheld information.

Spotting Garl outside of the Great Hall, Igdahven cleared his throat loudly. Not sure where to begin he announced, "I have good news and bad news."

Garl turned to see Igdahven fidgeting where he stood. Eagerly awaiting the spirit-seeker, he abruptly dismissed the Elders he had been conversing with.

"Did you find the answers you sought in the *Chàlgraäden?*" Garl asked anxiously, having hardly slept the previous night while he waited.

Sighing, Igdahven knew there was no way to tell Garl without him charging a straight line south, "Jvard is still alive, I didn't see him but was able to draw close."

"He's alright then!" Garl exclaimed, a gleam in his eyes and hopefulness in his voice that had been absent for many days, "tell me where he is."

"Peace, Garl," Igdahven begged, trying to slow the hulking barbarian who was already beginning to gather his things, "we need you here. If you leave, the group will look to Dagard, and he is no replacement for either you or Jvard."

Garl slowed down readying his pack, coming to a stop altogether.

"So be it," he growled, a scowl spreading across every inch of his face, "where did you find him then?"

"He is at the Jun'tirh Outpost," Igdahven informed him, "the town appeared mostly empty, but it was surrounded by the Risen. He was safe inside of the walls."

With a touch of nervousness, he added, "I have to tell you Garl, he was with a Fel-born."

Garl's scowl deepened, his face growing as grim as a dark winter's day. Hurriedly, he resumed throwing items into his pack.

"Garl, we need you here, not off running around the southern lands," Igdahven reiterated, "perhaps Jvard has a good reason for being away with the wizard."

"There is never, never, good reason to be with one of the Felborn. You understand? He needs our help," Garl said with finality as he slammed the canvas top of his pack shut.

"You realize what will happen if you leave?" Igdahven shouted back, standing his ground, "That will be it - the end of our tribe that has endured since the time of the Gods."

Garl sat heavily to the ground, deeply conflicted. He rested his face in his large hands, his shoulders slumped under the heavy mantle of leadership. Igdahven breathed a sigh of relief that the big man appeared he was no longer on the verge of doing something irrational when Garl sprang back to his feet.

"If we can't bring Jvard back to the tribe, then we'll be bringin' the tribe to Jvard!" Garl shouted through his grin, nearly knocking Igdahven to his knees with an enthusiastic pat on the shoulders, "start gettin' everyone gathered, we'll take a vote at the *Ingdaärðendvhel* straight away."

Igdahven sputtered, a hundred reasons crossing his mind on why that was a bad idea, but Garl was already off before he could choose which one to present first. He had seen Garl set his mind on many occasions; there would be no stopping him. There would be argument, but it didn't matter. Igdahven knew that by the end of the day the tribe would be vacating the Ridges, heading to Jun'tirh Outpost if Garl had to drag them there.

First Impressions

"I'm telling you," Walt insisted for at least the fifteenth time that day, "the Stricken rely on their noses quite heavily."

"Uh huh," Jvard responded dismissively, still looking over his shoulder constantly.

It had been nearly three days since Walt claimed they lost the mindless ones, but Jvard still wasn't ready to take his word for it. After two days of frantic pursuit upon leaving Big Bear, constantly gaining ground and losing it back whenever they tried to rest the animals, they grew exhausted and worried that their horses would die from exertion. Walt managed to talk Jvard into heading west towards the river, and gradually southeast back towards Creekview's Crossing rather than taking a direct southern route. During the flight Jvard outright refused to ride the horse until he was almost unable to take another step, saying he trusted in his own legs more than some foul beast. Walt imagined if he could read the horses thoughts, it was probably thinking something similarly unflattering about Jvard.

The added travel time irritated the barbarian, but he had to admit it seemed as though they were no longer being chased after crossing the Tinindraüg and cutting through the water for a time. His mistrust of Walt made him constantly question the true motive for the detour, but after many days they finally reconnected to Longpost Road, only a few hours away from their first stop in the long journey south to Dalesford.

"This isn't right, barbarian," Walt said from his wagon over to Jvard, who was still leading the horse rather than riding.

"Which part of this isn't right, *old man*?" Jvard asked, pausing.

Before allowing the wizard to answer he continued, his voice growing louder with each word, "Is it the part about our dead kin rising as cannibals, or the part where we haven't seen a single, solitary traveler out here in four days? Or is it the part where I'm entwined in the schemes of a self-serving, feltouched magician!"

Walt harrumphed loudly, setting his beard into an oscillation.

"The second one!" he retorted, "more people should be out on the road on a typical day like today, this suggests to me we're going to run into the same problems we had back home."

"And don't think your company is like a holiday with the Queen, barbarian," Walt added, "I wasn't going to mention it out of kindness, but until we went traipsing through the river you smelled worse than the horses."

Jvard ignored the insult, pushing ahead until the city was in view. The low-lying region of Creekview's Crossing sprawled out before them. Marked by a web of tributaries, some small brooks, others gushing streams, a series of bridges connected each segment of land. Mouth agape, Jvard couldn't hide his astonishment at its size. The buildings seemed as if they were constructed with no space between, there was hardly any grass or open land to be seen.

"This is nothing," Walt noted at Jvard's gawking, "just wait until we get all the way south."

"It's no way to live," Jvard said, shaking his head, "we keep livestock penned like this. Men need to roam."

"Not everyone lives as you do, barbarian. Most people of the world have no need to venture about. The things they need are brought to them," Walt answered with a chuckle.

"You could fit the whole of my tribe at least ten times over down there," Jvard remarked, "put these people onto the tundra of the Blue Fold Range and most would die in days from the elements. But if you put my people down there they would surely die from complacency."

"Well, I'm sure on our trip through there will be sufficient excitement to keep you from keeling over of boredom," Walt jested, "and besides, remaining in one place can have its advantages. Most people pick up a trade and excel at it in a way your people couldn't dream possible."

Jvard grunted in response.

"No offense intended, of course. Come, we need to get to that middle island there," he added, pointing with his finger, "and unless my eyes deceive me we're going to have a time of it."

Small dots cluttered the streets in the surrounding islets, beings slowly meandering through the city. At their distance it was difficult to discern any distinct features of the people, but the odd, aimless behavior was particularly telling.

At the center of the disjointed islands sat the Inner City, surrounded by water on all four sides and a high wall made of stone. A small palace in the Inner City marked the seat of power at Creekview; if any location in the kingdom of Luskir were still safe, Walt knew that would be the place. The only problem was how to get there.

***

There was no longer any doubt in his mind that he was in full favor of his God, nameless ruler of all, the one true deity. At first he feared for his life, praying as he ran to fend off his feelings of hopelessness, but as time and the miles rolled past those worries gradually faded. Whenever Daro Ildaradi found himself trapped with no way out, a door was opened to him. If endless miles of road threatened to overwhelm him, a passing wagoner offered a ride. Should a river block his path, he found a raft. If he looked closely, what he needed presented itself. His struggle for survival seemed inconsequential to him now; he simply knew he would always prevail. He had run from the Stricken who pursued him at first, but since his awakening he smote them just as readily.

Over two weeks had elapsed since he began his harrowing flight out of the mountains, following the river back to civilization. Having no one to converse with but himself, he discovered many truths. God would listen to a pious man who fully put his faith in Him. Forced to leave his possessions behind, Daro realized the things he thought he needed were no more than unnecessary burdens. Abandoning his belongings left him clean of conscious and spirit.

The magical nature of the affliction was not lost on Daro as he contemplated his fallen town. His most important revelation as he fled was to leave that which could not be understood to Him, and have faith that the mechanisms of the world ran as they should. That was Walt's mistake, dabbling in things that should be left in God's hands. Somehow, that conjurer was behind all of this. Even if it wasn't him directly, people like him were surely to blame. How else could the dead have risen? Not through the natural order of things, that was for certain.

His suspicion of Walt Whirten intensified to a burning hatred towards the man he once called friend. He had seen two flyers with the wizard's face upon entering Creekview's Crossing, both mocking him and reminding him that one day he would see the wizard again, and make him account for the wrongs he suffered upon his own people. Charlatans, magicians, and tricksters – they would have nowhere to hide once Daro spread his enlightened message. He had never felt so clearheaded, how had he once been so foolish as to befriend one such as Walt?

As he sat at the steps of the Inner City palace, a smile found its way across his lips while he viewed those holding onto his every word. Many stood near him, captivated by his presence, curious, or otherwise looking to please him in some way. He rejected all offerings of comfort; when they tried to give food, he would take only a small portion each day, rejecting the rest. When they offered blankets he chided how could he be cold when he had the warmth of His light? The gathering of his newfound followers were not insulted at his rejections, and remained by his side should he find need of something. They watched him, waiting anxiously for him to erupt into his next fervent speech.

But Daro didn't feel much like speaking at the moment, instead he continued admiring the one item of which he would not relieve himself. It was a blade-gauntlet, an entire sleeve of armor extending up his arm into a shoulder plate, and running down to his wrist where it ended in a covered handle which provided him a solid grip. The corpse he procured it from almost seemed as if it were still trying to grasp it. Aware of the sinful nature in coveting a possession, he reminded himself it was not the fine craftsmanship of the weapon he admired. Like a farmer granted the ability to provide for himself and family through his implements, so too did the weapon grant Daro a means to survive and ultimately serve Him.

The blade-gauntlet was an unconventional, mostly impractical weapon in normal circumstances, but in the recent state of the world he found it quite devastating for piercing the skulls of the Infected Ones. On his other hand, he wore a standard gauntlet, providing at least his hand and forearm some measure of protection from the ungodly beings.

Arriving at the Inner City had not been easy, though he never doubted or lost faith. The struggle he overcame seemed to earn him the title of Daro the Bladefist among the citizens. As long as they accepted his doctrine, they could feel free to call him whatever they wished.

Guards patrolled regularly, always eyeing him as they passed by. Their large stature and blackened leather marked them as belonging to the "Empress." Daro paid them little mind, though they were at least equally as fanatical about demonstrating her benevolence as he was about spreading His message.

Each day more arrived at the palace steps, to seek out the preachings of Daro the Bladefist and embark upon their path to salvation. By the end of his first week there, more than half of the thousand survivors within the walls would show up to hear Daro speak, while the guards were instructed to keep their distance.

Atop the palace was a small tower, the highest point within Creekview's Crossing.

"We should have never let him through," Lieutenant Kempf remarked to his watchman as they completed their sweep of the palace grounds, the pair returning to their command post.

From this spot they had a full view of the entire city, which the Empress's elite guard quickly put to use. Thankfully the Inner City, the center most isle, was quiet and contained after being cleansed of the Infected. The same could not be said for the remainder of Creekview.

The Infected dotted the visible roadways, aimlessly wandering, looking to feed. Patrols methodically set about purifying sections of the city, but it was a slow process.

"Captain Ramnar asked we keep a close eye on him," the other guard remarked as they looked over the landscape.

Not interested in discussing the vagabond priest, Kempf ignored the comment and handed over his looking glass, "Hey, over there. Two silver marks says he doesn't make it."

Nearly a mile away, on the next adjacent isle, a refugee fled to the shoreline in a desperate attempt to get back to his boat. At least ten of the Infected were giving chase as he dove into the river, narrowly escaping their grasp. The Inner City was at maximum capacity, no one else had been allowed through the gate. Pockets of survivors, however, were occasionally seen managing to stay alive on the other islands, while a few stayed on boats anchored in the river. Occasionally they had to risk returning to land to scavenge food or supplies.

"Bah, double or nothing for the next one," he said with disappointment, losing the wager.

"That fellow we let in though, that was quite the display at the gate he gave last week," the guard again remarked, returning to the topic he wished to discuss.

"Nothing more than a beggar," Kempf replied derisively, though half-heartedly.

Despite Kempf's blustering, he had to admit it was an impressive feat that earned Daro the moniker of "Bladefist" among the people. The previous week, guards first spotted Daro nearly half a mile away, crossing the bridge to the center island holding the Inner City. That particular area, just outside of the protective walls was especially dangerous because the Infected knew living people were near, yet just out of reach.

Watching the robed figure's approach, he strolled through as unconcerned as if he were browsing a farmer's market in midsummer. More guards came to watch over the wall as he progressed. By the time he reached the gates, nearly the entire Inner City was watching. They all assumed he had crawled out of whatever hiding hole he found in the city and was giving up, until they saw the trail of corpses sprawled out behind him in an endless, scattered line.

His clothing tattered and dirty, he sauntered up the hill towards the gates, almost regal despite his garb. With disinterest he disposed of any of the Infected Ones who ventured his way with a swift thrust through its eye, the blade striking so smoothly it truly seemed an extension of his hand. The noise began to attract more of the Infected, as well as more onlookers from the safety of the Inner City. By the time he reached the gates, the curious newcomer had his back to the wall, a sizeable contingent of walking corpses upon him, his end seemingly apparent. To the surprise of all, except for Daro who had no doubts as to the outcome of the skirmish, he did not fall at the gates.

With a lack of emotion that unnerved the onlookers, he delivered a killing blow that pierced the forehead of the first of the Stricken to approach him. His arm extended, and the blade still embedded in the creature's head, he grabbed another by the throat with his gauntleted arm to hold it at bay momentarily. Withdrawing the blade from the first one, its jaw still working soundlessly as it collapsed, he methodically repeated his attack until both corpses fell at his feet.

In the instant it took to kill the two, many more approached. He struck out again and again, skewering the Infected as they drew near. Still, dozens were upon him, crowding and jostling each other to get at Daro. Instead of retracting his weapon from the last victim, he angled the blade slightly to pull the unmoving creature into him, using it as a shield. The Infected began to press in on him, keeping the corpse on his blade aloft from the pressure. Nearly surrounded from all sides he wrenched his arm down and back, pulling the blade free to strike another, and again used his free hand to hold off his next target. With three corpses squeezing against him, the others were unable to get in close.

The crowd watching thought for certain he had been overrun, but after many long seconds as corpses began to fall it was apparent the lone man held his own, while maintaining his chillingly calm demeanor. Those first few moments were challenging, but Daro never lost faith. It was not his fate, or even logical for him to die just yet. His God had chosen him to deliver His Word, and if he were dead, how could he fulfill his mission?

Falling into a comfortable rhythm, the pile of corpses accumulating before him provided a convenient barrier allowing no more than a few to approach him at a time. With the battle well under his control, to the astonishment of the spectators, including the guards, Daro continued fighting and at the same time addressed those along the wall in what seemed like a practiced oration. After all, he hadn't been delivered to kill, but to enlighten.

"This is the manifestation of your sins," he projected, jabbing out and barely taking notice of the additional corpse added to the heap.

"Your jealousy, sacrilege, and worship of false deities," he continued, driving each word home with a thrust of his sword-gauntlet and the falling of another Infected, "all led to the dark times that are upon us. Each and every one of you bears the shame and burden of responsibility!"

If his words alone were not enough to gain the people's attention, doing so while cutting down foe after foe made up the difference.

Accentuating his point, he turned away from his enemies for a moment, and looked up to address the watchers, "You may believe we are at the end of times, but perhaps you have only been tested. Those who are still standing, are you ready to atone and find salvation? Can you abandon your sinful ways to bring forth a new era of righteousness?"

He shot his plated arm out blindly in mid-sentence, not taking his eyes off the crowd to catch one of the creatures by the throat. Even he wasn't sure how he had done so. Returning his gaze to the fight, he stabbed his sword-gauntlet through the Infected's eye. Deftly he repeated the motion into another pair.

"From the cleansing fire new growth shall rise…"

Out of enemies, he again looked along the wall to address the Inner City, "I am a beacon of light in this great time of darkness, illuminated by the one true God. Mankind is lost, I alone know the way forward."

By the end of his speech there were thirty-four bodies at his feet, Infected that had been cleansed to never rise again. Countless more were along his path from the river leading to the city's center.

"You will grant access now," he stated, awaiting the gates to open.

To Daro, it was not a request, question, or demand; it was the will of God.

The gates remained firmly sealed.

He burned the faces of each of the soldiers into his memory. Daro could forgive them their transgression, they would not be so lucky when they had to answer to Him.

A thought came to the preacher then, a voice from deep within his mind lending him guidance, "I can deliver the conjurer you seek."

Gears creaked over the sound of metal grating against wood, and Daro was allowed to pass through to the Inner City.

***

Questioning his wisdom yet again for placing his trust in the wizard, Jvard walked alone across the first bridge towards the archipelago that comprised Creekview's Crossing. Tall, grey buildings loomed, obscuring the low evening sun. Golden-red rays filtered through small alleyways where it could, giving sections of cobblestone the illusion of being on fire in contrast to the otherwise colorless road.

It occurred to Jvard as he walked the empty streets that there was no pulse to the city. Whether it was a tribal site, village or outpost, or anywhere that people lived, the land took on a life of its own. To see the people suddenly removed was like extricating its spirit.

Jvard played the last conversation he had with Walt over in his mind as he walked, searching for signs of deception. The wizard reasoned that most of the roadways in town were too narrow for the wagon if they needed to escape quickly, and it had to be temporarily left behind. But of course, Walt refused to leave it unguarded.

"Why bother even stopping here then, wizard?" Jvard had protested, "We should keep going south if that is where we will find answers."

"There are a full twenty thousand people who reside in this city, Jvard. Aren't you the least bit curious if any of them are still alive? Or maybe you're content with it being just you and I left alone in this great big world. Is that it?" he paused, his words seeming to have an effect on the big man, so he let them sink in a moment. "The two of us shall keep each other company for the rest of eternity, wandering around trying to not get eaten. Doesn't sound like much of a life to me."

"Fine, I'll go," Jvard grumbled, "but I'm not taking one of those foul horses. And as far as spending an eternity with you, it feels like I already have."

"The big island in the middle, that's where you want to get to," Walt replied, ignoring the surly barbarian, "I'll wait here and watch our things. You find out if anyone is still alive."

Jvard questioned his sanity in following the wizard's directive and walking the seemingly empty streets alone, while Walt so valiantly offered to guard the wagon. He tried to take a mostly straight line across the islet to the bridge that would lead to the next. It was much easier to map his route when he was back on top of the hill with Walt looking down, and the entire city was visible before him. Having no clear view, at times he felt unsure if he was taking the most efficient course. Praying his sense of direction was still as dependable among unfamiliar streets as when he was on the tundra, he pressed ahead.

The distance was deceptively further than he had expected before reaching the bridge to the next section of land. It was a blissfully uneventful walk, but after crossing the bridge his luck ran out upon hearing the shuffling and dragging of feet on pavestone. The small roads and multiple alleyways made it difficult to pinpoint the source of the noise, each time he came to a corner he expected to run headfirst into a pack of the Stricken. He turned down a few streets, thinking he was getting closer to the source of the noise. It began to seem impossible to discern its origin, there were too many pathways too close together to determine where it was coming from. He soon began to worry about venturing off course and losing his way, the maze of unfamiliar streets all beginning to blend together for him. When the solution came to him, he felt foolish for not thinking of it immediately.

Walking to one of the buildings at the end of the street, he noticed a sign hanging over the entranceway, gently swinging back and forth in the breeze. *The Silver Lady*, it read, along with an image of a woman shrouded in silver. At least that's what he thought the sign said. He wasn't the worst among his tribe with letters, but certainly not the best either. Having never seen an inn before, he thought the sign quite odd. Why would someone name a building? Perhaps it belonged to someone who called herself the Silver Lady. *Still, an odd thing to call one's self,* he thought.

He carefully pushed the unlocked door inwards until he was able to slip inside, grimacing at the high pitched creak it caused. With this building taller than most around it, he figured the roof should grant him a view to the next bridge at least, and maybe even allow him to find the source of the noise he heard. He quickly scanned the first floor, it looked to be a communal area with a counter, some tables, and a door towards the rear. A thin layer of dust indicated no people had been through in a while. Spotting a staircase to the right, he quietly proceeded through and headed upstairs.

Only pausing at each floor long enough to look down the hall, he continued upwards until he reached the fifth floor where the staircase came to an end. Maybe a large family lived here, or it was a meeting house of some sort, like the halls back on the Ridges. Dismissing the thought, he continued into the hallway. It didn't matter who had lived here; they were either dead or long gone at this point.

Confused, he looked up at the ceiling. There didn't appear to be an access point for the roof, and he was out of floors. There was a window, but it was of no use to him as it faced the direction he had come from. Having no other option, he forced it open, straining slightly from its apparent lack of use. It was a tight fit to squeeze his torso through, but he managed. Looking up, he thought he might be able to reach the roof by standing on the sill, if he didn't fall and break his neck in the process.

Cursing Walt once more, he repositioned himself and crawled through the open window, hoping he didn't lose his precarious footing while five stories in the air. He reached up, able to grab the edge of the roof with both hands. It was a terrible angle to pull himself up at, with both of his hands flat against the rooftop and nothing to grip them around. Pulling himself up using little more than his fingertips, he managed to hoist his waistline above the roof and quickly swung his legs over. Breathing heavily, he lay down for a moment and thanked the Gods he hadn't fallen.

Now that he was again outside, the scuffling sound returned in the distance. Walking across the flat roof, he saw he had been more or less heading in the general direction of the next bridge and islet, while beyond in the distance rose the walled palace of the Inner City. Pleased with his decision to come onto the roof, he spotted what was causing the noise. Based on what he saw, had he gone two streets further, he was certain he would have gotten himself killed.

The sounds he heard in the street had been deceptive; it wasn't a handful of Stricken close by, it was nearly a hundred further off, breaking the lifeless silence of the city.

"Maëk," he muttered silently, a word belonging to the tribes that roughly translated to 'bear dung'.

No longer able to proceed along a direct route, he had to decide whether or not to turn around and head back to Walt. The sun was rapidly descending in the sky; once darkness fully set this was not the place he wanted to be. While trying to think of any way forward, he looked along every direction and another option presented itself. Down along the nearest waterway there was a canoe tied off to a dock. One of the various rivers should lead him directly to the Inner City, or at least drop him nearby. Carefully he lowered himself from the roof, slipping back into the building through the window and returning to the street.

Moving at a jog, he backtracked for a time across the islet until he was able to veer east through a maze of alleyways towards the river line. Refuse cluttered the pathways, whether the accumulation was a result of the recent problems, or if it had been neglected for many months he could not tell. He grimaced and cursed each time he unavoidably bumped into a pile of garbage, most of the time causing it to crash to the ground with a clatter. With the buildings rising oppressively to either side of him there was barely room to swing his hammer if the need arose; he prayed he remained unseen at least until he was in a more open area.

The houses became increasingly dilapidated the further along he ran, until arriving near his destination by the waterfront. At any other time Jvard may have stopped and considered the drastic, sudden change in the condition of the houses. The city blocks he had previously been through looked to be in disrepair, hastily arranged with little planning, while the small townhouses along the river were designed with obvious care. Stone archways framed the entranceways behind latticed verandas, each house down the street identical to the next overlooking the water. Despite their opulence, Jvard found them unappealing. He had difficulty grasping the southerner concept of wealth, why in the name of Kuldárhik would someone waste their energy on mere decorations?

Movement caught his attention from one of the porches, almost directly across from the small dock where the canoe was landed. He hoped to be in and out of the city quietly, but based on the number of people Walt said lived within Creekview, he knew encountering the Stricken would be inevitable. After his experiences over the previous weeks, he didn't have fear of them individually or in small groups; he did, however, fear the disease they carried, and didn't want to risk them touching him if he could avoid it. Seeing the large crowd from the rooftop, the thought crossed his mind that a small encounter might grow out of hand if the noise attracts more enemies than he could handle.

Appraising his current situation, he tried to determine whether or not he could reach the boat before the Risen lingering about the porches saw him, and if he could row faster than they could swim. If he did have to fight how quickly would the noise attract others towards him?

His deliberation was cut short when a band of the creatures stumbled down from a veranda, leaving his instincts to make the decision for him. Rather than fighting, he sprinted towards the canoe. The Stricken, growling, drooling and groaning, lumbered towards him with surprising speed considering their awkward gait, but Jvard was quicker, his initiative paying off as he dove headlong into the boat.

In his hurry, he did not see the thick rope securing his means of escape to the pier. To undo the knots lashing the boat to the dock would have taken him minutes, and he only had seconds to spare. Without his axe, he berated himself for not at least carrying a knife. At home, he would never have gone off without one; it was impossible to tell when a small cutting blade would come in handy, or even be the difference between life and death. This certainly was one of those times. No less than twenty of the Stricken had arrived at the pier, the wood groaning and creaking under their combined weight. Hopping out of the boat, Jvard improvised and pulled the sledgehammer from his belt, slamming it against the pylon where the vessel was moored. The entire dock shook from the blows, wood cracking and shattering, small splinters bursting outward with each strike.

Each swing of the hammer further separated the dock from the supporting beam, its integrity diminishing. It wasn't his intention to sunder the entire section of the structure, but it began to appear that might happen. Only footsteps away, the smell of rotting death washed over him; he was running out of time. One last hammer fall put a large indent into the pylon, and split the top of it into a jagged edge. The rope, no longer tight around the damaged beam, slipped off easily to free the boat.

It pushed away several feet as he lunged back into it, giving him enough room to gain his bearings and seat himself properly for rowing. Many of the Stricken plunged into the water, but lacked the coordination to swim or even stay afloat. They sunk rapidly, whether to disappear forever or walk along the bottom until they reached the nearest shoreline Jvard did not know; thinking about it he wondered if they were even capable of drowning. Others appeared confused by the water, returning to the road and following the boat along as best as they could from the street.

Jvard allowed himself to breathe easy for the moment, safe if only temporarily. Rowing in the direction of the center isle and the walled Inner City, he took note that the Stricken were following him doggedly along the roadways. He expected nothing less after having been chased by them for two straight days, those weeks ago during his initial flight from the Blue Fold Mountains. His concern grew when he saw the mob had increased in size, more of the Stricken adding to it the further along they went.

"Kiévnar daer maëk," he cursed, his concern growing for the inevitable moment when he had to come to shore.

The only course left to him was to continue onward, heading towards the palace in the distance with the horde of Stricken following, getting larger with every passing moment.

***

"By the spirits, would you look at that?" the newly appointed soldier muttered to the True-Blood on lookout with him.

Squinting, the senior officer grunted, "Go inform Lieutenant Kempf, he should be aware of this."

Over the last few days, in an effort to maintain peace the force from Dun'Aldir recruited a few citizens to help with guard duty. That's how Davil, only a few weeks ago a well-to-do gilder, found himself with a helmet on and a bow in his hands keeping watch from atop the wall.

He didn't begrudge his newfound duties, on the contrary, he was grateful for the effort the soldiers were putting forth to work alongside the residents. With food running low and fights erupting at increased frequency, tension between the citizens and the True-Blood was becoming palpable. If that didn't change, Davil was sure a massacre would ensue.

Many of the guards would have liked to place blame on Daro Ildaradi, the evangelical who arrived in extraordinary fashion and was rabidly gaining followers. Although he preached for peaceful resolutions, if he wished it, he likely could incite a riot beyond the scope of what the limited number of guards could handle. What bothered the Dun'Aldirans the most was the preacher knew he held this power. At some point, he was going to become too dangerous and need to be dealt with.

"What is it?" Kempf roared, arriving at last, fastening the notches of his armor tight around his ample girth.

"It's down there," Davil said gently, removing his helmet briefly and running his hand through the few strands of hair left on his head.

Kempf groaned, peering over the wall while fiddling around for his looking glass, "Just a second."

Directing him towards the disturbance on the next isle over, Davil added, "Something's got the Infected all riled up."

The First Lieutenant chuckled, "We got a fool taking an evening river tour. Look, they're following him along the bank."

The action caused quite a spectacle among the guardsmen along the wall, giving them a reprieve from the tension they felt within the Inner City. What they didn't realize was their increasing callousness was the main source of disharmony around the palace. While most of the residents were worried for the stranger in the boat, the Drakvnar seemed to think of it as sport, wagering whether or not the man in the boat would escape alive.

Their levity sank however, when they realized the rower determinedly was headed towards the center islet, to the Inner City, consequently drawing hundreds of the Infected near the walls.

"Of all the slack-brained..! You know the rules, no more are allowed up here," Kempf bellowed, reminding his guards the city was at capacity.

They waited a time, watching as the solitary figure slowly inched his way along the river towards them.

Feeling things were as well in hand as they could be, Kempf made to retire back to his quarters, "You should be able to handle this, don't bother me again unless the walls gets knocked over. You understand?"

He turned, and stopped short when he came face to face with Daro.

"One of the flock is lost," Daro said, gesturing towards the river, his concerned voice dichotomous to the inciting gleam in his eyes, "are you not the shepherd when the good Captain Ramnar is away?"

Kempf, unsure whether to yell or growl, made a noise somewhere in between.

"Kempf and his men represent the 'Empress' who claims to lead us out of this darkness we find ourselves in," Daro sermonized, and seeing an opportunity to further drive a wedge between the people and the True-Blood he grabbed ahold of it, "one can be judged upon how they treat those by whom they have nothing to gain. Let us all bear witness to the mercy and sympathy of the grand Empress."

Kempf, not liking Daro from nearly the first moment he saw him, reared back and struck him on the jaw with a closed fist. The blow knocked Daro off balance, but he kept his footing. In return Daro did not fight back, or even appear unnerved, but he did smile at the Lieutenant. Nearly the entire city watched, and most seemed to be on Daro's side. Kempf realized then he had been baited, and the error in his judgment could very well cause an uprising. Just as quickly as the crowd prepared for violence, they stopped at an upraised hand from Daro. It was at that moment the guards understood the amount of control the preacher had garnered over the Inner City. Authority slipped through Kempf's clenched fists before their very eyes, landing firmly in Daro's pious hands.

"It is to God we owe our salvation, not your Empress," Daro whispered to Kempf, leaning in closely only for him to hear.

Kempf wished nothing more than to kill Daro then and there, until he looked about, not thrilled by the prospect of the five or six hundred men on Daro's side rioting against his force. The Lieutenant was no longer as sure of himself and the implied control the Drakvnar held over the Inner City.

Daro diffused the situation he caused, for the moment at least, by gesturing towards the man in the rowboat, "You have a guest approaching, Kempf. Let us see the hospitality we've grown accustomed to."

With the lone boatman in earshot, Kempf addressed him, and with all eyes upon him made an attempt to be less crass than usual, "Traveler, we can't have you... regrettably can't let you through to the Inner City. You'll need to continue east, to the island we've secured."

Jvard frowned as he looked to the guard who addressed him, and then over to the shoreline where hundreds of the Stricken had gathered, blocking the path to the gate. He wasn't sure how he would get in even if he wanted to.

"I am not looking for sanctuary," he answered, "I only seek information. Seeing other people alive, that in itself is good news. I'd only like to speak with you for a time, is there another way up?"

"There is, but rules are rules. You have no need to visit here. If you are looking to stay, continue eastward to the island, otherwise continue on your way wherever you were off to. May the Empress watch over you."

Jvard furrowed his brow in annoyance at the dismissive attitude, and when did the lands of the south proclaim an Empress? Admittedly he was poorly versed in southern politics, but the extent of his knowledge had always been that these lands were ruled independently by region. Surely Walt would have mentioned an Empress in the weeks they had spent together.

Raising his voice, with no attempt to mask his anger he asked, "Well is it too much to ask for the answers to a few simple questions, at least tell me who is in charge here? Or do you have some rules against that as well?"

Kempf stopped himself short of reacting in one of his typical outbursts. The unrest still felt like it could escalate into upheaval at any time, like a dry patch of grass waiting for the smallest spark to set it ablaze. The tension did not go unnoticed by Jvard.

"I'll answer your one question, I'm in charge," Kempf shouted, puffing out his chest with a swell of self-important pride, "now be gone, my throat is getting hoarse from this shouting. I'm sure any other questions can get answered at the lake island."

Thinking the discussion at an end, and that he handled the events with great tact, Kempf turned to leave. Of course everyone in the city had to lose their minds on his night off-duty. A good number of people were going to be flogged tomorrow for disrupting him, that much was for certain. He needed to remind everyone exactly who was in control of the Inner City.

As he was leaving, a shout rang clear over the murmuring crowd, "That dungpile Kempf isn't in charge, Daro Ildaradi is!"

Kempf's face grew red with anger, but his outrage was overshadowed by the bedlam that followed between the Dun'Aldirans and sympathizers of Daro the Bladefist. The two sides rushed towards each other, many with no choice but to move with the flow of the mob, caught like flotsam in a crashing wave.

The fighting abruptly came to a stop not much sooner than it began, the emotions that had been running high brought to a dead halt when a guard and two other men inadvertently fell from the wall. Jvard, able to see most of the turmoil, watched the entire display unfold from the safety of his canoe. He hoped the men who fell from the wall died on impact as the mob of the Stricken flew to them like crows to carrion.

Jvard had seen enough. He began rowing away, but wanted to make one more stop before darkness fell and he returned to Walt. As a leader himself, Jvard had a clear understanding of what was transpiring, at least in this particular city. The disorder of the last few weeks left this place without a clear, firm rule.

Whoever the 'Empress' was seemed to be trying to step in to fill the void, and poorly if she thought to do so by delegating to the handful of delinquents he saw on the wall. Kempf was a self-serving man to his core, someone who would be followed by force, not choice. This Daro person, on the other hand, had seemed to earn a fair amount of respect and it was causing contention. Walt would be happy to hear that there were other survivors, but Jvard thought it best to suggest they leave as soon as possible to continue on their quest.

"The spirits take you what took so long!" Walt rebuked as Jvard suddenly emerged from the darkness near the wagon.

Evening had come and gone, and it was well into the middle of the night by the time Jvard returned. The scant moonlight gave some visibility, but it was difficult for Walt to determine who was approaching until they were upon him. Two bodies lay on the ground near Walt's makeshift camp, while the old man leaned back against the wagon, puffing away on his pipe. Jvard didn't see the corpses until he nearly stepped on one.

"What happened here?" he asked, bending down to inspect the body.

"There's another one over that way," Walt answered offhandedly, "on the other side of the road."

"They were diseased?" Jvard asked.

"I should hope so, unless they were just two people with a late night hankering for a bony old wizard," Walt joked, and upon seeing Jvard's concerned expression he added, "oh I'm fine. I'm not completely defenseless after all."

Jvard shrugged, wizards did have their way he supposed.

"I meant to return sooner, but I had to visit a second location after the Inner City," Jvard began to explain before Walt had the chance to ask.

Seeing he had Walt's full attention, he continued, "Other people have survived, there are many hundreds at the palace, and hundreds more yet on the small island on the lake, east of the city. That's where I stopped after speaking to the guards."

"The city guard was able to protect Creekview to some extent then, that is good," Walt commented.

Jvard began to shake his head, "Something was odd about the guard, the people did not seem to accept them wholeheartedly. Tell me, I am not familiar with the ways of the south, does the Empress rule all the land between the Blue Fold Mountains and the southern deserts?"

"Empress?" Walt asked, genuinely surprised, "where did you hear such a thing?"

"The guards, they were dressed in black armor and spoke of an Empress. They didn't tell me much at the Inner City," Jvard said, relaying the conversation he had with Lieutenant Kempf, and his denial into the city, "but they did mention an island was secured to the east and I was welcome to go there. At each location the guards in black armor seemed to be in control, and spoke of an Empress."

Walt was not one to believe in random coincidence, and it took him only seconds to begin drawing conclusions he hoped were not correct. The order he abandoned many years ago spoke of the end of the world as they knew it, and a mad woman, Sevra, who sought to reign over the new land. He thought they had lost their senses, yet here they were. To Walt, the dead returning to attack the living could very well be constituted as the 'end of the world'. Now there were whisperings of an Empress. Walt's heart began to sink as his monumental mistake began to dawn on him.

"Wizard, are you alright?" Jvard questioned, snapping his fingers in front of his face when Walt appeared to have stopped listening, "as I was saying, I wouldn't keep my enemies on that island. People are walking in their own filth, and criminals are preying on the weak with impunity. A guard I spoke to told me of a barge project that would alleviate the overcrowding, but it's the guards themselves I do not trust. We should leave, there is only trouble brewing here and nothing to gain."

"Did they give a name, for the Empress?" Walt asked, feeling ill.

"I did not hear one," Jvard answered, "though they seem to favor someone else here. The Inner City, it nearly erupted in battle for a man named Daro Ildaradi, some seem to think him as their leader."

Walt picked his head up and furrowed his prodigious brow, certain that he could not have heard the barbarian correctly.

"You said Daro Ildaradi?" Walt asked, confirming he wasn't mistaken, "tell me did you see him?"

"No, I told you they did not allow me into the Inner City," Jvard answered, "again this place is beyond dangerous and we should leave, the Stricken roam the streets and the people themselves are ready to commit war amongst each other…"

Walt stopped Jvard's protestations, insisting that they attempt to visit the Inner City, "Daro was one of the few people from Big Bear that I could call friend. I thought everyone from my town was dead, if he survived and made it here maybe others did as well."

Jvard was unsure of the wisdom in lingering at Creekview's Crossing, he had one single purpose left to him – revenge for his tribe. Any move that didn't contribute towards that goal did not matter to him.

"We have to make a quick visit and find out, he'll speak to me," Walt continued despite Jvard's attempt to voice his concerns, "it won't take long. Then we'll continue on, maybe Daro will even come with us."

"You've told me much, Jvard," Walt added, seeing the barbarian was not convinced, "this will be a short detour, and once I have a name for the Empress I might know from whom you seek redemption."

Jvard put his disagreements aside. He had sympathy for Walt wanting to see if this was the same person from his town. Had the situation been reversed, Jvard would not be swayed from seeing the members of his tribe. By itself, that wasn't enough to convince Jvard into staying here any longer than necessary, but he could tolerate remaining for a time if it meant finding who was responsible for the demise of his people.

Midao

Pushing the horse to its limits, Myrna and Devin quickly covered nearly a mile, gaining distance from their pursuers. A thick lather of sweat accumulated on Honey from the exertion, her chest rising and falling rapidly as she drew air into her lungs. Slowing the horse to a stop, Myrna jumped off and instructed Devin to do the same.

"C'mon!" she said, pulling Honey along and pushing Devin into a jog.

"Why'd we get off?" Devin yelled, frantically looking over his shoulder, "we gotta keep going!"

"The horse needs to rest, she can't go all out for long with both of us on her. We'll get back on when we can't run any further," she said.

Myrna wasn't too sure the full extent of how far the Greymen would pursue, however, she did remember their first night out of Shady Vale and that they were followed to the farm the next day. She didn't want to risk stopping until they reached the next village. They ran for nearly three miles through the woods before Devin had to stop, a stitch in his side bringing him to a walk.

"Back on the horse, quickly now," Myrna instructed.

She looked back as she helped hoist Devin up, not able to see anyone following. The thick foliage and mildly curving road limited her vision, leaving her with the feeling that at any moment they would be set upon. In many places it felt as though they were running down a tunnel, the branches from either side of the road extended out towards each other to nearly touch while the full bloom of the trees filled in any gaps.

Hopping back on the horse in front of Devin she led it at a fast trot, perhaps only slightly faster than they had been jogging. While the horse seemed to be rested and moving comfortably, the same could not be said for Devin and Myrna. Each of Honey's strides set them bouncing, and though it was less strenuous than being on foot they had to constantly use their leg muscles to avoid slamming down in the saddle. Coupled with the exertion from running, they were gradually wearing down.

Many miles went by as they eventually fell into a rhythm. Honey could maintain the pace they were at for hours yet, and even though their discomfort grew, so could Myrna and Devin if they had no other choice.

The weather had not yet relented, a near two full days of rain leaving the ground muddy and saturated. Up ahead, a large pool of water had formed in the road, extending all the way up around the next bend and out of their view. Myrna promptly pulled to a stop; riding over the slick ground had been risky enough, to put the horse through that much standing water could easily result in a broken leg.

"Keep moving," Myrna insisted, though Devin didn't appear to need the prompt as he hurried ahead.

"Do you think they're still coming?" he asked.

"It'd be safer to say so, unless you wanted to stop and find out?" she stated crossly while breathing heavily.

With only a moment's hesitation they proceeded through the dark, dirty water. Though it wasn't deep, it was unsettling to not be able to see what might be in it or where the ground actually was. Honey even snorted with displeasure as they coaxed her along, unsure at first where to place her feet. A few times they lost their footing, nearly rolling an ankle or stumbling over an uneven patch of ground they could not see.

Myrna was glad she decided to dismount. Riding through at anything faster than a walk would have been disastrous, even though having to slow their pace troubled her greatly. As they wound around the bend, both Devin and Myrna groaned when they saw the entire path ahead was similarly flooded as far as they could see. They ran through as quickly as they could, but the unsure footing was an unwelcome impediment.

Every time they reached the next curve in the road, whether their visibility was limited to a hundred feet or five hundred, the entire path was pooled over from the heavy rain. Their anxiety grew as the minutes elapsed and they slowly moved along the road, Myrna insisting they not ride again until they get out of the water. After almost an hour of traipsing through the muck, Myrna was constantly looking over her shoulder and expecting to see the Greymen in pursuit. A flicker of motion caught her eye as she looked back, though with the rain, distance, and trees obstructing her view it was difficult to determine what it was or if she imagined it. Biting back a curse she abandoned caution and hurried forward, not interested in slowing to get a better look.

"Run faster, Devin," was all she said, her fear speaking volumes.

She ran alongside him, placing her hand at his back to urge him along. Despite their fatigue they hurried through the standing water, hoping the ground didn't take any unexpected dips.

"Are they close?" Devin gasped out between breaths.

"I think so," Myrna replied, equally winded.

"I can't keep going," Devin answered, slowing down and breathing heavily.

Myrna stopped, she would have tried to force him along but she herself was exhausted. They had already run for several miles, she didn't have many more in her.

"Alright, up," she said, giving Devin a hand climbing into the saddle, "we'll have to risk it. These woods aren't that deep, we should be out soon."

Devin was grateful for the break from running, the riding wasn't so bad either as Myrna daren't take the horse much faster than a walk.

"I need you to keep checking behind us. Count to five, every five seconds turn and look," she instructed Devin as she guided Honey, "let me know if you see them coming."

Dutifully Devin counted, every time he reached five twisting in the saddle to peer behind. After a while he tried to make a game of it, counting how many times he had turned in order to stay focused. Somewhere around four hundred he lost track, his mind starting to wander. He had looked so many times he almost expected to see nothing on each check. When he did finally turn around and saw movement through the trees it jolted him back to attention.

"Finally, I think the road is clearing up ahead," Myrna commented. Devin hardly heard her, intent on the trail behind them. Again he thought he saw some rustling through the trees, but couldn't tell for certain.

"Oh, good," he answered absently after a moment, "I thought I saw something but it was probably just a deer…"

His words trailed off into a terrified moan when a band of Greymen came crashing through the trees only twenty yards from their side. They did not give thought to the trail, overgrowth, rain or flooded path. While the road winded and curved, the Greymen pursued in a straight line, disregarding any obstacles. Many were cut or scratched from trailblazing through the woods, and one even dragged its leg behind it, bent at a disturbing angle below the knee. If their injuries caused them any pain or discomfort, it did not show.

Devin yelled, Honey let out a neigh that sounded close to a scream, and Myrna spurred the horse forward, praying that it wouldn't twist a leg in the next few hundred yards until the road became more passable. Water and mud kicked up from the horse's flight, until they came to a gradual incline and left the flooded area behind. Myrna distanced themselves for an additional minute or two before slowing Honey down to a more moderate pace.

"I think we'll be in the clear now," she said, breathing a sigh of relief, "Honey can go for a while yet if we take her easy, and they shouldn't be able to catch up. We'll be in town before then."

Relaxing muscles he didn't even notice he was clenching, Devin exhaled heavily. He was utterly exhausted, and thankful that the worst of this ordeal was over. Eventually they exited the woods, the rain slowing to a drizzle. Many trees were cut down at the edge of the forest, stumps dotting the fields before them. Myrna wondered if the villagers of Midao recently chopped them down to gain some visibility of what might be coming their way.

Looking back again over the field of tree stumps, Devin saw the Greymen were still giving chase nearly a half-mile away. In front of them, the blackened remains of a large fire could be seen in the center of Midao. It must have been enormous, to see it so clearly from this far away. Myrna didn't think about why they had lit such a large fire, she was just glad to see carts moving in and out from the north and other signs that the town was active and alive.

***

Replaying the previous night over in his head as he methodically worked, Baerne wondered if there was something he could have done differently. It did him no good to linger on what was, but he gave up trying to stop thinking about it, allowing his mind to wander off through various scenarios of what might have been.

He found the steady fall of his hammer on the smoldering ingot soothing; it was straightforward work, and it made sense to him. His thoughts drifted as he brought his arm down, the dull ring of the strikes carrying across the village like a mournful knell. He imagined that he stayed by his master's side longer fighting the creatures off, or at other times the two of them retreated together back to the family and brought them to safety.

Inevitably his thoughts wandered back to the reality he wasn't able to prevent, returning to find three of his brothers dead and his mother and remaining siblings cornered. He blamed himself for hesitating, if he had only made a decision Master Aberfeld might still be alive, or he could have gotten back to his family in time and saved them.

He had never hit something so hard, so many times without it dying. The thought of the excessive violence caused bile to rise in his throat, concentrating on the work helped alleviate the sickening feeling at the pit of his stomach. Pounding the steel flat, that's all that mattered. How long had he been at it, ten or twelve hours, it didn't matter so much as long as it gave him a task in which he could lose himself.

No more than the son of a poor farmhand, abandoned at a young age Master Aberfeld had taken him in and cared for him as his own. The master's children were not of Baerne's blood, but he viewed them as such. He stopped his incessant pounding at the thought, grief overwhelming him anew. The worst part of the ordeal was losing the man he called father after thinking he had survived the attack.

"I'm all right," Master Aberforth had said later in the night as they mourned the loss of the three youngest, "It's only a bite on the shoulder."

Baerne continued to hammer away at the metal, slowly drawing it while reliving the remainder of the previous night. That evening, already a living nightmare, somehow managed to worsen as it progressed. The village was just beginning to comprehend their losses when those blasted guards gathered them up; the villagers, his friends and family, trusting of the soldiers, obliged.

"Did the Infected touch any of you, bites or scratches?" they demanded to know.

Before long, they had ten men and women lined up and separated from the other villagers, the townsfolk unsure of what was happening.

"Everyone return to your homes, except for this group," one of the guard commanded, a decorative helmet marking him as the captain.

A few argued but most cooperated. Anyone with a family member singled out stayed behind, insisting they be told what was happening, Baerne among them. More guards in black armor swarmed in, pushing them back in an attempt to maintain some semblance of order. Unseen by all were the additional guards along the rooftops, bows trained on those segregated out from the rest. The captain raised his arm, bringing it down to his side in a sudden motion. There was an audible twang of a dozen or more bolts firing, followed by the thud of impact and bodies falling to the ground.

Screams came from every direction, one arrow straying to nick the mayor in the shoulder and incite more violence between the guards and some of the villagers. Master Aberfeld was among the fallen, an arrow straight through the center of his head, eyes open and staring into nothingness. Baerne struck with his fists at anyone in the way between him and his foster father, unbelieving of what had transpired. He vaguely sensed the guards grabbing at him as they converged, but it did not stop him from moving forward.

With a mostly average build, if slightly muscular from his work, he wasn't as tall or wide as the imposing soldiers. Blows rained down on him, jolting him back and forth, but he continued to fight back. His only thought was that he had to reach Master Aberforth.

Not knowing the other villagers were already subdued, it didn't occur to Baerne that he was the only man still fighting. Despite his best efforts, he was pinned to the ground as five separate guards reached him, one restraining each arm and leg, and another at his waist. He lay on the ground with his mouth in the dirt and a knee in his back, four of the men in black armor sprawled unconscious around him.

The Captain's voice rose above the commotion, explaining with as little emotion as if he were telling why a sword needed to be oiled, "Anyone injured by the Infected must be put down immediately. On order of Empress Sevra, for their own sake, and for the good of all it must be done. The disease is contagious, it is the only option."

That was the worst memory of the evening, being held powerless while they justified their massacre.

The sound of the hammer smiting steel continued to ring throughout the workshop. He vowed to never be caught unprepared again; this was his town, his home and his people.

A sword would do. Continuing to pound the steel flat, he decided that's what he would make.

***

Not wasting any time, Myrna guided Honey towards the village in hopes of sanctuary. As they approached, many of her worries were immediately alleviated upon hearing the typical bustling of a town that was still alive. There was no wall around the village, but a small blockade consisting of wagons and loose scraps of wood hastily piled across the main road leading in.

"Halt!" a guard cried out as they neared.

Upon hearing the voice, three men with bows trained on them peaked up from above the barricade.

"Please, help us," Myrna responded, "We've been running for weeks, we're on our way to Creekview's Crossing…"

"Look alive they've got Infected trailing them," one of the guards interrupted.

"Get a few more men up here now!" another yelled out.

"Come around to the house over there, we'll let you through," the first guard hurriedly instructed Myrna and Devin, pointing at a house adjoining the makeshift blockade.

They ran over to the house and momentarily heard scraping on the floor from inside, followed by metal grating against wood. A gargantuan man, dressed fully in the black leather they had seen on a few occasions over the last few days opened the door. The only difference was this person wore a meticulously sculpted, horned helmet that made him seem even taller.

"Get in, be quick," was all he said as he ushered them through, horse and all.

In a hurry he closed it, swung the latch shut and began shoving the furniture back into place to block the door.

"Follow me," he stated, removing his helmet while he walked through the opposite door leading into the town.

On the other side, he signaled to another guard, instructing him to take the horse.

"She'll be at the stable for you in the morning," he said, as Devin reluctantly handed the reins over.

Following the man brought them behind the barricade into the village proper. Myrna and Devin were able to see the entire town was similarly cordoned off, all of the houses along the perimeter connected with improvised barricades. It looked like they used anything they could get their hands on; tables, furniture, wagons, scrap wood and downed trees all were gathered to fill in any gaps.

Men were scattered about standing watch along the barrier, while more of the huge guards in black armor were interspersed among them. The soldiers clearly looked to be in charge, and Myrna noted anger, uncertainty, and a hint of jealousy among the town watchmen as clearly as if it were rolling from them in waves. On one hand they looked as if they wanted the foreign guards to leave their town, but there was something else there too. A sharp salute, or quickened step to follow an instruction showed a small part of them wanted to earn their superior's approval. In addition to the soldiers, groups of villagers sat off by themselves, looking ragged, lost and disheveled. Overall, the town exuded an aura of fear that told Myrna the soldiers were not entirely welcome.

The most prominent sight as they were escorted across the street was the charred remnants of a pyre at the center of the town square, still bearing a few burnt corpses.

"Where in hellfire did you come from?" the guard demanded, breaking Myrna and Devin away from the perturbing image.

"From the farmlands, to the south," she told him, only looking to him briefly before her eyes returning to the macabre, charred heap.

He grunted absently, appearing to be lost in thought for a moment, "You're lucky to have made it so far north then, it's grown dangerous on the roads. We haven't had any new arrivals in a few days now."

Their conversation was interrupted by the twang of bows from the barricade behind them, followed by a few cheers and compliments for well-placed shots.

"We saw a few men, dressed like you in Byrn and on the road, are you of the same group?" Myrna asked.

"Several battalions were dispatched under orders of the Empress, may the Gods watch over her, to help restore order," he responded, "we are ushering this group north to the Crossing, along with the lumber. You can accompany them if you wish."

Myrna noticed a slight accent to the man's words. He placed extra emphasis on the hard consonants, as if he were attacking the words as he spoke them.

A few of the soldiers withdrew from the barricade, coming over to inspect the newcomers as their escort walked away, apparently no longer interested in her or Devin. Myrna frowned at the dismissal, hoping for further explanation from the guard. Who in the spirits was the Empress?

"Wait!" she called out.

The man turned, with an obvious look of displeasure.

"Um, just one more question," she said, lightening up her tone at his reaction, "is it bad everywhere, I mean…"

"Were the Greymen here too?" Devin interjected, unable to contain himself any longer.

"Greymen?" the guard asked, emphasizing the word with a derisive chuckle, "I'm afraid what's been through here was worse than a children's tale. But if you mean the mindless savages that'll tear the flesh from your bones without a second thought, then yes the damn things have sprung up everywhere. Now if you'll excuse me, I am a busy man, and there is much more aid to be delivered in the name of Empress Sevra."

Nearby, one of the recently displaced sprang to his feet and began shouting, "Aid? So this is what your Empress calls aid? You're nothing but a bunch of murderers!"

"You've already been warned; we've heard enough from you!" the guard shot back, signaling to the other watchmen and waving them in.

They surrounded the man, dragging him off as more onlookers began to gather and murmur.

Fragments of his shouts could be heard as they forcefully escorted him down the street, Myrna distinctly heard the words, "They were still alive!" and "murdering bastards!"

The tension in the gathered onlookers was palpable. The guards watched the crowd, waiting to spring into action, and the crowd looked for the smallest excuse to break into a riot. Like a pot that was ready to boil over, the anger and fear of the group was close to erupting in violence. Apparently, the man being dragged away wasn't the only one who was upset with whatever had transpired here. Myrna wanted nothing more than for her and Devin to be away, this was none of their affair. Maybe if she grabbed the boy, and made a break for it through the ring of people...

A crying infant disturbed the volatile silence, breaking the entrancement. The bloodlust of the group faded as quickly as it had developed, and they disbanded with only minor grumbling. Myrna let out the breath she had been holding, and began to wonder what they just walked into the middle of.

"It could be worse," Devin said.

Myrna looked at the boy, and slowly nodded, "That's true I suppose," she agreed, looking back towards the woods they came from, "let's find somewhere to turn in for the night."

Every house in the village was occupied, most filled with more people than usual in a town that was already bursting at the seams. Many refugees out on the street settled down wherever they could find a dry scrap of ground. As the crowd dispersed, Myrna and Devin were left standing near the center of the town, unsure of where to go.

The village itself was not very large, in a few minutes they had walked its entire area. Myrna began to grow frustrated on their second pass through while she looked without success for somewhere they could sleep for the evening. Because of the recent rain, the streets were nothing more than a pool of mud. It looked as though staying in a house would be out of the question, but she hoped at least to find somewhere clean and dry.

Given the circumstances and current atmosphere, she was beginning to worry about wandering around and drawing attention to themselves. They simply wanted to find somewhere to sleep, and then head north in the morning.

Nearly ready to give up and lie down where she stood, a woman waved out to her from a porch across the street. Myrna had noticed the house on their first pass through the town; it was hard to miss.

More of a small mansion, wide and long with two stories, it was much bigger than any other dwelling in the town. The porch fully wrapped around its perimeter, with small columns evenly spaced. Furniture scattered across it suggested the owners were used to entertaining. Somehow the house was a model of elegance without looking out of place in the small village.

The lady in a fine yellow, frilled dress greeted them as they approached, "Hi there, you two must be the newcomers," she stated, greeting the pair.

"That's right," Myrna answered cautiously.

"No need to be alarmed," the woman said with a disarming smile, "my husband makes it his business, even with things as they are now, to know the comings and goings of everyone in his town. Please come in, we don't have as much as is customary to offer, but we still want to show new guests some measure of hospitality."

Devin looked to Myrna and shrugged, "Thank you," she replied, placing her hands on the boy's shoulders and walking to the porch.

"I'm Sarah," she said, extending out her hand to both Myrna and Devin.

After exchanging pleasantries they followed her inside, the interior of the house as impressive as the outside. There was a fireplace in the living room, expensive furniture, and various works of art adorning the walls. No fewer than thirty people must have been inside, some sitting and chatting, others standing and engaged in ardent discussion with one another. They quickly looked to the newcomers, but went back to what they were doing as if unexpected guests were nothing out of the ordinary.

"Let me introduce you to my husband, the mayor," Sarah said as she guided them through the house.

Through the dining room and kitchen, and beyond the second living room which was also full of people, was a small study where a man sat busily penning a letter. A large bay window was behind his desk, looking to the fields outside of town. There was another fireplace in this room off to the side, with an ornate-handled rapier mounted above the mantle. They stood there for several long seconds as he wrote, either unnoticed or unacknowledged. Myrna and Devin began to grow uncomfortable in the silence, when he finally looked up and smiled to address them.

"Welcome to my home," he said, setting the letter aside and tucking his pen away.

If Myrna had to define the man in one word, it would have been distinguished. With short cropped, jet black hair that had hints of grey creeping in and a neatly trimmed goatee, along with finely pressed, expensive clothing, regarding the man's appearance there wasn't a single thing out of place. His angular cheekbones and hawk-like nose added to the air of nobility he put forth. After hearing the man speak only a few brief words, Myrna had the impression this was a person accustomed to wealth and authority. She also noticed the corners of a bandage peeking out from under the collar of his shirt, and the way he held his left arm slightly high across his body indicated he might be favoring an injured shoulder.

"It's been a few days since we've had any new guests, I hope you haven't suffered too many hardships along your way. Unfortunately, hardship seems to be all too common of late," he said.

"We lost our entire village, Devin and I," Myrna answered, lightly touching Devin on the arm, "we've been travelling for weeks, and had a few close calls."

He nodded slowly, seeming to fully understand their turmoil without need of further explanation.

"Well you've made it this far, and are still alive. That is something for which to be grateful," he told Myrna, adding a brighter tone to his voice.

"Allow me to introduce myself, I am Radford Roltain. What brings you so far away from home, if I may ask, miss?" inquiring for her name.

"Vitano," she told him, "but please call me Myrna, and this is Devin. After everything happened I thought our best option would be to go to Creekview's Crossing. I lived there many years ago and have hope a larger town might be safer than living in the middle of nowhere."

He offered her a weak smile, with strain evident in his eyes as if he had something unpleasant to say but wasn't sure how to deliver it.

"Did you have family there, dear?" he asked, sorrow evident in the way he spoke.

"Yes, well, I did. Not since my parents passed though," she answered.

"Well that is fortunate, I was afraid you might be... expecting to reunite with people," he said, looking for the right words, "I have to tell you, Creekview was badly overrun and much of it is still unsecured."

He continued at their surprised expressions, "You see, there were about twenty thousand people living there when the plague, sickness, whatever you wish to call it, struck a few weeks ago. Only about a thousand have survived."

Myrna blanched, while Devin thought he was going to be sick. He still hadn't quite gotten passed his idea that he was responsible for the Greymen.

"But we're heading up there tomorrow with the guards, I don't understand…" Myrna began to ask, shaking her head.

"Those guards," Radford said derisively, "well they are effective, that can be said for them. Nearly three hundred of them showed up over a week ago at Creekview, along with too many soldiers to count, and they helped secure the Inner City. They've slowly been clearing out the outlaying islands, but it's still a mess. There are pockets of survivors throughout the city, but how long they'll last on their own, who can say?"

"Where did the guards come from?" Devin asked, mildly fascinated by them, "I've never seen anyone like them really."

"If you ask me, I'd steer clear of them," Radford responded quietly, leaning forward, "they are fully devoted to a dangerous, scheming woman, the so-called Empress Sevra. From what I've gathered, they're under orders to regain stability in the major cities. While it sounds good, we had an incident here three days ago that's put everyone on edge."

"You've probably noticed how tense it was in the street," Sarah chimed in.

Radford shook his head, continuing, "Three nights ago we had a problem here, some of the Infected, probably stragglers from Creekview wandered down and attacked. We lost a few people."

"I'm sorry to hear that," Myrna offered, "I'm sure that would put everyone on edge."

"It wasn't just the attack that upset the town, it was what happened immediately afterwards," Radford continued, growing visibly agitated, "the guards executed many of our citizens."

Myrna was shocked, she had hoped the guards were providing protection, and could be trusted. Upon entering town, for the first time in weeks she had felt secure. After hearing Radford's words, the feeling didn't even last an entire evening, and a sense of dread crept through her that she would be accompanying them north in the morning.

"Their leader, Captain Ramnar claims that a bite from one of the Infected will spread the sickness," Radford explained disdainfully, "he has a well-deserved reputation for brutality. You may have seen him, he was manning the line as you entered town. The soldiers call him the 'left hand' of the empress. He was only a young officer nearly fifteen years ago during the time of troubles in Dun'Aldir where he earned that reputation. He's running the Inner City at

Creekview now since it's been secured. Lately he's been spending his time between here and there, monitoring the barge project."

Radford stood and looked out of his window for a moment, appearing to be deep in thought. A flash of anger tightened the corners of his eyes, but disappeared as quickly as Myrna noticed it. He reached up and gingerly touched his shoulder, before drawing his hand back down as if just remembering there were people still in the room with him.

"We've heard a similar story across the farms, about the bites," Myrna offered, breaking the silence.

The Mayor nodded his head, as if her input added some validation to the claims. He had little trust for the guards, and didn't know if he could believe their words.

"Ah well, I've kept you far too long already," Radford said as he rubbed his fingers over his temples, "if you like, you can set up on our porch for tonight. It's not much, but it will at least keep you out of the mud."

"Sorry just one more question," Myrna asked before being dismissed, "what is this barge project you mentioned?"

"Right I suppose you should know what you're getting into up at the Crossing. As I've said, the Inner City is secured, its high walls and surrounding waterways make it an ideal location to set up a defense. But it can only hold so many people. The 'Empress' has ordered the steward to provide safe lodging, and building the barge is the plan they came up with. I'm sure you saw the trees cut down, they're pulling them back north by oxen and building the giant rafts right in the river," he answered.

Myrna looked puzzled, while Devin found the idea somewhat exciting.

"You see, the Infected can't swim. They'll walk under water longer than anything should be able to, so destroying the bridges and staying it out on the islands isn't an option. But they can't reach the rafts," he explained.

The plan he described didn't make Myrna feel much better about heading to the Crossing.

"Thank you for your hospitality, we'll take you up on your porch offer," Myrna said sincerely, gathering Devin to leave.

Feeling less than certain about the following day, Myrna walked back outside, finding an empty spot on the porch to lay out their sleeping rolls as it began to grow late in the evening.

Devin didn't know what to think as he lay down to sleep. Myrna hoped all along to get somewhere safe, with guards for protection, but the mayor made it sound like they were bad men. He rolled over and was able to feel the heat emanating from his stone all the way through his pack. Far too tired to worry over it, he struggled to keep his eyes open while Myrna's thoughts remained focused on how far she could trust the guards. Both exhausted, they fell asleep before the sun had even fully set.

The following morning they awoke to the sound of footsteps falling heavily on the stairs leading towards the house. It was Ramnar; like all of the other guards they had seen he must have stood well over six and a half feet, his great horned helmet bringing him closer to seven. With legs like tree trunks and thick arms, he was heavily muscled and covered with dense hair on his arms and shoulders. From their vantage point laying down he seemed even more imposing. Stopping briefly, he looked to Myrna and Devin, allowing his gaze to settle on the boy for a long moment. Frowning, the guard rubbed the back of his neck and proceeded towards the house.

"That was weird," Devin said, glad to no longer feel like he was under scrutiny.

"What's that now?" Myrna asked.

"The guard, he was staring at me," Devin answered, surprised that he had to explain to her.

"Was he?" she responded, "I don't know, I think he just looked over at us for a moment."

"I thought he was staring," Devin reiterated.

"I'm sure it wasn't anything," she said, patting his arm as she stood up and stretched.

It seemed Ramnar didn't make it far into the house before he was intercepted by the mayor, Radford. Myrna could hear their mumbled voices coming through the door, sometimes rising in ire.

"…Have to give him over. One of the men he assaulted didn't make it," she heard Ramnar saying with a voice like gravel.

"Truly sorry to hear that… But he is a decent man… nothing more than an unfortunate accident. Given the circumstances an exception should be made…" she gathered from the mayor's part of the conversation.

Growing more curious about their discussion she moved in closer to listen, but Devin made it difficult because he was still trying to talk to her.

"I don't think I liked him very much, that staring gave me chills," he rambled.

Myrna unsuccessfully attempted to hush him without making noise herself.

"Can I go down to the stables to get Honey, aren't we going off soon?" he asked.

Giving Devin her full attention for the moment, she looked around. The town was fairly small, and the stables were in sight of where they stood. With the streets mostly empty, except a few people going about their business, it wouldn't hurt to let him go there on his own.

"Okay, be careful though. Straight there and back, no dallying," she instructed.

A big smile spread across his face, he nodded to Myrna and hurried excitedly down the street. He hadn't been able to do much of anything on his own of late. Being able to go off by himself, even if it was only a small ways, made him happy.

Myrna, grateful for the silence, pressed up against the door and continued to listen in on the conversation.

"There is no room for argument, my men are on their way to take the blacksmith now. He'll be executed, and the Empress's justice will be served," Ramnar said, considering the matter closed.

Myrna cursed and rushed away from the door, appearing disinterested when Ramnar emerged. She'd have to go after Devin; guards were heading to the blacksmith's and it sounded like there was going to be trouble brewing soon. Unbeknownst to her, the smithy was directly connected to the stables where she had just sent him.

***

Baerne was busily placing the final touches on his creation. He was entering into his third straight day, now tempering the blade and preparing to quench it. He had to be careful; one small mistake at this point could ruin the entire blade and all of the care he had put into it over the last forty-eight hours. The work had given him a sense of control, granting him a reprieve from the instability of the past few weeks.

It was also a silent vigil for his late mentor, Master Aberfeld. Baerne felt as though his effort held special meaning; toiling away to the point of exhaustion at the craft that had been taught to him by his adoptive father was his way of saying goodbye.

With the blade glowing over the embers at a dull orange, it was time for quenching. Expertly lifting the blade from the fire he turned it over, and submerged the formed steel into the barrel of oil.

Smoke and steam rose up as he held the blade in the quench. Upon removing it, the residual heat from the metal reignited the thin layer of oil still on the blade, giving a very brief appearance that the metal was on fire. The sword wasn't the finest weapon he had ever seen, but certainly looked like it had been crafted by one with much greater skill than he. Nearly finished, he felt utterly drained as a result of the depth of his concentration over the past few days. More accustomed to shoeing a horse or molding a wedge, he wondered if he could ever duplicate his efforts shown in the blade in his hands. *Not likely,* he thought. He had worked on instinct and feeling, and now that he was done, the feeling was gone and he couldn't seem to conjure it up again.

Wide at the base, the blade tapered to a fine narrow point and was well balanced, not too heavy. It would perform the job it was built to do, no more and no less, just like any other tool he had proudly built over the years. Baerne held it upright, admiring his work.

He lifted it at the right moment, otherwise he would not have looked up to see the form rushing towards him. Caught completely by surprise, it was luck that he had the blade in place to deflect most of the impact from his assailant's club. The force of it knocked him off balance, pushing him back so his hips were against a table set near the wall. With only a split second to gather his bearings, Baerne saw it was one of the True-Blood who attacked him. Towering over Baerne, the guard charged back in immediately, placing his right hand at the opposite end of his club and driving forward and down onto the blacksmith.

Baerne was exhausted, the sudden onset of adrenaline coursing through him battled against his fatigue, making him feel momentarily nauseated. The guard pressed in on him, driving Baerne's torso flat on the table while his feet remained on the floor. The full weight of the guard bore down on him, making it difficult to draw breath. His sword was trapped against his body, luckily not yet sharpened, otherwise it could have sliced through his smithing tunic and into his flesh.

Trying to fend him off, Baerne was nose to nose underneath his attacker. The guard's face was bruised over near both of his eyes, his nose bent crooked and a split traversing his lip. It wasn't difficult for Baerne to piece together why he was under assault; this must have been one of the Drakvnar he had been fighting with on the night the Infected attacked.

"They're coming for you blacksmith," the guard said in a low voice through his wicked grin, "one of our brothers you attacked didn't pull through, and now we're gonna put you down like an animal. Maybe I'll just take care of it now, a little payback for the other night."

The guard shifted his weight high, either to get to Baerne's throat or gain some leverage to strike. For an instant, it freed Baerne's leg, and desperate to get out from under the brute he took advantage of the free space immediately. Not a time to be concerned about fighting dirty, he made the only move available to him, and drove his knee up hard into the man's groin twice in rapid succession. The guard groaned loudly, exhaling all of the air in his lungs and briefly relaxing his grip on the blacksmith.

That was enough of a break for Baerne, using the opportunity to take both of his hands and shove the guard upright off of him. Quickly he sat up from the table, and dove in low as the guard came back at him high with both arms out. Baerne drove into the guard's waist hard, wrapping his arms just below his opponent's hips and lifting him a few feet from the ground despite the difference in their sizes. Crashing through the wooden door separating the workshop from the stables, Baerne landed heavily atop the guard. His momentum was too great however, and the guard, no novice to grappling, went along with the motion. With a quick twist the guard rolled Baerne, trading positions so he was again atop the blacksmith.

Baerne knew he was in trouble this time. His surge of energy had played itself out, leaving him struggling for breath and completely drained. The only strength he could summon was used to try and protect himself, wrapping one of his arms over the guard's neck and his other around the guard's arm, trying to lock it in place. He wrapped his feet around one of the guard's legs, attempting to keep him still. After nearly a minute they had reached a stalemate; Baerne was as comfortable as he could be with three hundred pounds of guard on him, while the guard was trapped firmly in place. Though he had an arm and a leg free, he had no room to move them with Baerne pulling him in so tight.

Growling in frustration, the bruised guard made another effort to pull free of the blacksmith and pummel him. Baerne no longer had the strength left in him to hold on. After struggling, the guard managed to extricate his leg, and he sensed his impending victory as he reared up to deliver a blow. Baerne reflexively squinted and gritted his teeth in anticipation of the strike when he heard a sickening, tearing sound, followed by a gush of blood spraying his face. The True-Blood fell limply onto him, completely still.

Devin entered the stable, his spirits high now that he and Myrna were somewhere relatively safe, and about to set off on the last leg of their journey to Creekview's Crossing. Maybe he'd even get to sleep in a real bed again soon, the thought of having a mattress making him happier than he would have thought possible from something so simple.

He spotted Honey in her stall right away, as she seemed to be the only horse currently in occupancy. He approached her, and she gently nickered and nuzzled her head to his hand. Nearby hanging on the wall were her tack and saddle, entering the stall he began to prepare her for the day's travelling. A loud bang and muffled voices distracted him from his work, but it went away as quickly as it started, leaving him to wonder if he imagined it.

Returning to the straps and buckles, again the ruckus continued, this time unmistakable. Devin carefully exited the stall to look across the stable from where the noise came from, but again it subsided. Holding perfectly still and silent for a few seconds, he waited to hear if the clattering would start back up again. To his relief, the only sound was the gentle snort of the horse. Satisfied whatever disturbance caused the noise was over, he turned back towards the stall. As soon as he did, the door at the end of the stables violently smashed outward, splintering and sending it free of the hinges.

Jumping behind a bale of hay, he watched as two large bodies stormed through the opening and crashed to the floor, rolling over and over. Nearly crying out in surprise, he put his hand over his mouth to stifle the noise. One of the men was dressed in the black leather armor, marking him as a soldier, while the other he didn't recognize. The second man wasn't as tall as the guard, but heavy set, with a short, thick beard. Once the initial burst through the doorway ended, Devin was able to overcome his startlement as the two men grappled to the floor. Though neither looked to be moving much, they were both straining mightily against one another.

The man in the leather grunted and growled as he exerted himself, the inhuman sounds sending a shock of alarm coursing through Devin. He risked peeking over the bale while the two struggled, and saw the guard on top, looking like he was about to get the better of the shorter man. In the dim lighting he saw the guard's face was distorted, bruised and discolored.

Devin recalled the attack when he and Myrna were on the road, the primal sounds and battered flesh reminding him of when the Greyman almost took them. There was no doubt in his mind, this was one of the Grey before him. Somehow it got beyond the town's barricade. The guard's animalistic growls intensified, and he finally pulled free of the other man.

Over the days he thought a lot about how his panic had gotten the better of him at that time, almost costing them their lives. Devin saw his chance to redeem himself. Taking a deep breath, he pulled the crossbow from his hip with shaky hands. He lined up a shot at the Greyman's head, just above its ear. Muscle memory took over as he loaded the bolt and cranked back the lever. It wasn't the smoothest motion, but much better than the last time he tried to shoot the weapon. Picturing he was back in the barn with Harrington shooting cans, he squeezed the trigger.

"No!" Myrna screamed in disbelief, having just entered the stable to witness Devin shooting the bolt.

"I got him!" Devin exclaimed, proud that he was able to save the stranger from a Greyman.

Blood began to pool around the body of the guard, the blacksmith hurriedly pulling himself out from underneath.

The three stood, staring at each other, trying to make sense of what just happened. The blacksmith dropped his gaze first, retreating to the other room to pick up the sword he had dropped.

"I think more guards are coming, you two shouldn't be here," the man said to them, breaking the heavy silence.

Myrna nodded.

"Was he infected?" she asked.

He looked over to the boy, watching the confusion in his face beginning to take hold.

"No," the blacksmith said softly, thinking he was beginning to understand why the boy shot the guard.

"But he was a bad man," he added, as if in consolation.

That fact did nothing for Devin, who seemed to be in shock upon realizing his mistake.

Myrna was aghast. She didn't know what to say or do, all the while their time running low. The blacksmith, unable to wait any longer for either of them to act, spoke up.

"You two can't be here, the guards will kill you too if they knew this happened," he said, addressing Myrna.

"What do you suggest, they can't find out that Devin…" she began to yell, then finished more quietly, "killed the guard."

The blacksmith began to form a plan, it wasn't the best option but it would give him a shot at staying alive and keep the woman and boy out of trouble.

"This is what we need to do. Son," he said, speaking to Devin, "he took my bow, shot the guard, and stole the horse. That's what you need to say."

"Give me this," he added, putting his hand on the crossbow.

Devin gave slight resistance before letting go of the weapon, but obliged. The blacksmith wasn't even sure the boy heard him. Looking to Myrna, she nodded her consent. Without a plan of her own to offer, she didn't seem to have a choice.

"Again, hey look at me," he said to Devin, "he took my bow, shot the guard, and stole the horse. Can you repeat that? Say it."

With some coaxing he repeated what the man told him, though he said it mechanically as he stared off into the distance. The blacksmith hoped the boy would be alright, he couldn't imagine it was easy for the young man, child really, to have someone's blood on his hands.

"I'm going to need to take the horse," he said to Myrna apologetically, "they'll be less suspicious."

Myrna hated to give up Honey, and nearly thought twice about doing so.

"Get going, they'll be here any second. I showed up just as you were riding away," Myrna stated, finishing the story they would shortly tell the guards.

"He was a bad man, son. You did the right thing today, remember that," the blacksmith said as he hopped onto the horse, exiting the stable.

Myrna sat next to Devin, who was on his knees still staring at the dead guard on the floor. He hadn't spoken yet, and didn't look like he would be ready to anytime soon.

"Don't look at him, Dev," she said, turning him gently to face away, "remember, he took your crossbow, killed the guard, took the horse and ran off."

She lightly repeated the lie four more times as she sat there with her arms around him, gently rocking back and forth. In only a few minutes, more guards arrived, followed by Mayor Radford as well as the Guard-Captain, Ramnar. Soon the room filled up, the Drakvnar inspecting their fallen soldier.

The mayor spotted Myrna and Devin in the corner. Surprised, he approached them to see what they were doing here. She explained their concocted story to him. Finding him much less intimidating than the guards, she was glad he came over first.

"Really, so that's what happened?" he said quietly, his eyes revealing a hint of suspicion.

"You, woman, what do you know of this?" Ramnar asked, seeing the trio and making his way over.

"The fellow you were looking for, the blacksmith?" Myrna said, putting on the most innocent voice she could muster.

"Yes, he was here? You saw him?" Ramnar demanded.

Devin looked to the looming guard, nodding his head vigorously.

He appeared as though he was about to speak, but Radford intercepted the question, "Yes it looks as though the boy's been carrying a crossbow around, concealed under his cloak. He came here to retrieve their horse when the guard arrived through the workshop."

Continuing over the captain's growing scowl, he added, "Devin here, had set his things down to prep the animal when Baerne and the guard's scuffle spilled over to this area. The blacksmith took the crossbow and killed your man, then stole the boy's horse."

"Was that an accurate depiction, Myrna?" Radford asked her as Ramnar looked between the mayor, the woman and the boy.

"Mm, yes that is what happened, thank you," she said, clearing her throat and averting her eyes.

"I believe your belongings are still at my place, Myrna? Why don't you two go begin getting ready to depart, we'll take care of things here," Radford asked before the Guard-Captain could inquire any further from them.

"They are, yes mayor," she answered.

"Try not to worry, we have things well in hand," he assured Myrna.

Quickly she took Devin's hand and exited the stable, not looking back.

"Despite this you'll all be heading off soon still I presume?" Radford asked Ramnar, changing the subject slightly.

His attention diverted from Myrna and Devin, Ramnar responded, "Correct. Ultimately this won't slow us down much this morning. We'll send a few men to track Baerne and bring him to justice, and leave a few behind here to clean this up."

Ramnar looked at the bloodied floor in disgust, doing nothing to hide his anger at one of his men dead. "For your sake, mayor, I hope you aren't thinking to protect the blacksmith," he threatened in his thick accent, "I'm keeping my eye on you."

"Likewise," Radford responded, already at the doorway. Alone with so many of the guards, he couldn't get out of the stable fast enough. Meeting Ramnar's hateful gaze he was uncertain of how much of an 'accident' that stray arrow injuring his shoulder was three nights ago.

"Best pretend this didn't happen. Let's not speak of it, we can't risk being overheard," Myrna implored Devin in hushed tones while they walked down the street towards the mayor's house.

Devin in turn said nothing, staring off into the distance as if looking at something only he could see. They gathered their packs in silence, and soon joined the throng of people headed north. More guards, at least a hundred, and several dozen workers arrived from Creekview leading teams of oxen. Massive tree trunks were piled and organized, encircled in heavy chains attached to the beasts' yolk. Lines of oxen were grouped to each fallen tree, ready to drag them northward. The men moved with practiced efficiency, having done this many times over the past few weeks. Hardly noticed among the guards and workers, the pair slowly walked north, beginning their two day escorted journey to Creekview's Crossing.

***

Only miles from Big Bear, Garl was filled with anticipation as he and his remaining tribesmen passed through Darcláw's gap, onto the Laskouth Plains. They had argued long and fierce over the decision to leave, and in the end the vote had been close. Garl persuaded many that Jvard would do the same for them, but it was Igdahven's rationalization that won over the majority; Big Bear still had its walls, while the Ridges had become unsecure after the Risen attacked and destroyed the gates in the process.

With the outpost in view, Garl called the crew to a halt and surveyed the area before them.

"Keep sharp everyone, once we're in we can rest," he instructed.

They had maintained a strong pace on their journey out of the Blue Fold Mountains, arriving at their destination in just over four days. Though they weren't completely fatigued, the prospect of a respite was welcome. Their spirit-seeker had warned it would be dangerous directly outside of the outpost town, but it looked to him as empty as the land they had covered the last several days.

"What do you make of this, Igdahven?" Garl asked, hesitating to move ahead based on the spirit-seeker's earlier warnings.

"As far as the Risen are concerned, I can see only as much as you. If I had to guess, it looks as though they've moved elsewhere," Igdahven answered, speaking quietly back to Garl.

Garl grunted absently at Igdahven. "Everyone forward!" he hollered, impatient for answers.

As they neared the sturdy walls of Big Bear it was easy for the barbarians to confirm what Igdahven had seen in the *Chàlgraäden*. The last remnants of snow stubbornly clung to the ground, and visible in it were hundreds of meandering footprints.

Leaving three men behind to make sense of the tracks, the rest of the tribe approached the wall. Working as a team they managed to get two men over, and soon the gate creaked open to allow the rest through.

"We're all in, close it back up!" Garl yelled from the opening, letting the pair working the mechanism know to resecure the entrance.

Garl looked to Igdahven who was leaning against the gate, lost in thought.

"I don't think he's here any longer," Igdahven answered to Garl's unspoken question, "I don't sense him or the wizard anywhere near."

Garl sighed heavily, and as he expected, heard the voice of Dagard begin to once again undermine him.

"Fine adventure, chasing a ghost over two hundred miles away from our ancestral homeland," the Speaker pointed out.

"We've been over this, Dagard," Garl growled, "even if he is no longer here, we're still in a better position behind these walls."

Looking to reignite their previous argument, Dagard continued to push, "Do you intend to stay here forever? We should have remained and rebuilt, what's to stop another tribe from walking into the Ridges and claiming it as their own?"

"I've not the time for debatin' things we've already decided, I suggest you get in line with the rest of us and give a hand. Why don't you start by lookin' into one of those houses over there, see what you can find?" Garl responded dismissively.

His face growing red with anger, Dagard stormed towards Garl. But halfway to him, his gaze drifted to the side and he stopped short with his mouth open, reaching his arm out. A startled cry spun Garl about, and he saw Igdahven drawing his arm back from the gate, holding it close to his body in pain. On the other side of the gate stood a small child, its mouth covered in blood. Igdahven held his hand out to inspect the wound, revealing a large chunk missing beneath his thumb.

"My hand, it's ruined," he uttered to himself, pushing down the sickening feeling in his stomach as he moved away from the gate and hunched over in pain.

Garl issued a stream of curses, watching the girl with vacant eyes reach her arm desperately through the gate. Yellowed skin showed through under the layer of dirt and tattered clothing. She growled unintelligibly, her frustration at Igdahven bounding away the only emotion evident within her.

The barbarians nearby gathered around Igdahven, looking at him with concern and sadness.

"Garl," Dagard spoke quietly, but intently as he drew closer to the man, "you know what will happen to him over the next day. We saw it before at the Ridges. Put him out of his misery now, we can't risk having him harming anyone else later."

Garl knew he had to take care of the problem this time; he could look back to the terrible day on the Ridges and justify his inaction as a result of ignorance. Now, however, they all knew too well what was in store for Igdahven. He had no excuse in delaying what must be done. Still, it didn't make it any easier. Sensing his hesitation, Dagard drew a small blade from his belt.

"Fine, if you don't have the fortitude to keep the tribe safe," he said obstinately and approached the injured spirit-seeker.

He moved two steps before a strong arm grabbed him by the collar and threw him backwards, sending him crashing against the side of the house behind them.

"I'll deal with it, Dagard!" Garl yelled, "I make the decisions that need to be made, not you."

More of a crowd began to gather, many stopping what they were doing to form a ring around the three men. No one dared interrupt or speak to Garl, they only waited to see what Garl would do. Drawing the great axe from his back, Jvard's weapon currently in his safe-keeping, he slowly stalked towards Igdahven.

"Hold on," Igdahven implored, falling over himself trying to back away, "stop and think a moment."

Garl shook his head, "It's got to be now. I'm sorry, lad."

"Garl, you don't have to do this," Igdahven pleaded, his voice becoming frantic as he saw the resolution in Garl's eyes, "there has to be another way."

"Put your face to the ground, my friend. It'll be easier for the both of us if you don't see it comin'," Garl demanded.

Catching up to him with three large strides, Garl placed his foot to Igdahven's chest, stopping him in place. With a nudge from Garl's gigantic boot, Igdahven shifted onto his stomach, submitting. He felt Garl's foot press against the back of his shoulder, causing his right arm to extend out to the side.

"Hold still," he heard, the icy voice freezing him in place as Garl removed his foot.

Closing his eyes tight, the spirit-seeker couldn't believe this was how it all ended for him. He survived for years on the unforgiving tundra, living through savage attacks from rival tribes, enduring the elements, and made it through the most trying of times in the last few weeks; it was now over because he left his hand carelessly on a gate for a brief few seconds. He felt the shadow of the axe rising high, heard its swift downward arc as it sliced through the air with the speed and power only a barbarian could generate.

A tremor ran along the length of his entire arm, followed by heat and an explosion of pain that radiated from his elbow up to his neck. Distantly he heard screaming, and was surprised to realize it was himself.

"Bandage him up, and keep an eye on him," were the last words he heard before slipping out of consciousness.

Creekview

"I'm telling you again this is a bad idea," Jvard reiterated, "the way the soldiers and city-dwellers were at each other's throats, the Inner City is one misplaced coal from becoming an uncontrollable wildfire."

"We will be fine. In and out, hardly noticed," Walt reassured him, brushing away the northman's concern, "this is necessary, and if we can catch the name of this 'Empress' while we're there, it will have been worth the detour."

That was the only reason Jvard hadn't taken control and dragged Walt south by the collar, and agreed to walk back into the hornet's nest that was Creekview's Crossing. Though he didn't care to admit it, he was largely at the mercy of the wizard in the southern lands. He had to trust in Walt's decision that to head to the Keep of the Magicus Celesti in Dalesford was their best course of action, and Walt would be able to lead him there. The implied promise of drawing closer to revenge was a powerful motivator for the barbarian.

Rather than winding through the streets along the same path Jvard took on his last trip to the Inner City, they walked east below the bluffs outside of Creekview until they reached the small boat Jvard had used. Jvard rowed silenty, handling the oars while Walt sat at the stern and viewed the city. He had always liked Creekview's Crossing, the vast network of rivers and creeks broken up by large islands made the city one of a kind. Not to mention with access to both roads and rivers, it was ideal for trading.

Walt was concerned at first about how he should approach the guards at the Inner City, but it seemed they were already aware of his presence and he had no need to worry about getting their attention.

As they drew closer, a guardsman on duty at a crenellation shouted to address them, "You in the boat, state your business."

Walt answered back, his voice resounding richly across the river. To Jvard it seemed he spoke at a normal level of volume, but his words magnified outward over the water, echoing unnaturally. Jvard's skin crawled at what he could only assume was the wizard magically amplifying his voice.

"I understand a man by the name of Daro Ildaradi is residing here. I wish to speak with him," Walt responded.

"And why would he want to meet with you?" responded the guard, "be off. We cannot accept any more refugees."

Annoyed at having to explain further, Walt answered curtly, "Just tell him his dear old friend Walt is here, he'll know me."

Jvard touched his palm to his face and shook his head. They would hardly be noticed, Walt had said. Practically everyone who could get to the wall came to see where the boundless voice that seemed to come from everywhere had originated. In a matter of seconds there were well over a hundred spectators. The guards began speaking amongst themselves, before a few ran off.

"Come around to the front entry. We'll cover you," the soldier shouted, pointing over towards the gate.

"See my friend," Walt murmured quietly to Jvard, "you just have to know how to talk to people a bit, not walking around puffing out your chest and making demands."

Leaving Jvard to his incredulous expression, Walt hopped from the boat and waded to the grassy shoreline. It didn't take long upon them making landfall for a small contingent of the Stricken to gravitate towards them.

"Just keep moving!" the soldiers shouted from above as arrows rained down behind Walt and Jvard.

The gates slowly began to open as they raced up the narrow streets, Walt allowing Jvard to overtake him and lead the way. A door to a house burst open up ahead, three of the Stricken coming forth to try to cut off the wizard and barbarian's progress. Jvard continued running full tilt, swinging his sledgehammer in an upward arc as he ran by to catch the creature under the jaw. A resounding crack split the air, leaving Walt's ears ringing from the intensity of the impact that had resonated so closely to his head. The thing's chin was blasted away, and head nearly torn off from the blow, yet it did not die as they ran past it. It stumbled into the other two and flailed wildly while trying to regain its bearings, but could not see where to walk with its head lolled back and to the side.

Continuing their dash up the hill, they made it to the monolithic, twenty foot stone gate as it opened slightly to allow the two of them through.

"All clear, close gates!" came a loud call, and immediately the guards on duty began working the cranks to again secure the passage.

Upon entering the Inner City, Jvard and Walt were immediately hit by a wall of foul odor that hung thick in the air. With a thousand people in an area meant to accommodate roughly two hundred, and the fact they were all essentially trapped in the confined space and had been for weeks, the conditions were deplorable. Tents were pitched everywhere; what had once been an elegantly constructed district that housed the seat of power for a major city was now a disorderly, filthy camp. One section, more oganized only in the sense that the tents were in straight lines, looked to belong to a group of soldiers. Large guards dressed in black armor walked among them, occasionally stopping to address other soldiers.

"This way," a guard gestured to Walt and Jvard as he approached from a lookout point along the wall.

More accustomed to fresh air and open expanses, Jvard grew increasingly uneasy while passing through the crowded encampment. It was beyond his comprehension why anyone would live this way, even under these circumstances.

Further and further they were led, heading towards the palace that sat at the center of Creekview's Crossing, in the middle of the Inner City. Groups of soldiers and women sat around cooking fires, washed clothes and pots, carried pails of water, and performed other tasks to keep their day to day lives tolerable.

The barbarian noticed several men walking in a group nearly a hundred paces behind them, going out of their way to try to appear they were not together. Jvard looked to Walt, who continued looking straight ahead and seemed not to notice those behind them. Whether it was intuition or paranoia, he had a sinking suspicion they were not going to be allowed to leave.

"Come, Daro is awaiting you in the meeting chambers," their escort told them as they approached the palace.

More soldiers lined the entrance to the royal manor, stretching out between the colonnades at the top of the steps. They opened up their ranks to allow the pair to pass, and efficiently fell back into place after letting them through. A layer of perfume hung heavily in the air, only masking the odor of the city but not completely eliminating it.

There was no crowding within the palace; the only people to be seen were the guards in black armor, all men nearly the same size as Jvard. It appeared as though they took this place over as their headquarters and kept everyone else out.

Jvard kept his misgivings to himself, not caring for the fact there were now dozens of the special guard and countless soldiers between him and the way out. Walt seemed at ease in the stranger's hall, either incognizant or unconcerned of the small army between themselves and the exit.

"Through here," the soldier leading them instructed, standing to the side of the doorway to invite Jvard and Walt in.

A narrow stairway brought them down into a dimly lit room. More of the elite soldiers stood at attention along either wall, as well as a group of men plainly clothed. At the table in the middle of the room sat two individuals, Daro, and a very heavy, broad man also dressed in black armor. Walt spoke first into the silence, surprised at the amount of people present and the feeling of tension in the room.

Concerned, he approached his old friend and asked quietly, "Daro, have you gotten into some sort of trouble here?"

Jvard lightly put his hand to his forehead again. So Walt wasn't being aloof, he truly didn't see the noose tightening around their necks.

"No," Daro answered, glancing over to the other seated man and giving a quick dip of his head, "I am very well, Walt. Please, have a seat."

Cautiously he pulled out a chair adjacent to Daro and sat. Jvard stood unmoving, arms crossed underneath his chest.

"So this is your friend Walt," the man next to Daro asked, standing up and moving uncomfortably close to the wizard.

"Walt, this is First Lieutenant Kempf. He manages the soldiers here most of the time. Kempf, this is the heretic you've been looking for. You'll become well acquainted I'm sure," Daro told his former friend.

"Heretic?" Walt exclaimed, "What exactly are you talking about Daro?"

Kempf ignored the two for the moment, his gaze falling upon the northman, something about his resolute stance oddly familiar. Looking over to the scowling barbarian, Kempf added, "There a problem, is our hospitality not to your liking?"

Jvard had sensed coming here was a bad decision before they even stepped foot in the Inner City, and it seemed his suspicions were coming to light. There was a game the barbarian played as a child with his friends on the tundra involving a particular insect, the achoyid. Small with oversized pinchers, and highly territorial, it formed small mounds of dirt where the colony lived. They would take turns reaching their hand in, while another poked around the area with a stick to agitate them. Whoever could keep their hand in the longest won the game. Jvard always held his hand in the longest. He and Walt now seemed to have inadvertently stuck their hands in the achoyid mound, he might as well give it a good whack with a stick.

"I have no opinion of your hospitality," Jvard answered grim-faced, shaking his head, "you in particular, are not to my liking."

Kempf's face darkened, angrily he rushed over to stand in front of Jvard. Slightly shorter, perhaps as heavily muscled but much fatter, he stared off with Jvard, neither breaking the other's gaze.

"You should mind your tongue, stranger," he warned.

Walt, trying to salvage the quickly deteriorating meeting, continued speaking to Daro. Why had his old friend called him a heretic, and what did he mean by the guards were searching for him? Kempf walked away slowly from Jvard, moving over to block the stairwell with his prodigious girth.

"Daro, I came when I heard you were here. What happened, did anyone else from town make it here with you?" he pleaded.

"I am the only survivor of your malfeasance, conjurer," he replied coldly, "everyone else turned to one of those abominations, or succumbed to them. You are to be given over to the Empress and questioned."

In the next moment, everything happened at once. Guards converged on Walt and Jvard, leaving their positions against the wall. The second they twitched, Jvard reacted, grabbing the heavy chair in front of him and twisting to hurl it into the group. It did no real damage, but hit with enough force to trip them up and buy him a few seconds. At the same time, a flash of light exploded out with a concussive blast of air, leaving the men close to Walt lying on the ground. Rivulets of blood ran from their ears and noses as they writhed back and forth, temporarily senseless.

Walt stood, breathing heavy and struggling to move from the manipulation of energy it took to create that blast. Unfortunately, the guards further away were less affected by the shockwave and quickly overtook the wizard. Jvard looked back to see Walt helplessly surrounded, and ahead to the clear path towards the stairwell. For the second time in his life, he made the difficult decision that to head back and fight would be reckless. With Walt subdued, he would be outnumbered nearly fifteen to one. Not fleeing would only serve to get himself captured as well.

Jvard dashed for the stairs, leading out from the way they had come in. There was only one obstacle in his way, in the form of First Lieutenant Kempf blocking nearly the entire exit with his mass.

"You're not going any..." Kempf began to bluster, indicating he didn't intend to let the barbarian leave.

But like so many others Jvard had engaged, Kempf greatly underestimated how explosively the barbarian could propel himself, and how far he could extend his long arms. Jvard's fist slammed into Kempf underneath the chin, sending him reeling backwards up the stairs. Before he even fell all the way to the ground, his momentum was reversed as Jvard grabbed his chest piece and pitched him back down into the room, landing squarely on the other guards in pursuit. The chase was on as Jvard darted up the stairwell with the Drakvnar and soldiers in tow. Outraged and embarrassed, Kempf got to his feet and brought up the rear of the procession.

Luckily for Jvard, most of the palace was empty during the day with soldiers out patrolling the city, or off procuring food in the surrounding countryside. His footsteps fell heavily on the marble floor as he worked his way back outside, while the armored guards giving chase created a cacophonous echo throughout the hallways. Because of all the noise, the soldiers guarding the main palace entryway were not caught totally unaware when Jvard spilled out with a dozen men close on his heels. Stopping short, the barbarian saw he'd never make it down the steps with all of the soldiers in the way, so he continued along the portico until he reached the end of the line of pillars. With no other choice, he didn't hesitate to jump over the railing and drop over a dozen feet below, down into an alley.

Rolling with the fall, Jvard bounded back to his feet and continued running towards the rear of the Inner City. On his last trip here, he remembered seeing the guards using a manual lift to enter and exit the city in that direction along the wall overlooking the river. He could only hope he wasn't trapping himself into a corner.

"An extra month's pay to whoever brings me his head!" Kempf bellowed when he made it outside, putting his hands to his knees and allowing others to continue the pursuit.

Alarm cries began to spring up throughout the camp, and though they initially appeared disorganized, the soldiers easily spotted Jvard as the source of the disturbance and began to mobilize faster than he hoped. By the time he neared the edge of the line of tents, he met resistance from soldiers that were able to see him coming and ready themselves. Jvard did not slow, dipping his head under an arrow and unlatching his hammer from his belt loop. In a smooth motion of his wrist he brought the hammer up to his shoulder, crashing through the defensive line. With a wide, arcing swipe he slammed the head of the weapon into the shoulder of the nearest soldier, sending him spinning and flying through the air. Jvard, never slowing his frantic run, was already ten paces away by the time his victim hit the ground.

Upon seeing the vicious blow, a few of the guards lost their enthusiasm for the chase. None of them wanting to be the first to approach, they collectively slowed as he sprinted beyond their reach. With only a thin line of enemies between him and the wall, Jvard was close to making a clean escape.

In a final effort, three guards set in a triangle formation managed to position themselves to intercept the charging barbarian. The point man bore a short sword and tower shield, his weapon angled to strike. But as Jvard approached, it became apparent to the soldier that he was not slowing, if anything the mad barbarian gained momentum. At the last moment the soldier decided to fully brace himself behind the shield, and attempt to slam back against the charge.

Jvard had only one thought coursing through his mind, and that was making a straight line for the wall regardless of whom or what he had to trample. As the soldier before him set to block his charge, Jvard's focus narrowed onto the shield. All other sights and sounds faded away in the instant before impact, the wild rhythm of his pulse thundering across his temples. The defender faltered slightly at the sight, unsure if his mind was playing tricks on him or the barbarian actually seemed larger than he had a moment ago, if that were possible.

With a deep, loud growl Jvard lowered his shoulder and slammed into the shield, wrenching the soldier's arm and launching the man back into his two supporting guardsmen where they collapsed in a heap. Jvard, on the other hand, was slowed only so much as an ill-tempered ox might be after running down an unwitting traveler unfortunate enough to hop the wrong fence. Forging ahead, he ran straight over the prone men and continued unimpeded to the nearest tower.

Bursting through the unlocked door he rushed up the stairs, ignoring the startled guards sitting and playing at cards. Hoping he judged correctly that he wasn't headed towards a dead-end, and that there was an access point to the top of the wall nearby, he rushed headlong through another door at the end of the stairs. Knocking over two more guards in the process, he proceeded through a short hallway before he was again outside, looking down over the river. Along the side of the wall were a series of lifts the guards used to enter and exit the Inner City, but he did not think he would have the luxury of using one for a safe trip down.

Arrows flew over his shoulder while a line of guards clattered up the steps behind him. A brief glance below revealed the sheer cliff face, and river flowing swiftly underneath him. It was a very long ways down, and looking from this angle, the water was out further than he thought on his way into the city.

Instinctively he ducked under a bolt that would have otherwise taken him through the throat. With no time to second guess, he could only hope the river was deep enough to support his fall and that his leap was far enough to avoid slamming into the side of the cliff.

***

Walt wrinkled his nose, feeling a droplet of water tickling as it ran down his face. The sensation mercifully did not wake him; he was having an uncharacteristically wonderful dream that would have been a shame to leave. It was a mild winter day in Big Bear, much of the town off to one of Daro's uplifting sermons. He had remained behind, staying in bed while the scent of eggs and chips frying drifted in to wake him. The vividness of the scent memory made his stomach growl loudly, nearly causing the dream to shatter.

Carefully he got out of the bed, trying to concentrate on not waking up. Being back at home was much more pleasant than his current whereabouts, even if it wasn't real. The thought forced an impending sense of dread on him, which he immediately pushed away lest it bring a premature end to his machinations. As he walked into the kitchen a women wearing an apron stood at the stove, busily toiling away over the pots and pans.

Her back was to him, and though he had no clue as to who she was, she seemed altogether familiar. She wasn't a dainty thing, but he always preferred women with a bit more substance; it usually meant he could trust their cooking. At least that was in his younger days, he hadn't had time to bother with such foolishness in many years. Another drip of water gently splashed his forehead, running down the tip of his nose causing him to scrunch his face.

"Oh dear I was trying to surprise you with breakfast in bed," she said to him.

Though she turned to look at him, he couldn't quite make out the features of her face. He smiled anyway, enjoying the feeling of domestic bliss he had never actually had the opportunity to experience. That was by choice of course, the day Walt chose to have someone around to answer to would be the day he had his head examined.

The woman joined him at the table, sitting down and taking his hand in hers.

"You do work too hard, don't you?" she said to him sweetly.

Closing his eyes, he sat back feeling more relaxed than he could remember, until another bead of water landed on his forehead, interrupting his tranquil state and threatening to pull him from his dream. He didn't want to wake, but felt the inevitability of it sinking in. The woman squeezed his hand increasingly tighter until it felt as though it would break his bones, causing pain to radiate through his fingers until it became unbearable. He rationalized it was impossible for someone to apply that much pressure with their hands, and with that realization he awakened.

Staring up at the ceiling, Walt sighed at his current predicament, betrayed by one friend, abandoned by another and locked away in a cell. He couldn't quite blame Jvard; if the situation were reversed he supposed he would have acted in much the same manner. His head and part of his robes were wet from a steady drip coming through the ceiling, the foul smell of it leaving him to wonder what exactly was leaking. He didn't care to try to solve that mystery, thinking he was probably better off not knowing.

Wiping some of the slimy water from his face, he drew his hand back reflexively once his fingers touched his skin. Looking at his hands, each finger was horribly mangled, all broken at the middle joint. He was glad he was already lying down, because if he were standing, his legs would have given out from the pain. Unable to use his fingers, he gritted his teeth and began to examine each of his digits as gently as he could with the heel of his palm.

After a brief inspection he was reasonably sure two on his left hand and three on his right were fractured, while the others were only dislocated. He stood up, placing the flat of his hand against the wall as best he could. Pushing against the displaced joint of his thumb, he popped it back into place, grunting in pain. He repeated the process for his pinky and ring finger; the two broken ones he'd have to worry about later. Nauseated from the agony in his hands, he had to lie back down before he tried to tend to the remainder of his injuries.

Walt knew where he was, locked away in the Inner City, but he had a hard time recalling how it came to be. Snapshots of being beaten by a small mob flashed through his mind, but the fragmented images were fleeting and incoherent. He entered the city with Jvard, but couldn't remember much else beyond that. Now why had he wanted to come to the city, and what had become of Jvard? It seemed he was able to remember only a moment ago.

His thoughts felt muddled and unclear, trying to logically connect the sequence of events was like piecing together a puzzle that was missing some of the pieces. To his dismay, the only conclusion he could reach was that something was obviously not right with his brain. He sat back down and tried to clear his thoughts, and ignore the throbbing ache in his hands. He had no spell to help him with his current dilemma; even if he could concentrate enough to call upon his magical abilities, the precise hand movements necessary for most incantations were all but impossible with his fingers mangled as they were.

A loud clank and sliding noise came from the other side of the fortified steel door to his room, bright torchlight from the hallway invading Walt's cell as it creaked open. He put his arm up over his eyes, the light flooding in silhouetting the frame of a person standing at the doorway. A man dressed in black armor cautiously entered the room, followed by a smallish, nervous person carrying a tray of food. His scrawny, pointed features, and the skittish way he looked about reminded Walt of nothing more than a large rodent.

The guard stood off to the side, while the overgrown weasel set the tray down in front of Walt. Grabbing Walt by the hair and craning his neck back, the man examined his eyes, pulling up each eyelid one at a time with his thumb and peering into it. Taking the cup from the tray, he pressed it up to Walt's mouth. He struggled as much as he could as a bitter liquid came into contact with his lips, prompting his examiner to ask the guard for assistance. A big meaty hand grabbed Walt on either side of his jaw, forcing his mouth open, while the ratty fellow poured the contents of the cup down his throat. They forced every ounce of the foul concoction down as he gagged and coughed.

Instantly Walt's thoughts became even more incoherent than they were before. The profound sense of worry he had been experiencing also seemed to vanish; he knew he should be concerned about his current situation but couldn't seem to summon the energy for it. Examining his eyes again, the man nodded in apparent satisfaction and exited the room along with the guard. Walt felt an urgent need to stop him from leaving, but couldn't muster more than a raised arm in his direction. He had questions to ask of them, didn't he? Overwhelmingly tired, he couldn't give thought to it at the moment. Closing his eyes, just for a little bit, he'd think about it later.

***

First Lieutenant Kempf listened disinterestedly to the sermon at the steps to the palace. This had become nearly a daily occurrence, practically every citizen residing at the Inner City standing along the steps intently focused on Daro's preaching. It was a shame they hadn't killed Daro when they had the chance, Kempf thought not for the first time.

Before he even arrived at the Inner City, Daro had demonstrated he was dangerous; now he had a fervent following and was under constant protection. Kempf wasn't even sure they could kill the preacher at this point, and each of his speeches grew increasingly rousing. He hated to be on duty this time of day, with most of the trouble they've had occurring in the hours following one of Daro's religious rants.

On the bright side, any dissent he had to contend with gave him an excuse to do what he did best, make an example out of troublemakers. He had been excessive in his peace keeping efforts of late, his long-time compatriat Captain Ramnar going so far as to instruct him to ease off. It was part of an effort to salvage their suffering reputation with the citizens of Creekview, he was told. Kempf disagreed, these people needed to be constantly reminded who was in charge. He saw the way they stared at him now, a little less respect than his station deserved, the huge bruise under his chin still prevalent. Anyone making eye contact for too long with him was given a painful remembrance he was to be feared.

The crowd erupting in cheers drew him from his rumination, the strong reaction to the speaker souring his countenance. As much as he had grown to dislike Daro over the past weeks, he couldn't help but listen to the mesmerizing oration.

As the crowd died down the preacher spoke, "The cleansing fire has shone light onto the sinners, exposing them in their dark, hidden corners and recesses, forcing them out of the shadows to face atonement. There is still evil walking among us, but we have captured one of the sinners, and it will be a good day for justice when he pays for his crimes!"

Again the crowd cheered, and he waited a moment before continuing in a somber tone, "We've all experienced loss recently, some of us entire families. As for myself, everyone from my town perished. All of the people gone, whisked away like dust in a wind upon the plain. The world is no longer the same, and may never be what it once was. But how do we continue on? Do we even continue on, or lie down and give in?"

Sporadic cries of 'no' came from the audience, while others emphatically shook their heads.

"Many of you might not know, but there are forests in the world, large forests that extend as far as the eye can see. Nearly every decade flames rampage through the trees, devastating them, much like we have been devastated. But these fires clear deadened brush to make room for fresh growth, and new life arises from the ashes. You have survived the cleansing fires – and it is you who will reseed Luskir. Be wary of who you choose to lead you in this new age, for many will come along and try to lay their claims over people and lands."

"The only one to whom your sovereignty belongs is the one true God, He who has created the ground you walk on, the endless sky, and all under its domain. Beware any person who elevates themselves to this position, for they will use you to their own ends. The only ends you need concern yourself with are His. You may ask yourself, how do I know what course is just, who's path is righteous, what are His ends?"

All eyes were upon him, hundreds of people, even some soldiers, craving the guidance only Daro could provide.

"If you listen carefully for Him, the way forward will present itself to those who are pure of mind and spirit. His is a course of selflessness, not self-indulgence. Avoid those who seek the power to rule, for they will lead according to their ambitions. Especially avoid those who seek knowledge of the arcane, secrets that should be known only to Him, for those conjurers seek a different kind of power that is more dangerous by far than any politician could summon forth. Seek out the rule of the reluctant, those who bear the burden of responsibility with a grim face and heavy heart."

At that moment, Daro looked directly to Kempf who stood hundreds of yards away, somehow locking eyes with him among the sea of people, "For unless they are greedy or foolish, carrying the fate of a people is a hardship no man or woman of virtue would willingly impose upon themself," Daro said, ending this day's sermon on a darker note than usual.

The gathered crowd mostly appeared thoughtful, and largely remained silent rather than breaking into their typical applause. Kempf stood long after everyone departed, seething with anger. He knew what Daro was up to, even if all of these witless people couldn't see the dung he spat forth for what it was.

Since they captured the wizard that Sevra sought, Daro had grown increasingly brazen. The preacher wanted to kill Walt on the spot in the very room that they took him, and nearly did as he had the unconscious wizard in his hands, demanding to know why the Drakvnar wouldn't allow it. When they informed him that Empress Sevra intended to tear every last secret from the wizard's mind, and assured Daro it would be most unpleasant, rather than being pleased he reacted in a peculiar manner. To Kempf, it now made sense. It wasn't only the wizard that Daro abhorred, it was anything linked to magic, which Daro surmised included the Empress. The preacher was becoming dangerous indeed, and he needed to be dealt with before he grew beyond their reach.

A disturbance along the tents demanded his immediate attention; it looked as though the post-sermon quarreling was beginning early today and he would likely be busy attempting to keep the peace for the remainder of the afternoon. Tomorrow he would speak to Captain Ramnar about readjusting his level of leniency; at the very least they needed to put an end to Daro's daily preachings.

***

Their arrival at Creekview's Crossing was an anticlimactic moment for Myrna. For weeks, she and Devin had been running scared, unsure of whom they might meet or what disaster was waiting for them around the next corner. She convinced herself that Creekview would be a safe place, a large protected city that would have more stability and structure than the countryside and backwoods villages they were accustomed to. In a way, she was correct. But the city had many drawbacks that she didn't consider, most notably its overcrowding.

When Myrna was younger, she had lived on one of the small islets, immediately west of the Inner City. Each day, boats and caravans streamed in and out, a constant hustle and bustle of goods moving off in all directions.

How different it looked to her now.

A few boats dotted the rivers and surrounding lake, while the islets themselves were void of life. The only travelers on the road were the soldiers and wagoners she accompanied north, on their slow two day trek from Midao. What would take one person on horse only a few hours took nearly two days as the teams of oxen pulled the heavy lumber.

"What do you think Dev, isn't it something?" she said to the boy, trying appear cheerful and prompt a few words from him. He hadn't spoken for the entire trip since the incident at the stables. Nodding vaguely, he left Myrna unsure if he even really heard her.

The True-Blood escorting the laborers led them around the cliffs to approach the eastern end of Creekview, rather than following the main road to the middle of the city. As they stood high on the cliff, they could see the entirety of Creekview's Crossing and its many rivers and bridges sprawled out in the valley below. Apparently most of the sections were still unsafe; the guards informed her that only the walled Inner City and the most eastward island were secure.

As they skirted around the city, Myrna was able to see the main road had been completely excavated near the entrance. The hill leading towards Creekview was dug into a sheer cliff face, preventing any of the Infected from directly accessing the route between Midao and the city.

Trotting close to the nearest guard, Myrna asked, "I beg your pardon, sir, but what happened to the roadway?"

"It keeps the Infected from interrupting our business between here and Midao, ma'am," he answered, "now if they wanted to bother us they'd have to go all the way north through the city and sweep back around for miles. It looks like they haven't quite figured out how to do that yet."

Myrna frowned, but thanked him. She had seen how persistent they could be; a few miles acting as a barrier did not inspire much confidence in her.

If it was possible, the island they were led to appeared even more crowded than when she viewed it from high on the cliffs. Their entourage funneled across the lone bridge, squeezing shoulder to shoulder as their lane of travel narrowed. Once connected to the rest of the city at many points, the islet was now segregated with the remnants of destroyed bridges jutting out of the river like half buried skeletons. Only the one crossing remained at the eastern end, leaving a sole point of access that was heavily guarded.

Finding a small patch of dirt for themselves, they set down their belongings and disappeared among the sea of tents.

"At least we'll be safe for the time being," Myrna offered, trying to remain positive, even if it was a bit forced.

Devin shrugged, "It doesn't really matter."

Myrna was taken aback, the boy hadn't said more than two words since leaving Midao and now the only words he had to say was their safety didn't matter?

"How could you say such a thing?" she whispered back harshly, filled with disappointment, "All the running, the terrible things we had to see. We're still alive and out of danger now. That should count for something."

"Don't you see?" he yelled back, "it's only a matter of time! You don't know what's waiting around the next corner. And all of these people here, we'll have to sleep with our eyes open."

"You're tired, and you've been through a lot Devin, you need to rest. I know this isn't ideal, but we can stop running now for a bit. Things will get better here, the guards told us they are working on clearing out an additional island, and look at the barges they're building," she said, pointing over to the construction area.

Massive trees, at least a hundred feet tall were being treated and lashed together as a temporary plan to alleviate the overcrowding. One was nearly complete, with several canopies built onto it to offer protection from the sun and rain.

"We can move onto one of those when it's ready if you want," Myrna offered, "they're saying here that the Greymen can't swim, those rafts will be safe tied out near the island. I know it's not the best here now, but given some time who knows, maybe it'll almost be normal. Devin?"

She stopped talking when she realized he had rolled over, fast asleep. He would feel better, she was sure, once he had some rest.

Cornered

Make it look like an accident, those were the instructions given to Captain Ramnar and his Drakvnar for dealing with the absentee councilman, Radford. Their hunt for the instigating blacksmith may have provided them with a means to do just that. Deciding to stay in Midao and deal with this problem rather than follow the caravan north, Kempf would have to handle things on his own at Creekview for just a few more days.

Once again out searching for Baerne, the Captain and two of his men returned empty handed. They had seen signs of him, a small campfire deep in the woods, some footprints, but he continually stayed one step ahead. It appeared he had not yet completely left the area, which was good; he would slip up eventually and be captured. Catching Baerne was of lesser importance to them anyway, and while out looking for him, Ramnar found something potentially better.

Returning to Midao, he ordered all of the remaining Drakvnar and soldiers to quietly leave town throughout the rest of the day, a few at a time to move to Creekview until further notice. As long as his plan eliminated all of the villagers, there would be no one to refute whatever story he chose to fabricate. Even if any survived, it would still look like no more than an unfortunate incident. He told his men to find fresh horses from the stables; the solution he stumbled upon was a few hours ride out, but would be well worth the time.

Baerne watched as the soldiers returned for the second time that day to the patch of forest he had been occupying for the past week. He was lucky to escape the village alive after killing two of the True-Blood. Well, technically he only killed one, but gladly took credit for the second to draw attention away from the boy. At first he thought he would continue running until the horse couldn't take another step, but after gaining some distance he realized he really had nowhere to go. Midao was his home; everyone and everything he cared about was there from the woman he thought of as his mother, to his siblings, and the workshop where he felt he most belonged.

Instead of fleeing entirely, he wound up circling the surrounding woodlands, always staying perhaps ten miles away but constantly moving while the soldiers searched for him. The expansive forest stretched north to the Tinindraüg, and southeast to encompass many of the outlying villages, giving him no shortage of hiding places. Staying out for so long didn't bother him much, he tried to think of it as a prolonged hunting trip.

When he was a few years younger he would frequently go out for days on end, and was glad of the basic tracking skills he picked up to help keep him out of reach of those who now pursued him. Unfortunately it looked as though he was going to have to change locations sooner than he wished, they had homed in on him yet again, much faster this time than he would have liked.

Leaving Honey tied off to a tree several hundred yards away, he watched quietly from the bushes while they moved through his small campground. He expected them to stay and dawdle about the area, but was surprised when they passed straight through, appearing hardly concerned that he may have been there recently. They were men moving at a determined clip, with a destination in mind. He recognized two of the three men, one of which was the actual Guard Captain; that certainly didn't bode well to Baerne.

Common sense told him to go the other direction and continue their game of cat and mouse, but a mixture of curiosity and a growing sense of tedium got the better of him. Retrieving Honey, he let them gain a small distance before finding their easily discernible trail.

He tracked them for miles, and miles more through the woods northwest of Midao. Hoof prints and other signs of their passing, broken twigs and flattened grass, allowed him to give them space but still follow along without difficulty. After hours of tracking, he began to question the wisdom of coming so far out with the men who intended to hunt him. As he began to wonder if he should return to his senses and go back, they reached the end of the wood line on this side of the river, the strong flowing Tinindraüg stretching out before them to divide the forest. He stayed hidden in the woods, watching with confusion.

Before him at the river bank were the three guards, along with what had to be nearly two hundred of the Infected lumbering aimlessly – that is, until they saw Ramnar and his two men. What began as a slow approach quickly turned into a stampede when the Infected caught wind of the trio. Further adding to Baerne's confusion was their size; even at his distance he could see the group was once comprised of large, rugged individuals. The Drakvnar were collectively the biggest people Baerne had seen up to this point in his life, and this group of Infected rivaled them in stature to a man.

Ramnar and his men stayed on their horses, moving away fifty paces as the Infected drew near them, in Baerne's direction. Cursing silently to himself, Baerne retreated a small distance while still trying to see what the guards were playing at. After nearly a half hour of watching the guards' dash away, then stop and wait for the pack to catch up, he was certain they were stringing the Infected along. He feared to think about where they were leading the monstrosities.

He continued to watch for many miles as they baited the Infected to follow along, back towards his home. There was nothing else for miles in this direction; he had no choice but to accept they were leading the throng to Midao. If the Drakvnar decided to stop defending the town, this group would overwhelm his people in a matter of minutes. But why had they chosen to betray them after providing protection for so long? It made no sense to Baerne. Spurring Honey to a gallop, he made haste back to the village, hoping he could give them ample warning.

The woods gave way to open fields as Baerne raced south, the houses of Midao becoming visible in the distance. He hadn't been this close to home in many days, causing a mixture of emotions within him. The guards were going to give him problems, there was no doubt about that. He also missed his family and was looking forward to seeing them again, but greatest of all was the feeling of urgency to alert his people of the danger heading their way. He pushed the tiring horse for the final stretch, approaching the barricades along the western perimeter of the town.

A few soldiers dotted the edge of the village, though it seemed much emptier than he last saw. Immediately a few of the men recognized Baerne and came to attention at seeing the wanted blacksmith storming back to town.

"You have a lot more brass than brains, I'll give you that," one of the soldiers shouted to him as he approached, "Ramnar'll be pleased when we deliver your head…You, halt now!"

Ignoring the guard's directive he charged ahead full speed, jumping a lower section of the barricade and continuing on. The soldiers cursed and backed out of the way, setting off after him immediately.

"Radford!" he yelled, heading along the road with the soldiers chasing behind him on foot.

By the time he reached the large, white mansion the mayor had already heard the commotion and was out on the porch along with his wife. Surprised to see the blacksmith, he firmly directed her back inside, shutting the door behind her.

"Alright, you showing up makes one too many strange things going on today, what's happened?" Radford asked bluntly.

Pulling Honey to a stop and approaching the porch, Baerne began to answer before he had even dismounted, "You need to gather everyone up and get out of here, the whole town's in danger."

Radford's expression changed from curious to deeply concerned, "Is it the Drakvnar?" the mayor asked.

"Not all of them, I don't think at least," he answered, shaking his head, "it's Ramnar, he's herding a group of Infected this way, him and two of his men. They could be here in minutes."

Radford blanched, "Get everyone ready, armed and prepared to fight…"

The blacksmith interrupted, putting up his hand, "No, this group will overrun the whole town, they're too many. If we stay we're all dead."

By then the three soldiers caught up to Baerne, seething with anger and drawing their weapons.

"Peace!" Radford yelled, "There is a larger problem to deal with. Any minute a large contingent of the Infected will be here to ravage this town."

The mayor's typically kind eyes were steel now, and his voice carried an air of authority more fitting of a general than the head council of a backwoods village. Even the soldiers, not under his command, hesitated in their desire to apprehend the blacksmith.

"If all the damn guards hadn't left maybe…" Radford began, "well that explains why you've all been sneaking off today. All day long I've been watching you head north in small groups, as if you didn't think I would notice."

The three soldiers looked to one another, consternation written on their faces.

Catching the awkward exchange, Baerne asked, "Why are there so few soldiers here now, you know of this?"

The lead guard who appeared to be in charge answered back simply, "Don't know what you're talking about."

Standing in a tense silence, the five men stared at one another. The level of distrust between both sides prevented either from wanting to divulge any further information.

Gesturing to his guards, the soldier told his men, "C'mon, we're due back in Creekview. We never saw you today."

They departed, leaving Baerne and the mayor to wonder what part, if any, they had in this.

"What can we do? Can you get everyone up to Creekview?" Baerne asked, and thinking aloud added, "What would be the point if the guards are trying to kill us all anyway?"

"The guards aren't in on it, only a few of them I'd bet. We'll have to start moving everyone immediately. Creekview will be safe enough for everyone, it's me they want," Radford answered, carefully, "but that alone won't do. To get all of us up there, women and children, we'd be dead before making it halfway. Those damn things don't tire, but we will."

"Wait, what do you mean it's you they want?" Baerne asked, not understanding.

Radford shook his head, "On a few occasions I've met this so-called Empress Sevra the guards have been singing their praises of. She was the advisor to one of the Luskiran Council, of which I'm also a member. A few weeks back she requested a meeting; I was too busy here to attend. Then guards start showing up around Creekview, declaring the woman as ruler, not to mention the bastards 'accidentally' shoot me in the shoulder the night of the attack... No, the Council would never have allowed these declarations. I fear something terrible has happened to them. Wait here, I need to inform my wife."

In a matter of seconds Radford was back outside, walking up the road informing anyone he saw to meet at the town center immediately. Sarah, his wife, exited the house and headed around to the other side of the village, while Baerne hustled to keep up with the mayor.

Answering the blacksmith's unspoken questions as if he could read his mind, Radford continued, "Stay by my side, my wife will take everyone north, and we need to get them moving quickly. You and I will deal with Ramnar."

Soon the entire town had gathered, and Radford kept the instructions as simple and succinct as possible while cutting off any discussion. He told them plainly that a large group of the Infected was on their way towards them, and they needed to depart in minutes, his wife would lead them there.

"Move!" Radford yelled as his people hesitated, some beginning to ask questions, "The time to leave is now, your very lives depend on it!"

Wagons and horses were gathered, people scrambled back to their homes to get what they could carry, and soon the group was ready to head out. Baerne felt as if his head was spinning, with so much happening all at once, and how quickly Radford managed to get everyone mobilized. He always marveled at the mayor's ability to lead; he didn't need to explain himself, he told people what needed doing and it simply happened. Baerne could skillfully hammer metal into any shape, but how to form a group of people to his will in such a way was beyond him.

"We're going to need to head them off before they reach the fields. We'll catch them at the edge of the wood," Radford instructed Baerne as everyone else departed.

"What exactly are you planning to do?" Baerne asked incredulously.

"C'mon, go get yourself a pair of fresh horses, you're going to have a lot of riding to do. I'll get my bow, meet you at the stables and explain it on the way. Hurry along, no time to waste now," he answered.

As Baerne prepared the horses, Radford shortly arrived outside of the stable. The mayor had a bow slung over his back, and the pommel of his rapier was visible underneath his travelling cloak. With a fresh pair of horses, riding one and guiding another, they departed from the side of town.

"Do you think Honey will be alright left back at the stables?" Baerne asked, the thought suddenly occurring to him, "She belongs to that woman and boy, I would have hoped to return the animal to them at some point."

Even though it was necessary at the time, he felt guilty about stealing the crossbow and the horse.

"Oh, not to worry, I'll swing by and grab the mare if I can afterwards. Should everything go correctly I'll deliver the horse to her myself," he answered, understanding Baerne's concern.

"So how are we going to handle this?" Baerne asked, try as he might he wasn't sure what the two of them might do against so many Infected.

Ignoring the question, Radford asked, "I assume that crossbow of yours is in working order?"

"Aye," Baerne answered, "it's been keeping me fed a good part of the week."

"We'll hide at the tree line, if the guards are on horses as you say they'll have to be exiting near the road. They won't be expecting us; we'll take out their mounts and then see just how far then they can tease the Infected along. Once the guards are out of the way, you'll need to return the horde back north, lead them away just as those despicable men tried to lead them here. I'll be right behind you and join you for a bit, to make sure none slip by."

Baerne's face soured, thinking Radford made it sound much easier than it was going to be.

Slapping him on the shoulder, he added, "You'll be fine. If you can, swing back down outside of Creekview, the eastern edge. I'll check for you there in two mornings and the morning after that."

"Let's get to it, then," he said, the thought that he didn't have much to lose providing Baerne a touch of courage.

As they arrived into position off the road, they did not have to wait long before they heard the stampede of men nearing exit to the forest. The three True-Blood came through first, followed soon thereafter by a stream of the Infected. One after another they emerged; though it only took seconds for them all to pass, it seemed for a moment they would continue to pour endlessly out of the woods. Riding another hundred yards out, Ramnar and his men again slowed to a stop, allowing the Infected to catch up slightly before leading them along further. With their attention elsewhere, the Guard Captain and his two Drakvnar didn't see the two men lying in wait by a small crag away from the road.

"Now Baerne!" Radford whispered heavily as Ramnar and his men began getting ready to move once more.

Radford's bowstring twanged and Baerne's crossbow recoiled as they released their bolts, two of the animals along with their riders falling heavily to the ground. Ramnar's horse reared, and though he was able to avoid a bad fall there was nothing he could do for his men on the ground. One was pinned down, trapped underneath his horse. The other struggled to get to his feet, and appeared to have a badly twisted ankle. Ramnar pulled hard on the reins, steering his horse back around to flank the horde as they rolled over his prone men in a frenzy.

"Quickly! Get their attention, start leading them away and I'll deal with Ramnar!" Radford shouted to Baerne over the screams of the guards and horses.

Radford paused to see what course of action was least likely to get himself killed. Though many of the Infected were occupied devouring the two fallen men and horses, there were too many of them to all join in. A small group towards the rear broke off to pursue Ramnar, while another dozen spotted him and advanced hungrily. He watched as Baerne spurred his horse forward, shouting and waving his arms, doing everything he could to draw attention onto himself. To his relief, and likely Baerne's dismay, it worked exceptionally well. A large wave of the Infected trailed after the blacksmith, leaving him and Ramnar with only a score of the creatures.

"You're a dead man Radford, you hear me!" the Guard-Captain shouted to the councilman, spotting him and the blacksmith as the cause of the disturbance.

He drove his horse forward towards Radford, but was cut off by the Infected and forced to stop short and turn in retreat. Likewise, Radford had a small group impeding his way to Ramnar.

"Twice now you've tried and failed, I'm afraid you won't get a third opportunity," Radford retorted, nocking an arrow as Infected loped towards him.

They were nearly upon him, arms outstretched, almost grinning with anticipation of tearing into his flesh. He kicked one in the face that had gotten too close, sending the creature stumbling backwards and briefly stunning it. Their stench was overwhelming, but Radford held his ground and took aim. Firing, the arrow flew a narrow line between the Infected, missing many of them by inches to drive into Ramnar's horse above the shoulder. The animal reared and thrashed violently, throwing Ramnar from the saddle. He became lost to Radford's view as the mob of Infected circled in on him. Satisfied Ramnar would no longer be a problem to him or his town, he sped north to assist Baerne.

Following the trampled grass, it took several miles before the mayor caught up and sighted the group chasing his friend. Baerne was doing a fine job, resisting the temptation to speed away and allowing the Infected to stay on his trail. Not wanting to draw any of the throng onto himself, Radford swept out wide to the east, and began to arc back towards Baerne once he was in front of the group.

"Alright there Baerne?" he called out as he finally drew close to the blacksmith.

"Just fine," he answered, slowing to a trot, "should be able to keep this up a while as long as I don't do anything careless."

Radford nodded, "Good, I'm going to go ahead a ways, and then double back to the village, and see that everyone got away alright. Make sure they stay on you. Try to lose them at the rivers, but if you can't, bring them right to the soldier's door, let them deal with it - and switch out your horses so they don't tire as fast! I'll see you in a few days outside of Creekview, right?"

"You got it," he answered, confident in the plan, "do me a favor, and tell my Ma I'm alright."

Radford nodded and rode ahead through the fields, shrinking to a small figure in the distance until he disappeared from Baerne's view altogether.

***

Scowling atop her throne, Sevra had difficulty hiding her amusement as the messenger's leg began to quiver involuntarily while he delivered his report. A minor tremor slipped into his voice as well, though he did his best to clear his throat and continue as if it didn't happen. Unfortunately, she couldn't fully enjoy his discomfort. She was not happy; by all reports the deep south was nearly an uninhabitable disaster, and now she had to sit and hear that Creekview's Crossing was contentious as well. At least they had captured the wizard, that was a spot of good news. To her dismay, the same person instrumental to his capture was also the main instigator against her soldiers. The more she listened, the more she began to realize she would need to get involved personally and either rein in or destroy Daro Ildaradi.

"Enough!" she shrieked, cutting the messenger short and dismissing him with a wave of her hand.

Stopping in mid-sentence, the messenger bowed, and turned on his heel. He walked away so quickly he might as well have run.

Almost with a pout, she exhaled heavily and slumped in her seat. She knew the repercussions if she did not bring stability back to Luskir and gain validity as ruler among the people; her God had made that painfully clear. Yes, she decided, she would go to Creekview personally and deal with the unrest before it grew further out of hand; it should take her no more than a fortnight. With both Ramnar and Kempf absent, Urstaag was fully capable of keeping an eye on Aubur and directing the forces here in that brief period of time. Though she abhorred the thought of travelling without him, she would inform him of her departure and in the morning set off to secure her reign.

***

"My name is Walt Whirten, I'm being held as a prisoner. I'm Walt Whirten, I'm a prisoner," the wizard repeated over and over during his brief moments of lucidity.

It was the foul liquid they poured down his throat that turned his memory to soup, he realized as the effects of his last dosing started to wear off. Of course, that meant it would soon be fed to him again. On the bright side, the growing sense of doom he was beginning to feel anew would soon fade once he received the next mouthful.

No, he had to intervene and break this cycle of forgetfulness. Sooner or later they were going to proceed with whatever it was they were going to do to him, which he was reasonably sure would not be pleasant. He had to find out why he had been captured, and a way out of the mess he landed himself in.

While his memory started to return, so too did the throbbing in his hands. The fingers that were only dislocated, while they hurt, did not bother him nearly as bad as the ones that had been broken. He had done his best to set them, but they would likely never be the same again once healed.

As expected, the door soon opened and the small, familiar man that reminded Walt of nothing more than a tailless, overgrown rodent came through with a plate of food and a cup filled with the mindnumbing elixir.

"And how are you today, Mr. Whirten?" he asked cheerily.

"Roses and sunshine, my good jailor," Walt answered, becoming more alert with each moment.

The weasily doctor paused and issued a frown, seemingly surprised that he received more than an unintelligible mutter for a response. Placing the tray on the ground, he walked up to Walt, putting his face close to the wizard's.

After an inspection of each eye, he shook his head and hummed quietly to himself.

"My-oh-my, I think we'll need to begin upping the amount we give you," he said, grabbing the glass and forcing it to Walt's lips.

Reluctantly, Walt obeyed. Trying to fight the little rat man off right now would have gained him nothing more than a beating from the guard standing outside of the door.

"That's better now," he said brightly, sitting down to watch the drug slowly take effect on Walt.

A stream of chatter issued forth as Walt began to nod off, jarring him awake. *Must be a lonely fellow*, he thought, nearly forgetting that each of the visits ended with a forced discussion. Well, not a discussion so much as Walt being someone for the strange man to talk at.

"And then the cook nearly lost it when the bowl of peas spilled to the floor..." Walt heard through the fogginess forming in his mind.

It went on for several minutes, and then several more. *How could someone talk so much without actually saying anything?* Walt wondered. Usually he would have fallen unconscious by now, it was remarkable to Walt the person was able to talk for so long. On his previous visits had this man stayed and continued to chat even after he fell asleep? Walt began to suspect that was the case. If he didn't pass out soon, he was going to have to find a way to hang himself to bring an end to this conversation.

"And you remember what I told you about my sister, well, no maybe you don't, I'll start again..."

He prayed for the concoction he was forced to drink to kick in and provide the sweet relief of sleep, to give him a brief escape from the pain in his hands and more importantly from the inane chatter forced upon him.

"But like my pappy said, 'you can't force an oak back into the acorn'…"

By the spirits why am I still conscious, Walt wasn't sure if he could take another minute of the witless rambling, but unfortunately could do nothing to stop it as the poison had done its job in preventing him from forming his thoughts to speech.

"Really is gonna be a shame when they pack you off to Dun'Aldir in a few days…"

Walt wasn't quite sure, but he thought the imbecile might be saying something relevant. He tried to force himself to pay attention.

"Yeah it'll be a real shame, won't have no one to talk to again I won't. Empress Sevra will be sure to get what she wants, she always does. Sure must be good to be King - errr, Queen."

Sevra. The name struck Walt like a hammer on steel, momentarily galvanizing him to his senses. There was something about the name, but he couldn't recall why it was important. If only his thoughts would clear out and the person before him would end his ceaseless banter! Trying to tell the man to seal his lips, Walt groaned something nonsensical before finally succumbing to the foul liquid and collapsing to the ground.

The wizard sat with his back to a tree while he thumbed through a large volume, mostly daydreaming as he made a halfhearted attempt at understanding the text. A few clouds dotted the sky, lazily drifting along as the afternoon grew late. He sighed audibly as another day seemed as if it was going to slip through his fingers, but it didn't concern him greatly; there was always tomorrow. The keep grounds were his favorite place to whittle away the time. Perfectly manicured hedges formed elaborate patterns, the sound of fountains providing a dull, ambient noise, and there was just the right amount of trees to fill in the landscape and find a shady place to sit without feeling like he was in a forest.

Turning a page, Walt glimpsed at his hand, and his long, thinly elegant fingers. No, that wasn't right. His hands should be mangled, and the skin he saw had the smoothness of youth to it, not the wrinkles he was accustomed to. A gentle breeze stirred, flitting auburn locks in front of his face, the color it had been in his younger days before it all turned to gray and silver.

The realization that he was dreaming nearly woke him, prompting him to quickly close his eyes and empty any thoughts from his mind. Walt often achieved a lucid dream state, and that was one of the little tricks he had mastered to keep himself from waking. Carefully he opened up his eyes again, and was pleased to find he was still among the grounds of the Magicus Celesti, in the gardens high among the bluffs overlooking the city of Dalesford.

What could it have been that prompted him to dream himself into this place? Though he did remember fondly spending any free time he could find among the gardens, in general he didn't think twice about his decision to leave the order. Perhaps he was feeling some trepidation from his intentions to head back there with Jvard.

He looked at the book, curious if he could actually read anything. Now there was an interesting dichotomy to Walt; could he learn anything from a book in a dream, or would it merely be a reflection of knowledge he currently possessed? Unfortunately the words continually changed or arranged themselves into meaningless patterns, putting an end to that question.

As he picked his head up he saw a group walking across the gravel path towards the Keep. It looked to be four members of the order escorting a woman and a hulking fellow who followed her every step. One of the men he recognized as Glaedrin, the leader of the Magicus Celesti. He had met the old wizard only seldomly, and couldn't say he regretted their lack of interaction during his stay with the Celesti. Glaedrin was known to be both shrewd and cunning to the extreme, and was perhaps the only person Walt ever felt off-balance around. As to who the other men were, Walt could not say.

There was something familiar about the procession. The pale, petite woman with dark hair and a shock of white at the front, coldly beautiful like morning frost draped over a barren garden, and a bear of a man who followed her teased the edge of his memory; he looked a bit like Jvard come to think of it, though that wasn't what struck a chord of recognition. He couldn't be quite sure, but he thought he might be looking in on a day from his past.

Deciding to follow, he motioned to set the book down until he saw it was no longer in his hands, and took off after them. The pursuit was futile; no matter how hard he ran they continued walking away from him, gradually moving out of sight. When he stopped running, he found he was no longer among the gardens, or anywhere near the Keep for that matter. He stood in a sea of blackness that slowly materialized into snowy mountains on the horizon, along with a vast network of currents flowing through the sky. If a river had suddenly floated up into the air and shimmered with a translucent film of black and white, it would be close to what he saw before him. Even though it struck him as odd, the currents seemed in a way as natural as the mountains in the distance.

Looking down, he could discern that he had been placed just outside of the Blue Fold Mountain Range, and far below him was his chosen home of Big Bear. There were people down amidst the streets, reminding him again that he was still dreaming, and he forced himself to bury painful emotions that tried to surface. Pangs of shame and remorse crept through him as he thought about everyone who had perished. There was nothing he could have done for them, but still that fact did little to lessen his feelings of guilt.

A pungent, sickly sweet smell suddenly overpowered his senses as rain began to fall. Drops of liquid spattered onto him, singeing and burning into his flesh. It was not rain, but acid he noted with horror, looking up to see the corrosive liquid falling from the rivers in the sky. Even as far away as he was, he could hear the screams from the town below, the vividness nearly making him forget he was within a dream.

"No, no, no," he whispered, shutting his eyes tight, trying not to succumb to the fear and sadness he felt.

The world spun around him, Big Bear disappearing and the landscape swirling into a blur. When his equilibrium returned, he found he had journeyed northward, into the plateaus that the wild men of the north, the barbarians, called home. The same scene greeted him that he had just left; many lay dead on the ground, the smell of decay nauseating him while the rivers in the sky continued to emit the acidic substance.

Walt lost count of how many times he changed locations, the scenery rapidly rotating and reforming to reveal more of the same. Villages across the Laskouth Plains, southward through the Golden Terraces all the way to Dalesford, and east to Dun'Aldir were all devastated by the aberrant particles raining down. He didn't want to see anymore. Certain this particular dream was a reflection of the current catastrophe that struck his town and beyond, seeing its far-reaching consequences so bluntly laid bare was nearly paralyzing.

Deciding he had all he could take, Walt had sufficient control of the dream to bring it to an end and awaken. Similar to working with magic, but a fully mundane ability, it was merely a matter of purposefully maneuvering from one state of consciousness to another. To Walt, it came as naturally as breathing.

This time, something went wrong. In the small space between wakefulness and sleep, he was seized by a firm grasp that prevented him from rousing. The experience caused him to feel a jarring rebound, like he was shot out of a catapult and yanked backwards by a rope in mid-flight. He landed on the ground of his cell in the basement of the palace at Creekview's Crossing, but he was outside of his physical form which lay only a few feet away. Walt immediately recognized he was in the strange realm he sometimes found himself in upon falling asleep, and he was not alone in the room.

Standing across from him, watching with trepidation was the oddest looking person Walt had ever laid eyes on. His attention immediately set on the stranger's belt, which had a wide assortment of skulls of varying shapes and sizes dangling from long leather cords. The man's right arm flickered, vanishing and reappearing so quickly Walt wasn't sure if it was only his imagination. Looking up to meet his eyes and seeing his wolf-skin cap, Walt remembered having seen this person once before, chasing him through a dream outside of Big Bear.

"Be still, wizard!" the man shrieked, the change of pitch in his voice undermining the confidence he tried to put forth.

"Easy," Walt said carefully, still trying to gain his bearings after the abrupt change in his surroundings.

Walt slowly sat up to face the one who extricated him from his dream. He remained still on the ground, trying to discern anything he could about his adversary.

"How is it that you pulled me here?" Walt asked, hoping to at least delay any confrontation in a place he didn't understand.

"You walk among the spirits, wizard," the robed figure said cryptically, "a dangerous place to find oneself unguarded."

Walt stood abruptly, ignoring the visitor's unease and allowing his insatiable curiosity once again to get the better of him, "Are you saying you grasp the workings of this world?"

The wolf-capped man nearly jumped out of his skin when Walt stood, bumping the wall and scurrying backwards. Before he could tell him to relax, Walt felt an invisible hand grab him roughly, throwing him back to the floor.

"Do not move, Fel-born," Walt was instructed, "your very essence is in my hands. Tell me, what have you done with Jvard?"

Admittedly, Walt had very little knowledge of the pseudo-dream world he occasioned. Realizing he was at the mercy of the stranger, Walt did his best to appear more appeasing. However, many questions ran through his mind, and he didn't want to reveal information that could ultimately harm his travelling companion.

"Jvard was with me, but is no longer at the moment, as you seem to have already guessed," Walt answered matter-of-factly.

"If you've gotten him caught up in your scheming, wizard," the stranger began, his ire rising.

So this person knows Jvard, and is concerned about his safety, Walt thought. If this was a misunderstanding, he needed to do something quickly to correct it.

"Please tell me who you are, and how you know our mutual acquaintance. If I believe you, and it doesn't put his safety at risk, I'll gladly tell you everything I know about him," Walt interrupted.

The stranger looked taken aback, expecting Walt to be less cooperative.

He appeared to think it over for a moment before answering, "Igdahven, spirit-seeker of the Frostwrynn. Jvard was lost to us many weeks ago and we have been searching for him. Now tell me everything, and I will let you live."

That seemed satisfactory to Walt, especially the part about allowing him to live. In his weakened condition, and in this unfamiliar place governed by rules unknown to him, Walt didn't think he'd have much of a chance in a confrontation with Igdahven. Making themselves comfortable, they had what turned into a lengthy discussion.

***

After all the long years, he sensed his time was nearing its inevitable end. He now saw his life and sacrifice for what it truly was, a fool's errand. The gem he had willingly imprisoned himself in almost two millennia ago, helping to seal away a being more evil than the world had ever known, would be in the hands and protection of a mere boy. He was the last one, he knew in the depths of his soul. The other twelve wizards and gems had long been destroyed. All alone for centuries, he solely maintained Kubathu's prison, managing to keep the sorcerer's destructive force from acting on the final seal. Were the people of the world even remotely aware of the calamity that was soon to be unleashed upon them when he faded away?

It was a thankless task, and one he was able to accomplish only because he had somehow become separated from the cursed necklace. The distance was his saving grace, greatly dampening the brute force Kubathu could direct towards him. Even though most of the original covenant, save one, had high hopes, he feared it would end this way. Their solution, though long-lasting, was in reality only temporary as they were warned.

Kubathu had transcended to something more than human, the countless souls he took granting him a state of near immortality. The group of wizards he was part of who stymied Kubathu, despite their knowledge and ability, were only men. With their best efforts and intentions, all that they were able to accomplish was to buy the world a little time.

Volunteering to this task had cost him everything: his family, sanity, and his very identity. After so many years, he could no longer even remember his own name. Despite the enormity of his sacrifice, they were facing their moment of failure. If he still had a body, he would have laughed, or maybe wept, at the futility of it all.

Of late, his lucidity was particularly fleeting; some days he couldn't figure out where he was or why he had been confined. Other days he could not comprehend the sheer amount of time that had passed. Often he forgot the world outside was not the same as that of two thousand years ago, the same people no longer alive as when he originally encased his soul in the diamond. Remembering felt like losing them all over again.

A ripple passed across his limited range of awareness outside of the diamond, a familiar signature that tested the limits of his recollection. The warmth of it caught him off guard, and it took him a while to even recall what it was, though he instinctively knew it to be good.

It was a feeling that caused him great discomfort because of how foreign it had become.

It was hope.

He dared to believe his senses weren't deceiving him, and after the sensation remained for many minutes it could no longer be mistaken. A shimmer of hope shone through his despair. He felt his master nearby, the founder of the Magicus Celesti. Somewhere close he felt magical traces coming from two men, the emanations as unique as the lines on one's palm. He could not remember the master's name, or the last time he had even seen him, but the imprints of energy were unmistakable. Surely the master would know what to do!

There was not much life left in him as he struggled to maintain the barrier that had been his charge for the last two thousand years. He had to act fast, and prayed the master remembered him and would take on his burden. With no other options, he would need to reach out and use his caretaker, the boy Devin, one last time to bring him to the eldest, wisest of wizards.

***

Igdahven returned to the physical realm, where he was greeted immediately by the pain of his severed arm from days before. He felt fortunate to have passed out before they cauterized it, and that the wound did not grow infected. Oddly at times, he still felt where his fingers should be. He couldn't begrudge Garl for the loss of his arm after the bite, surely his life had been saved by the stand-in chieftain's decisive action.

What he didn't care for was that as soon as he woke up, he was forced to move once again despite his condition. When Garl's scouts returned, informing him that they found two old sets of footprints heading away from Big Bear, he wasted no time in going after them. Before anyone had time to disagree, Garl took twenty-five men, Igdahven included, and headed south.

"Any news?" Garl asked as Igdahven emerged from his tent and approached the campfire.

He had asked the same question the previous two mornings, hoping the spirit-seeker was able to find answers that were hidden to the rest of them.

"Yes, as a matter of fact," Igdahven replied, "I did not find Jvard but I was able to locate the wizard."

Garl leaned forward with anticipation, gesturing Igdahven to continue.

"He is currently imprisoned," Igdahven began, and clarified himself as he saw Garl growing anxious, "the wizard, that is, by the name of Walt Whirten. They travelled to Creekview's Crossing together, where they were ambushed by one of the wizard's former acquaintances. Jvard may have escaped, the fel-born wasn't sure what became of him after they separated."

"And you believe this tale?" Garl asked skeptically.

"I do, at least this much of it," Igdahven replied after hesitating only a brief moment, "he seems genuinely concerned for Jvard. It's the rest of the wizard's story that I hesitate to trust."

Garl, though he grew impatient permitted Igdahven to continue. He was sure whatever he was about to hear would be no more than lies concocted by the wizard to serve his own ends, whatever those may be.

Pleased that Garl wished to hear the rest, Igdahven continued, "The wizard claims he knows who is responsible for the disaster that befell not only our people, but all people across the entirety of Luskir. It is a witch, named Sevra. She has some of her army at Creekview and is trying to appear a savior, even though in reality she was the cause of all the problems."

"So what's this to do with Jvard?" Garl asked gruffly, his frown growing deeper.

"Jvard returned to the Ridges and believed everyone had perished, and was then harried south where he became entangled with the wizard at Big Bear. Walt, the wizard, informed him that further knowledge may be available in a place far south, a keep in some place known as Dale's ford. Jvard, having no other purpose agreed to accompany him," Igdahven answered.

The story seemed plausible to Garl, though he still had his doubts.

"So now the wizard has been captured, and Jvard's on his own somewhere outside of Creekview," he confirmed.

"That's how it seems," nodded Igdahven, "and, the wizard warned that what he last saw of Creekview looked like an achoyid den after a silverfrost stuck its paw inside."

Garl raised his eyebrow at the use of the northerner's expression.

"Not his words exactly but it sums up the sentiment," Igdaven clarified.

"Good work then, Igdahven. Keep trying to locate Jvard, we'll find 'em even if we have to scour the entire city," Garl said confidently.

The affairs of the southlands belonged to nobody but the southerners, as far as Garl was concerned. Finding Jvard was all he cared about. With their tribe nearly decimated they needed him back where he belonged, now more than ever.

A Time for Action

Perhaps Devin had been right all along, Myrna wondered while they patiently awaited their turn for food to be rationed out. Much of the rest of the crowd did not show similar restraint. Staying at Creekview was slowly revealing itself to be no less risky than had they taken their chances on their own in the wilds.ABOUT Fights, like the one breaking out that very moment, were becoming increasingly common.

"There will be enough this time, I promise," Myrna said as they waited.

"You said that yesterday," Devin replied glumly, watching the dwindling supply of goods at the heavily guarded wagons.

Based on the number of people still crowding around, he did not have high hopes. The entire town of Midao arrived the previous evening, along with Mayor Radford that very morning. He and Myrna spent most of the day with them, enjoying the familiarity the villagers provided. Radford apologized profusely for not bringing Myrna's horse, Honey, back to her, stating that he intended to but the animal must have run off before he could retrieve it.

Though the guards came by to dispense food regularly, it usually ran out early, especially now that the island was so greatly overcrowded. Two massive barges were nearly finished to alleviate the crowding, but it did nothing to help feed everyone. Many hadn't eaten in days, and the general mood of the mass of people began to grow dark.

"That's it, all out for today," came a shout from the wagon, which was followed by groans and angry shouts.

Every day, the announcement that the rations were depleted caused sporadic skirmishes to ripple across the island before they were quelled by the soldiers. This time, the fighting did not die down; instead it spread like a wildfire over parched grassland. Yells mingled with cries of terror created a sound the likes of which Devin never experienced before or hoped to again. The guards formed a perimeter with their shields around the wagons, and runners were sent to the Inner City for reinforcements. Over the past few days, they grew accustomed to controlling the crowd, but today was beyond their ability.

Devin had never been in a place with so many people before, and found the experience frightening. Having always lived in a small village, he could only assume this was how people acted in the big city. It made him wonder why anyone would ever want to stay somewhere like this.

Where he once thought that wishing everyone dead had caused them to become Greymen, he began to question if that was possible. Rather than cheer him up, it was almost a depressing notion. The world was far too big, bigger than he could have ever imagined and filled with more people than he could count. He was small, insignificant.

A tug at his arm stole him away from his brooding, the mob of people and violence was yet to be quelled and grew dangerously close. He allowed Myrna to pull him along, somewhere safer, if there was such a place they could reach. It seemed as if half of the island had worked itself into a frenzy, while the other half moved to the edges trying to get away from it. Radford futilely tried to organize the people of Midao, but they were spread out and the rioting too intense.

More guards began to file out of the Inner City, what must have been nearly every Drakvnar as well as most of the soldiers on their way to help stem the rioting. Devin watched in quiet shock as a man was hit over the head from behind and collapsed to the ground only thirty feet away. What was the point of going on in a world like this? People killing each other over food, they were hardly better than the Greymen.

Myrna wrapped her arms around him protectively as soldiers rushed by, and did her best to move both of them further from harm's way.

"It can't stay like this forever, Devin," she said softly, offering herself some comfort as much as him, "nature has a way of correcting itself, this is only temporary. Just follow me and we'll be okay."

The two of them had been through so much to get here safely. She had to believe the disorder at Creekview would pass, there was nowhere else for them to go.

***

Jvard followed the rivers northward to the outskirts of Creekview, staying underwater and out of view as much as he could after escaping the Inner City. It was a precarious position he found himself in, weaponless and alone in an unfamiliar land. He was pleased to see the horses still alive where they left them, and that their wagon hadn't been ransacked. Jvard lay down in the back, behind their supplies while he tried to think of what he should do. He couldn't abandon Walt; not only would it be dishonorable, he needed the wizard if he was going to find and eliminate the one responsible for the destruction of his tribe. With the Inner City walled and heavily secured, he didn't know where to begin in trying to free Walt.

He closed his eyes for a time, exhausted. It was dangerous being alone these days; at least when he had a travelling companion they could sleep in shifts. As Jvard lay there, he nearly drifted off several times, his eyes popping open in his effort to resist falling asleep. He needed to stay awake and form a plan, but none was forthcoming in his sleep deprived state. A faint thumping sound drifted into his thoughts, the rhythm of it nearly lulling him further towards slumber. As it drew closer and became louder he jumped awake, realizing someone was approaching. Banging his head on the canopy, he fumbled over Walt's belongings to stand up and get out of the wagon, cursing and accidentally kicking over one of Walt's barrels of explosive powder. He winced when it thudded onto the floor, and breathed a sigh of relief that its lid remained tight.

Exiting the wagon he saw a man on horseback galloping by. Jvard could see the rider's exhaustion by the way he held himself, slumping forward as the horse jostled him heavily. As the rider saw Jvard, he gave the barbarian a panicked look and began to wave his arms frantically.

"Run! Go! Go!" he shouted as he neared and rode past, flying by a confused Jvard.

It didn't take long for Jvard to catch on and see the source of the rider's dismay, as a stampede of the Stricken rounded the bend further up the road.

But Jvard did not run, and was frozen in place by what he saw.

"By the Gods," he whispered, recognizing each of their faces when they drew closer.

His former tribesmen that had given him chase from the Blue Fold Mountain Range, all those weeks ago, were again before him. Shoving down a sick feeling rising into his throat, and channeling his anger into action, he set into motion. Quickly rummaging through the wagon, he found and pocketed Walt's flint striking stone as well as a flask of oil. A rusty, short sword was the only extra weapon they packed away, it would have to do for now.

Jumping back out, he reached in and hoisted one of the hundred pound barrels of powder as if it were lightly packed with feathers, shouldering it and mounting the larger of the two horses. It neighed in protest at the sudden, heavy burden of rider and barrel. The other horseman came to a stop further along the road, slowing to allow Jvard to catch up to him.

Baerne's eyes seemed to be playing tricks on him while the stranger from the wagon rode in his direction. He couldn't quite pinpoint what was out of sorts, but it was like looking at a painting where the subject was drawn too large for the background. It took Baerne a moment to catch on that the person was simply very large, and that he was also riding an enormous draft horse, further playing tricks with his perception.

Afraid he was going to be run down, Baerne spurred his horse out of the way, but the giant simply rode past with the focus and determination a hammer might have while pounding an ingot flat.

"Follow me!" the stranger barked, galloping off while balancing a sizable barrel in the crook of his shoulder.

Glancing back at the Infected gaining ground, he needed no encouragement. He set his hesitation aside and followed after the stranger, his fatigue temporarily alleviated now that he was no longer alone. Riding hard for far too long, he had been rotating his horses until only a few hours ago when his spare succumbed to overexertion. It was worth the cost, successfully leading the horde away from his village, foiling the Guard-Captain Ramnar's plans and keeping his town safe. He hoped they weren't going too far now, though; this horse was on its last legs as well. Baerne caught up and rode at the stranger's side, not quite sure of what to make of him.

"You should slip away when we get into the city, take a side avenue and double back around if none follow you," the man told him.

"What is it you're doing?" Baerne asked after riding for many minutes, growing concerned.

"Leading my kin to their final battle," was the only reply.

"But my people are here!" Baerne said fiercely, a fire igniting within him as he realized this person could be, intentionally or not, using the Infected to put his family and friends once again in danger in much the same manner as Ramnar intended.

If he had to fight this behemoth to keep everyone he knew safe, he would do so.

Jvard eyed the simple, rustic man at his side and the resolute set of his jaw. He looked to be a down-to-earth, earnest person, perhaps a farmer or field hand. Intent was what now drove Jvard, any indecision, either his or this newcomer's, would be disastrous. He needed this person on his side or out of his way. There wasn't time right now for an argument, but he could tell one was coming.

Growling and pulling the horse to a stop, Jvard took control and issued an ultimatum, "The ones calling themselves Drakvnar and their soldiers in the city are holding someone I owe my life to, they are the only ones I intend to hurt. I've seen men like them before, if your people are here they will only be subjugated by them. I am not your enemy. But mark my words, they are whether you realize it yet or not. Choose a side."

The words rang of truth to Baerne, he had seen it first hand. Suddenly he felt ashamed; here he had been, hiding in the woods after watching his village occupied and his father cut down. He knew nothing about the individual before him, but it only took one look to see he wouldn't have tolerated the same. Though Baerne didn't consider himself a coward, he began to feel like he had acted like one.

"This group chasing us, they were intended to be unleashed upon Midao by the Guard-Captain of the Drakvnar," Baerne explained, "I know full well who the enemy is."

The Infected again began to gain ground, and it was time for Baerne to make a decision.

"Lead the way," he offered.

"Good," Jvard answered and began to ride ahead, "do your best not to get in the way. I still suggest you leave when you get an opportunity to do so."

"We'll see," Baerne answered, "my name is Baerne, by the way."

"I am Jvard, son of Helstajvan. Let's be off, it's not very far."

Jvard wound through the streets of Creekview's Crossing, maintaining as straight a line as possible along the meandering roads towards the Inner City. After turning a corner he pulled his horse short, grimacing at the street full of the Stricken. Many were in the uniforms of soldiers, and some even in the black hide leather of the Drakvnar, indicating to him they had made an ill prepared effort to retake parts of the city.

Turning down several alleys and side roads, they emerged closer towards their goal with even more of the Infected in tow. By the time they neared the gate, their numbers had nearly tripled.

"This is growing far too dangerous to ask you along," Jvard advised, "you should head back around the city and out."

Baerne shook his head. After all the running he'd done, for the first time in days he no longer felt powerless or hunted. Having already made up his mind, he answered, "No, I brought those things this far, I will see it through."

"Once you've made enemies of these people there is no going back," Jvard reminded, giving him one last opportunity.

"I've already made enemies of them back at my village," Baerne said flatly, "I'm beyond the point of being able to go back."

"Very well," Jvard stated, understanding the sentiment and not feeling the need to inquire further, "the next street up, take a right and then another left. I'll meet you around the side of the gate, move!"

The massive horde relentlessly approached from behind, filling the entire roadway. Jvard raced up the avenue toward the gate, barrel still on his shoulder, watching Baerne disappear across the side street as instructed. On their original trek south to Creekview, Walt had made quite a bit of conversation to pass the time. Much of it was about his 'famous' black powder, used mostly to clear the mining shafts. Just a teaspoon would do the trick for most any job, he had said with the same pride a warrior would hold for his prized weapon. Jvard hoped an entire barrel would take care of the job he had in mind right now.

Davil sat atop the gate of the Inner City, reflecting on the life that seemed so long ago to him now, though in reality it had only been several weeks. How much things could change in a few short weeks. He was a soldier now; his business was no more, and family lost to the wild creatures outside of the secure walls. What need did people have for his fine gildwork when they were preoccupied with finding food and the simple act of survival? Before he had time to grow saddened once again by his loss, a crazed rider making a wild approach brusquely reminded him of his new duties.

"Hey, easy there fellow, what business have you here..." he began to shout.

The gilder-turned-soldier trailed off when he saw the army of Infected in the rider's wake as they emerged from around the buildings and houses. He began to run for the alarm bell, and realized nearly all of the soldiers and Drakvnar were off dealing with a riot on the eastern island – but Daro and all of his followers were still within the Inner City. Resisting the urge to panic, he would go to Daro to get as many bowmen together as he could, surely the preacher would cooperate under these circumstances. Nothing terrible had yet happened, nor would it; they were safe behind a solid gate and protective walls.

Jvard nearly laughed at the terror he saw in the fleeing soldier's eyes as he vacated his post at the wall. Unfortunately, he was in no mood for mirth while he led his tribesmen to their last battle. They would meet an honorable death in combat as they were meant to; it was the least he could do for those he abandoned. He set the barrel down in front of the gate and hurriedly set to work before the Stricken caught up to him. Hesitating only briefly, he uncorked the oil and began spreading much of it around the base of the barrel, and some along its sides. There were surely innocent people he would be placing in danger, but it was the Drakvnar and soldiers he was after. He needed them distracted while he retrieved the foolish wizard. Already having his mind set, he pushed forward with his plan.

Running away to what he thought would be a safe distance, he picked up a fair sized rock along the way, just the right size so he could throw it comfortably with both hands. He removed some of the animal hides that served as his chest armor, hastily wrapping and tying it around the rock. Dousing it with more of the oil, he lit it on fire with Walt's flint striking tool. With a grimace, he grabbed the flaming ball at chest height, and heaved it forward at the barrel.

His thick, callused hands prevented them from getting terribly burned, though he felt they were red and tender from the flames. Praying his aim was true, he waited with anticipation until the flaming rock rolled by the barrel, catching the oil around it on fire. He watched as the Stricken piled up against the gate, and then funneled down the tight pathway towards him.

Panic, or a feeling as close to panic that Jvard could ever reach washed over him as he thought his plan failed; he had hoped for more than just a few flames. He'd still have to try to carry on with his attempt to rescue Walt, but now had no diversion and would likely meet heavy resistance after somehow gaining access to the Inner City. He began to run, signaling Baerne who was slightly further ahead to do likewise.

An odd sensation ran through Jvard when he began to move, a vibration that coursed through his entire body. It happened so fast he hardly had time to think about it before hearing the loudest noise he ever heard in his life. He had nothing to compare it to, if thunder were to fall from the sky and strike near his head he thought it might come close to the violence of the sound. Disoriented, he had a vague notion that his feet were no longer on the ground and he was flying forward, while Baerne stood a safe distance away with his mouth agape.

Bodies of the Infected flew in Baerne's direction, while Jvard launched forward, away from a dust cloud of smoke and debris.

Both horses bolted at the loud noise, Baerne's running away after rearing up and throwing him. A small section in the middle of the immense stone gate shifted slightly, dropping several feet. The entire structure paused and held there precariously for a tense second, and in the span of a breath the entire gate collapsed in on itself, taking part of the adjoining wall down with it.

Jvard thudded to the ground, close to Baerne's feet after careering along the alley. Pushing himself up onto a knee, he attempted to stand. His very bones felt sore from the concussive explosion, leaving him struggling to get to his feet. Finally with his legs underneath him, he shook his head, trying to clear the daze while he staggered to the wall for support. The ground beneath him would not stop spinning.

Baerne was pointing, shouting and trying to tell him something, but all he could hear was a high pitch ringing that slightly oscillated in tone.

"C'mon, we can't stay here!" Baerne yelled frantically, some of the Infected still coming at them.

Many of the Stricken were blown into pieces, severed limbs landing far from their owners, but many more weren't within the blast radius, and continued onward either over the rubble of the former gate into the Inner City or along the wall towards Jvard and Baerne. The blacksmith tugged at Jvard's arm, nearly pulling the big man over while he tried to regain his sense of balance. With a curse he ducked his head under Jvard's shoulder, catching most of his weight to prevent him from falling, and buckling his knees in the process.

"You're a madman!" Baerne yelled, and was left wondering what kind of person he got himself mixed up with.

Jvard still only heard the loud, discordant hum, watching Baerne's lips move with no sound. When battle was upon him a glorious song unerringly coursed through his veins, guiding him and providing strength. Still trying to gather his senses, there was no song, only the dissonant clatter of a cavernous echo reverberating throughout his skull.

With his head still spinning from the blast he was of little use, and Baerne didn't know where to go as they retreated from the main gate. Jvard pulled away, nearly taking both of them from their feet when he realized his cohort was leading them away from where he needed to be. The barbarian found a wall to lean against while he continued to try to regain his bearings, but there was little time. Though many of the Stricken had broken off to head into the Inner

City and some were caught in the explosion, a small group remained in pursuit of the pair.

Jvard focused on the one thing he still had full control over, his breathing - in for four heartbeats, then out for four more. He repeated the exercise twice as the Infected loped towards them down the alleyway.

"Hey, you," Baerne said, snapping his fingers under the nose of the semiconscious barbarian, frustration outweighing his nerves caused by the oncoming horde, "we can't stay here!"

Indicating his agreement, Jvard motioned they continue, pointing Baerne northward along the wall. He remained focused on his breathing; though he still didn't quite feel himself and was seeing double, he found it easier to put one leg in front of the other. Once he had a foothold to the rhythm of his breathing, he shifted his concentration into coordinating his movement. Increasing his pace he put one foot in front of the other, slowly recovering and moving under his own power. Soon he relied less on Baerne for support, and they regained a comfortable distance from their pursuers.

The separate, clashing harmonies within Jvard began to resolve themselves, converging together into a solitary, unified chorus. His strength began to return in earnest, a determined fire burning in his eyes once again leaving Baerne somewhat shocked from the speed of his recovery.

"Alright, then?" Baerne asked as they continued to flee, Jvard pulling away from the blacksmith's support and moving on his own.

Jvard nodded, still in pain but continuing to feel better with each breath he drew. The first part of his plan didn't go exactly as he would have wished, but then again, he supposed that was the way of most things. He embraced the need to be adaptive, and would accept each turn of fate and turn it to advantage, as he had ever done. Right now, the wizard he owed his life to needed the favor returned, and he would do whatever it took to see that debt repaid.

Baerne could no longer ignore his confusion as they ran around the wall, if they intended to go into the Inner City there was only the one entrance.

"Where are we going, Jvard? There's nothing back here but the river. Looks like it's at its widest point too for that matter," Baerne asked doubtfully, the thought of swimming across it not a pleasant one.

"The soldiers constructed lifts at the back of the city, bringing goods in by boat and over the wall to avoid using the front gates and streets," Jvard answered between heavy breaths, confident this was a better way in than running straight through the front.

Arriving towards the rear of the Inner City, as Jvard hoped some of the lifts were down on the ground. The nearest was still ten feet in the air, which Jvard found both curious and fortunate. He jumped up, easily grabbing the edge and pulling himself onto it. Leaning down, he reached his arm towards Baerne and assisted him up as well. Quickly they began to climb, Baerne following Jvard's lead. The Infected were soon underneath the lift, reaching up in frustration as their quarry eluded them once again.

Before pulling himself onto the wall, Jvard lifted his head over only so much as to peek above the ledge. He wanted to avoid confrontation until it was absolutely necessary; hopefully with the disorder he created they could slip in and out with Walt, unnoticed. Looking over the wall, he couldn't have done a better job of inciting pandemonium. Infected streamed through the front gate and for some reason there seemed to be very few soldiers at hand, though many of the residents of the Inner City had taken up arms.

He grimaced at the lack of guardsmen, not anticipating their apparent absence. Where in the Fel-waste were they? The thought that he might cause innocent people harm brought him grief, but he didn't allow himself to dwell over it. What's done was done. A few fires broke out as well, whether purposely or by accident he couldn't tell.

"All is clear along the wall," Jvard said while he hoisted himself over and offered a hand to the blacksmith.

He turned away, nearly ready to proceed from the heights when he saw the crankshaft connected to the lift's ropes.

"Just a moment," he said.

He worked the lever, hoisting the lift up towards them as the Stricken stood some hundred feet below like a pack of wild animals fenced out of a farm. Before Baerne could ask what he was doing, Jvard instructed him to bring up a second lift. He followed the order without asking questions, not sure of what Jvard might be thinking but deciding it would be best to just do as instructed.

As Jvard's elevator neared the top of the wall, he locked the shaft in place and drew his sword. With a quick slice, the rope was severed sending the lift crashing down below. He watched its descent until it slammed into the group of Infected, driving them down to the ground where they did not rise again.

Still confused, Baerne drew his weapon and made to cut at his rope as well.

"Not that one!" Jvard whispered harshly, "In case we have to come back out this way, we'll have a way down."

Baerne nodded, feeling slightly foolish for not thinking that through himself.

"Trust me, you don't want to have to jump from up here," the barbarian told him with a wry smile.

"So where are we going?" Baerne asked, thinking that though the Inner City was not particularly large, trying to find a single person without knowing where he was seemed impossible.

Jvard surveyed the disarray along the streets, and watched as what he intended to only be a distraction grew increasingly out of hand with each passing breath. The Stricken were pouring into the city now, it seemed even more had crawled out from their hiding places and were attracted towards the ruined gate. He didn't have every action planned and thought out. Generally if he knew his starting point and end goal, all things inbetween were merely minor details that would work themselves out. Those minor details were beginning to add up.

Despite his increasing concern, so far it was going as well as he could reasonably expect. The rear section of the city had not yet been overrun as most of the fighting taking place was near the front gates and slowly spreading in their direction. It gave him a few moments to plot his next course of action. He knew Walt was still somewhere nearby, and he would find him if he had to turn the city upside down in the process.

"He's still in this city. I've been watching the last two days and saw no signs of him brought out," Jvard answered, thinking aloud more than talking to Baerne.

But where did they bring him? Was he in a room at the palace, locked in a cellar, or tied up and thrown on the floor of a tent somewhere in the middle of the army's encampment?

As he looked across the open expanse of the Inner City, he spotted a small group of soldiers gathering together, led by a particularly rotund captain that Jvard encountered once before. The thought of meeting him once again pleased Jvard; they had unfinished business.

"Follow me. Don't engage with anyone, let them stay busy fighting the Stricken," Jvard instructed to Baerne, "I don't know where Walt is, but I know who can tell me."

Finding a way down from the wall through the nearest tower, Jvard took a path to intercept Kempf and his group of soldiers.

A Debt Repaid

Myrna turned away for only a moment, looking for somewhere to run and hoping the fighting on their island would die down. No area seemed to be safe. Reaching out to take Devin's hand, she panicked when she noticed he was no longer there. In the split second she turned her head, he simply disappeared from sight. Frantically she called out to him, scanning the area to no avail.

"Devin!" she screamed at the top of her lungs, what would possess the boy to run off at a time like this?

The violence only escalated in the last hour as soldiers poured out from the Inner City. Myrna was surrounded by bedlam, mostly with the Dun'Aldirans battling the original residents of Creekview's Crossing, though she thought she noticed some of the villagers of Midao joining in against the guardsmen. Many lay dead on the ground, including soldiers, Drakvnar, or residents of Creekview who joined in the rioting.

A resounding crash echoed across the valley and shook the very ground they stood on, causing a brief halt to some of the bloodshed while both sides looked around in startlement. Amidst all the chaos, Myrna thought it within possibility that the earth just might be falling apart. It was a fortunate break for her though, because only one person was still moving determinedly, his little head bobbing up and down as he ran. She sprinted after Devin, but spirits save her she forgot how fast the boy could run.

The fighting resumed in pockets across the islet. Some skirmishes continued straight through the disturbance, the combatants paying little or no mind to the blast, and some even taking advantage of their opponent's distraction. Devin continued running directly across the battlefield, heedless of the danger as if he lost his faculties. Myrna noticed him becoming more withdrawn of late, especially since the incident at Midao.

Maybe something inside of him finally snapped, she supposed. She'd have to save that worry for later; presently, she needed to get both him and herself out of danger before one of them was accidentally stabbed or decapitated.

She continued to scream out to him, but either he couldn't hear over the din or was altogether ignoring her. He was shorter than most of the men fighting, and seemed to be able to slip through largely unnoticed and untouched. She on the other hand, had a difficult time keeping up with him while trying to skirt around any conflicts. Many times she lost sight of him, but was able to find him again because he moved in such a direct path. The challenge for her was avoiding getting accidentally clubbed over the head by one of these buffoons fighting each other.

Devin continued unerringly towards the destroyed bridge that once connected the sections of land, in the direction of the Inner City. Mercifully, the number of combatants began to thin out when they reached the edge of the isle. Diving in the water after Devin, she arrived on the other side of the narrow river shortly behind him. They may have left the battlefield, but the boy was leading them into a different type of danger. She knew soldiers had retaken some parts of the city, or at least intended to, but she had no idea where they had been successful as of yet. She prayed this area was safe, and Devin wasn't leading them towards an army of Greymen around the next corner.

Why would he run away, what could have possessed him to do such a thing? She had half a mind or more to give him a sound thrashing should she ever catch up to him, but she was beginning to grow tired and fall further behind. Worse, they had attracted a few of the Infected as they ran through the city, and because she was behind Devin they were more of an immediate threat to her as they pursued. She couldn't bear the idea of leaving Devin to fend for himself, but could not keep up this pace much longer and her position was becoming precarious.

"Devin," she breathed out sadly, not much louder than a whisper.

She couldn't do it; he had gotten too far ahead and ran as if he were driven by the devil's own whip. A small tributary was not far to the south, and with a heavy heart she had to make for it. If she could reach it, she might be able to stay alive.

***

Up there, onto the hill is where you need to be. There's plenty of food over the river, many houses, soft beds – you could probably slip in there with no one even noticing. Devin was unsure if the thought was his own, or came to him from somewhere else. It seemed to originate from inside of his head, but it felt like another person speaking to him. Whether his own thought or not, it sounded like the best idea he had heard in a long while. His feet began to move before he even realized it. They did not stop until he was at the outskirts of the Inner City.

Devin saw that the big gate keeping everyone out of the Inner City was no longer there, replaced instead by a large pile of rubble. *Perfect*, he thought, his worries easing about how he was going to get in. Finally luck was in his favor for a change. Looking back he saw Myrna chasing after him, and a fair sized group of Greymen they had attracted on their flight to the city. His legs trembled as he tried to turn around and run to her, but for some reason he couldn't get them to cooperate. Another thought came to him, prompting him onward; he felt bad to ignore her, but she didn't understand. They had been stuck living in the mud and their own filth, while people here behind the gate still had nice homes and safety.

Devin took a step forward, but hesitated after hearing the terrifying wails of men and continued sounds of battle.

Wait! The voice came to him again, *There's probably another way in, safer. Go around, keep looking.*

Now Devin felt a chill run through him, that was definitely not his thought.

"Hello?" he thought and asked aloud, unsure of what he expected to hear back.

Devin felt the response as a surge of annoyance, mingled with urgency. A sudden compulsion to move along the wall and find another way in overwhelmed him, and again he set off. It was then he realized he didn't leave the field to come here of his own accord. Distantly he recognized he was moving - probably to somewhere he shouldn't be, but could do nothing about it.

***

The wizard confined to the diamond currently in Devin's care had never made such a direct exertion on the boy before, or any of his previous bearers for that matter. He once reached through Devin in a dream, trying to warn the woman watching over him of the impending doom. That was much easier to accomplish; the boy had been directly touching the gem at the time and also sleeping, his mind more open for him to enter. In the end he reproached himself for that particular decision. Since then Devin hadn't handled the gem at all, making it much more difficult to assess anything going on in the outside world.

It was a great risk the wizard took just by reaching outside of the diamond, breaching the magic's protective encasement. Outside of the gem he was exposed and vulnerable, and subsequently placing the binding spell that sealed Kubathu at risk. He supposed it didn't matter, his end was soon approaching and he was desperate. Suffusing his essence into the gem had greatly extended the life of his spirit, but it was still finite and the inevitable end was upon him. Despite that knowledge, he felt good this day, clear of thought and full of purpose. He needed to do whatever it took to find the master nearby and pass the burden onto him.

Firmly entrenched in Devin's mind, he saw what the boy saw, willed him to move as he desired. The sounds of fighting at the front entrance and piles of rock and strewn debris indicated that way was too dangerous, there had to be another access point over the walls. If his estimation was correct, the person he was looking for was further towards the rear of the enclosed part of the city. It would be much better to get in as close as possible.

There was a difficult balance for the wizard to strike; he needed to take control of Devin's actions so they were performed without hesitation, but also needed to be careful not to cause any permanent damage or complications. Sharing a mind was a delicate task, one he was far out of practice with, and even more difficult when one of the participants was unwilling. Pushing Devin's thoughts to the outskirts of his psyche, he was careful not to eject them altogether. Occasionally they crept back in as the wizard ran Devin around the wall, looking for any place they might be able to get in.

What was most overpowering to the wizard was Devin's concern for his travelling companion, Myrna. Many times he looked back involuntarily as Devin's worry bled through into their shared consciousness, revealing her in pursuit followed by a pack of Greymen hungrily giving her chase. She looked to be slowing, and eventually he no longer saw her or the Greymen when looking over his shoulder to check. Stifling a surge of distress originating from Devin, he continued forward in search of a way in. The wizard felt remorse for forcing Myrna into danger, but he could not linger on it. The completion of this task was paramount, and more important than any one person's safety.

As he reached the rear section of the fortified area, the smell almost brought him to his knees. There was a series of lifts and ropes on a small ledge of land he nearly had to climb to, and crushed under one of them was a pile of corpses. The lift shifted slightly as some of the bodies struggled to move, and both the wizard and Devin felt a wash of relief when they realized it was more of the Greymen, not people, trapped or destroyed under the machinery. Again he pushed Devin's thoughts aside, ran to the next lift over and began to arduously climb one of the ropes. He could sense the master was near.

***

Bruised and battered, and walking with a mild limp, the Guard Captain saw the city of Creekview's Crossing appear on the horizon as the sun began to set. Though he was haggard and thoroughly exhausted, he was still alive and driven onward by an intense hatred. He was going to personally skin Mayor Radford and stretch his hide across a pole. The Infected nearly took him when the two last parted ways outside of Midao, after Radford felled his horse leaving Ramnar to fight for his life and scramble to safety – and fight he did. After all he had been through to achieve his rank and abilities, it would require more than a few mindless husks to take him down.

He ventured over to Midao shortly after his skirmish with the Infected to find the village completely empty. The damned blacksmith, he must have spotted him and his men baiting the Infected towards the village, and went back to warn them. Taking the only horse available in Midao he set off to Creekview, hoping the mayor sent his people there and would likely try to join back up with them. Regardless of where the mayor had gone, it was time for him to resume his duties at Creekview. There was no doubt that his second in command, Kempf, had many uses, but successfully managing the entire force for an extended period was not one of them.

Unfortunately for Ramnar the mare turned out to be completely untrustworthy and skittish. Likely startled by a snake, it threw him and bolted away, leaving him with only his own two feet for the final half of the excursion to the Crossing. Spitting grass from his mouth, he resigned himself to the fact that just about everything that could have gone wrong in the last two days had gone wrong. After picking himself up, he used the time spent walking to further feed his anger for the mayor and blacksmith.

As Ramnar drew close, the pile of dust rising above the Inner City and mixing into the hazy pink-tinged sky of sunset prompted a surge of alarm through his veins. His vantage point from the cliff also revealed the eastern island was in the midst of a battle. It looked like every blasted one of his men was down on that island. He cursed loudly, wondering how in the name of the Empress that Kempf allowed things to deteriorate so rapidly. He decided to make for the Inner City first. Many possibilities of what might have happened crossed Ramnar's mind, but mostly he suspected to find Daro at the center of the turmoil. If he wanted to find the preacher, that would be where to start looking.

As Ramnar approached the ruined gate, running through unimpeded into the Inner City, the anarchy was far beyond anything he could have imagined. As he suspected he saw very few of his True-Blood or soldiers from Dun'Aldir, it was mostly the fools who followed Daro fighting for their lives against a legion of the Infected, and fighting poorly at that. These people were not trained warriors, just regular citizens fighting with the desperation of an animal backed into a corner.

Drawing his flambard, the undulated, black blade was a unique piece upon almost any battlefield. Crafted to match his stature, the two handed sword was so large most men would not have been able to handle it effectively.

The Infected appeared to be gaining the upper hand as they spread throughout the Inner City, leaving pockets of men to fend for themselves. There were nearly as many men dead or near death on the ground, being feasted upon, as there were alive and still in combat.

Two of the Infected drew too close to Ramnar, and with a single swipe he lopped off both of their heads. Each generated a fountain of blood, their bodies dropping to the ground in a heap. The heads landed soon after, their eyes still alert and jaws working soundlessly. At the western end of the open area before the palace, he did see one figure darting in and out among the throng, enemies falling wherever he went.

Begrudgingly, Ramnar had to admit that Daro the Bladefist lived up to his honorific. The man truly believed he had been chosen by a God, and watching him in motion Ramnar could see why others might be hesitant to doubt. It was like he had an extra set of eyes guiding him as he landed blind thrusts at odd angles, or dodged attacks that he should not have been able to see coming. He would love to take the opportunity to cut the preacher down amidst all the chaos and confusion, but it was far too dangerous to find a clear path to him at this time.

Ramnar saw all he needed to here. Disgusted with everything, the dead rising, the Inner City overrun, Daro's prowess, and Kempf allowing it all to fall apart, he decided to gather what was left of his troops at the eastern isle and attempt to salvage what he could.

***

It was days like this that made Kempf loathe being the one in command. He couldn't envision circumstances unfolding in a worse possible manner than they had during the course of the afternoon. It was bad enough that a full scale riot was taking place on the only island they managed to secure; if that were the only problem he had to deal with it would have been no more than a nuisance. His confidence in quelling the riot greatly deteriorated when some new devilry, the likes of which he had never seen, obliterated their front door. It was as if the Gods shook the earth and hurled a ball of lightning and fire at his gate, then spewed forth the dead to devour them.

Worse, if that were possible, some of the Plague-touched they battled were unlike any he had encountered before. They were enormous, powerful creatures – many even larger than the elite Drakvnar. Kempf himself was bigger than most men he came across, with an unrivaled girth, but even he found some of these Infected difficult to manage. Battling with a flail and kite shield large enough that it would have served as a tower shield for an average sized man, the First Lieutenant was a formidable force against the Infected. Most of his men were away securing the isle, but he was able to find and lead a ten man contingent that fared better than most in the Inner City.

After dispatching a few stragglers, an entire group of the fel-spawned creatures approached. They seemed to be pouring through the gate in an endless stream, and this particular batch was mostly the large ones. Some neared or maybe even topped seven feet tall, their decomposing flesh not yet detracting from the thickness of their frames.

Kempf did a double take when he assessed the new enemy, seeing another man approaching from off to the side that moved too fluidly, had eyes that were too vibrant for one of the Infected.

"You!" Kempf roared, enraged by the one he saw before him.

It had been a few days, but he certainly would not forget the wizard's odd companion that bruised his jaw during his escape from the cellar of the palace. Another man seemed to be fighting in tandem with him, keeping away any of the Infected that came too close.

"Where is the wizard?" the barbarian demanded, bringing his sword up into a ready position as he moved in towards Kempf, skirting around the Infected.

Jvard's focus was solely on the bulky officer that assisted in Walt's capture, trusting Baerne to watch his blind spots for as long as necessary.

The two men were left to square off with one another while Kempf's men were fully occupied trying to fend off the most recent incoming attack. Tired and outnumbered nearly two to one by physically larger enemies, they were hard pressed to merely stand their ground, much less make any progress towards dispatching their foes.

"Of course you'd have to show up now, on top of everything else today. I knew you were going to be trouble the moment I laid eyes on you," Kempf spat, "I'd love to see you die slowly, but as you can see I've not the time for that."

"Release the wizard to me, and I'll be out of your way," Jvard told him honestly, frankly nothing would have made him happier than to leave this forsaken city behind.

Raising his shield and proceeding towards the barbarian, Kempf made one last remark before launching into an attack, "You should have gone back to wherever you came from when you had the chance, wanderer."

The strike came with surprising ferocity, leaving Jvard to sidestep rather than making an attempt to parry. He approached the fight cautiously at the start, not having direct experience in battling a flail-wielding opponent. Among the Blue Fold Mountains, it was seen on occasion but not a commonly used weapon. As the swing came up short, Kempf turned to remain facing Jvard, whipping his arm back down to kill the momentum of the failed attack.

Jvard noticed that Kempf remained well defended during the attack, keeping the shield high and tight while barely peeking over it. They repeated the routine a few times, with Kempf slightly changing the angle of his delivery on each attempt. Continuing to allow Kempf to be the aggressor, Jvard remained elusive as he evaluated his adversary. The First Lieutenant pivoted well to either side, and was persistent with his shield work, never leaving himself vulnerable.

After taking a solid measure of his opponent, Jvard weighed two strategies for handling his fight with the First Lieutenant. The cautious route would have been to allow Kempf to tire himself out and then pounce. Knowing his own skill to be superior, he chose to attack.

As Kempf came in to make another strike, Jvard barely turned his neck, allowing the flail head to whistle by and miss by a hair. Because he had been lulled into the routine, Kempf instinctively began to turn to where he thought Jvard was going to move to, and was caught off balance as Jvard plowed forward instead.

Unleashing a barrage of blows, the barbarian nearly caused the unsteady commander to lose his footing. Jvard lamented the loss of his great axe, or even the sledgehammer he had used since Big Bear and had to abandon after diving into the river. The rusted toothpick of a sword he now used was largely ineffective against the well armored First Lieutenant.

With a poorly crafted weapon and time working against him, Jvard pressed the one advantage he currently held over Kempf – his speed. As he saw Kempf's flail arm come up, Jvard ducked under the strike practically before it was even thrown. Kempf remained off balance as Jvard came back up on his other side, relentlessly raining down blows. Again, they only landed harmlessly onto the shield, but it did serve to prevent Kempf from retaliating and left him struggling to defend himself.

Ending the attack sequence, Jvard allowed his opponent to again bring up his flail arm. Instead of ducking, this time Jvard slammed his shoulder into Kemp's shield before he was able to launch another strike. The Lieutenant stumbled back several feet, resulting in a temporary break to their confrontation.

Their eyes locked for a moment as they stood a dozen feet apart, reevaluating each other's abilities. Kempf found very few weaknesses in Jvard's technique, and knew in his heart that should the skirmish proceed, he would not prevail. That did not give him much motivation to continue their fight. Taking a second to smash the skull of one of the Infected that drew too close, Kempf casually reset the momentum of the flail and returned his gaze to Jvard.

"Soldiers! Fall back and flank!" he yelled suddenly.

Quickly his men disengaged and fell into line around Kempf. In an instant the cluster of Stricken that Kempf's soldiers had been fighting firmly separated Jvard and the First Lieutenant. Baerne was busy fending three off while more steadily approached.

Growling in frustration, Jvard was forced to pull back. He might as well have had a solid wall between himself and Kempf.

Sorely pressed, Jvard watched Baerne decapitate one of the Stricken, and plunge his sword upward under another's throat and through the base of its skull. The strike ended the creature, but he struggled to extricate his weapon as a third grabbed at him from the side. Toppling down with his sword still stuck and the body on top of him, the remaining Stricken followed them down to ground while trying to tear at the blacksmith. Jvard hurried over, kicking it in the head to temporarily stun it as it fell over onto its hands and knees. With one hand he threw the corpse from Baerne, including the implanted sword and hurriedly assisted the blacksmith back to his feet. Baerne rushed forward, setting his foot on the body and jerking his weapon free.

"This way!" Jvard yelled, knocking the stunned Stricken prone while he ran by, taking an extra second to splatter its skull with his boot.

"What's the plan?" Baerne asked as they were forced to circle back around again towards the rear of the city.

Jvard tried to look around, it was becoming increasingly treacherous and crowded with each passing second. He had thought the guards and soldiers would do a better job of handling his improvised diversion. He didn't think that most of the soldiers would be away and the group of Infected he led into the city would grow considerably on their way. What Jvard intended to be a momentary distraction so he could sneak in was beginning to turn into the loss of the Inner City.

"Kempf got away, I wasn't able to get any information," Jvard informed his comrade.

He looked back towards the wall feeling disgraced, it would probably be best to just leave while they still could. He had no idea where Walt was and time was running short. The Inner City wasn't particularly large, but trying to find one person amidst all the fighting was a fool's errand. He hated the thought of coming so far to abandon the rescue, not to mention the destruction he caused. He was able to justify it to himself when he thought he led the Stricken to the soldiers and Drakvnar, but it turned out there were a good number of innocent people who would lose their lives because of his actions. As he looked around, most of those he saw were just regular townsmen fighting to survive.

"By the Gods," he uttered, his jaw dropping as he saw a mere child drop down from the wall and begin sprinting towards the palace with no apparent concern for what was before him.

"What is it?" Baerne asked, cautiously peering about to see what got Jvard's attention while he chased after the barbarian.

"Boy, stop!" Jvard yelled, trying to overtake the youth.

In Jvard's eyes, the entire effort had been a failure. The least he could do was get this lost child to safety, and it would be one less death on his hands. But try as he might, he had no chance of heading him off. The boy was too far ahead and did not hesitate in the slightest as he ran.

"He's moving towards the royal grounds," Baerne noted, stopping next to Jvard as they reached the long stairs leading up to the palace.

They were far enough away from the destroyed gates that they were not amidst the terrors rampaging through the Inner City, but that certainly wouldn't last much longer as the Stricken began to propagate throughout the area. The boy had run himself into a dead end that he wouldn't be able to escape.

"C'mon, we go in after him," Jvard decided.

Baerne shrugged resignedly. He had agreed to follow Jvard's lead at the start of the venture, and as a man of his word wouldn't back out now. Something also seemed familiar about the boy, but he couldn't quite place what it was. It grew eerily quiet as they dashed up the steps, the palace area of the city being nearly empty. Occasionally someone ran by going the other direction, paying no mind as they passed by the boy, then the barbarian and blacksmith.

Entering the building, the main foyer split into a hallway running left to right for nearly a hundred feet either way before dissappearing around the corner. They lost sight of the child, but could hear the telltale pitter-patter of his feet rushing down the corridor.

"This way," Jvard said after pausing to listen, discerning the direction of the echo.

To Baerne's amazement, Jvard pulled ahead of him as they sprinted down the hallway. He would not have guessed the towering northman could outrun him, but that seemed to be the case as he struggled to keep up. After several twists and turns he lost sight of Jvard, and found it necessary to follow the crash of his booming steps.

The sound of footfalls ceased, prompting Baerne to move with more caution. Why had the barbarian stopped running? Pausing at the next turn, he carefully peered around the corner before stepping out. He felt both relief and trepidation when he heard muffled voices not far ahead. One he recognized as Jvard, the other having the signature rasp of one greatly advanced in their years.

"There is no time," the unearthly voice muttered, disturbingly quiet yet clear as a bell at the same time.

Baerne then heard a loud groan and a crash, and hastened beyond the next corridor to find Jvard slumped against the wall breathing heavily. Every hair visible on the barbarian's body stood on end.

"Jvard!" he yelled, approaching the seated giant.

As he came near, Jvard shook his head clear and looked up at him, a seething hatred evident in his eyes.

"Ah, are you alright?" he asked haltedly, suddenly uneasy from the look on the barbarian's face.

From whatever the boy did to him, Jvard felt nearly as rattled as he had immediately following the blast at the gate.

He snarled something unintelligible, Baerne only able to discern the words 'boy', and 'demon spawn.'

Pushing to his feet with a roar, denying his injuries, Jvard abruptly returned to his senses. The latest bang on his head seemed to jar him just enough to restore his faculties, giving him a clear-headedness he hadn't felt since blowing the wall to pieces. Driven by anger, the beat of his heart thundered in his ears and his vision excluded all else except for the demon boy running away down the hall. His muscles swelled from the influx of blood as a rage fell upon him, heightening his senses and narrowing his focus to a blade's edge. There was only the wild drumming of his heartbeat, and his footsteps landing in sharp succession as his legs carried him after the fel-spawn. Few men outside of the northern lands had the frightening honor of seeing a barbarian in the midst of a battle rage; Baerne was presently receiving that honor.

That was no boy, Jvard was convinced. It may have looked like one, but it spoke as if possessed and had an evil magic within him that made Jvard's hackles rise. He couldn't remember a single time when anyone took him from his feet, but the thing masquerading as a child managed to in the hallway. Distantly, he may have felt an innate fear that his people held towards untamed magic and those who wielded it. If he did, he buried it deep down. Resuming the pursuit, he followed the sound of the boy's steps down the stone stairs into the bowels of the palace.

***

Walt awoke once again, surprised at actually feeling refreshed for the first time since his imprisonment. Other than the pain in his fingers, he felt nearly right as rain. Moreover, he remembered well who he was and had a restored sense of urgency that he needed to escape – as soon as possible. It occurred to him that the odd doctor must have missed the last scheduled drugging, and he needed to take advantage of his momentary clarity while he could.

The dream he awoke from was still fresh on his mind, along with the ramblings of the strange, lonely fellow that kept him medicated. Empress Sevra, it must be the very same Sevra of whom the Magicus Celesti forewarned. The connection from the conversation to his dream was vividly clear. The young woman who arrived that day when he was no more than a lad at the keep grounds, it had to be her. Her relationship to the Celesti at that moment hadn't quite yet seemed to be adversarial, leaving him to wonder how and why she had grown into an opponent of the magical order.

He had much to tell Jvard, the barbarian would be pleased to know their enemy was identified. The barbarians! More memories flooded back into Walt, his meeting with the enigmatic spirit-seeker, Igdahven, and their discussion. Jvard had thought them all dead; Walt could imagine how thrilled the ox would be to hear they were on their way to him.

But first things first, he had to get out of this cell. Finally clear of mind, it was difficult to imagine how complacent he became being locked away like this. The small room was damp and dark, and filled with various foul odors. Whatever poison they were giving him must have greatly dulled his mind to make him content with the living conditions. The downside was the poison had also dulled the pain in his hands, which returned with a vengeance now that it was out of his system.

Fighting through the pain he tried to open and clench his fists a few times. He grimaced when only a few fingers closed all the way, while most moved a little and some not at all. That was going to be a problem if he wanted to work any type of spell manipulation. Some of the motions were fine and precise, and needed to be exact if they were to work properly. He'd have to figure that out later, one problem at a time and his foremost need was to escape.

He moved to the door, pushing against it with most of his meager weight. As he expected, it did not budge. Against his better judgment, he rammed his side into it, earning him no more than a bruised shoulder. Circling his arm around to work out the stiffness, he tried to think how he could get out. A blast of air might do the trick, but trying to control it could be unpredictable with his mangled hands.

The metal hinges, after years would succumb to rust. Perhaps he could speed that process along to several days or a few weeks by guiding air and traces of water at them, unfortunately he did not have weeks to spare.

It looked as though he would need to put some thought into this. Exhaling heavily to set his mustache bouncing, he regretted his lack of a pipe to help guide him through the process. Simple solutions were always preferable, and it quickly became evident he would not be able to find one to get himself out of the room.

Many minutes elapsed as he stood staring at the door, thinking up conceivable resolutions that grew increasingly far-fetched. While he pondered the likelihood of turning a section of the stone wall to mud and pushing his way through, a noise from the other side of the door broke his concentration.

Upon hearing footsteps he stood back from the entrance, fighting against the urge to panic at the thought of being dosed once again with the mind-numbing agent. The thick steel door rattled mildly, accompanied by two light knocks. Walt tilted his head curiously when the door remained closed and there was no further sound from the hallway.

As soon as he began to think it was just his imagination, he was forced to dive for his life when the door flew clear of its holdings, crashing noisily behind him. When the dust settled, he looked up to see an adolescent, no more than a boy really, standing in the doorway. The wizard felt power emanating from him, vast and cold as he tried to meet the boy's omniscient gaze. He walked into the room, not blinking or breaking eye contact and moving directly towards Walt. Slowly backing into the corner, Walt only realized he had moved when his back was against the wall with nowhere else to go, so unsettling he found the boy.

"You are a prisoner," the boy reasoned aloud, in a voice more fitting of an old man than a child.

Walt couldn't remember a time when he had been as unnerved as he felt at that moment. He tried to think of any defenses he could or should prepare, but gave up on the thought, sensing he was far outmatched and completely caught off-guard.

"Yes," Walt answered cautiously, unsure of what the boy was or what his intentions might be.

The boy continued his unsettling stare as he continued slowly towards Walt, who could not move any further backwards. Finally releasing eye contact, he looked to the wizard's broken fingers. He took each of his hands in turn, and Walt gasped in simultaneous pain and relief. After seconds that seemed an eternity, he released Walt's hands and nodded slightly, looking intently as if he were admiring his work.

Walt felt the bones of his hands crack and straighten. Though they were still tender, difficult to move and deeply bruised, he was reasonably sure his fingers were no longer broken.

Meeting the boy's eyes again, Walt felt his mind pried open against his will. He tried to rebuff the intrusion, but was overpowered as he felt the additional presence enter his thoughts. He sent a barrage of random ideations at the being in guise of a boy, hoping to confuse it and allow him to retreat while he cordoned off the section of his psyche that had been compromised. It was useless; he was the child when matched against this foreign presence.

Stop, master why do you resist me? Please, you must listen. I do not have much time remaining.

Walt paused in confusion upon hearing the thoughts that were not his own. He remained quiet as he weighed his options and realized his best course of action was to at least listen; perhaps it was his only course.

Sensing it had Walt's attention, the boy reached back into his pack. Procuring a small bundle wrapped in cloth, he held it out in his palm for Walt to see. With his other hand, the boy mechanically uncovered the top portion of the cloth, exposing an opaque, light blue gem roughly the size of a large coin. Walt felt the energy pouring forth from the diamond, and though it wasn't particularly bright he had to resist the urge to shield his eyes.

I am dying, I'm sorry but I've failed you in my task, master. This is all that now stands between the world and its complete domination, it thought aloud to Walt, referring to the stone in the boy's hand.

The sealing dweomer imbued in my stone is going to fail soon. For ages I have dutifully been its caretaker, master. I can no longer sense the eleven others, and can only assume they have been destroyed. Please, I beg you master, maintain the spell in my stead. Kubathu cannot be allowed to walk the earth once again. I can feel him drawing near even as we speak! Please, I beg you take back this burden and flee far from here!

Walt hesitated. Though he was the one hosting the foreign presence, the sharing of minds was a reciprocal, exposing process for each member. He could tell the being believed to the depths of their spirit in what they were saying, but he could also sense that its mind was addled and compromised from supreme old age.

The entity seemed to think it knew Walt, and whether it meant 'master' literally or more as a title of honor he wasn't sure. Either way it was obviously mistaken, but Walt debated whether it was safer to play along and placate the being or if he should deny its request. After experiencing the raw power it could wield, he was leaning more towards the former.

Before he could respond, another clamor outside of the room interrupted the sharing of the pair's thoughts, as well as prompting the boy to turn around. Walt nearly didn't recognize the figure filling the doorway, his face contorted with anger.

"Jvard!?" the wizard exclaimed, surprised by the barbarian's sudden appearance.

Jvard stood in the doorway, his eyes momentarily diverted from the thing masquerading as a child. He was equally surprised to see Walt, so surprised it almost deflated his rage. Almost.

"Demon spawn!" he bellowed, charging and switching his attention back to the boy.

The boy held his hand up in defense as the barbarian barreled in, aiming a slash of his sword directly below the boy's throat.

"No!" Walt yelled, largely confused on why Jvard was even here, much less why he would attack.

A concussive force with no sound originated from the boy's palm when Jvard was only inches away. Walt felt the peripheral vibrations run through his bones, making him unsteady on his feet and sending him to the floor. As he tried to pull himself back to his feet, he noticed a second man had entered the room behind Jvard and was rendered unconscious from the blast. A large crack ran through the floor underneath the focal point of the magic. Concern ran through Walt when his head stopped spinning. If the indirect force of the attack had been that disabling, how had Jvard fared after receiving the brunt of the impact?

Remarkably, Jvard was still alive, though greatly disoriented. It felt like a solid wall slammed into him before he reached the boy. Any normal man would have been blasted backwards, but in his heightened state he denied much of the force directed at him. He slowed as the wall of soundless energy collided into him, but bore down and kept his feet moving, crashing into the boy and bowling him over. Unfortunately for Jvard, the boy recovered before everyone else. Narrowing his eyes, he directed another jolt towards the barbarian. This time, Jvard could not brace against the attack, and was sent crashing against the wall, barely able to maintain consciousness.

Walt gathered his bearings and luckily still maintained his linked mind to the other being. It felt anger and annoyance, as if something terribly important had been interrupted. But mostly it felt vengeful.

Wait! Walt cried out with his thought.

The boy paused, his hand outstretched towards the prone barbarian.

My time is too short for these impediments, he answered telepathically.

That is my friend and fellow traveler, Walt continued, *I need him, alive*.

Walt could feel the entity contemplating his request, and leaning towards disregarding it.

Spare him and I will take on your burden! Walt bargained, thinking quickly.

This time the boy lowered his hand and looked to Walt, giving greater consideration to the appeal.

"Jvard, do not move. Leave this business to me," Walt said, whether or not the barbarian heard or understood him at the moment he did not know.

The being continued to hesitate, looking between Jvard and Walt. Pressing the advantage, Walt added, *Ignore him. Should you further harm him there is no bargain*.

"Very well," the boy said aloud, in the disturbing, raspy voice that did not belong to a child.

Let me show you now, I am beginning to fade, Walt again heard in his head, weariness evident in its tone.

Agreeing, Walt beckoned the child to proceed with whatever it was he needed to see. The essence began to withdraw from Walt's mind, returning to the gem resting in the boy's palm.

Follow, it thought to Walt, *I will show you how to maintain the spell.*

Trepidation filled Walt. Was the spirit asking him to try and fully separate his mind from his body? He wasn't quite sure if he could accomplish that, and was even less inclined to make the attempt.

I, I'm sorry, Walt began, *I must remain in my body. Unlike you I am flesh and blood, more than only spirit.*

No, master, it replied, *you must abandon the flesh. It is inconsequential. Maintaining the spell is all that matters.*

Incredulous, Walt stifled a groan. This thing was asking him to essentially end his life. His mind racing, he tried to think of some way to appease the entity while avoiding this requirement. Throughout the conversation the other being elevated Walt's status, presumably mistaking him for someone else. Perhaps he could bluff his way safely to a compromise.

Walt thought back, *that is unacceptable. I do not have the luxury of abandoning my duties. There are other dangers present in the world I must tend to. I cannot simply disappear and fully devote myself to this task.*

The entity paused, Walt's nerves increasing in the ensuing silence.

Finally it responded, *Very well. I will show you, but it will be taxing. Eventually the stone must be occupied or maintaining the spell will leech every last bit of your strength. See to your tasks with haste, my master. Then you or another of the Magicus Celesti will need to assume my responsibility from within the gem.*

Ice flowed through Walt's veins at the mention of the obscure order to which he once belonged. What could the Magicus Celesti have to do with this? He greatly wanted to inquire further, but couldn't risk abandoning his façade.

I understand, Walt answered, *show me.*

Nearing the last of its strength, the entity rejoined Walt's mind and guided him through a specific manipulation of energy aimed towards the gem. It wasn't particularly complex, and though his hands ached fiercely, Walt felt he had a handle on it in a short amount of time. His mind was clear for the first time in many days, and it felt good to work magic once again. However, the particular spell was indeed a mildly draining, constant feed of energy.

It may not seem like much at first, the entity thought, re-emphasizing his point, *but trying to maintain the spell from outside of the gem, much like walking a great distance, will slowly but surely sap you of all of your strength. Now you try, alone.*

Walt hadn't realized the entity was assisting him. Upon attempting himself, he found the endeavor significantly more taxing. Masking his concern over how he would do this over an extended and indefinite period, he acknowledged to the former caretaker that he understood what was required of him.

Just before passing the spell back to the entity, Walt felt a sudden jolt slam into the shield he was tasked with maintaining, nearly compromising the integrity of the gem. The amount of power the shield extracted from him to try to regenerate itself nearly sent him to his knees. Immediately the entity returned to the gem which had made its way into Walt's hand, leaving both Walt's and the boy's minds back in their sole possession. After several long moments alone, the boy began to stir as well as Jvard and the other man who accompanied him. Walt was drenched in sweat from exertion, concentrating fiercely while the others came to.

Before Walt could go to them, the entity reached out once more to him, *He has somehow placed himself within our reach! Much like the boy and his descendants have been my bearers, He too must be using another as a vessel. This gem and its binding magic is all that remains to prevent him from fully entering the world. Master, if Kubathu escapes all will be lost! Flee far from here! It does not matter where, just get away from Him. I will fight as long as I can, but it will be over for me soon. When I die he will overwhelm you at this proximity, go now and farewell!*

The voice again fell quiet as the entity resumed its work inside the gem. Walt could feel the hum of energy coursing through the stone, and the heat it emanated through the cloth it rested on resulting from its endeavors. Half of Walt's focus assisted the entity in maintaining the shield against the attack which was still in progress, while any attention he had left went to Jvard, who was getting back on his feet, though shakily.

Slowly standing, the barbarian disregarded his injuries and immediately stalked forward, setting his sights on the boy.

"That was no demon, you oaf," Walt said harshly, quickly moving in front of the child.

Regaining his bearings, the boy wobbled slightly and looked around, seemingly lost. To Walt, the child looked as though he had no idea where he was. Jvard paused in midstride as well, seeing the change coming over the young man. Walt had much to say, but it was the third man in the room who spoke first.

"Hey, I know this boy!" Baerne blurted out, finally placing why he looked familiar.

"Son, remember me?" he added, catching the boy's attention as he came to.

Devin did remember meeting the blacksmith, at the stable in Midao where he shot the guard, thinking it to be a Greyman. Not responding, he looked around like he wanted to run, but settled for shrinking back against the wall in fright upon viewing the other two men he did not know.

"Easy, easy," Walt interrupted, approaching the boy slowly from the side, "can you tell us your name?"

"Devin," he finally answered, his terrified eyes not leaving Jvard.

"Good," Walt answered through a strained smile, having a difficult time concentrating at pouring magic into the gem and having a conversation at the same time, "that's a fine name. Jvard, for spirit's sake would you give the boy a little room?"

Jvard nodded awkwardly and took large strides towards the exit.

"I'll be in the hall. Hurry up, it's dangerous out there," he said, realizing he probably scared the boy senseless, looming over him as he was.

Devin looked longingly to his gem resting in Walt's hand as Jvard and Baerne exited the room.

"I'm afraid I'm going to need to take this for a time, it's a very important stone you see, full of magic," Walt said, responding to the boy's disappointed look at no longer possessing the gem, "it's not doing very well right now. I'm a wizard who understands such things and I'll try to make it better for you. Is that okay?"

Frowning at the proposition, but unable to deny something was amiss with the stone, Devin agreed.

"Excellent!" Walt said cheerily, pleased the boy readily agreed to pass on his ownership of the item, "come along now, we'll help you get home."

In the hallway Jvard waited impatiently with Baerne at his side. As Walt and Devin exited the room, the wizard abruptly spoke over Jvard who was trying to bark instructions.

"There's no time, just listen," Walt said, waving his hands to cut off the barbarian, "I need to get far from this city immediately."

"No argument there," Jvard answered, thinking along the very same lines.

"What of the boy?" Baerne asked, "we can't just take him along, I'm sure someone must be wondering where he is… there was the woman watching over him back at Midao. Was she still with you Devin, what was her name?"

When Devin didn't answer right away, Walt stepped in to begin issuing directions. He didn't have the time to argue over the details of what everyone in the group was doing. If what the entity told him was true, it was past time for him to leave.

"I do not know you my good man, but I'm going to ask you to watch over the boy and get him back to his family. Can you do that for us?" Walt asked.

When Baerne nodded, the wizard continued, "Good, Jvard you and I can get back to our wagon… By the spirits! I nearly forgot, Jvard some of your people have survived!"

"What? How could you know that?" Jvard asked, shaking his head and furrowing his thick brow; news about his tribe was the last thing he expected the wizard to mention, much less they were alive.

Memories raced back for Walt as the last traces of the mind numbing poison left his system. The dream he had that was not a dream, meeting the spirit-seeker, and his last conversation with the man who had been drugging him.

"One called Igdahven, he came to me in a dream," Walt explained, "they are on their way here to find you."

Jvard was stunned, his kinsmen had survived!

"They're alive!" he roared in excitement.

Unable to contain himself, he grabbed Devin under the shoulders and hoisted him high in the air.

"They're alive!" he yelled again and laughed, overjoyed and oblivious to the boy's terror.

"I have more to tell you – but let's get moving first. Will you put the boy down before he has an accident for spirit's sake?" Walt admonished, already moving down the passage.

They encountered no one else on their way out of the palace, Jvard taking the lead and back tracking his earlier path through the maze of hallways. Leaving the main entryway, moving beyond the palisade, from high upon the stairs they could see the Inner City had nearly fallen to ruin during the short time they were inside.

Walt paled at glimpsing the desecrated Inner City, "How did this happen?" he whispered.

"I'm afraid it's my doing," Jvard informed him, "things didn't exactly go as planned."

"…Indeed," was the wizard's only response.

There was very little resistance left in the open courtyards, and the only sign of survivors was a small group leaving through the rubble where the gate once stood. Aside from the fleeing survivors, the area crawled with the Infected.

"Stay along the wall, we'll take a lift down over there," Jvard said, pointing towards the rear of the city where he and Baerne entered, "stay quiet and move fast, we should be able to slip past them."

The others signaled their agreement, observing that the perimeter was mostly clear if they hurried along. Instead of taking the stairs, they hurried to the edge of the portico, dropping the fifteen or so feet to the ground. Jvard went first, smoothly jumping down and landing low, then springing forward to expel the momentum gained from falling. Baerne followed next, hanging from the edge to decrease the distance to the ground. He landed cleanly, if not gracefully. Devin went next at Walt's urging, and though he seemed hesitant, he dropped down into Jvard's hands after only a brief pause. Walt came last, actually taking a running leap and jumping clear over his three companions to land as cleanly as if he jumped over a small puddle.

To his friend's stunned looks he simply stated, "Quit your gawking, I am a wizard after all. Are you coming along or not? Don't just stand there."

They snuck towards the guardhouse at the furthest point along the rear of the city, aiming for the access stairs to the top of the wall and lifts. Jvard took up the rear as they drew the attention of a few of the Stricken, fending them off and cutting them down with well-placed blows. The barbarian ran to catch up to his group and urgently spurred them ahead, the noise of his fighting seeming to attract more and more of the undead horde. Walt held the door to the gatehouse, imploring Jvard to hurry. The army of the Stricken continued to converge, sweeping more members into its ranks with every frantic step. By the time he reached the entrance, only fifty paces separated Jvard from a growling, frenzied mob.

Once he crossed the threshold, Walt slammed the door shut and threw its lockbar into place.

"That won't hold them very long!" he shouted, nudging Jvard in the back to encourage him up the stairs with the others.

They spiraled up the steps, leading towards the next door and access point to the top of the wall. As they crossed through, they could hear the cracking and splintering of wood from below, signaling that the Infected managed to breach the door.

"Onto the lift!" Jvard yelled, gesturing wildly towards the elevators.

Behind them them the clamor of the Infected made a racket so terrifying that Devin fell to his knees, covering his ears and yelling for it to stop. Baerne, directly behind the boy, wordlessly scooped him up and flung him over his shoulder without missing a beat.

They reached their destination with very little time to spare. Jvard escorted everyone else onto the lift, waiting until they were all aboard before releasing the latch on the left-side gears securing the ropes. They cried out in alarm as their container began to slowly tilt, hanging precariously hundreds of feet above the ground along the wall. Realizing that two men were probably needed to work the mechanism, Jvard ran to the other gear and released its latch, allowing the lift to start lowering safely, if slightly lopsided. He leaped down to join Walt, Baerne, and Devin, the elevator already lowered nearly ten feet as the cranks slowly turned from their combined weight. It sped up moderately when Jvard landed, causing the others to struggle to keep their balance.

Looking up, the narrow wall overflowed with the Stricken. Many fell, plummeting far down to the rocks below while they jostled one another forward. Some descended directly next to the lift on their way down, growling and hissing as their faces flew by, leaving the group to pray that none fell on their lift.

"We'll be safe once we get to the ground. We're almost there," Baerne offered, "even they can't survive a fall like that…"

As he spoke, three bodies careened down, landing heavily on the elevator. The group instinctively fell to the floor, trying to get out of the way of the inhuman projectiles in their limited space. Worse, the force of the impact stripped the tension in the ropes, sending them barreling the rest of the way down at a dangerous speed.

There was nothing they could do as the ground rushed up to meet them. The lift slammed into the dirt, breaking apart to send its occupants rolling down the hill towards the water.

Jvard was the first up, shaking off the dust and testing his battered limbs. It wasn't long before everyone else was able to stand, bruised but not badly injured from the short freefall. The Stricken that dropped on them had not fared so well, breaking their arms and legs in the initial fall onto the lift. As ruined as their bodies were, they seemed to feel no pain or even notice their bones were shattered. Their only concern was to get to the living flesh walking away from them.

Ignoring the ruined creatures trying to drag themselves towards him, Walt immediately set to task, "We'll need to part ways here. You'll look after the boy?"

"Of course," Baerne agreed.

Speaking to the barbarian, Walt added, "Good, Jvard let's be off to the wagon and continue our way south. I'm all but positive the 'Empress' Sevra whom the guards here follow is the same woman my former order quarreled with, and this catastrophe is her doing."

"So she is the one we seek?" Jvard asked, eager to place a name onto his enemy.

"That would seem to be the case. It is imperative we get out of here now, something is coming for this gem. It's sapping nearly all of my strength even as we speak trying to fight it off. I'm sorry we ever stopped in this Gods-forsaken city," Walt answered.

"Wait!" Jvard shouted to the wizard who was already setting off, as well as Baerne and Devin who began trekking east towards the island they thought was safe.

He continued as they turned, "The horses are gone, Walt. They bolted away during the last attack, you won't get very far with the wagon. And I cannot come with you just yet."

Walt's face soured at the multiple pieces of bad news, especially his horses running off.

"Be at ease, I have an alternative," Jvard continued, aiming to stop Walt from going into a fit, "there is no shortage of abandoned boats nearby. Take one of those south through the river. If what you say is true and my people are searching for me, I need to be here to see them. In the meantime I'll help Baerne find the boy's home and get some horses for the wagon. Try not to go too fast and I'll catch up with you in a few days along the river bank."

Walt thought for a moment and reluctantly accepted the revised plan.

"Very well, it looks as though we say goodbye for now," Walt remarked.

"At least for the moment. I'll set off from here as soon as I can, and I'll hold you to your promise of vengeance," Jvard commented with a grin, "let's find you a boat."

Matters of Honor

The ancient spirit of Kubathu grew agitated within his crimson prison. He could sense the increasing frustration in his bearer, Sevra, upon hearing consistent reports of bad news from Creekview's Crossing. The way she saw it, she no longer had any choice but to go there and personally bring the city under control; whether it was the people themselves, the leadership of her army, or the instigator Daro Ildaradi at the root of the problems, she was unsure. Regardless, the contention had to come to an end. She was supposed to be seen as their savior, not the cause of their strife! By all accounts, if that area wasn't stabilized soon there very well might not be any people left there for her to rule.

Kubathu, still filled with anger over Sevra's blunder, did not concern himself either way with her success or failure in the endeavor. His interests currently lay with Aubur, back in a prison in Dun'Aldir. Somehow the spell had not fully destroyed his mind, though his body had been somewhat transformed. Those transformations were what captivated Kubathu; from what he observed the man had a constant hunger but practically no physical need to eat, and slept very little with no ill effects. It seemed as if his body had become exempt from the biological processes that require normal individuals to rest or refuel themselves. Should he ever escape the gem, taking over a body without those limitations could be very useful indeed.

At first hesitant to be out of Aubur's vicinity, he decided it would be good to allow Sevra to follow her plans through. It would give him a chance to see firsthand what was going on elsewhere, as well as help him determine if his interests with her were any longer worthwhile. Prodding the edges of her mind as they wound to the northeast, he felt anxiety within her, but also a rigid determination. That was both her strength and flaw he supposed, too prideful or stubborn not to know when to give up.

His mood turned sour as he thought of Sevra's unforgivable errors in judgment. Never in his wildest dreams would he have purposely concocted a magic so terrible, so devastating as to exterminate what was rapidly becoming more than half of the population. It wasn't that the act of killing displeased him; on the contrary he enjoyed it quite thoroughly, but Kubathu's desire was to rule and subjugate, not commit genocide without purpose.

His anger spiked suddenly as he thought about the witch, all of the years he spent molding and shaping her, guiding her to allow them to achieve greatness. When it came down to it, he chose her because she was convenient, not because he found her particularly talented. The thoughts continued to pester him, pressing in on his mind until it felt as though they were going to cause him to suffocate. But the feeling did not subside when he focused on other matters; it continued to increase, the weight of it smothering and grasping around him.

A cage began to close in on Kubathu as they drew near to Creekview's Crossing, the walls of his gemmed enclosure seeming to become more imposing. A sense of panic reignited within him that he hadn't felt since he was first imprisoned, so long ago. His initial reaction was to cower back to the center of his confinement, like a hunted, cornered animal with nowhere to run.

The seconds elapsed and all of the freedoms he currently held remained intact, and he quickly regained his composure. When first captured, he had been so utterly subdued he couldn't even recall his own name or connect two thoughts together. What he felt now was similar, but the power of it significantly diluted to no more than a mild pressure.

Cautiously, he again projected his mind outside of the gem, prodding the edges of Sevra's consciousness. So subtly he brushed against her psyche that she didn't even notice he was there. Still present was her nervousness and pinpoint determination, but most importantly he found nothing directed his way. Whatever was trying to restrain him wasn't coming from her.

With great effort he extended his will out further, across the plains. He found many tracings of magic resembling the binds that weakly tried to subdue him, their unique signature unmistakable. The tracks grew clearer in the direction of Creekview's Crossing. He wasn't usually one to hesitate, but this gave Kubathu pause. What could have narrowed in on him and how? When the only possible answer came to him, a jolt of excitement rushed through his spirit back in the gem about Sevra's neck. He dared to believe he could be so fortunate.

Seething hatred overwhelmed his senses, driving him to reach out even further. Following the trail that became increasingly clear within the city, he travelled over the rivers, streets and buildings of Creekview at the speed of thought. Approaching the limits of how far he could extend himself, he located the source of the emanation within the bowels of a palace atop the hill at the center of the islands. He needed to push just a little further to confirm his suspicion; the last diamond maintaining his prison was at hand.

Kubathu attacked it viciously, throwing the full weight of his strength against the integrity of the gem. His strength was by far the greater, nearly overwhelming the one who opposed him from within it.

How long it had been since he had the pleasure of crushing one of those pathetic beings to dust; finally, freedom was near!

After all the long centuries he could be free of his accursed prison. His joy was short-lived, however; the rival wizard nearly beaten, he felt a second fount of power join against him to quell the deluge of energy he wished to rain down upon his captor.

A throbbing sensation formed in his mind from the exertion of reaching over such a vast distance and trying to overcome the combined power of two wizards. In truth he would not be able to continue the assault much longer, but stubbornly he refused to cease his barrage on the two souls defending the diamond. It became a war of attrition with both sides tiring and neither gaining any ground. He couldn't believe his stroke of good fortune that this encounter presented itself, and lamented his inability to capitalize on it. Despite his efforts, he felt the opportunity slipping through his fingers.

He cried out in frustration at his failure. The gem was on the move once again, beyond his reach. Soon its powers over him reverted back to a mere physical confinement, leaving his will to float along a river south of Creekview's Crossing where their battle came to a temporary end. With no alternative he returned to his spirit within the ruby, the prison still in the same condition it had been for the last several hundred years.

Sevra, go west to the Tinindraüg! he commanded, booming in her mind like a thunderhead and breaking his silence to the witch once again.

She stopped, startled at the sudden reappearance of the voice she thought of as a God, demanding that she suddenly change direction towards the river.

"But I am so close to my destination," she stammered, hesitant to make a last minute change to her plans.

Do it now! he snapped, encapsulating her mind with his own and squeezing it as if he had it in his fist.

"Yes, as you desire! Please, stop master!" she responded immediately, the sudden pain unbearable.

Much to his dismay, the detour proved to be a fruitless endeavor. Taking Sevra and her personal escort hours out of their way, Kubathu did not feel the presence of the diamond or move within its proximity again.

Perplexed, Sevra stood at the swiftly flowing river she was led to. There was not a soul to be seen as darkness began to fall. Somewhere distantly an owl hooted, solemnly welcoming the evening.

"We are here," she said aloud, drawing stares from her small group of guards.

What is it you want of me here? she asked through her thoughts.

Do whatever you wish, Kubathu replied glumly, breaking off his connection to her once more and retreating into solitude.

She stood there, confused at the edge of the water wondering what the purpose might have been for the small excursion. Turning north without a word, her contingent followed behind, unquestioning of the Empress.

***

With the city nearly overrun, it was all Daro could do to save those around him. The true problem was the disorder, with most of the guards dealing with yet another riot, there was no organized response to the breach. If there was one thing he learned from his tumultuous upbringing, it was that panic and confusion ran hand in hand, and often those were more dangerous than any potential enemy – so too they were often caused intentionally for someone else's sinful benefit.

The wave of Infected steadily approached in his direction, slowed only slightly by a scattered, desperate defense. Men near him began to scurry off, some towards the fighting and others away.

They were helpless lambs led to slaughter; poor fools who could not find their way.

God shone His light and provided the righteous course for Daro, His chosen. He only need follow it.

"Hold!" Daro called out, raising his sword-arm high in the air.

Every person in the Inner City, whether they revered or despised him, knew the name and face of Daro the Bladefist. Most bore witness to his spectacular entrance to the city, instantly elevating his reputation at the Crossing. When Daro spoke out, people stopped and listened. When he held his blade aloft and illuminated their way to salvation, they followed.

With the attention of those nearby, the preacher began to put the men into some semblance of formation. Though he was no commander, he had the sense to know it was better to fight side by side than getting caught away on one's own.

"Gather around, here!" Daro demanded, "Able-bodied men right here in front, form up a line!"

Confusion turned to order as he progressed with his instructions. Those around him were desperate for some guidance, any at all, and drew to him like wayward sheep to their shepherd. Some armed and some not, he gathered roughly forty men, women, and children to follow his lead.

"The three of you," Daro continued, "go find as many more people as you can in the next two minutes. Bring them back here, only look from here to the west wall. Anything before us in the other direction is too dangerous now."

"You three," he added, pointing to another group, "find as many weapons and return as quickly as you can. Whatever you can get – knives, clubs, swords, or pitchforks it doesn't matter."

While they ran off with their tasks, the rest of the men were put into two straight lines surrounding those who wouldn't be able to defend themselves. Soon the runners brought more people in, and more still followed them when they saw there was a rallying point to congregate to. By the time they set off towards the ruined gates, the company grew large enough to form a square, fully encompassing any folks who wouldn't be fighting.

"Stay together! For no reason break your lines," Daro demanded, "watch the man to your left and right, protect each other. We are getting out of here."

Daro forged a path through the makeshift encampment, skirting around as much of the fighting as he could while the block of men behind him followed, plowing straight over the empty tents. A few stragglers fell into his ranks as they passed by, relieved to find safety in numbers. From what the preacher could see, it was going very badly for the people of the Inner City.

His face was grim as he carved a meandering trail through the carnage. What could have reduced the solid gate to a pile of stones? The concussive force of it shook the very ground he had been sleeping on. Foul sorcery was at work, of that much he was certain. The only sensation he had ever similarly experienced was at the mountains behind Big Bear. Walt and the black powder he used to expand mining operations caused similar tremors, but it was nothing compared to the blast felt here.

So many lay dead or dying, scattered across the field, bleeding out from the mangling attacks of the Infected. Groups of the beasts hunkered around some victims, consuming their flesh to the bone. Daro methodically drove his blade through the skulls of any of those feasting that he came near, taking advantage of their preoccupation to deliver a precise, permanently fatal blow.

Amidst all of the scattered fighting and disorder, Daro's group was a sanctuary from evil. The jumbled nature of the Infected's aggressions broke apart whenever one reached their line. Working as a team, three or more men pounced if one came close, keeping their defenses from becoming overwhelmed. Only Daro didn't adhere to the formation, moving ahead to clear the way when necessary. Single-handedly he dashed into small pockets of the Infected, expertly weaving through and slashing out his sword arm in precise movements.

Battling his way through yet another batch, he jabbed his blade straight out to thrust it through the eye socket of the lead creature. As he tried to pull the blade free, it caught along the thing's orbital bone, yanking it in close to him. With his free arm, protected in steel from shoulder to gauntlet, he struck another with his fist. It stumbled backward, falling over to land unmoving with part of its skull bashed in. Deftly, he shoved his sword out again, corpse and all, and at the end of its range snapped his arm back towards him. The momentum released the body from the blade, freeing up his arm to meet an oncoming rush.

Four more advanced on him, one to his left and right, and two directly in front. With a wide swipe he severed the head of the rightmost assailant, and pivoted to face the others. Turning to meet the one on his left, he caught it high under the throat, controlling its head as it crashed into him. Knowing God to be with him, he had no sense of fear even with one arm occupied and two more Infected coming in from his side.

Its teeth gnashing and breath putrid, he ignored it for the moment and raised his blade high once again to chop a downward arc over its shoulder. He struck the one behind it, causing it to slump to the ground, while the last of the bunch pushed in from behind to press the still-thrashing one he had by the throat even closer against him.

Using their momentum, Daro dipped down suddenly, dropping his hand from its neck to its clothing and pitching both Infected behind him. Following in immediately, he stabbed one through the back of the head before it had a chance to stand up. He didn't even bother with the fourth of the Infected, trusting his company to finish it off before it got back on its feet; instead he continued forward, intent on leading the group out of the city with all haste.

As they closed in towards the gate, if they stayed close by the wall and buildings Daro thought they might be able to slip out unchallenged. There was a large gathering of the Infected, but they were already a few hundred yards ahead of the ruined wall, occupied with those unfortunate enough to be caught in the middle of the Inner Ciy. Holding up his fist, Daro commanded everyone to a stop and signaled for silence.

"Go through, down the alley to the left. Wait near the bridge," Daro whispered several times as he motioned his company across the gates.

Waving them through, he waited until each man had passed, keeping an eye out that they were not drawing attention. As the last of his group exited, he took one final look back. Before turning to leave, the silver gleam of a shield caught his eye. Smiling to himself, there was no mistaking the hefty figure of First Lieutenant Kempf, fully surrounded with his back to the wall. For an instant, Kempf turned his head and the two men's eyes seemed to meet. Satisfied that God's work would be done, Daro smiled and turned to follow his men out of the ruined Inner City.

***

The conditions for Radford's villagers rapidly deteriorated as the morning slipped into afternoon. Though he managed to collect most of them together and withdraw away from the fighting to a corner of the island, many had been injured. The soldiers and Drakvnar of Dun'Aldir finally seemed to gain back control and suppress the rioting, but at what cost? There was no repairing the damaged relations caused by today's events. The people of Creekview and the occupying troops had been toeing the line of civility for days, finally crossing a point of no return. The smell of blood hung heavily in the air.

"So many needless deaths today," the mayor whispered to no one in particular.

He stood near Baerne's saddened mother and siblings. She did brighten at the news that the blacksmith was alive and well, and as of yet uncaptured. But it was only a small blessing, after having lost so much in the past few weeks. Giving her a small kiss on the head and consolingly touching his hand to her shoulder, Radford moved off to remind the rest his people to be complacent in the following hours. He hoped their cooperation would allow them to be spared as the guards began rounding up the remaining civilians. By the end of the day he intended to be guiding his townsmen back to Midao. The Dun'Aldirans could go burn for all he cared. His people survived just fine before the guards showed up in their small village, and would continue to do so.

A lone figure approached from across the river at the southeast end of the island, dressed in the telltale black armor of the True-

Blood, and Radford's heart sank. Soldiers paused in their duty to offer him a salute, which the towering soldier returned curtly.

There he was, unfortunately still very much alive. The Guard-Captain Ramnar stalked about the field, barking orders and sending men scurrying in nearly every direction. Soon a small contingent followed him about, while others began tying the hands of the rioters behind their backs and seating them.

"Allow me to handle this," Radford stated gently to the people of Midao, walking out to meet the incoming Guard-Captain.

Ramnar's demeanor further darkened upon seeing the man who had left him for dead outside of the village, the one he had been commanded to silently eliminate.

"Prepare this group to be executed for treason to the Empress," Ramnar bellowed for all to hear upon seeing Radford approaching.

The Drakvnar paused only briefly, looking to the Guard-Captain as if verifying they heard him accurately. After their hesitation they moved in towards the people; if they were given an order, they would follow it. Cries of shock and protest came from the villagers, many resisting when the Drakvnar attempted to subdue them.

"Wait!" Radford yelled, "It's not them you want Ramnar. You want to take my life? Here I am. You have me."

"No, not anymore," Ramnar replied, his lip twisting into a wicked smile, "I'm going to kill you last so you can watch everyone else die before you go."

"You're nothing but a spiteful coward, I've seen more honor in a mangy dog than what you possess," the mayor shouted, hoping to bait the Guard-Captain.

He moved in towards Ramnar, and was immediately intercepted by two guards, grabbing him behind the elbows while a third disarmed the blade sheathed at his hip.

"Surely you're not afraid of a silver-tongued politician, Ramnar," Radford continued, ignoring those restraining him, "or is it you don't want your men to see you bested by someone half of your stature?"

"Just what do you think you'll accomplish? You want your village to see you soundly beaten before they go? Get him out of here," Ramnar demanded.

His men began to pull Radford away, while any resistance his villagers offered was firmly quelled.

"How many innocent people have you butchered to help that charlatan usurp authority in Dun'Aldir?" Radford continued, further trying to rile the Guard-Captain.

Ramnar's face grew red with anger. He only executed those who stood in the way of Sevra's mission. It was their right and duty to see it done.

"Your 'Empress' is nothing more than a delusional crone, and you her pathetic lackey," the mayor shouted, unrelenting seeing that his words were having an effect.

"She is driven by the mandates of a God Himself!" Ramnar shouted, an uncharacteristicly zealous gleam in his eye.

"Then surely if you and your mission are driven by the desires of a god, one such as myself could not stand in your way. Prove your claims of divine favor. If you truly have faith, that is," Radford stated with all the calmness he could muster.

"Okay, I'll entertain you. Let him go, give him back his pig-sticker of a sword," the Captain commanded his men, hatred contorting his face, "I'll make sure to leave you alive just enough to see your town killed to a child."

Radford had gotten his wish, effectively goading Ramnar into a fight and buying himself and the town a little more time. As the near seven foot tall Guard-Captain drew the massive, curving flamberge from over his shoulder, he questioned the wisdom of his decision. A ring of guards soon formed around the two combatants, a primitive rush of excitement coursing through the soldiers at the spectacle that was about to unfold.

With no buckler at hand, Radford angled his left arm lightly behind his back, squaring off with a mild flourish of his rapier. The son of a nobleman, fencing was a part of their life as much as discussing boundary disputes or taxation. Only they practiced and demonstrated for sport, and it was rare to suffer an injury during a match. Now, he was without protective gear and faced someone intent on killing him. He supposed not having a shield was to his benefit in this particular encounter; he would be foolish to attempt to block a strike from Ramnar. Not only would the force shatter his arm, the particular style of weapon Ramnar wielded was known for causing excessive reverberation whenever it struck anything.

To his dismay, the Guard-Captain was expertly able to control the weapon. He had hoped because of its size, Ramnar might be sluggish with his strikes or find himself off-balance, but as the flamberge swooped dangerously close to the side of his head, any such hopes were dashed. Scrambling out of the way, Radford repositioned himself to the right and even attempted to return a thrust before Ramnar could fully turn. The attack didn't come close to landing, and the mayor realized he was going to have a difficult time overcoming his disadvantage of reach in this fight.

Ramnar led the aggression, while Radford was doing all he could to avoid being struck or tying in close with the larger, stronger opponent. Trying to form any kind of strategy, he saw a few chances where in a typical contest he could have landed some counter-strikes. However, due to the expansive arm span of the Guard-Captain, it would have been foolhardy to move in for the attack. He simply couldn't close the distance to his opponent in time. Dodging another swipe at his head, and two more in rapid succession, he poked his rapier straight out to buy himself time to regain his footing, managing to nick Ramnar's arm.

Radford's evasiveness and the cut infuriated Ramnar, sending him into a wild flurry of attacks that kept the mayor on his heels. Ducking and side-stepping, a strike finally came that he could not avoid. Frantically he stepped in towards it, placing his blade upright in front of him to cause the blow to land nearly handle to handle.

The vibration in his hands almost caused him to drop the rapier, numbing him up to his elbow. Ramnar shoved out violently, sending Radford a dozen paces away. The strength of the Guard-Captain diminished Radford's spirit for the fight, but he was glad to gain some space from his adversary. A quick glance to his weapon showed it was functionally undamaged from the deflection, only a small dent was present in the guard. Breathing heavily, Ramnar stalked forward once more, determined to put an end to the contest.

Radford again began to dance away, avoiding the wide swings of his opponent. The second barrage of the Guard-Captain did not nearly have the same level of intensity as the first, and Radford gained hope he just might be able to defeat his larger opponent if he could keep the fight going long enough. Confident that Ramnar could not best him at swordplay, and would continue slowing down, he would allow his adversary to tire himself out a bit more before chipping away at him. He needed to draw this fight out as long as possible without making any mistakes; once it reached the conclusion he expected, he was not optimistic about how the rest of the soldiers and Drakvnar would react.

***

"I told you we should've been takin' the road all the way south," Garl snarled not for the first time throughout the afternoon, "now you've gone and gotten us lost in this overgrown thicket."

Realizing they travelled too far east after detouring away from the Longpost Road, Igdahven guided them back in a southwestern direction. He again assured his fellow tribesmen that they were making a straight line to Creekview's Crossing and Jvard, hoping they weren't counting that this was his third such reassurance. He thought he had it right this time; it wasn't his fault a dense forest happened to lay in their way.

"We're almost there, I can sense Jvard's presence without even seeking his spirit in the *Chàlgraäden*. He is close by, and alive," Igdahven reiterated. He kept to himself that the *Chàlgraäden* was still in an unusual state, the flow of the *Duchstraüm* veering off course from where it should be.

The news that they were drawing close and would shortly reunite with their chieftain gave the barbarians a renewed vigor, allowing them to pick up their pace as they blazed a trail through the thick woods. As Igdahven promised, they soon reached the tree line along a high bluff, affording them a view of the sprawling basin below. Rivers branched off to intersect the land at more points than they could count. The barbarians, who lived a fair distance from one river which was frozen over for the majority of the year, had never seen so much flowing water. Its beauty was marred by the scene of a battle unfolding before them on the nearest piece of land, many armored men fighting against people who looked nothing like soldiers.

"Jvard's down there? What's he gotten himself into?" Garl wondered, calling his men to a halt.

"I think he is," Igdahven answered, "if not down in that mess he's very close to it."

"Seein' any other way around?" Garl asked.

A nearby path led down to the island, other than that it was miles upon miles around the ledge before the land sloped in any way that made it traversable into Creekview's Crossing.

"We'll just have to cut across and that's all there is to it, then," Garl responded when no suggestions came forth, "be on your guard. Unless my eyes deceive me it looks as though the black-clad warriors are gainin' a handle on the battle."

Moving along the cliff they took a small path down leading towards a bridge to the island. Garl paused before crossing, uncertain of the reception they might receive at this particular time. The fighting was nearly through, but the last thing he wanted was to be harassed by a southern military.

"Are we going down there?" the youngest member of their scouting party asked.

"Of course Adran," Garl answered gruffly, "that's what we've come all this way for isn't it?"

The young man shrank back. At the Ridges, Adran had shown some promise in being able to make rational choices. His confidence was another matter; Garl had hoped bringing him along would help him find some measure of fortitude.

"Igdahven, you're smaller like most of them, why don't you go investigate. They're more likely to not notice you than all of us," Garl suggested.

Igdahven scowled at the thought, but upon hearing murmurs of agreement from everyone else he begrudgingly accepted. It didn't seem to occur to any of the barbarians that the wolf cap atop his head and dangling animal skulls adorning his belt made him stick out far worse than anyone else possibly could have.

"Wait here," he muttered, resignedly shaking his head and setting off across the bridge.

Upon reaching the other side he ran into a sight he found rather curious. Two men, whom he surmised were the leader of the armed force and the other in charge of the city dwellers, were squared off with one another and ringed by a large group of onlookers. He pushed his way in to see the combatants, drawing double-takes and odd stares from those near him.

Truly surprised, Igdahven risked asking a question to a burly soldier at his left, "You follow the ways of *Kleïntòr* here?"

"What?" the man shouted, scowling at the disruptive, strange person that seemed to have appeared from nowhere.

"Decision born of honor, to settle a dispute," Igdahven responded less than cordially, offering the literal translation.

"Who... where did you come from?" the guard asked, his attention beginning to fade from the fight and onto Igdahven.

"Very interesting," Igdahven answered introspectively, ignoring the guard's question and threatening demeanor, most likely no longer even aware he was under scrutiny.

Before the soldier could inquire further, with a quick turn of his heel Igdahven returned across the bridge to report to Garl. The guard shrugged, shaking his head and rejoining the crowd to watch the duel.

"It looks as though they've decided to settle the matter through individual combat," Igdahven told the rest of the band who eagerly awaited his return.

The barbarians nodded their approval at the unexpected news. Unbeknownst to the villagers and guards, the northmen held this type of duel in the highest regard. Known as the *Kleïntòr*, for generations many feuds between rival tribes were settled through a contest between the chieftains, sparing themselves from unnecessary bloodshed. Just at the beginning of the season they had observed Jvard's victory over the chieftain of the Denórvja.

Ultimately, the entirety of the northern tribes realized that without the system they would all fail as a people, unable to battle the elements as well as each other. To ignore the results of the *Kleïntòr* was a great dishonor, equivalent to sacrilege, and guaranteed to bring the greatest displeasure from the Gods.

"That means they will spill no more blood once the duel is complete," Garl suggested, assuming they followed the same tenets that surrounded the familiar ritual.

The others expressed their agreement, using the same reasoning as their expedition leader. Of course, not one of them had ever previously travelled further south than the Laskouth Plains.

"It should be safe to approach them, in that case. We are only passing through, after all," Adran chimed in.

"So be it," Garl decided, "we shall bear witness to the result of their *Kleïntòr*."

His men grinned at the thought, typically a day or more of celebration came after the ending of hostilities.

"No festivity for us mind you! Once their fight is done we will acknowledge the victor and head off on our way," Garl reprimanded, seeing where his men's minds were, "we're here to find Jvard and that is it. Our only goal is to get by this pack of soldiers without stirrin' up more trouble than we need to."

All in agreement, the twenty-five men set off across the bridge. They were disappointed they wouldn't be joining in the celebrations afterwards, but looked forward to at least glimpsing some of the fight before it was over. To the barbarians, there was no greater testament to a man's strength than a display of one-on-one combat. A *Kleïntòr* in particular held a place in their hearts in which nothing else could compare.

Igdahven's mind was elsewhere compared to the rest of his kinsmen. He could sense Jvard was very close, and only hoped the southerners paid honor to the *Kleïntòr* in the same way as the tribes of the north.

***

Myrna had done her best to look after Devin and keep him safe, and felt a profound sadness that she could no longer protect the boy. After chasing him to the Inner City and becoming separated by an entire swarm of the Infected, it was all she could do to keep herself alive. Running through the streets, she was continually driven in the opposite direction she wished to go.

The thought occurred to her that the Drakvnar must have done a poor job at securing the rest of the city; every street she ran to had at least a few of the decrepit monsters lurking about. As much as she wanted to reach the Inner City and follow Devin, each turn brought her further away until her own safety became jeapordized. She wasn't even sure where she was going after a time, but she knew she had to keep moving or they would catch up to her. She was forced to shift her priority from saving Devin to saving herself.

Pausing at the corner of an intersection she looked behind her to see more of the Greymen loping along, sniffing at the air and heading her way. Peeking around the building she saw many more, further ahead, wandering with apparent aimlessness. She couldn't go back, and moving forward towards the outskirts of the city didn't appear to be an option. Nearly cornered once again, her only choice was to doubleback eastward across the river, heading again towards the center of the city and pray she didn't attract more of the Infected towards her.

She felt as if for every two steps forward she had to take one backwards. If she ever even managed to reach an edge of the city, she wondered if she would have every single one of the cursed animals on her heels, chasing her through the woods until the spirits knew when. It was a game of cat and mouse she could only play for so long before it reached its inevitable conclusion.

Drawing a deep breath and summoning what remained of her courage, she made a break towards the street, across lawns and passing abandoned houses in hopes of reaching the river. If she could just get across the water she'd buy herself a little time from her pursuers. Halfway there, her foot caught on a root and she fell to the ground hard, badly bruising her knee. She gasped as she struggled to her feet, pain radiating up her thigh, and found she could hardly put any weight on the leg. Frantically she tore off her shirt, hastily tying it tight around her damaged knee above and below the joint to give her some stability.

The added bracing allowed her to hobble along somewhat, if painfully so. Looking behind her she saw it was hopeless; the Greymen were gaining on her and she would not make it to the river in time. Refusing to give up she continued along as fast as she could, ignoring the injured leg that shot waves of agony along her body. The pain of the injury demanded that she stop and tend to it, but to do so would be the end of her. Unable to take any more abuse, her leg finally gave out and sent her tumbling once again. Rolling downwards towards the river, she came to a stop at the edge of the water.

Maybe it was the injury to her leg, or the knowledge her life was nearly over and her mind wanted to make it as painless as possible, because as the Infected bore down on her she fainted away without a struggle. Her last memory was that of a brilliant light, so bright that it pierced stingingly through her closed eyes. Before succumbing to unconsciousness, she wondered if this was what it felt like to die.

***

Having found Walt a boat he would be able to manage and saying farewell to the wizard, Jvard escorted Baerne and Devin across the islands of Creekview's Crossing. Finally able to coax some information from Devin, he and Baerne discerned that he last remembered being with Myrna at the eastern-most encampment, with all of the others who were unable to stay in the Inner City. Until his tribesmen showed up, Jvard had no other responsibilities to see to for the time being. He hoped they would arrive and find him soon, not looking forward to being idle for some indefinite period.

Wherever possible, the three took to the rivers to swim their way closer to the refugee area. The streets had grown unsafe; nearly around every corner they crossed paths with a wandering 'Greyman', as Devin had taken to calling them. If they stayed along the roadways, Jvard knew it was only a matter of time before they would run into a larger group than they could handle.

As they crossed the final waterway that would bring them to their destination, Jvard instructed Baerne and the boy to hold their position along the bank. Peeking up over the grass, Jvard now understood why the Inner City had been emptied out. It looked as though the entire army was on the field before them, most of them lying dead along with the majority of the civilians. He couldn't even begin to count the fallen, at least a thousand if he had to guess. Groups of Drakvnar walked along the remaining soldiers, rounding up and detaining any people still alive.

Jvard wasn't sure which was the greater disaster, the loss he caused at the Inner City or the slaughter that occurred on the island before him.

"Myrna!" Devin sobbed, dashing forward.

The barbarian reached out to grab him with one hand by the collar, stopping him in his tracks.

"Shhh," he signaled, not releasing him until he was sure the boy wasn't going to try to run again.

"But what if she's out there," he began.

"Use your head," Jvard whispered harshly, "there's nothing to gain by dashing out there. We will watch, and wait until the guards clear out."

"I'm afraid Jvard's right. As much as I'd like to go over there myself, it's not safe," Baerne agreed, peering his head over the bank to have a look, "everyone from Midao was here last I knew. I wonder if they're okay."

"It will be dark soon, we will investigate then," the barbarian decided.

The three settled in along the high grass near the river, allowing the time to pass and watching as the sun began its descent beyond the western horizon, bathing the entirety of Creekview's Crossing in a golden dusk. It wasn't long before raised voices drew their attention; solitary yells of battle, the subtle ringing of steel, and the occasional hollers of approval or groans of disappointment carrying across the air.

"More battle?" Baerne questioned.

Jvard concentrated on the sounds, furrowing his brow and finally shaking his head, "No, I do not believe so. Those are not the sounds of war."

Deciding to get a closer look, they stayed along the water's edge, moving northward along the rim of the island. Their new position afforded them a clear view of the commotion. Many soldiers and Drakvnar were formed in a rough semicircle around two individuals engaged in combat.

This time it was Baerne's turn to be stopped at the collar by Jvard as the blacksmith cursed and darted forward, though it took both of the barbarian's hands to halt his momentum.

"What is wrong with the two of you?" Jvard reprimanded, "The boy is excusable, but I thought you would have more sense…"

"That is our mayor in the fight," Baerne spoke in a hurried, hushed tone, "and that is my village sitting under guard!"

Jvard took another look around, and it became clear to him that not everyone shared in the revelry that the Drakvnar felt. Another group, the people of Baerne's village, sat subdued and distressed.

"The one he is fighting, he's the commander of the forces here at Creekview. I've aided you when I could have just ridden away, I'm asking you to return the favor now," Baerne implored the barbarian, "help me kill him and get my people out of here."

Jvard sighed heavily, knowing the outcome was currently in the hands of the Gods and beyond his control. To interfere with a battle of honor, on the field of battle nonetheless, Jvard was frankly surprised Baerne even considered such a thing. The request seemed so out of place coming from the blacksmith; though Jvard didn't know him long, he thought Baerne to be a man of principles.

"Why do you hesitate?" Baerne remarked, "Without their leader they would crumble. We can cut off the head of our enemy, here and now!"

"You know well we cannot interfere," Jvard began to state carefully, feeling odd explaining something to a grown man that every youth should know well.

"I don't understand," Baerne snapped, "with or without your help, I'm not going to let them force my people to watch Mayor Radford slaughtered. I've seen your exploits, you are no coward. Let's rally my people and put an end to the Drakvnar now!"

Jvard took a closer look and began to catch on; Baerne's people simply didn't pay homage to the ritual taking place. To the soldiers and Drakvnar, this was no more than grizzly entertainment – they've already beaten their enemy and were adding insult to injury. Even so, the duel before them had too much in common with the rite of *Kleïntòr* for Jvard to consider interfering with it.

"Your intention is honorable, but in the end a duel between chieftains is sacred among my people and cannot be interrupted," Jvard told Baerne regretfully, "have faith in your mayor, he is holding his own by the looks of it."

Incredulous, Baerne asked, "So you're just going to sit here? I've heard stories of the northmen's bloodlust, but didn't know your people enjoyed killing for sport."

"The point of the *Kleïntòr* is just the opposite, to bring about peace with the lowest possible loss of life," Jvard answered without hostility, "when this contest is over it will mark an end to the violence. Among all the dead here today, one more life lost – whether that life is your mayor's or not, it is worth the price. Had they come to their senses and done this earlier, not nearly so many would have perished."

"You think it's going to end with those two?" Baerne told him, "Once that fight is over the soldiers are poised to massacre everyone from my village."

Again Jvard couldn't believe what he was hearing. Surely they wouldn't kill an enemy that was already defeated. For the people of the Blue Fold Mountains, violating the results of the *Kleïntòr* in such a way would unite every tribe together to eradicate the offenders.

"If that is the case, I can assure you it will be our duty to interfere, but only when the contest is over," Jvard promised the blacksmith, "for now let the Gods hear your prayers for your chieftain the loudest, and they will answer."

Baerne couldn't believe the misplaced sense of honor displayed by the barbarian, but in the end decided he didn't have much of a choice but to do as Jvard instructed. If he ran out alone, maybe he could catch Ramnar by surprise, but he would surely be cut down soon after. Even if Jvard agreed to rush into battle, he had to admit they would have little odds of surviving. Realizing now wasn't the right time to act, he forced himself to calm down. It was the same as shaping a piece of steel; try to skip or hurry through necessary steps and the piece would be ruined. Patience was needed to do the job properly.

"I will wait then," Baerne relented, "but should the fighting spill over beyond Ramnar and Radford, I will be where I belong beside my people."

Jvard nodded, "As will I."

***

Radford was soaked in sweat and his breath came labored, but he believed he was faring better than his opponent. After nearly twenty minutes of fighting, his strategy seemed to be working as Ramnar's reflexes began to slow, his attacks arriving with decreased frequency and fervor. He could never have matched the intensity or strength of Ramnar in a direct exchange, so instead he slowly dragged the Guard-Captain out into deep waters during the course of the fight. Now it was time to let him drown.

The two men stood roughly a dozen feet apart, Ramnar eyeing the mayor with hatred, and what looked like incredulity that he hadn't managed to kill him yet. Radford decided that at the next interchange he would make his move. The onlookers were beginning to grow concerned by their Guard-Captain's inability to finish him off, and at any moment he feared they might interfere with the fight. With Ramnar's strength deteriorating, Radford reasoned he should be able to follow his opponent's weapon hand back inside and counterattack unchecked.

As intense as his focus was on his adversary, Radford couldn't help notice a growing commotion among the guards and soldiers who were playing spectator to the contest. Their shouts and jeers turned into concerned whispers, and many had turned their heads to view something else. Radford's distraction cost him dearly as Ramnar, who had not taken notice of the outside events, charged in and barely missed a strike that would have cleaved the mayor in half. The Guard-Captain stayed on the backpedaling mayor, unrelenting. After missing a third blow, he continued his forward momentum, driving his shoulder hard into Radford and sending him sprawling to the ground.

During the latest trade of attacks they pivoted around, and only now did Ramnar see what had diverted everyone's attention. A fair sized number of the dirtiest, most uncouth group of men he had ever laid eyes upon crossed the bridge and stood off a distance behind the villagers. There was something jarring about their presence, and it took him a moment to realize it was that the shortest man among them still stood well over six feet tall.

Luckily for Radford, the minor delay allowed him to get back to his feet before Ramnar could press in again. Ramnar visibly showed signs of fatigue, his mouth open trying to take in air, and his movements no longer as sharp as they once were. It was time for Radford to end the confrontation. Pretending to favor his front leg as he stood, he beckoned Ramnar in, holding his blade slightly low and to his side. It was an open invitation for a high attack from the left, and the Guard-Captain predictably tried to take advantage. The crowd showed a renewed interest in the fight, the soldiers believing Radford injured and sensing their leader closing in on victory.

A stunned silence ensued when Radford nimbly recoiled onto his back leg, dodging under a devastating swipe and lunging forward in one swift motion to pierce Ramnar's shoulder between the seams of his leather tunic. The single blow stymied the Guard-Captain, but wasn't fatal by itself. However, Radford persisted with two more strikes in rapid succession, the first parried as Ramnar managed to get his sword up to make a feeble block. With a spin to the outside, Radford again struck the same side from a different angle within the blink of an eye. Bringing his rapier straight across it slipped behind Ramnar's weapon, opening up a slit across the Guard-Captain's throat.

Ramnar fell instantly, dead before his soldiers could even reach him. For the first time that day, it was quiet enough to hear the gentle babbling of the rivers flowing alongside the island. The silence was only a fleeting thing, shattered when the True-Blood dashed forward to their fallen leader and others began to attack the people of Midao.

With their backs to the river, Radford's people had nowhere to run. They were outnumbered and not nearly as well armed as the remaining soldiers. Desperately he continued fighting, trying to make his way towards them despite the futility of it. His village was going to be massacred, and there was nothing he could do.

He nearly lowered his weapon and forgot to defend himself when he saw the True-Blood begin fighting with each other. Then he looked closer. Another group of men joined in the fray, nearly the same size as the Drakvnar, give or take, but each of them donned in various animal furs rather than black armor. Fully bearded with long hair extending halfway down their backs, they contrasted sharply to the clean shaven soldiers despite their similar stature.

Even with the unexpected assistance, the villagers were highly unorganized, and Radford feared for them as he fought for his own life. Though every one of his people was a target, the mayor in particular drew much of the attention after slaying the Guard-Captain. It seemed any nearby enemy wanted him in particular to achieve some semblance of revenge. Five men advanced, and he thought with certainty the end was upon him. But before they reached him, three of his assailants were bowled over by a mountain of agile muscle, wielding a rusty sword that looked more like a knife in his large hands.

"Get back to the bridge!" the man boomed at him; his size, devastating motion, and the gravel in his voice leaving Radford to think he was viewing the embodiment of an avalanche.

Not questioning his fortune, he skirted to the left around the two remaining attackers, deflecting one sword strike and moving entirely out of range of another. He didn't even bother to stop and fight, moving as quickly as he could towards his people and a defensive line that was beginning to form. Amidst the disorder of the villagers and soldiers, one group worked in striking harmony to guide the course of the skirmish to their desire.

Radford wasn't sure who the newcomers were, and though he didn't know if they could be called allies, it was clear to him they shared the same enemy. With a practiced efficiency and minimal communication he watched them systematically herd the soldiers back across the field, forming a partial perimeter around Radford's people and slowly backing towards the narrow bridge. Allowed to squeeze in through a gap in the defense, the mayor rejoined them, some fighting side by side with their rescuers while others were escorted away from the battle.

Once again Radford saw the person who had saved his hide only moments ago, bursting his way back across the field. It was to whom he spoke that surprised the mayor. He watched as the bear of a man issued a few commands to the blacksmith, Baerne, before once more diving into combat.

"Baerne!" the mayor shouted, heading towards the blacksmith.

The last they had seen each other, they were parting ways with a horde of the Infected chasing after Baerne. Radford was greatly relieved to see him alive and well.

"Are these men with you?" the mayor asked, perplexed as to who they were.

Baerne shook his head, "No. Well, I just know the one I was speaking with a moment ago, and they are with him."

Seeing the mayor still didn't understand, he added, "I'll explain later, for now they want to get everyone back across the bridge. They can defend it easier."

He noticed this new group, though deadly efficient, was much smaller than he originally thought and only succeeded by the slimmest of margins. The way they moved together, weaving in and out of each other's space to swap targets looked almost like a dance, and allowed them to do the same amount of work as a much larger conventional force. Though he wanted to inquire further of Baerne, Radford put his questions aside and began to take charge of the people from Midao. Many shook his hand, congratulating him on his victory against the Guard-Captain. Others asked him what they were going to do next, or frantically asked if he had seen someone important to them who was missing, or another dozen questions he didn't have an answer to.

"Please," Radford implored those gathering around him, "we aren't safe yet. Our first order of business is moving across the river. You'll have to have faith and meet up with your loved ones there if you're not all together right now."

Slowly everyone started moving, either voluntarily or because they were caught in the flowing crowd and didn't have a choice. With the area somewhat stable, the barbarians slowly began to move backwards, funneling everyone all the way across the bridge and spreading out along the opposite riverside. Only two men could fit across the width of the walkway, creating an effective chokepoint that counteracted the superior numbers of the soldiers. Jvard and Garl stood shoulder to shoulder, rapidly dissuading any attackers from approaching at the far end of the bridge. The two were an impenetrable wall, piling up the bodies of any foolish enough to try to break through. A few soldiers fell or jumped over the side of the bridge and began swimming towards the shore in hopes of flanking the Northmen, but their attempt was too scattered and half-hearted to make any headway against the fierce barbarians waiting for them.

By the time darkness fell, the two sides reached a stalemate. For the soldiers, crossing the bridge proved to be impossible against the stoic defenders, and the river was stained with pools of red from any who were caught defenseless trying to swim over.

Essentially leaderless and soundly beaten, the soldiers' thirst for battle looked all but quenched. Retreating to the field, they regrouped, waiting until the light of morning to decide their next move.

The immediate danger passed, Radford could finally get a few answers about the evening's events. Baerne found his mother and siblings, pulling all of them into a tight embrace. Allowing them to have some time together, the mayor decided to wait and see how everyone else had fared before drawing the blacksmith away to talk.

As he walked among the villagers he took the time to observe the force that came to their aid, northerners by the looks of them. He was surprised to only count twenty-five men; during the course of the battle it was difficult to discern their number. Some of the younger, able-bodied men from Midao stood near to the barbarians along the bank to feel as though they were being useful, but next to the grizzled warriors they almost looked like children playing at soldiering.

Standing watch, they had broken into three smaller teams. Five guarding the bridge, fifteen stayed along the river, and the rest watched the trail that led up a rocky pathway towards the bluffs to their east. Occasionally one of the barbarians offered him a dip of the head, or a light touch of their fingertips to forehead in what he assumed was a salute. Unsure of what he might have done to earn their respect, he awkwardly returned the gesture when it was given.

Feeling as though he waited an appropriate amount of time given the circumstances, Radford intruded upon Baerne to find out what relationship he held with the strangers. Adding to his surprise, he recognized a young man standing off to the blacksmith's side, close enough to be in Baerne's vicinity but far enough away that he looked like he was unsure of where he belonged. Wherever he was, usually Myrna hovered close by.

"Devin? Are you alright lad?" Radford asked, concerned for the boy.

Devin looked to him, but put his head back down without answering. Hearing his voice, Baerne turned away from his family and the campfire to greet the mayor.

"What can you tell me about all of this?" Radford asked, not sure where to start and hoping for answers.

"I can explain some of it," Baerne assured Radford, "come with me. Let me introduce you to Jvard, assuming he's not too busy."

Turning he added to Devin, "You too. Remember our talk? Until we find Myrna I have my eye on you."

Baerne began to fill the mayor in on what he could as the three walked towards the barbarians at the bridge.

Trying to think of the most important place to start, he informed Radford, "The Inner City has been lost. I can't imagine we'll be safe here long."

That news gave Radford pause, his concern had been to smooth over his relations with the Drakvnar and soldiers of Dun'Aldir. As

Baerne continued to talk, it seemed like that might no longer be necessary, and he should begin thinking about where to take his people.

"What of the barbarians?" Radford asked, still not understanding their presence here.

"They are here for their chieftain, and nothing more," Baerne answered, "from what I gather the only reason they appeared to be on our side is the Drakvnar violated some code of conduct that the northmen rigidly uphold."

"It had to do with your fight with Ramnar," Baerne explained further, seeing Radford wanted to know more, "they have similar duels of honor, and the result is viewed the same as a peace treaty."

The barbarians stood alert as they approached, until one waved the others down and came forward.

Radford recognized him as the one who earlier barreled into a group of attackers so he could escape, though he now carried a great axe instead of the rusty sword he held before. Meeting the barbarian's eyes, they had a subtle, yet striking difference compared to what he would expect to see in a person. They held the steel of an instinctual creature; it was the difference between staring at an animal from the wilds and a domesticated house pet. The mayor found himself feeling unsettled, to see that quality in the eyes of a person. Looking to the others, he realized all of the barbarians possessed a similar gaze.

"Hail, my friend," Baerne said, approaching the barbarian and grasping his forearm in greeting.

Turning to Radford, Jvard offered out his hand, "The Gods have shown you favor this day. Well fought, champion."

The mayor returned the gesture, extending his arm. His hand wrapped nearly a third of the way around the barbarian's forearm, while most of Radford's disappeared into Jvard's oversized palm.

"Let us sit and talk, there is much we should discuss," Jvard said, signaling towards a few large stones near the bridge.

"I suppose I should start by thanking you," Radford offered, "should you have not intervened my people would likely be dead. You have my gratitude."

Jvard nodded, accepting the acknowledgement.

"We are not aware of the customs of your people. Back home, sometimes it is necessary to shed the blood of a rival tribe. But we do not kill each other excessively. If a dispute grows out of hand, we resolve it through the *Kleïntòr*, an honor duel. The outcome is sacred. It is the duty of every tribe to respond swiftly should the

Kleïntòr be disregarded. My people responded here in the only way they knew how," Jvard explained.

Radford let out a soft whistle through his teeth. It was one thing to claim to be principled when someone was watching or your own well-being was at stake, and quite another to follow through on it when there was little benefit to be had.

"What will you do now?" Baerne asked, the fate of his town essentially still riding on the protection of the barbarians.

Jvard shook his head, "I do not know. As soon as the enemy admits defeat my people can move north again. I had thought them all dead, now knowing some survived is more than I could have hoped for – but I cannot join them just yet. I still have promises to fulfill, one of them to help this boy find his mother."

"She's not my mother," Devin interjected, speaking for the first time in many hours.

The barbarian turned his head to the boy, "Then you are especially blessed, to have one not of your blood care for you as such."

Devin opened his mouth to speak again, but instead closed it, deciding to keep the thought to himself or reconsider it altogether.

"Then again, with so many of the Risen nearby, we might not have the choice of staying to uphold your victory. I've discussed it with my men, and we're willing to escort you to the Jun'tirh Outpost if it comes to that," Jvard added.

Radford began to protest but was interrupted by Jvard, "Let us all sleep on it. This entire city has been pushed to the verge of collapse, and we do not know what tomorrow brings. Things will be clearer in the light of morning."

Last Stand

Winding through the maze of rivers that intersected the islets of Creekview's Crossing, Walt guided his small boat along the waterways in a generally southwestern direction. Eventually these small tributaries would rejoin the wide Tinindraüg River flowing out of the city, and could carry him all the way south to his destination of Dalesford. He hoped the order of the Magicus Celesti could provide him answers there, because he sure didn't have any.

The warm air and setting sun would have made for a pleasant evening drifting along the channels, had it not been for the silent battle raging inside of the gemstone or the gathering of the Stricken who followed him along the embankments. Beads of sweat trickled to the floor of the boat, and his head felt like it might collapse in on itself at any moment from the pressure of his magical efforts. If not for the assistance of the other wizard currently residing in the gem, Walt would have long ago been overpowered. It assured him once they gained enough distance, the assault would cease. Walt prayed that to be true; he knew he could not keep up his current level of exertion for much longer.

Along the banks a frenzied bustling of activity stole part of his absolute concentration from the gem, demanding he pay attention to the world around him once again. There was a woman, toppling down a small hill to land roughly along the dirt and mud by the water, while no less than a dozen of the once human monstrosities eagerly pursued her. She still had all of her faculties; the fear in her expression made that perfectly clear. Struggling to stand, she managed to scuttle a few more feet towards the water where she finally collapsed, unmoving.

Walt was closer to her than they were, and moving swiftly with the current. Landing the boat he moved on instinct, barely aware of his actions as most of his effort was still directed at the contest within the diamond. The Stricken approaching from the opposite side of her emitted a powerful stench, and the smell of rot and decomposition hit him like a wall as he landed the boat and ran to the prone woman.

Lifting her from under the shoulders, he dragged her towards the craft as best he could. Bare from her waist to her shoulders, Walt saw that her shirt had been tightly tied around her leg. Though modesty wasn't his greatest concern at the moment, or many other times during the course of his life for that matter, he did his best to avert his eyes.

Greatly overestimating his own strength, Walt was struggling more than he anticipated along the shoreline. Over the years, the wizard leaned towards activities and endeavors that were mental in nature; if physical work was necessary he would simply hire someone to do it. He paid for that now as his scrawny arms and legs protested while he strained to carry the unconscious woman to safety. Misjudging how long it would take him to get back to the boat, nearly two dozen drooling, rotting, walking corpses bore down on him well before he reached the water. Distantly, he recognized that he overextended himself. Engaged in two separate struggles, Walt had to decide which one to fully commit to or they would both fail.

Inside of the gem, the entity sensed Walt's attention was elsewhere, and the power of Kubathu threatened to overwhelm them.

Master, the entity called out, still under the impression Walt was someone else, *why do your efforts wane? We are nearly beyond his reach, but you must focus.*

I have a problem here! I can't deal with both things at once! Walt thought back urgently.

Their minds still linked, the spirit within the gem viewed the world through Walt's eyes. Concern filled him as he saw the wizard dragging Myrna's unmoving form; though he was so accustomed to the healer's presence through Devin it didn't strike him as odd that she was here now. He also saw more of the men who were not whole in body and mind, suffering the same ailment he once viewed when he was under the boy Devin's charge. Except this time there were much more of them. Even given their numbers, they were still merely unthinking creatures.

He did not understand why his master, so wise and powerful was having difficulty with them along the river bank. Surely he would gather his senses and incinerate them at any moment, but as the seconds elapsed he did not. They moved in closer and closer to the wizard, dangerously so.

I see - you are trying to conserve your strength, it assumed, having no explanation to Walt's inaction.

Only he sensed that Walt's thought pattern was not in a rational state; if anything, it felt panicked and wavering. With only moments away from being set upon, the entity decided to act. Whatever the reason for his master's inaction, he seemed to need assistance.

The entity, as tired as he was and as implausible as it seemed, felt it was necessary to intervene. Calling on what remained of his strength, he drew the very air in towards the mindless ones, condensing and igniting it. Tremendous heat emitted from the Stricken, causing a blast of wind that knocked Walt backwards and singed his beard and eyebrows. White fire erupted from the eyes, nostrils, ears, and various locations on the bodies of the Stricken as they burned to ash.

The fire threatened to rampantly spread outwards, causing Walt to throw his arm over his face in a meager attempt to protect himself. To his astonishment, the flames reached a point close in front of him and simply stopped, hitting a thin layer void of oxygen that the entity had used to fuel the fire.

Able to once again put most of his attention to the gemstone, Walt distractedly brought the woman onto the boat and covered her over with a spare cloak before setting off. His escapade had cost them dearly, leaving him and the spirit scrambling to restore their defenses. The effort grew so arduous for Walt that he no longer saw what was physically before him, fully devoting himself to maintaining the spell of binding within the stone.

His strength continued to drain while feeding the protective spell, and diminished to a dangerously low level. His only concern became drawing energy forth and transferring it to the structure of the magic. It developed into a rote pattern for him, and the consistency of his method was all that allowed him to keep going; one slip and it would come to a crashing end. Just as quickly as he tried to fortify the spell, the one the entity referred to as Kubathu dismantled it. Walt could feel the raw power, anger, and purified evil within the being assailing them, and in that instant he fully understood the urgency of the responsibility he had been given.

At the height of its intensity, when Walt thought he could hold out no longer, the assault simply ceased. His boat drifted lazily along the river, Creekview's Crossing fading to a small point behind them. Not even aware he had been gripping the sides of the boat, he unclenched his hands and rolled onto his back, allowing unconsciousness to wash over him.

***

A solitary boat wound along the river, the long white beard and slightly hunched stance of its passenger unmistakable to Daro who stood atop a hill at the northern entrance to Creekview's Crossing. The wizard was long out of his reach at this point. It did leave him wondering just what role the conniving Walt Whirten might have played in the downfall of the Inner City. He'd love nothing more than to hunt down the blasphemous conjurer and bring him to task for his sins, but he had a more pressing responsibility to ensure the safety of his newfound flock.

Passing by a wagon on the road outside of town, he brought his group to a brief halt. Something about the wagon struck a chord of familiarity, but he found it difficult to focus fixated as he was on the image of Walt floating to freedom along the river. The thought of the wizard once again roaming freely burned at Daro's conscience, creeping into his every thought and turning his mood dour.

He laughed aloud when he finally figured it out, startling those next to him who waited patiently as he stared at the cart. The wagon belonged to none other than his former friend Walt. The telltale dings, scratches, and its general wear and tear marked it as clear as the good Lord's light of day.

Going in for a closer look, he inspected the ground carefully and wasn't surprised by what he found. A few flecks of black powder were scattered on the ground. It was a small amount, probably only so much as might dust off from the top of a lid. Inside of the wagon he saw four more barrels and a few grains of the volatile powder around them. Most noticeable was the empty spot where another barrel would have fit perfectly. Daro knew well of Walt's explosive powder, having lived alongside him for many years. A full barrel would have been more than enough to blast through the gate of the Inner City. But Walt had been captured and imprisoned in the cellars of the palace; he couldn't have been the one to destroy the wall.

"The barbarian," Daro said lightly to himself, remembering the formidable figure from Walt's initial capture.

His men looked to him expectantly, anxiously, and he realized he had spent too much time dawdling here. He didn't have the luxury of time right now; in any minute a trail of the Infected would track them out of the city.

"Let's move on," he decided, hesitant to leave the wizard's belongings intact but not having much of a choice.

The men and women were tired, but appreciative when they finally found an area they deemed safe to stop for the night. After leaving the Inner City, Daro concluded that it was too dangerous to remain anywhere within the entirety of Creekview's Crossing. With mobs of the Infected roaming freely, they were forced northwards where Daro led the group out of the city altogether, and all the way back around south onto the bluffs surrounding the river basin of Creekview.

In the morning he would follow along the cliff to get a view of the island camp from a safe distance. Not knowing the state of the rest of Creekview's Crossing, he believed it prudent to evaluate it from afar first. The people he led followed him unequivocally; if Daro thought it best, than it was so.

The evening had long turned to darkness before the weary group came to a halt. With no tents or supplies, they settled in and slept on the open grass. Daro lamented the lack of warriors within his company while he considered securing a watch. With well over a hundred people following him, perhaps a dozen might be able to use a sword properly without stabbing themselves in the foot. It would be difficult to defend themselves, he realized, if he had to keep them on the move for long.

"Unfortunately there will be no sleep for some of you tonight. Spread out along the perimeter," he instructed those he felt capable, "if you see anything, call out."

The night passed slowly in silent darkness as Daro patrolled along the line of watchmen to check in periodically. It seemed to help keep them awake, not knowing when he might stop by to stress the importance of being diligent in their guard, or offer his thanks for their service. The compliments were always well-received, leaving the guard standing a little taller after the preacher passed by.

Along the way to the next set of watchmen, he stopped to stare off into the darkness. The way ahead for him was unclear; if the entirety of Creekview's Crossing was no longer safe, he was unsure of where to go from here. Maybe north, back to the seclusion of Big Bear would be a wise choice.

A sound along the southern edge of the perimeter brought his head up sharply. Was it a baby crying? It was amazing how alike that could sound to a yowling animal. Still wearing his blade-gauntlet, he raised it slightly and looked about. Moving ahead a dozen paces, he stopped where he thought he heard the noise. Perplexed, he saw nothing and the crying ceased. Just as he was ready to dismiss the sound and continue along it started again, another ten paces out. The perpetual scowl that he wore lately deepening, he approached the source of the noise again, only to be drawn out further. Daro stopped, sensing something amiss. He was no fool, someone was trying to lead him out and he saw through the ploy.

"You might as well show yourself. Deceipt is a game for cowards and thieves; I am neither," he said in a clear, confident tone that alluded towards a person who trusted in their ability.

The sound of distress came once again, slightly in front of where he stood.

"Have it your own way then!" He hollered and moved ahead, his patience quickly at an end.

The thought crossed his mind to go back for assistance, which he promptly rejected. That would only serve the purpose of unnecessarily putting others at risk. Stalking forward, he ignored the cries that came at such regular intervals he could have predicted where and when they would arise. Not too far away, a copse of trees stood in line of the direction he was heading, and he guessed that would likely be his destination.

Crossing the tree line, he entered a wide but short clearing with a denser scattering of trees further ahead. The only sound was the distant prattling of birds, calling out to greet the predawn grey of early morning. A cold, empty feeling settled upon him as he looked towards the woods. If he were to continue on, it would not be much further until he entered miles of forest that stretched nearly to the southern farmlands. Just how far had the destruction spread, he wondered? Expect the worst, and hope for the best – he had to assume the entirety of Luskir had been ravaged by the unholy blight. Those who had already succumbed paid the price of atonement, now was the time to bring forth a world that reflected His image.

He straightened his back at the thought; it was a challenge of which he was up to the task. His flight from Big Bear was merely a test to see if he had the strength of what would be asked of him in the days to come. There were many times that he could have given up and lay down to die, but he did not. The true God saw he was capable, and now he had been chosen by Him to lead those who survived. Daro believed in his calling, he would not fail or give in to despair.

Shadows closed in around him, bathing him in an unnatural darkness and abruptly ending his thoughts of what was to come. He felt no fear in whatever manner of evil it was that attempted to subdue him, knowing the light that guided him to be the stronger. His God-given instincts saved him once more as he darted his weapon out to the side and felt the soft resistance of flesh meet the blade. He leapt forward while three men converged on him from behind, and one fell to the ground, sputtering and grasping his ruined throat. Up ahead, more emerged from the woods and walked determinedly towards him.

The men looked very much like the Drakvnar, with subtle differences. Where the Drakvnar had obvious physical gifts and displayed superiority in battle to the regular soldiers, these men looked like they were handpicked from the very best of that elite group. Impossibly large men, they carried their weapons like they were born with them in hand. Turning to meet his attackers, Daro backed away as they advanced, keeping in line with the left most man in an effort to avoid being surrounded.

Suddenly lunging forward in an attempt to put his attacker off balance, his blade was cleanly deflected. The strike bought him a little distance, though, and he used it to fend off a blow from one of the other men. Daro realized he would soon be in trouble as the three men spread further out and continued to move in, while another ten came from the other direction and likewise converged. The circle of Drakvnar tightened around him, drawing in close until he had nowhere to move and points of steel gently pushed against his flesh.

"Don't move," a strong, deep voice instructed him from behind a faceguard.

Each man was clad in full blackened steel armor, with a helmet and faceplate that did not allow him to recognize his assailants. Through the small gaps between the soldiers, he saw a woman approaching, though he wasn't quite sure where she had come from.

"At ease," she commanded, and the guards slightly backed away to open up a path to him.

Standing before him was a petite woman he might consider beautiful, if not for the snowy paleness of her skin, and the chilling set of her eyes and voice. She was the dreariest of winter days come to life. The only shock of color about her was the blood red ruby set low on a necklace adorning her delicate shoulders. A single streak of silver ran through her hair, making it difficult to place an age to her. Halfway towards him she paused and glanced to the side, seeing the one fallen guard that Daro managed to strike.

"A pity," she muttered absently, walking towards the dying guard.

Daro couldn't hide his disgust at the display of magic as she reached out towards the fallen soldier, not quite touching him. A subtle, greenish hue surrounded her hand, followed by a more tangible mist leaving his body and flowing into her. She tilted her head back in apparent pleasure while the man's skin tightened and shriveled until the features of his skull were easily discernible. He gasped and struggled violently for a final breath before his head fell back to the ground, unmoving.

So there it was, another foul magician, Daro thought. A pleasant fantasy flitted across his mind of cutting off her head, bringing a smile to his lips.

"Amused, are we?" she remarked, seeing his expression lighten when she moved within only a few steps of him.

Not receiving an answer, or expecting one she continued with her business, "Not many men carrying such an unorthodox weapon match your description. I can presume you are Daro Ildaradi?"

Again, he did not offer a response. Unsure as of yet how this new development fit into God's plan for him, he would not give this woman the satisfaction of seeing him off balance.

"You've given me quite a bit of trouble," she continued, unfazed by the silence, "undermining the authority of my men at Creekview and garnering quite a following of your own. I think I'll turn you over to Kempf and let him do as he sees fit with you. I'm sure you've become well acquainted with him by now, yes?"

Daro's smile faded as it dawned on him it was Empress Sevra who stood before him, and that she was a sacrilegious witch. How he longed to strike her down! To think that a foul sorceress was so close to coming to power caused bile to rise up into his throat. He quickly pushed the feeling down, collecting himself. God delivered the witch to him so he could prevent that from happening… yes, that fit very seamlessly into His plan, once Daro gave it a moment's thought. Everything under the sun had a time, place and purpose, and surrounded by Sevra and her guards was exactly the place he needed to be right now. His purpose was obvious.

"Though it would probably be simplest to be rid of you here and now," she contemplated aloud, continuing over the silence and leaning towards the decision that eliminating Daro was her best option.

"You don't know yet then, do you?" Daro asked, his apparent disinterest in her threat eliciting a frown from Sevra.

She appeared calm as she waited to hear him out, but the tightness around her eyes told Daro it was only on the surface. Boiling underneath he could see a cauldron of fury burning to be released. At delicate times such as this, the preacher put his trust to Him, seeking guidance. The response came back to him almost immediately; in order to execute His designs, the ability to demonstrate meekness was sometimes required. This was one of those times. He would have to present what he was going to tell her delicately, and shift blame elsewhere so that the volatile woman didn't react dangerously towards him.

But how he wished to plunge his blade into her! Immediately he put his desires aside, showing pious restraint. God told him to stand down, that now was not the time to put an end to the witch, and he held faith that he was not being led astray. The snake he sought to eradicate had many heads, and Sevra was but one of them. Walt Whirten was another. Come to think of it, the two were probably conspiring together, that's why she insisted on taking the wizard alive. He grimaced at picturing the conjurers working in tandem with one another. The last thing Daro wanted to see was the two of them forming a vile covenant.

"Creekview is in turmoil, it happened hours ago," the preacher began after his brief contemplations.

Her expression remained blank, though her eyes remained thunderheads ready to bring forth a storm without warning.

He would turn those two against each other; if she needed to have him captured then they obviously had a tumultuous arrangement to begin with. There was an opportunity for him to drive a wedge further between the sinful pair.

"The wizard your men were holding seemed to prove more capable than they estimated. He escaped, I saw him rowing away from the city with my own eyes. His companion likely assisted him, a northman by his looks. They brought untold death and destruction into the city," he continued.

He thought it irrelevant to mention how the enlightenment he spread onto the masses allowed them to see that their fate was not set in stone, and his sermons only added to the existing tension in the city until it reached the breaking point.

Again he issued a subtle pause, not wanting to offer too much until he saw if Sevra viewed the information favorably or not. Her brow furrowed slightly upon hearing reference to the wizard, and that told him all that he needed to begin guiding Sevra to His ends.

***

Kubathu raged and roiled inside of the ruby for allowing the key to his prison to slip out of reach. Vaguely monitoring the conversation through Sevra, he went still as he heard the talk turning towards the escaped wizard. Could this person be a link to the one securing his imprisonment? Gently reaching out he touched upon Daro's mind, and was quite impressed by what he found.

This was a person of great cunning before him, quick of wit, self-righteous, and calculating. He was everything that Sevra was not. Slowly he sensed Sevra's mind viewing him more favorably as he continued to speak, while he partially read Daro's thoughts throughout the entire process. The only concern Daro had at the moment was self-preservation, and then trying to garner status with the witch once he convinced her she no longer wished to kill him. To those ends, he manipulated her masterfully.

Unfortunately he gave no real indication of where the wizard, Walt Whirten by name, might be currently heading. Desperate for that information, Kubathu risked delving slightly deeper into Daro's mind. He treaded carefully, not wanting to risk alerting the self-proclaimed preacher to his intrusions as he probed for the knowledge he sought. Not surprised, he found the presence of Sevra vainly trying to wrap her tendrils around Daro's thoughts to determine his truthfulness. He nearly laughed at her inability to do so. Though she was competent at this particular art, Daro was able to subconsciously evade the witch like a greased eel slipping through her fingers.

Having invaded the minds of untold thousands throughout the course of his unnaturally long years, he had seldomly encountered those like Daro, with a seeming natural ability to protect their thoughts. Of particular interest to Kubathu, however, was how he did so. All was not well within the mind of Daro Ildaradi. A second, distinctive personality sat there, working together with the man to help him evaluate and refine his actions or thoughts. As he explored the far recesses of Daro's complicated mind, he discovered there was no phenomenal explanation for the two personas. The two distinctive personalities both belonged to the preacher, and Kubathu found the man's madness fascinating.

Even though he couldn't divine from Daro's knowledge where the wizard might be, he did find that Daro knew a great deal about Walt Whirten, and held an evaluative mind demonstrative of someone who was attentive to detail. It would be worthwhile to keep this one around, Kubathu decided. The man was wildly ambitious, more specifically one of his personalities was. Having made up his mind, he contacted Sevra to let her know how important it was that this man be kept close by and alive. The preacher's mind was far too interesting for Kubathu to pass up on. Having only scratched the surface of Daro's psyche, he intended to spend far more time unraveling all the secrets it had to offer.

Daro would have breathed a sigh of relief, had he not had an unwavering faith that his God protected him. His will was of ultimate precedence; no man or woman had the power to see it undone. It was no surprise to the preacher that Sevra would choose to keep him alive for now. In time he thought she may even come to offer him a small degree of deference, assuming an opportunity to kill her didn't present itself first. For now though, he faced another dilemma as he was forced to march back to his people, tightly guarded, and explain that they would be returning to the island under Sevra's guidance and protection. He viewed it as a small concession towards her, considering he was still alive and not in chains.

***

"Do you s'pose they'll be admittin' defeat this fine mornin'?" Garl asked Jvard, more to make conversation than out of concern there could be more battle.

"I can't say," Jvard answered carefully, "they are unpredicatable, leaderless and without purpose. Without someone to tell them what to do, I'd suspect they would soon realize they're free to leave and seek their own future. On the other hand, one straggler wishing to prove himself could turn the day bloody for all."

Garl issued a disdainful grunt in response, noting his agreement. That was the problem with hired soldiers; they fought with their heads and not their heart. He'd rather face five of them than any one of his men. Just by looking at the fragment of the Dun'Aldiran army on the other side of the small river, Jvard's words showed hints of truth. The sporadic arrangement of the tents, and the scattered groups they split themselves into spoke towards a lack of command. Without discipline, they'd likely dissemble to small bands of vagrants scavenging from the countryside.

As they watched trying to determine their enemy's next move, an approaching vanguard from the west caused a scurry of motion among the soldiers that spread through their ranks like a whirling dervish across an open plain. Two rows of ten men on horseback accompanied a woman standing atop a chariot, followed by scores of men on foot. Soldiers dropped to their knees as she passed, placing their heads to the ground. One person in particular caught Jvard's attention; a robed figure he had seen once before when he was nearly captured along with Walt at the Inner City. The two locked eyes for a moment, Jvard scowling as recognition set in on the man in simple brown robes.

"Maybe they still have a leader after all," Garl remarked to Jvard.

Looking as though the army would hold together, the chieftain responded, "Perhaps you will have your battle after all, old friend. Gather up the men for me. Bring the mayor Radford and Baerne too, this will concern them as well."

The barbarians watched as the woman was escorted around the island, speaking occasionally to a soldier or issuing an order. Eventually she convened with what they assumed were the higher ranking officials that remained on the field. Jvard began to wonder what they might be deciding, and if they should ready themselves for more combat. He could simply order his people to begin heading back north, but that was not an option he would even consider and likely a directive his people wouldn't follow if he did. The force on the island had lost the *Kleïntòr*. Whether or not it was a ritual these southerners observed, it was a matter of honor to the barbarians that the result be upheld.

As Jvard's company began to congregate, he decided on a course of action to give them the best chance for survival should the day turn to battle. Keeping in mind that the villagers of Midao were not fighters, he would give Radford the option of leaving. The entire band of barbarians filled in a circle around Jvard, with Baerne and Radford awkwardly taking the cue and falling into place.

"There was a time when I thought everyone dear to me was gone," Jvard began, "the song of our people was lost to me. Vengeance filled my heart, and I saw myself as no more than a vessel for exacting revenge."

The men nodded their heads slightly, understanding and approving of Jvard's perspective.

"When I learned that not everyone had perished, I too felt alive again. It is more than I could have hoped for. But now, here we are, outnumbered and fighting a battle that is not ours. Let us put it to vote, do we appease the Gods by upholding the victory of Radford Roltain?"

"Aye!" the group replied as a single unit, each man ready to uphold the sacred *Kleïntòr*.

"Very well," Jvard stated, expecting the response, "Radford Roltain, your victory was well fought. But this is not the place for you and your people. You should take your town and go. I would suggest the Jun'tirh Outpost, it will soon be empty and the walls are fortified."

"I will send the town north, then," Radford responded, "but I will stay behind and see this through."

Jvard intended to give the mayor a way out while allowing him to maintain honor. From what the barbarian knew of southern leaders, most sat safely behind palace doors while allowing others to do for them. He apparently underestimated this one's courage.

"Then your sword is welcome," the chieftain told him.

Directing his gaze to Baerne, he added, "I have a special task for you. Take Devin to the south, out of Creekview along the river. Find a pair of horses any way you can, and if the wagon you first met me near is still intact, take that with you as well. Find the wizard, tell him I will catch up soon."

At that a murmur grew among the barbarians. They thought their leader would rejoin them again at Jun'tihr Outpost and lead them back to Boldstone Ridge, helping the tribe to rebuild. Baerne also began to protest, wanting to stay and fight if needed.

"I've made two oaths I cannot break. One was to seek revenge for the death of my kin. Though we've survived as a people, barely, I intend to see that oath fulfilled," Jvard spoke in grim tones, "the second was to watch after the boy. This is hardly the place for a child to be right now. You're the only one I can count on to do this."

Though he wanted to argue further, Baerne begrudgingly agreed. The barbarians, however, were still not pleased they had come so far to reclaim their chieftain only to hear he intended to run off again.

"What're you thinkin'? Garl argued, nearly flying into a rage at Jvard's claim he would leave once again, "Mixin' in your lot with a wizard? You have a duty…"

"My duty is to see to the safety and well-being of all of the clans of the Frostwrynn," Jvard interrupted, "that is exactly what I intend to do. Something terrible has happened to the world, and we are not unaffected, secluded as we are in the Blue Fold Mountains. The wizard claims to have knowledge of what has happened. I will help him put it right."

They grew quiet at Jvard's reasoning. Even though he intended to leave again, in the end it was to help protect them.

"What of the enemy? Should we attack before they have time to organize?" Adran asked, eager to deal with them one way or another and return home.

"For now we will wait and see what they do next. We do not know their plans, they still may decide to leave," Jvard answered, "Radford will begin evacuating his people now up the trail behind us. Should they attack, we will give them the bridge and fend them off in the pass to the east."

The men agreed, finding the trail behind them easier to defend should the soldiers decide to organize a full attack. Radford began to gather his village, instructing them to begin travelling further north. Though it drew some half-hearted disagreement, most of the people understood it would be far safer behind sturdy walls than the open countryside of Midao.

As the evacuation began, soldiers on the field took notice of the activity. Shortly after the line of villagers began trudging along the hill onto the bluffs leaving Creekview, six riders on large steeds approached the bridge, crossing halfway where they stood and waited. They remained there in a two by three formation, one man bearing a banner of a red sun rising; the standard of Dun'Aldir.

Unsure of their intentions, the barbarians spoke hurriedly amongst themselves, deciding who would fight the six riders. Selecting Garl and his four best men, Jvard set off. Every nuance of his movements expressed coiled fury, straining to be released.

"They wish to parley with you," Radford interjected upon Jvard, sensing the northman's misunderstanding, "it is a formality for the officers to meet before combat, to discuss terms, negotiate a last minute truce, things of that nature."

Jvard paused, rethinking his course of action, "Why don't you come along too, then," he asked.

As they approached the bridge the riders came forward; Jvard's group advanced until the two sides stopped only feet from one another.

"Who speaks for this band?" the front rider asked, his deep voice thick with the accent of Dun'Aldir.

"I do. Jvard, son of Helstajvan," the barbarian answered.

"On behalf of Empess Sevra, here are our terms," he dictated to Jvard, "we have knowledge that you have been in the company of one named Walt Whirten. You will surrender yourself immediately to Empress Sevra's questioning in regards to your knowledge of the conjurer."

Radford's face grew dark at the mention of Sevra, connecting the name with the slender form of the woman they watched all morning whisking around the isle. He was familiar with her as the advisor to the First Seat of the Luskiran Council, and as a member of the council had even been in the same room with her on several occasions. Her presence was always unsettling to say the least, the way she gazed at the other councilmen as though she could bore straight into their heads.

The name of the woman was also not lost on Jvard. It was the one Walt had suspected of unleashing the plague onto his people.

"The rest of you will swear allegiance to..." the delegate continued.

He was unable to finish the sentence as Garl stepped forward, his mountainous fist connecting to the horse's skull above its eye. It whinnied and stumbled sideways, falling over gracelessly while the rider barely managed to escape getting crushed. The horse shakily stumbled from the narrow bridge into the river, shaking its head fiercely and swimming away towards the shoreline.

"I want his head!" the felled man spat, his face red with anger and embarassment.

Sounds of weapons being drawn rang out across the bridge, the impending violence hanging heavy in the air as the two sides stood off with one another.

"These are our terms," Jvard said, prolonging the tension before it crossed a breaking point, "honor Mayor Radford's victory over your commander. Leave the battlefield, never to impose yourself upon the people of Midao or my tribe. My men will go where and when they see fit."

He glowered at Jvard and Garl, his desire to attack here and now tempered by the fact he had to crane his neck to look them in the eyes. Without a word he turned on his heel and stalked off, calling his men after him.

Jvard did likewise, though he was not nearly as disgruntled as his adversary. He hoped to avoid more combat, but if the Gods dictated there to be bloodshed this day, he would oblige them. Garl however, seemed to be as agitated as the rider of the horse he punched.

"Looks like we're in it now," Radford commented, expressing his displeasure as they left the bridge to return to the rest of the group, "I'd say that's the first time I've seen a horse knocked senseless at a negotiation, so much for avoiding a fight."

Garl fixed a stare at the mayor, his temper not yet abated. Knowing his large friend well, Jvard stepped in between the two to prevent any unfortunate mishaps.

"We're on the same side, both of you," he said to the two of them, but mostly to remind Garl.

"If your man hadn't," Radford began, but Jvard stopped him short.

"You know they had no intention of upholding their defeat," Jvard emphasized, "if there is a code they live by, it is different from our own."

"Code? They are honorless pigs," Garl growled as he stalked off.

"And only a southerner would allow the defeated to make demands of the victor. Every one of 'em deserves to die this day," he criticized of Radford as he walked away.

Radford again attempted to express his frustration, to which Jvard responded, "Nothing short of their surrender and acceptance of our conditions would be tolerated. This is out of your control. Accept it and aid us in the coming battle, or you are free to leave just the same."

Jvard too walked away, leaving Radford uncharacteristically speechless. The barbarian thought he understood the mayor's confusion; if the southerners were accustomed to negotiating in a certain manner, Jvard's people must have appeared exceptionally rigid. But there was no argument to be had, no ground could be given in this matter and they were out of time to dwell over it. Greatly outnumbered, he imagined the enemy would attack soon in an attempt to overwhelm his small force.

If he was concerned, it did not show while he gathered his men by the mouth of the narrow trail they had arrived from the previous day. With high bluffs tight on either side and no way around for days, their inferior numbers did not matter. From here, he was certain they could keep the other force at bay for weeks if necessary. His men had unrivaled endurance and the skill to match any of those soldiers one to one or even two to his one.

"We will wear them down if we must," Jvard told his men as they surveyed where they would make their stand.

There appeared to be few archers remaining among the enemy, but to practice caution he instructed the only two bowmen he had to take up position on top of the cliffs. The bows they held were made from the forearm bone of a massive beast that roamed the Blue Fold Mountain Range, and painstakingly crafted and cured to prevent splintering. It took a large amount of strength to achieve a full draw, but the distance the bow could send a projectile was without equal. Any men who carried a shield would take up the front to start, until Jvard was sure exactly what they would be up against.

As he suspected, it soon began when the Dun'Aldiran soldiers swarmed over the bridge and across the river to take up formations only a hundred yards away from the path the barbarians occupied.

"I've got them counted at fifty and two hundred, twenty mounted," Garl remarked, standing up the hill with Jvard as others took first position at the front lines.

"They will be choked down to four or five across at the pass," Jvard said confidently, "after a few hours, they will lose their heart for battle when wave after wave of their comrades fall."

The first tactic they tried was as the barbarians predicted, a row of archers stepping free from their company and unleashing a volley of arrows in unison. An anxious moment of quiet passed as the projectiles soared through the air, and was broken by the thud of impact. Overlapping their shields to protect one another, the barrage struck harmlessly against the barrier. The barbarians yelled and jeered as they stood up, unscathed from the attack. Two more volleys followed, with no more effect than the barbarians' shields beginning to resemble pin cushions.

As the archers began to nock more arrows to their strings, two bolts soared down to strike one below the collar bone and graze the wrist of another. Those around them looked about in alarm, finally spotting the two distant figures high upon the hillside with their own bows. At their distance, they couldn't hope to return fire.

"Fall back to ranks!" their officer called out, and the group of bowmen interspersed back to their respective battalions.

With Jvard's instructions to conserve arrows and only fire at the archers, having no clear mark the two men on the bluffs held their shots. A brief stalemate ensued as a few of the higher ranking officials conferred out in the field, shieldmen diligently guarding them and keeping an eye on the two barbarian archers.

"Watch for the charge coming next," Jvard reminded the dozen men guarding the mouth of the pass, "Garl, get your men ready."

Jvard took four men a hundred paces along the narrow pass away from the entrance, while Garl did likewise along the side opposite to him. Each group pressed their backs to the wall, and waited. If he were in his opponent's position, first he would have tried to break them from a distance.

If that failed, he'd try to punch through with a swift, intense assault. The tribes of the north had little use for the beasts of burden, but Jvard did understand their potential in combat and how others might try to utilize them. He wasn't sure if the Dun'Aldirans would try to shatter the blockade with a horse charge here; he certainly would not in this particular situation, but he hoped they would. As he heard the low thundering of hooves approach, he smiled in grim satisfaction.

Bracing themselves against the charge, the volume of their battle songs competed with the yells of the riders and the resounding stampede of twenty armor-clad horses. Just as the impact of horse crashing into man seemed inevitable, the wall of barbarians at the mouth of the pass disengaged. Splitting away to either side, they allowed the horses to ride straight through unimpeded along the path. Hurriedly they reformed and closed the gap, clashing against a band of men on foot who followed in behind the cavalry.

Perplexed, the horsemen continued along the trail for only as long as it took to comfortably bring their horses to a stop without colliding into one another and turn them around. The maneuvering proved difficult with the amount of men and animals cramped together along the tight corridor.

Before they could regroup, Jvard and Garls' warriors were upon them. They smashed and hacked at horses' legs, pulled riders down, attacking anything they could to devastate the cavalry before they became mobile again. Garl speared a man through the chest as he tried to turn his steed around, prying him out of the saddle and sending him lifeless to the ground.

Capitalizing on their brief confusion and the cramped space, Jvard's men decimated the cavalry. As the riders bumped into one another trying to turn and face their attackers, the barbarians darted in and out of the throng, shredding them apart like wolves loosed in a sheep pen.

When the dust settled, horses and men littered the ground, most of them Dun'Aldiran soldiers. A few of the animals ran off, riderless. Three of Jvard's own were trampled to death during the frenzied melee, and though their loss stung, the barbarian's risky maneuver was executed to near perfection.

More soldiers followed in on the heels of the cavalry, with the hope and expectation that the way through would be clear and the barbarians routed. Instead, the line had reformed, trusting Jvard and Garl to finish off the horsemen now at their backs. Forced to fight the barbarians man to man at the path's chokepoint, the Dun'Aldirans fell in droves, unable to match the strength or ferocity of the northmen. Bodies slowly piled before the barbarians, and the soldier's attacks throughout the morning were marked by hesitation and a tempered zeal.

The four surviving riders broke away, galloping east up the path to disengage from combat while Jvard followed them a small distance from his company to gauge their intentions. It seemed as though they would continue fleeing, their morale broken. One turned back halfway up the pass, Jvard recognizing him as the soldier issuing terms of surrender earlier. Hatred burned through him as he stared at Jvard, the barbarian tauntingly waving him in. Accepting the challenge, the rider reined his horse around, spurring it to a gallop towards Jvard.

Timing a strike as the horse charged in, Jvard misjudged its speed. The glancing blow did no substantial damage to the beast, and the force of its pass tore the axe from Jvard's hands. The rider swept out to the side and turned to face the barbarian again, the two only a dozen feet apart against either wall of the pass.

Jvard had one option before him, and he was ready to fully commit to it. The song of battle filled his senses, surging through him, giving him strength and fully entrenching him in the fleeting moment. He never felt as alive as when in battle, walking a razor's edge of life and death.

The horse kicked forward, throwing small rocks and dust behind it in a final charge at Jvard. Jvard also exploded forward, meeting the animal halfway before it could build a deadly level of speed. Tucking his head, Jvard drove his shoulder under the horse's chest in a horrendous collision. A sharp crack rose above the ringing of steel and cries of men.

The front end of the horse lifted momentarily as Jvard crashed into it. The two came to a dead stop, the force of their opposing charges negating each other. Its hooves kicked out, slamming into Jvard's face and slicing his chest as it whinnied and reared. Trying to fend off the blows with his forearms he stood his ground, despite the pain shooting down from his neck to the tip of his fingers after the initial impact. The rider attempted to get a few swings of his sword in, but it was all he could do to keep his seat during the exchange.

With a mighty heave Jvard shoved himself free and came back in at the side of the animal, grabbing the bridle close to the horse's snout to keep its head away from him. With its four legs firmly on the ground, Jvard had some measure of control on the animal, but the rider was free to use his sword arm. Quickly dipping his head down, Jvard felt the wind of the blade arc past his ear as it narrowly missed him. The horse jostled him back and forth as he tried to maintain his leverage on the beast's head, while he used his free arm to grasp at the rider's weapon to prevent him from striking out. All the while his injured shoulder throbbed.

In an instant the struggle was over, a fount of blood splaying in a line across Jvard's face. Radford's rapier jutted out of the far side of the rider's neck, the blade entering and exiting cleanly behind his windpipe. Immediately approaching from the other side were Garl and a handful of warriors, arriving to assist.

"You barbarians certainly have interesting methods for countering cavalry," Radford remarked, taking the reins as Jvard awkwardly attempted to keep the horse at bay.

Jvard ignored the comment that he was nearly certain was intended as an insult, allowing Radford to lead the animal away. His shoulder quickly grew stiff and began coloring to a deep purple.

"How is the line?" he asked, looking down the sloping path to his men still in combat.

"They're holdin'," Garl answered, "I'd say the enemy sent in their best chance at breakin' through, and failed. They'll probably send a few more men in on foot before they see they're only feedin' the crows."

That was as best Jvard could hope for. In a few days, the Dun'Aldirans would realize they've cornered a beast beyond their ability to break. With the woods and river behind them for foraging, and extra men to rotate holding the line, they could last as long as they needed to here.

"Good," Jvard replied, beginning to give out further instructions, "send out a few scouts behind us and around to make sure they don't begin moving a force to flank us. We'll need some fresh water too…"

He trailed off as he looked beyond his men fighting, and beyond the isle where his enemy sat, stymied by their inability to overcome Jvard's small band. Another force approached, larger than either side could likely handle.

"May the Gods help us all," he whispered.

***

For the moment, Daro was alive and his flock relatively protected. He had to focus on that, not on the madwoman driving soldiers to their needless deaths at the hands of savages. Seeing packs of soldiers fall to the barbarians one after another was like watching his lambs brought to slaughter.

Sevra, though she didn't quite trust him, did not view him as a threat either. That was a small advantage for the preacher. Though his weapon had been confiscated, he was able to avoid being shackled and had freedom of movement. Given the circumstances, he supposed it could have been worse.

Daro took a new measure of Sevra, a more cautious approach upon observing her for most of the morning in his efforts to find some weakness he might exploit. She was angry now, and the preacher could not deny some might find it a frightening sight. There was no mistake that she was powerful, and possessed certain abilities the likes of which he had never seen.

Earlier, she took his head in her hands and left him feeling like he had been stripped naked and doused with cold water. His entire soul felt as if it had been laid bare before her for judgment. Disgusted that she put her foul hands upon him, he had to restrain himself from striking out. His mind felt violated; he wasn't sure what he was able to hide from her, and he suspected not very much. That she hadn't tried to kill him immediately afterwards did bode well, however.

"I want those rats flushed out of their hole, do you understand!" the self-proclaimed Empress screamed.

It became a personal vendetta to her that less than thirty men could keep her entire force in check. She had thrown reason to the winds hours ago; to Daro, this entire exercise was one of sinful pride. He could have thought of a multitude of better uses to put the soldiers to, instead of thrashing against a raging band of barbarians to no purpose. The failed cavalry charge was the pinnacle of the disaster, yet Sevra refused to yield, growing more enraged with each unsuccessful attempt. Her clouded judgment made Daro begin to wonder if she would try to bully the corpses to do her bidding when she ran out of soldiers.

"Hammonds!" she yelled, calling over to her recently promoted first officer.

It was her fourth one that afternoon. After a few ineffective attempts to rout the barbarians, she began executing the squad leaders with her strange, life-stealing magic. Despite the powerful motivation of facing death upon failure, no officers had yet managed to break through the northmen's barricade. She was hesitant to go in and do their job for them, though Sevra was beginning to see she may have to. In her limited experience, barbarians could be a... difficult lot to deal with when working together.

"Don't be so nervous, young man," she said coyly, "this is your opportunity to make a name for yourself."

With a hunted look, searching for an escape and not able to find one, the youthful soldier saluted fist to heart and turned towards the battalion he would lead in next.

Their eyes held a seething resentment, and their solemn expressions spoke volumes.

In order to even reach the barbarians, they would need to climb over the bodies of their comrades who had already fallen to the formidable group they attempted to dislodge. It was clearly written on his men's faces that they too had no desire to try and take the pass. If anything they were likely weighing the risk of insubordination against a sure end by the hand of a barbarian.

"Well?" Sevra demanded, displeased by their lack of enthusiasm.

To her delight, cheers broke out among the soldiers along the edge of the isle and worked its way towards her.

"Reinforcements!" they cried out, "Coming in from the city!"

Only half of the men seemed excited, while others scrambled back in alarm.

"About time they crawled out from their hiding spots, I knew more of my True-Blood were here than this. They will show these pathetic soldiers how to fight a proper battle," Sevra boasted, not catching on to the panic.

Something wasn't right, she soon began to grasp. Daro became aware of the problem much quicker than she had, faster than almost anyone had, for that matter. The rambling line of men coming towards them from the next island over didn't seem to end, stretching back all the way to the hilltop of the Inner City. They continued adding in droves to the main throng, pouring in from every visible street across the islands. There must have been thousands of them.

"If it pleases you, I'll have my weapon back now," Daro stated flatly.

Most avoided the rivers, eventually finding their way towards the one western bridge remaining that would allow them to access the island.

"Where did they all come from?" the young officer murmured.

"The noise from all of the fighting yesterday and today, or maybe the smell of freshly killed flesh drove them out. That horde probably represents every single Infected in all of Creekview," Daro answered, his instincts for leading beginning to emerge once again, "forget the barbarians. Get your soldiers into a perimeter around the western bridge."

"Those are not your men to command," Sevra told him coldly, her eyes narrowing dangerously.

"Then you give the order!" Daro barked.

His voice dripping with sarcasm and offering a mocking bow he added, "If it pleases my lady."

He thought she might strike him dead where he stood, but instead she released him from her stare and gave the order. Even though she ignored him for the time being, he was sure she'd revisit his insolence at her earliest convenience.

The barbarians appeared interested in the sudden change to the battlefront, and Daro quietly reminded himself to not forget their presence. There may only be twenty or so of them, but he could well imagine the havoc they might cause if they chose the right moment to strike out. One in particular, towards the rear of their group stood head and shoulders above the rest, a wolf's head sitting atop his own. He blinked away the impossible sight, wondering if his eyes were playing tricks on him and focused on the immediate problem.

Hopefully Sevra was keeping track of all the pieces in motion as well as he was. But then again, he thought, maybe it better if she makes a fatal mistake for herself, or best still if he could orchestrate one in the upcoming chaos that was sure to erupt. In their short time together, she struck him as a person who might be so fixated on keeping a knife to her enemy's throat she would fail to see the assassin behind her.

"I can be of use to you here, let me help fight," Daro risked in response to Sevra's plight, leaving off that he would take his company and slip away should the opportunity present itself.

She looked to the preacher as if she was debating once again to kill him where he stood. Then she glanced back at his group of followers, and to the Infected threatening to overwhelm her force. She needed him right now, and Daro knew it. With a nod to one of her men, Daro's sword-arm and shoulder plate were tossed back to him.

What the Infected lacked in their ability to coordinate with one another, they made up for in sheer numbers and an absence of fear. If they felt pain, they did not show it. The soldiers tried to contain them at the west bridge, but they continually pressed forward, scrambling over one another in an effort to get at the army with their teeth or nails. Many of the Infected lost hands or arms, took strikes to the face or chest that would have felled a normal man, but they continued coming. Only decapitation stopped them, and even that left their mouths chittering and eyes looking about with a yearning frustration.

As they piled onto the bridge, many spilled over into the shallow river, sinking to the bottom. At first what seemed a stroke of fortune for the Dun'Aldirans turned into a nightmare when the water began to fill with the Infected's rotting, moving corpses. They shoved and crowded each other, cramping together until they were a submerged, writhing mass of flesh. Others following behind simply began to walk across on top of them, suddenly widening their lane of attack and the amount of area the soldiers had to defend. It was too much for them to handle, and the ranks of the Dun'Aldirans began to dissolve.

The world was crashing down for Sevra, the full disaster of her failed attempt to secure Creekview's Crossing culminating before her. Yet still, she refused to yield.

"My Empress, it may be time to call a retreat," her guard suggested.

"We're pinned," another answered shaking his head, "one way out is blocked by the northmen, and the other by those creatures."

Daro watched them mull it over, wondering if they would arrive to the only logical choice as he had. He knew how he would be getting out with his company, all of whom became more anxious as the trap closed in around them. It was just a matter of choosing the right moment; when the time came he hoped they could all swim.

"Enough!" Sevra cried out, growing tired of the bickering.

Sweeping her arm out, she blanketed her guards in silence. For a few brief seconds their lips continued to move, only no sound came forth.

"We will grind every single one of the Infected to dust," she continued, having their full attention.

Eyeing each man in turn and allowing her gaze to linger on Daro, she added, "Do your duty and protect the Empress."

They fell in behind her while she stalked forward, approaching the thinly holding line of Drakvnar and soldiers. Nearing the front, her body faded to something less substantial; if Daro were to reach his hand out he was suspicious that it might pass right through her. The air around Sevra grew dark, as if she had become a shadow that threatened to steal any approaching light.

Tremors rocked the field as Sevra flung her arms down at either side, large fissures spreading across the ground beyond her soldiers and rending apart any flesh they came into contact with. The bridge crumbled and fell to pieces, sending hundreds more of the Infected into the water. Dark bolts erupted from her fingertips, eight streaks of black and purple writhing out and disintegrating anything they touched. Out of all the inexplicable feats Daro had seen Walt perform in their years together at Big Bear, they paled in comparison to what he saw Sevra unleash before him. It sickened him to see a man or woman possess the hubris to wield such a power.

Yet the creatures still came onward, their solitary purpose to find living tissue to feed upon. With Sevra's assistance, her troops were able to regain some ground and battle back to an even footing, but it was only temporary. For every one they killed, two more moved ahead to take its place, and there was no shortage still trying to press forward from the back of the mob.

Daro moved among the line, finding places where he could jab his sword-gauntlet forward between soldiers and through the forehead of one of the plagued beings. He kept his eyes everywhere, signaling for his men to remain back. Very few of them were capable fighters, they had needed help getting out of the Inner City and it was his duty to take responsibility. By coming here with Sevra, though he didn't have much of a choice in the matter, he ultimately put them in jeopardy again.

For every passing minute, the swing of men's swords slowed and fatigue began to take its toll. The mass of Infected came at them, unrelenting, untiring. They could not keep this up much longer, Daro knew. Even Sevra was beginning to show signs of strain. Her wraith-like appearance faltered several times, her body returning to its normal state at frequent intervals. It must be taxing for her to remain in that ethereal form, he reasoned, and she likely slipped out of it for brief respites. She continued to whisper under her breath, whether she was talking to herself, reciting some incantation, or praying to whatever heathen Gods she believed in he could not tell.

He'd love nothing more than to run his blade through her side while she was distracted, but he'd never get close with those blasted guards of hers. There was nothing he could do about it for the moment; as events continued to unfold he would make sure he was ready when an opportunity presented itself.

***

Reaching for his elk-bone dagger, Igdahven cursed silently and put his truncated right arm back to his side. He still hadn't gotten used to losing his hand, sometimes it felt as if it were still there. Drawing the small blade with his left, he felt even more ineffectual at the moment. Average-sized by typical human standards, he looked, and felt at times such as this like a child next to his fellow barbarians. It had to do with being born into the *Duchàlg*, none of whom had the fearsome size that the southerners assumed was a characteristic of all of the peoples from the Blue Fold Mountain region.

Nevertheless, he was well respected among the tribe for his abilities – they just weren't particularly useful for fighting against men or beasts. He had done his part in tracking Jvard, but did his best to stay out of the way as the chieftain and Garl directed the defense of the pass. They performed well, and Igdahven welcomed the break in the action when the enemy's band grew distracted at their western flank.

The rest of his tribe stood near the choke point they defended, evaluating the cause of the disturbance that pulled the Dun'Aldirans away and debated what their next move should be. It looked like many hundreds of Risen approached, maybe even a few thousand. As their spirit-seeker, they would surely seek his advice shortly. Jvard often liked to make up his mind first and then present his decision to him for any feedback, and that often took longer than necessary. Either do, or do not, the right choice would always show itself to be the clearer. What was so complicated about that?

His thoughts wandered while he waited for his chieftain to arrive at a decision. The large creatures nearby drew his attention, most curious things they were. He was fascinated that the southerners rode them into battle – of course, leave it to a southerner to find a way to luxuriate warfare. Since when were one's own legs not good enough? Three of the animals survived the assault unscathed; two ran off a distance, but the last stood nearby. Stamping its hoof and snorting, it seemed to notice Igdahven staring at it.

Horses, that was what they called them down here. Some of the barbarians had seen them before in the area outside of Jun'tirh Outpost, but most of Igdahven's time was spent at the *Duchàlg* encampment on the Shadow Cliff or divining answers in the *Chàlgraäden*. This was a rare opportunity for him to observe something new, one he could not let pass him by. Was the beast angry, indifferent, or mourning the loss of its rider?

With a look back to Jvard, Garl, and the rest of the company still adamantly debating, he set off a short distance up the trail towards the animal. He'd have a few minutes to spare while they tried to make up their minds.

Excitement overpowered Igdahven's good judgment as he approached the horse, and he nearly giggled in glee at the nervous charge of energy between him and it. He reached his good hand out, and pulled it back on instinct when the beast tried to bite him with its large flat teeth.

No harm, no offense, he reasoned, not discouraged in the slightest.

Easy girl, he thought hard at the horse. Was it a girl? He continued trying to send his intent to the beast, willing to it that he came in peace.

"Ha ha!" he exclaimed, quite pleased with himself when it permitted him to pat its snout.

The noise drew a concerned look or two from the barbarians still discussing, but they intently returned to their business. Emboldened by his success, he wondered what the appeal was in riding one. A glance back at his comrades showed they were still occupied and would be for some time yet. Summoning his courage, he lithely hopped up, awkwardly straddling the saddle and grabbing the pommel with his hand. By the mountains it was uncomfortable! The horse bucked, sending a shooting pain through Igdahven and launching him clumsily to the dirt. He rolled back and forth on the ground, groaning over his injured groin.

A few more of his kinsmen looked, shaking their heads in disapproval as he got back to his feet. He ignored their quizzical stares and dusted himself off, determined to persevere and riddle out the secret of horses. Maybe if he positioned himself in the seat atop the horse slightly differently...

Much better, he thought, believing he had it figured out on his next attempt. Sending waves of approval at the animal, he communicated his delight. Slowly, he walked the horse towards the rest of the barbarians, joining the conversation.

"Good, we have agreed then that we cannot decide," he heard Garl bluster.

"Igdahven!" Jvard yelled, thinking the spirit-seeker was still wasting his time up the hill with the horse.

They were all startled as they looked back, craning their necks upward. Igdahven had already joined them and was standing on top of the saddle, the reins in his hand.

He understood the horse's appeal to the southerners. He felt very tall this way.

"We are at an impasse," Jvard told him, the strange sight only giving him brief pause before he explained the dilemma to Igdahven. He had seen the spirit-seeker behave more oddly than this on a few separate occasions.

Igdahven tapped his foot on the saddle and listened intently while the chieftain laid the barbarians' concerns at his feet. There was much to consider; Jvard suspected it was the blood of the 'Empress' that would fulfill his desire for vengeance, some wished to charge forth and slay as many as they could in a glorious frenzy, while others thought it best to leave but were concerned it might displease the Gods, unsure if leaving would be viewed as disregarding the *Kleïntòr*. Indeed, the way ahead was shrouded in uncertainty.

As the spirit-seeker it was his duty to find the true path and ultimately ensure the survival of the clans. Within the *Chàlgraäden* he could see what was hidden, what is, and what may become. Under normal circumstances he might take days to explore the possibilities surrounding an event, but out on the battlefield as they were, he did not have the luxury of time. Nevertheless, he would perform his duties.

The Risen began to push through the line of soldiers on the main isle, and the barbarians watched the one their enemy called 'Empress' join the fray. Most paled at the display of her raw power. They would face swords, shields, and beasts with stoic determination, but one of the Fel-born was before them, unleashing a fury unlike any they had ever seen. She moved like a specter in the winds, dark eddies obscuring her form and leaving swaths of destruction in her wake.

"I will be vulnerable while I am in the *Chàlgraäden*. Should anything happen," Igdahven began.

"Nothing will reach you unless it has killed all of us first," Jvard assured his friend, "go, and be quick about it."

Regretfully, Igdahven hopped down from the horse. Though he enjoyed the fresh perspective it offered, it wouldn't do to fall and break his neck while his spirit was away. Finding a comfortable patch of dirt along the pass, he leaned back against the ledge and tucked his feet underneath his knees. He needed no special rituals or components to venture to the realm of spirits. As long as he wasn't taking anyone along with him, it was as easy for him to visit the *Chàlgraäden* as it was to fall asleep. Breathing in and out to a slow rhythm, he began to separate his mind and body, leaving his form behind to sit against the cliff.

The world turned gray and muted. No longer did he hear the gentle breeze over the grass, the barbarians arguing, or the clamor of men fighting and dying in the distance. Sound didn't exist in this diaphanous reflection, only the land itself and the essences of those dwelling within it. Small whirls of pure white and deep blackness danced where men stood, representing their location in the material realm. Above him ran the *Duchstraüm*, the raging streams of darkness and light flowing across the sky. It was unknown to him exactly what purpose they served.

Igdahven often pondered their significance, and believed, at least in part, they provided balance. Good could not exist without evil, and there needed to be equal parts of each in order for the sun to continue rising. To the spirit-seeker, the *Duchstraüm* were an echo of that never ending struggle for harmony.

For the past few months, that balance had been disturbed and it left Igdahven baffled. Rivers of a black deeper than night jettisoned in one direction, as if merging to a singular location. He finally understood the mystery that had given him many sleepless nights as the point of convergence was upon him, the woman directing the force against the barbarians.

People did not exist in this place as they did in the physical world, or at least they should not. Most, except for the other *Duchàlg* and the occasional wizard, lived a life unable to even touch the *Chàlgraäden*. Igdahven himself only walked the land of spirits as an apparition of his physical form. Yet before him, fully corporeal, was the Empress; how she was here fully fleshed was beyond his realm of experience.

The storm of darkness gravitating around her was a tempest strong enough to strip the hide from a silverfrost bear, but she did not seem affected by it. On the contrary, she harnessed its power, guiding and directing it to terrible devastation against the Risen. Generations of stories passed down from father to son among the barbarians cautioned against those who could touch the elements, and the danger they posed. Not only could this woman touch the elements, she called them forth and bent them to her will. She had to be stopped before that maelstrom of destruction was wielded at his kinsmen.

She did not seem to notice his presence while she worked, tearing the ground asunder and calling forth deadly bolts of blackened light. While he knew he couldn't linger for long, he also didn't want to be hasty.

He risked moving in closer. Thinking of a spot behind her and a safe distance to the side, the landscape lurched as he took a single step to cross the distance. The woman was in a deep state of concentration, the effort she put forth splayed across every inch of her face.

Several times in the course of his observation Igdahven noticed that when the strain became too great she would momentarily leave the *Chàlgraäden*, returning to the physical world. Her re-entry was so subtle as to be nearly imperceptible, but after she had gone through the motion a few times he was certain of it. A small tear in the air appeared that she would step through, disappearing so quickly he would miss it if he blinked.

Igdahven believed that by bringing her body forth and leaving part of her spirit behind, it allowed her to draw power in a way he wouldn't dare attempt. If he could stop her somehow from stepping back through the portal she created every time she left and came back...

After observing her for several more minutes, he was fairly sure he reasoned out how she moved back and forth between the two worlds, piercing the veil between the realms to step into the *Chàlgraäden* at will. She used a fragment of the spirits from the storm around her, forming it to a razor thin wedge to create the tear.

The way she manipulated the whorls of dark and light gave him pause. He was certain he could recreate her feat if he attempted to, or seal a rift as she tried to make one, but to touch the elements in such a way was a thing of evil. It would be necessary to consult the *Duchàlg* before trying such a plan.

Then he remembered he was the last of the *Duchàlg*, except for his young apprentice Naÿrja. Which was worse, to stand by and watch the fel-born defile the sacred place that was his duty to watch over, or to break the rules set forth by his own people in order to protect them? Something of this magnitude should be considered for days before taking action, with the consultation of knowledgeable individuals; he had the luxury of neither time nor counsel.

The very existence of his people would be at stake once the Empress turned on Jvard and the rest of the men. Allowing his spirit to release back towards his body, he made his decision.

As he opened his eyes the warriors were already standing there beside him, eagerly waiting to hear what he discovered.

"To leave her alive endangers us all," he stated, answering their unspoken question, "she is an adder in the *Dhidvhel*, striking from the shadows without warning and moving away unseen."

Can our weapons even harm her?" Garl asked skeptically, "She is nearly a shadow herself."

The other men nodded in agreement, unsure of how to effectively fight a foe they've never seen the like of before.

"Watch for her to fully return to her body. When she does, attack on the count of ten if she remains unshrouded. I will stop her from reentering the *Chàlgraäden* where she is most powerful," Igdahven told them, sighing deeply at what was required of him and its repercussions. "She will still be dangerous, but perhaps not as much. Strike quickly while her focus is on the Risen. May the Gods forgive me for this."

Once again he closed his eyes and began falling into the state that allowed him to enter the *Chàlgraäden*. As his spirit began to pull away from his body, this time he did not allow it to fully separate, anchoring it in the physical realm. Gingerly he reached out with his thoughts and took hold of a fragment of a *Mináduchstraüm*, one of the small eddies dancing about his spirit.

It was like trying to grip a bolt of lightning. After struggling for seconds that felt like an eternity, he crudely shaped the energy to a knifepoint and jaggedly tore the air in front of him.

Igdahven disappeared into the rift, and to the rest of the barbarians it looked as though as he simply vanished. The barbarians cursed and jumped back at the display, looking about nervously. Jvard, having grown accustomed to being around a wizard for many weeks, was the only one to not recoil.

"This thing he does," Garl began to admonish.

"Is necessary," Jvard answered for him, "you heard the spirit-seeker, he does as he must to provide us a way forward. Wait for my command."

***

The hemorrhage of Infected passing through the defensive line was triaged to a slow trickle thanks to Sevra's efforts. She became increasingly confident her small force would hold as long as they needed to against the tide. Improvisation was her greatest asset in this fight; slowing the throng of Infected was a matter of finding what killed the most effectively without having to expend herself too greatly. The best solution so far was to create shrapnel. Harnessing the strength of the raging storm of energy that surrounded her, she hurled large chunks of the destroyed bridge into the air, bursting them into thousands of shards in a blast of light.

Most of her attention was directed many rows behind her men, the explosive force of the stone would have killed them as easily as it did the Plagued Ones. After the first few frantic volleys she found her pace, comfortable that she could maintain her attacks throughout the day if necessary. Exiting the realm of shadow and spirits only for a moment, she allowed herself to catch her breath. The flood of power she tapped into in the other realm was the lifeblood of creation itself; stepping away from it made everything feel so… mundane. Unfortunately, it had to be done. Guiding that torrent was pure ecstasy, but it was also exhausting.

Reaching back across the veil was second nature to her, and required only a miniscule amount of her strength to accomplish. Ready to return and leave only the smallest fragment of her spirit behind in the physical world, she sliced open a portal before her and stepped forward.

She nearly stumbled when her foot landed on the muddy ground in front of her. Her soldiers remained along the bank, fighting and dying, the grass solid underneath her feet. Frowning, she tried again, tearing open a doorway to the other realm where she was a true conduit of power. Again it closed instantly, before she could cross through. Her frown turning to a scowl, she tried a third time. Clearly visible through the entrance before it closed again was a man with the head of a wolf sitting atop his own. Looking her in the eye, he let out a startled squeak before sealing that portal too.

At that moment, the barbarians charged.

***

All caution was cast aside once Jvard and his men dedicated themselves to their course. Abandoning any conventional formation, they scattered in a mad rush towards the witch and her personal guard. There was no need for Jvard to issue a command for them to do so, all of them intrinsically understood they needed to spread out to mitigate their particular foe's devastating abilities. They were the embodiment of havoc on the battlefield when charging as a scattered group, like a swarm of bees that confounded their target while somehow working with an underlying coordination only they understood.

Dark, wavering bolts as thick as a man's arm flew in their direction, some missing, but the ones that landed dropping barbarians in mid-stride. A few struggled back to their feet and stumbled ahead, while others remained still in the grass. Their numbers slightly lessened, it did not curb the frenetic pace of their assault. Jvard made the first strike towards the edge of the guards hastily arching around Sevra, denting the man's shield and knocking him aside.

Rather than engaging, he spun beyond reach of a blade that jutted out towards him and brought his axe down onto another guard at the end of the formation. The blow was partially blocked, but still drove the soldier backwards. Similarly across the line, barbarians struck and moved, knocking the defenders aside and forcing them into an unstructured melee. The Dun'Aldirans were forced to put more effort towards watching where an attack might come from than actual fighting, greatly setting them off balance.

The barbarians' attack patterns, though random, had an element of coordination that went beyond what a unit could achieve through practice and repetition alone. Connected to one another in a deep, primordial sense, the barbarians shared a bond as old as the tribe itself. The hymn of battle flowed through their veins as one, originating innately in their ancestors and refined through centuries of conflict. A single barbarian was dangerous, an entire clan was a force of nature.

Jvard and Garl were the first to break beyond the line, hesitating only slightly as they faced a foe with weapons greater than steel. Moving off to an angle at either side of her, they attacked simultaneously, Jvard coming in high with his axe while Garl charged with an upward swing of a battlehammer.

Invisible bonds wrapped tightly around Jvard, locking him in place and sending a pulsing shock through every muscle in his body. Gritting his teeth, he refused to drop to his knees but found no strength to take another step. He watched as Garl too failed to complete his attack, cursing and reflexively dropping his weapon. The handle glowed white with heat, leaving deep blisters on his palm.

Ignoring the pain, Garl moved forward, weaponless, while Sevra danced back and conjured another bolt from her fingertips. The black, undulating mass sped directly at Garl, blasting him across the shoulder and chest. Jvard could almost feel the strength flee from Garl as his knees buckled from the impact. His arm on that side hung limp, but he refused be taken from his feet.

Sevra's shock was complete when the old barbarian fell upon her. He shouldn't have even been standing, but there he was, too close for her to escape his grasp. She was still unable to move fully into the other realm, the strange person blocking her at every turn. The torrent of power available to her was only a trickle of her potential, stuck as she was in the physical realm.

Fighting down the urge to panic, her feet left the ground as the aged barbarian lifted her with one hand, her face disappearing into his mitt-like fist. It became nearly impossible to breathe as her nose crunched in the vise-like grip, her mouth not able to take in enough air with his hand obstructing it. Frantically, she grabbed at his arm before she suffocated while blood streamed down her face from her ruined nose. Desperately she sunk her nails into his forearm. Using the ancient technique her God had shown her, she began to leach the vitality from him and take it as her own.

Why had her God not come to her aid during this battle? She knew he became dissatisfied with her ever since her original failure, but did not truly realize the depths of his abandonment until this moment. With her attention diverted, her soldiers struggled once more to keep the Infected at bay. They would have to hold while she dealt with this unwanted distraction. *I am alone in this conflict*, she thought, *he will not assist until I can prove I am still worthy of Him.*

She struggled for her life against the barbarian, revolted by the fact that one of the filthy beasts actually had his hands on her. Having to fight this band in her weakened state made it a true challenge. They were not normal adversaries, some trick of their minds allowing them to shrug off attacks that would have stopped anyone else dead. Driving her spells into them was as difficult as trying to punch through a piece of armor with a dull knife.

The barbarian's grip finally began to weaken, the air rushing back into her lungs like rain soaking into parched soil. Dropping her to the ground, he collapsed while she siphoned the strength from his body. She was back in control, ready to bring the northerner to his end.

Her impending victory was cut short when she had to hastily put all of her effort into constructing a shield of air near the side of her head. The sharp steel of a small throwing axe drove through it, but it served its purpose and deflected the projectile to the side. It seemed her other attacker had broken free of the bonds that by all rights should have left him incapacitated. This one she recognized as the leader of the small force of barbarians; killing him would bring her a great deal of pleasure.

"It's a shame we couldn't have met under different circumstances, barbarian. You would have made a fine pet," she taunted.

He growled in response.

"Tsk, tsk," she chided, "we'll need to take away those teeth and claws first."

She began to heat the great axe in Jvard's hands, affecting it the same way she had done to Garl's weapon. Bearing down and accepting the pain, he hefted the weapon over his head, then hurled it spinning end over end towards her.

The axe stopped in midflight at Sevra's outstretched hand, frozen in the air before her. She stared closely at the way it caught the light, bringing her back to a time roughly two decades ago. The old, though well-cared for axe with intricate runes carved along the handle was known to her, dredging up images from her not too distant past. Looking to Jvard she now saw the similarities. She bared her teeth in semblance of a smile at the shocking coincidence, thinking it a pity she would likely have to kill this one.

"Yes, perhaps I will take you as my own," Sevra purred, "my Urstaag grows old, and will soon need to be replaced. You may know of him, he once carried a weapon much like this one, if I recall."

Some of the fight seemed to leave Jvard as his weapon remained suspended in motion, and it took him a moment to understand the significance of her words. The telling look in Sevra's eyes revealed she knew more than she indicated, leaving Jvard unsure of himself. He did indeed know of Urstaag, that was the name of his father's father. That axe was passed down for generations, once belonging to Urstaag, then inherited by Helstajvan, and finally Jvard.

"Don't be listenin' to her Jvard. She is a lyin' witch, trying to put you off your guard," Garl coughed from the ground, his gray hair now white and the fine wrinkles on his face more pronounced, "finish her off and let the world be rid of her."

Jvard was torn, did this woman really have someone close to him under her dominion? His thoughts grew thick and muddled as she used the seed of doubt to plant a foothold in his mind. He heard her voice in his head, comforting and reassuring.

Soothing waves of pleasure rolled over him from the Empress. In all honesty, perhaps he had not given the woman a fair chance. What would it hurt to go back to Dun'Aldir with her so she could ease his worries? Their fight was a misunderstanding; two sides meeting at the wrong place and time.

"Urstaag was taken twenty years ago during combat with the Denórvja clans. Jvard, don't let her be twistin' up your head!" Garl yelled from the ground, seeing the insidious woman beginning to have some kind of effect over Jvard.

Sevra spun towards Garl and readied a deadly barrage, the pause in the mental assault giving Jvard a reprieve to see through the spell and clear his head. He felt the remnants of her tendrils in his thoughts, the vile roots at the edge of his consciousness like recently pulled weeds lying in the grass. He fed them to his anger, allowing the rage within him to burn unchecked. The sounds of battle around him carried across the air and gathered to him as a steady dirge, its somber clarity washing away Sevra's mind enchanting effects.

Immediately she turned back to him as she felt her connection to Jvard shatter, hastily sending a smoldering streak of blackness errantly over his shoulder. In that motion she had revealed much to the chieftain; she could not accurately divert her attention in two separate directions at once. He may not be familiar with the unique weapons at her disposal, but some reactions in battle were universal. She let a weakness slip, and Jvard planned on exploiting every inch of it. Without his axe in hand he'd have to rely on his fists, if only he could draw close to her.

"Can you strike us both at the same time witch, are you that fast?" Jvard bellowed, moving off to her side opposite Garl, "I'd wager I am faster!"

"I only need to kill you," she retorted, seeing through his strategy, "your companion can die at my leisure."

Jvard was concerned for his old friend, who remained groaning on the ground. He had never seen Garl off his feet, let alone struggling to get back on them. Garl injured was as implausible an image as a stone weeping or a mountain crumbling. There was nothing he could do for him at the moment, only trust the weathered man could ride out the storm of this battle as he had done so many times before.

He dodged another one of those strange bolts, constantly moving, strafing side to side in hopes of finding an opening. She kept him at bay, but could not coax him into making a fatal mistake. Similarly he could not find a clear path to strike out at her. It was too risky, getting in close where she might be able to inflict that leaching touch upon him.

"It is over for you witch," Jvard growled, "your guards will soon be no more, and you cannot defeat us all."

Even as he spoke, more of his men cautiously approached, having begun to dispatch the protective troupe around Sevra.

"Spread out and circle in," Jvard called out loudly to his men, "The glory of the Gods to the one who takes her head!"

Sevra could not deny the truth of the barbarian king's words. Her entourage was all but dispatched as she looked around, behind her the soldier's line precariously holding against the Infected by a hair's breadth. More of the barbarian's stalked forward, lions circling a wounded prey. Granted, she was still dangerous, but there was only one inevitable outcome to this encounter. She paced backwards, inviting them forward. The barbarians cautiously obliged, beginning to fan around her.

Slowly, as she backed away she funneled power from across the veil, reaching into the realm of spirits and drawing what she could, letting it accumulate within her. Still unable to enter fully, her diminished strength limited her options.

For what she had in mind, it would have to suffice.

She did not live several lives over and usurp an entire kingdom to be cut down in the dirt like a peasant in revolt. Nearly reaching her remaining soldiers, she gathered all the power she could muster for one last spell. It was time to extricate herself from the battlefield and salvage what she could.

***

"Fall back!"

They weren't sure who yelled it out, perhaps it was several of them at once. Whoever called the warning, it was unnecessary for the barbarians as they momentarily felt the air hum with energy yearning to be released, notifying them something was horribly wrong. The strain and pressure of it was palpable, discharging in a violent explosion of earth and thunder. They dove to the ground, protectively throwing their arms over their heads. Jvard was the first of his band to get his legs back underneath him, standing to survey the carnage. His ears rang in the sudden silence, all noise ceasing to exist. That didn't seem right; he should have been able to hear something.

The ground finally stopped heaving, and most of his men began to stand on shaky legs. Three lay staring with empty eyes at the sky, their legs mangled and torn apart. Jvard wasn't sure if they died from trauma or blood loss.

While the buzz in his ears began to undulate and fade away, sounds of the battlefield returned in full. Those sounds were mostly dominated by the moans and cries of Sevra's own soldiers, similarly affected by her blast. Unlike his clan, most of her people were not lucky enough to escape harm.

There was no time to mourn the loss of yet more of his kinsmen, as a sea of the Risen filtered over the bridge and streamed past the nearly eradicated defenses. The witch had sacrificed her own people to create a means for herself to flee. He caught a glimpse of her running north before she was lost to sight, an unending mass moving in between the two of them.

Behind him, at the other side of the field, Radford was busy escorting a terrified group of refugees up the eastern pass out of Creekview. He thanked the Gods Radford listened to his earlier instructions; though he was a good fighter, among the honed instincts that guided the barbarians as a collective force he would have been more of a hindrance than an asset.

"To the pass!" Jvard yelled, rallying his men to an escape.

The battle on the island rapidly deteriorated into a lost cause for both sides, and Jvard knew to stay would cost them their lives. Fleeing towards the same path Radford approached, he paused to help two other men with Garl who still struggled to stand on his own. The enemy's force was all but destroyed, it was time for his people to return home. There was no pursuit from the Risen on the battlefield, and Jvard assumed there would not be until they had their fill of those unable to escape. Jvard didn't intend to stay around to find out if that were the case.

Separate Paths

The spirit-seeker stayed to his task with diligence, preventing Sevra from directly entering into the realm of spirits. Closing Sevra's doorways to the *Chàlgraäden* was turning out to be quite the sport. She was good, randomly creating entrance points to slip past him, but he was always a step ahead. He could sense them the instant before they sprang into being, giving him warning of where he should expect one of Sevra's attempts at entry. Trying to convince himself he and the witch were merely playing at a game with one another almost let him forget his perilous position. Almost.

As he followed her away from the field of battle, many spirits surrounding Igdahven blinked out of existence in an instant. His vicinity to the sudden loss of lives while in this place jarred him to the bone. Much like a tree drawing water from the roots to its top most branches, the essences of the recently deceased were drawn upward into the *Duchstraüm*. The sudden pressure of it ripped and pulled at the spirit-seeker, threatening to tear him apart.

On reflex he leaped ahead as far as he could and withdrew from the *Chàlgraäden*, stepping onto the road somewhere north of Creekview's Crossing. In the future he'd have to remember to be more cautious if he entered the garden of spirits in both mind and body. That riptide of departed souls interacted strangely with his flesh, a danger that wouldn't have existed had he been there only in part.

Igdahven realized he was alone on the road, separated from his tribe, and Sevra would be approaching any second with unhindered access to the *Chàlgraäden*. Now he had really gone and prodded the Silverfrost; maybe he could risk slipping back to the spirit lands, but had that storm of souls abated yet?

He felt uncertain of what he should do, to retreat would allow Sevra to continue roaming free and unchecked. He was the only one standing between her and the Gods only knew what plans she may be brewing. No, to run and hide was not the way of the Frostwrynn. He would stand and fight, like a barbarian. He first saw the black wisps and tendrils streaming about her head, cresting the hill towards him. Those dancing shadows let him know she was in her full power once again, and Igdahven felt true fear.

***

The shepherd was once again without a flock. It greatly angered Daro, once the stars in his eyes vanished, to see his followers led away to safety by someone else. Up the eastern pass they went; the survivors he led out of the Inner City, soon followed by the retreating barbarians, faded into the distance and then disappeared from his sight altogether. Waiting for his head to clear, he recovered enough to remember where he was and that it was not safe. Most of the soldiers lay dead or dying around him, some still alive as they were consumed by the Infected.

Sevra had killed her own people to escape. Despite how lowly he regarded her, the level of apathy she had for those she ruled still managed to surprise him. Then again, who knew what despicable acts a blasphemous conjuress such as she might do? He supposed in a way it was good to know what his enemy might be capable of, less chance of being caught unawares that way.

Following the swathe of destruction before him, a trail of bodies, the ground torn asunder, it was easy to track where she went. As he retracted his blade gauntlet from under the chin of one of the creatures accosting him, he glimpsed Sevra fleeing across the river to the north, all alone. He saw himself standing at a crossroad, the moment of decision upon him. It came to him as clearly as the good Lord's light, one path leading to a meaningless life of meager survival and the other to glory and salvation. With renewed determination, he stalked after the witch.

***

Sevra once again failed miserably, and Kubathu couldn't help but pity himself for having to suffer through her continued incompetence. Perhaps incompetence was too strong a word; she had the far more dangerous qualities of being both highly arrogant and woefully average. An entire city was destroyed, and she lost a sizeable portion of her army in the process. Over the last few decades he had used her to his designs, and she served her purpose in that regard. Now though, until he could free himself, he needed someone with more vision and foresight.

There was one last task he would ask of Sevra, a possible impediment down the road that he would prefer to see eliminated before it became a larger problem. Ahead, in the middle of the road stood a defiant figure, one whose presence alone unsettled the mighty Kubathu.

He had watched cautiously as the walker of shadows hindered Sevra on the field of battle, dampening her strength and limiting her effectiveness. That was what they were built for, an antithesis to counter one born of magic. The being was a remnant from another age, the likes of which he had thought forgotten to existence long ago. His last encounter with one ended with him blocked from his ability while the wizards cast him away, imprisoning him in the accursed ruby that became his home for the past two thousand years. For the first time in twenty centuries, Kubathu felt trepidation. Filled with rage at the presence of the shadow-walker, he once again broke his silence to Sevra.

Sevra! he shouted through thought, anxious to eliminate the potential threat.

There was hesitation before she replied.

You choose to return to me now? she finally sent back to him, her typical enthusiasm in speaking with him absent.

The Shadow-walker no longer blocks you! Seize your power and destroy him! Kubathu commanded, *he is young and untrained. He will only grow more dangerous to you with each passing day, kill him now!*

That was Sevra's intention once she saw the fool wearing the wolf's head appear in front of her. He was the insect thwarting her every move on the island; there was no mistaking that one's distinctive appearance. If not for him, she could have salvaged her mission at Creekview's Crossing, and she hungered to make him pay for its ruin. The reappearance of the God who abandoned her stayed her hand. So the deity suddenly returned to demand this of her, but where had he been when she needed him?

Sensing her hesitation, the intensity of his urgings increased. So loudly the directive reverberated within her, she felt as if her mind were a piece of glass pressed upon to the point of shattering.

I won't kill at your order like some trained beast! she thought to him, defiant of the pain he exacted on her, *I do this because it is what I want!*

She felt the full extent of Kubathu's anger spike through her thoughts, driving a wedge into her mind where he could insert himself. She flailed and struggled against him, vainly trying to fend off his intrusion. In the past, she would willingly relinquish a degree of her control over to him, but this was the first time she was forcefully overtaken by her God. Stunned, she was helpless as she fought to take back control of her mind.

I will crush the shadow-walker myself, and through you rule as it should have been before your blundering actions! Kubathu ranted, his hatred clouding his vision to a singular point fixated on Igdahven.

Sevra could only watch as Kubathu, the one she thought to be of the Gods, drew in more power through her than she thought possible. Distantly she felt her bones ache from the strain of it, her slight frame struggling to cope with the vast amount of energy within Kubathu's grasp.

Blind to all else around him, he held Igdahven in place with a single strand of light, slowly crushing him with a constrictive force that grew ever tighter. He could not maintain this level of domination over Sevra's form for long, but he did not need much longer to sate his aggression. A few moments more and it would be over.

Far away he heard Sevra's pitiful wails, distraught at her impotence. She was an insignificant fly, her buzzing hardly registering as Kubathu increased his crushing pressure around the shadow-walker.

Sevra felt another presence approaching, within several dozen paces of her from behind. She turned around, or tried to but had no control over her movement while Kubathu invaded her body. Its malicious intent was palpable, why had he not noticed yet?

Ten paces, five paces.

She scratched and clawed to try and regain some measure of control - her mind, body, anything to meet the threat. There was a brief jolt, followed by a sensation of cold spreading through her limbs. A blade protruded through the front of her diaphragm, while she stared at it as if looking through someone else's eyes.

Kubathu did not notice until his connection to the spirits and his spells around Igdahven ceased.

***

The pressure suddenly ended, allowing Igdahven to fall to the ground gasping for air. So great was his relief, he wondered if it was a release into death that had brought him such a respite from the pain. His vision steadily returned, the blurred, dual images becoming clearer and merging into one. No, he was still very much alive, he decided as he looked up. Though he could not say the same for Sevra.

A figure in simple robes stood behind her, hoisting her in the air with a sword that protruded from an armored hand. With his other gauntlet he grabbed the blade, lifting and shaking her violently to further tear the gaping wound in her midsection. He nearly tore her in half before dropping her to the ground in a heap.

"And here's yet another one," the man muttered, stalking towards him, "the Lord's work is never done, is it?"

Igdahven fell back, the blade speeding over his head as the strike came in too high. Once more he risked entering the

Chàlgraäden, opening a rift as he rolled away and slipped through it.

Frowning, he felt a draft on his head, and looked through the closing portal to see his wolf-cap stuck on the end of the stranger's weapon.

Daro looked around cautiously, not particularly surprised by his target's disappearance. Someone vanishing altogether didn't seem so much of a stretch of the imagination after witnessing Sevra's terrible display. These people did things that were unnatural and evil, for humanity's sake they had to be put down. Face grim, he continued scanning the area so as not to be ambushed by the sneak.

"Come out and fight, coward," he coaxed, "let us see which one of us is in their God's favor, you heathen!"

A hand appeared in the air in front of him, quick as a mountain cat snatching the cap from the end of the blade gauntlet and disappearing once again. The surprise of it caused Daro to sputter a litany of curses.

Standing there perfectly still and fully alert near Sevra's corpse, his controlled breathing was the only sound. Quickly he mastered his residual nerves at being caught by surprise, but even so, for once, Daro was speechless.

***

Not wanting a repeat of the previous morning, Devin took a few bites of the porridge Baerne prepared. He wasn't really hungry, but when Baerne said he could either eat it willingly or be spoon-fed with his mouth pried open, he apparently meant it. Nearly setting the spoon down, he changed his mind and took another bite.

"You know you need to eat right?" Baerne asked.

Devin nodded, very slightly.

Baerne stood and looked further down the river, rubbing the side of his neck and working out a crick in his shoulder. He had to swing his sword an awful lot yesterday.

"Spirits only know what we'll run into today," he began, "you'll need to keep your strength up."

Casually he picked up their belongings, then threw dirt over the small fire and stomped out the remainder of it.

Without turning around he added, "Are you going to stay quiet all day again? Alright, suit yourself. Just a thought, both our days might go a little easier if you'd speak up every now and then. Let's get going."

In truth Devin didn't feel much like talking. Not that he had anything against his newest travelling mate. He seemed decent enough, if a bit rigid. Maybe the guy just didn't like children very much, some grownups were like that. Plus he didn't really need anyone taking care of him, he could look after himself perfectly fine. Sure, it was nice having him around yesterday when all the Greymen attacked, but Devin could have handled himself if he had to. Of course he could have.

Thinking about the Greymen sent a shiver running up Devin's spine. The pair was lucky to have stumbled into the creatures while they were feeding on a dead cow in the high grass. No surprise registered in their sunken eyes, though he and Baerne nearly jumped out of their skin. Those things were like vultures with the face of men.

He remembered their smell, and the faces of all the ones he had seen before began flashing before him. *No, no good thinking about any of that.* But the thoughts continued to trickle in as he struggled to push them away. He saw the face of the guard he killed, pictured Myrna being taken down by a pack of Greymen and coming back as one of them, the legless body of one of those monsters still moving forward, unaware that it should be dead. The images flooded over him, and he sat shaking in his bedroll as he succumbed to them. It was his fault; deep down he knew it didn't make sense, but he couldn't stop thinking it.

The guard came forward, leveling his sword as he pressed in. It was the same one he had killed with his crossbow back in Midao, his intent for revenge clearly written in his expression. He closed his eyes, hoping the vision would go away. A stray thought crossed Devin's mind that it was odd Baerne was the one fighting against that guard he shot all those weeks ago, and now here they were travelling together.

He tried to grab hold of the thought, but it floated away like a dandelion on the wind, *I'm here with Baerne, this isn't real.*

Devin risked a peek and the soldier was still there, stalking closer. Reflexively, his hand darted to the crossbow holstered along his leg.

"You're dead," Devin whispered over and over, shutting his eyes again.

It was stuck, a corner of it caught in the strapping. He moaned softly, helpless.

"Hey, you alright?" Baerne asked, genuinely concerned while he stood in front of Devin, his motion towards the weapon not unnoticed.

Devin snapped out of it, the phantoms of his imagination gone, leaving him alone with Baerne along the grassy river bank in the mid-summer sun. It was going to be hot today, he was already sweating and it was only early morning.

"Let's get a move on. With any luck we might catch up to the wizard today," he continued, trying to not put too much attention to Devin's odd behavior, "hopefully he stuck to the river; it runs slower in these parts."

***

Jvard once again made the difficult decision to leave his tribe, parting ways to the west as the rest of his group swept back towards the road to continue north. They protested, but Jvard was certain despite his unease that returning to Walt Whirten was the right decision at this time. Something had unnerved the wizard before he departed, and Jvard needed to understand what that was.

Garl was somehow on his feet again, his face a thunderhead as he barked orders. He looked like he had aged a decade after suffering the witch's attack, but seemed as vibrant and agitated as ever. Jvard nearly thought it was going to result in a fight between the two of them when he informed him he wouldn't be returning just yet. Eventually, Garl would come around and recognize it was for the best. Jvard knew, even if Garl couldn't see it, that as isolated as the tribes were they could not live unaffected by what was taking place across the land. Before leaving, he mentioned his grandfather Urstaag again, but Garl was dismissive of the idea.

"It's been at least twenty years, son. Don't waste your time chasin' a specter," was his only advice.

Venturing back to Walt's wagon, still intact and sitting on the outskirts of Creekview's Crossing, Jvard found a welcome sight. There was Walt's horse, Tulip along with the big draft horse grazing comfortably along a patch of grass. They looked up and their ears flickered as Jvard approached. He had a new respect for the animals after so intimately meeting one in combat, unconsciously working his stiff shoulder where he had met the rider's charge. The aching and deep purple bruise would take some time to heal, but fortunately he still had full use of his arm. All of the food was gone from the wagon, and one of the barrels of Walt's powder had tipped over to spill some of its contents, but other than that most of their things were where they left them.

A second sight, this one disturbing, met Jvard after he hitched the horses and began leading the wagon south. A body lay in a pool of blood along the road just outside of Creekview. Pulling the horses to a stop, he disembarked and hesitantly approached it. The once fine black dress was tattered and matted with dirt and blood, but Jvard surely recognized it.

The body of the witch his tribe battled was on the ground before him, he was certain it was her even though her head was missing. Perplexed, he returned to the wagon and wondered who might have accomplished such a feat; it had not been one of his people. Even though it wasn't by his hand, he felt a sense of completion, that the clans had been avenged and he could again proudly call himself chieftain of the Frostwrynn tribe. He sat there for several minutes, wondering if he should turn back to inform anyone, or at least move the body. Deciding that he could afford no delays, he took the wagon south, diverting to the secondary roads leading along the cliffs that surrounded the city. *May the crows feast*, he thought, leaving her corpse as he found it.

Days passed, and he could only hope that Walt did not deviate from his intended course along the river. South beyond the city, and beyond a few abandoned villages, occasionally Jvard saw two fresh sets of footprints in the muddier areas, one big and one small. With any luck, they belonged to Baerne and Devin. His only option was to continue on, trusting that he would find the wizard. If he didn't, he would find another road to travel, perhaps one that would lead him back to his tribe. He was not unaccustomed to adapting his plans as necessary. *Daün drovka du sôjn dravka* - as it comes, so Jvard would go.

***

Whistling a merry tune, Daro had a bit more spring in his step than usual on his way back into Creekview's Crossing. And why shouldn't he be happy? God granted him another victory against evil and at least one more day under the brightly shining sun, the rivers of Creekview glistening in its glory.

The blade on his right arm also glistened, slick with a tantalizingly red hue. In his left hand he carried Sevra's head, casually gripping it by the hair as it left a dripping trail of blood to mark his passage.

He called out, loudly, as he walked through the streets looking for survivors who would follow his righteous path. Mostly he found the Infected.

Rather, they found him.

Leaving a trail of bodies in his wake, he continued along any random avenue and side-through that struck his fancy, one hand holding the head, the other thrusting a deadly blade. Surprisingly, there were a few desperate souls that came to his call. Many crawled from their hiding places, feeling their first sliver of hope in weeks; they prayed for a savior and their prayers were answered.

Men who were soldiers, men who had once been thieves, honest men who at a time that felt so long ago were skilled tradesmen, and even a few Drakvnar with no army to return to began to congregate to the preacher. He blazed a trail of salvation, from one end of the city to the other.

Certain areas he had to avoid, they were too far gone, but he did what he was able. It was the burden of responsibility he chose to bear; he could not carry everyone, but he was strong enough to carry some. They left the city somewhere to the east, the men and women he led away singing his praises.

He would do for those he could, it was his litany against the ceaseless evil he faced. The thought gave him clarity of mind and focus unlike anything he felt before, guiding him as he guided those around him.

Absently he stroked the necklace he now wore tucked under the collar of his robe, the crimson gem it held nearly matching the hue of his blood-stained blade. It was far too ornate for him, something a king might be adorned with in his selfish avarice, and the thought of seeing himself that way he found revolting. He grimaced as he tucked it out of sight under his clothing. Earlier, he almost didn't pick it up when he saw it at Sevra's feet, but it occurred to him how many people could be fed and sheltered by the handsome sum it might fetch. After putting it on, only for safekeeping, the insights and revelations came to him as if divinely inspired.

Someone needed to reclaim this land. If it took an army to do it, and it would, he would raise one. The people were lost, in need of someone to guide them both spiritually and militarily through the dark days to come. He had no desire to be a ruler of men, but this was a responsibility passed onto him from a higher power that he could not ignore. The path before him was set. For the good of all, he would see it done.

*** The End of Book 1 ***

Thank you for reading, I hope you enjoyed the first installment of the Risen Lands Duology: The Witch's Catalyst. For information on the progress of the concluding book please visit:

http://www.risenlands.com

http://www.booksmithy.com

Quick Glimpse of Book 2 of the Risen Lands Duology

Fully in communion with his God, there was nothing Daro Ildaradi could not accomplish. He had never felt His presence so strongly flowing through him before, and because of that, knew his path to be a righteous one. Though he never would have sought to be a leader of men, other than in a spiritual sense, it was a role he found thrust upon him. Every person, in accordance with their strength, had to do as they were able to take care of their fellow man. He was both burdened and blessed with great strength.

His next charge had been to go to the aid of those in need at Creekview's Crossing. Wayward individuals could still be found and saved, though the city itself was lost to evil and would soon perish.

He did not allow it to die quietly.

Sevra's head in one hand, and the sword-fist extending from the other, the abandoned flock gratefully followed him along the trail he blazed to safety. With a few hundred strong in tow, he guided them from the ruined city and used the myriad of rivers to help obscure their passing from the Infected.

Camped outside of the city many nights later, those he delivered from evil continued to sing his praises. He never accepted the accolades, always redirecting the glory to the one who deserved it most, the true lord and savior who watched over all. Those who were true to Him would reseed Luskir, and find their way through their darkest of times.

In the early hours of the morning, nearly alone with his thoughts, Daro contemplated how best to accomplish his mission.

It came to him as a whisper, *Dun'Aldir...*

He froze.

Often Daro communed with the one true God, ever since his frantic flight from the mines north of Big Bear those months ago that led to his transformation into the embodiment of the Lord's word.

But never before had he heard Him so clearly. Immediately he was on his guard, scouring his thoughts, though for what he was not sure. He sensed nothing amiss; slowly concluding that he had attained a higher union with Him.

"I suppose Dun'Aldir would make sense," Daro answered, accepting the new level of intimacy.

In the den of sin that was Dun'Aldir, the preacher could find many opportunities to offer his guidance. He knew the city well; born there, he roamed the streets as a youth like so many nameless urchins. Many had lost their families in the turmoil that only resolved itself in more recent years. Battles of succession brought Dun'Aldir to its knees, driven by a woman of an obscure branch of the royal bloodline named Eldora Al'Deir. It had taken everyone by surprise, how someone with no reputation for warfare, subterfuge, or even a desire to lead could so adeptly maneuver herself to rule.

Sitting on the open bluffs outside of Creekview, he reflected on that thought. During the brief days he spent with the conjuress Sevra just before killing her, Daro wondered how she came to be commanding Dun'Aldiran soldiers. Absently, he thumbed the ruby at the end of the necklace tucked under his robes. The answers came partially in whispers, mingled together with his own thoughts. Sevra's attempted rise to 'Empress' did not happen over night, the devilish woman was likely behind the scenes for many years, biding her time. She had been the true source of power behind the First Seat of Dun'Aldir. It was a seat that was now vacant, and one he planned to fill.

***

Finally, he found a way into the thoughts of the madman that was now his bearer. Despite his malady, Daro Ildaradi's mind was calculative and structured in a way that would have made a wizard of the highest order envious. Trying to claw his way into that psyche initially seemed as daunting a task as gaining a foothold on a sheer wall made of glass. However, if anyone could find a weakness in one's mind, no matter how robust that mind was, Kubathu had the skill to do so.

Though Daro did not seem to be aware of it, two distinct personalities were lurking in the recesses of his consciousness. Kubathu found that he had to tread very lightly with him; any stray thoughts he tried to impress onto the self-proclaimed prophet immediately set him on edge. With Sevra, he could issue demands that she would almost blindly follow, or he could even directly infiltrate and take control of her thoughts if he felt it necessary. He was hesitant to try and exert that much force where Daro was concerned. Internally, the man questioned everything, carefully following choices through to logical conclusions. He simply could not be forced, so Kubathu adapted his plan and explored more subtle tactics.

Taking time to observe the preacher, Kubathu saw that the alternate personality within Daro was the true visionary, while Daro himself ultimately chose the course of action. Initiating a gentle contact to the other persona, he met no resistance. When trying this directly with Daro, it resulted in immediate failure each time, as well as having the effect of setting the preacher on edge. The God-Emperor of the Vermillion Sands had been approaching this situation all wrong.

He laughed to himself, or at least had the sensation of laughter.

Pleased that he had made some progress, Kubathu patiently watched the pattern of thoughts before him and their contents. If he had a mouth, he would have gaped openly.

Underneath the constant flow of plots and schemes was an incessant drone, repeated over and over - *There is but one true God, He the Creator. His ways...*

There was a desperate need within Daro to impose his set of ideals; he truly thought that through spreading his devout beliefs the world could be saved. The world was being cleansed, and his 'God' would reward those who forsook their own ways and adopted His.

Making a few improvisations to his own plans, ever so delicately Kubathu planted a thought into the alter-ego and waited tentatively.

Securing Dun'Aldir is the key.

Daro's alternate persona went silent. Moments passed, and just as Kubathu began to think he failed once more, he felt the notion passed on to Daro himself. Consolidating power within Dun'Aldir aligned with Daro's goals, and the idea was well received.

Kubathu helped Sevra usurp the power in the capital city when it was in stable condition. It had taken years, but he knew all the right moves for her to make. Amidst the current anarchy, he wagered he could have Daro climb through the political ranks in mere weeks. He did not lament the loss of Sevra; of late, she had not been able to perform to his expectations. She had served her purpose, and as his work began to approach its fruition she was unable to meet his increasingly demanding requirements. His encounter with Daro was fortunate, should he be able to leverage their relationship appropriately. In a sense, Daro was trying to consolidate power in much the same way Kubathu too wished to rule the lands. The only difference was Daro thought he was doing it in the name of God - Kubathu would be that god.

Glossary and Pronunciation Guide

Definitions:

Duchàlg – (Doo-Shalg): Shamanistic sect of the Frostwrynn tribe; spirit-seekers.
Chàlgraäden – (Shal-Grah-ayden): "Spirit Garden." Realm of spirits.
Duchstraüm – (Dook-Strah-oom): Current of spirits within the *Chàlgraäden*.
Mináduchstraüm – (Meen-ya-Dook-Strah-oom): Smaller branches of the Duchstraüm.
Kveösjá – (Vee-Oh-sya): A simple greeting among the northern tribes.
Dhidvhel - (Deed-vel): Large, hall-style dwelling on the Ridges that holds several families.
Daärdvhel – (Day-ard-vel): Large building on the Ridges designed for clan meetings.
Ingdaärðendvhel – (Ing-day-ard-end-vel): Great hall on Boldstone Ridge for tribe meetings.
Daün drovka du sôjn dravka – (Day-uhn-drohhv-ka-doo-sohn-drav-ka): As it comes, so shall we go.

Character Name Pronunciation:

Igdahven – (Ig-dahv-ehn): in 'dahv' the 'a' is short and soft, pronounced similar as in 'hall'.
Jvard – (jVard): very light emphasis on the 'j'.
Kubathu – (koo-Bah-thoo)
Myrna – (Meer-nuh)

Location Pronunciation:

Byrn – (Burn): Small village south of Creekview, southwest of Midao.
Dun'Aldir – (Dun-Aldeer): Large city to the east.
Jun'tihr Outpost - (Juhn-Teer): Outpost mining town also known as Big Bear.
Idehldivar – (eye-Dell-div-varr): Western boundary of Luskir, large mountain range.

Laskouth Plains – (Las-kooth): Expansive plain outside of Big Bear.
Midao – (mihd-day-oh): Small village south of Creekview.
Tinindraüg River – (Ty-nin-Dray-ugh): Large river flowing north to south across Luskir.

Made in the USA
Middletown, DE
11 February 2017